MW01382973

DISTRACTED
no more
ASSURED DISTRACTION SERIES
BOOK FOUR

THIA FINN

Distracted No More

Assured Distraction Series Book Four

Thia Finn

Disclaimer: The material in this book contains graphic language and sexual content and is intended for mature audiences, ages 18 and older.

Edited by Swish Design & Editing
Proofreading by Swish Design & Editing
Book designed and formatted by Swish Design & Editing
Cover design by Deranged Doctors Designs
Cover photo model: Matthew Hosea
Cover photographer: Wander Aguiar Photography
Cover image Copyright 2016

ISBN 13: 978-0997340754

To my faithful readers.
Thank you for believing in me, encouraging me, and pushing me to write the stories.

DISTRACTED
no more
ASSURED DISTRACTION SERIES
BOOK FOUR

-prologue-

"Why can't I go with you? I can do whatever the band needs."

"Sweets, you can't go with us. You're not part of the band. We'll be doing good to feed ourselves much less one more. Besides, you don't want to be traveling with a bunch of horny guys in a van. I'd worry about you all the time."

"I can do it. I know I can. I'll even bring my guitar, and we can continue practicing together." Her desperation came through loud and clear.

"Halo. Stop. It would never work. You can't quit high school to go with the band. It won't work. You'd be the only female with all of the guys, and we won't make enough to feed an extra person. They're valid reasons for you to stay here. Why are you acting like this?"

"I know you're gonna forget me the minute you head out on tour, Carter," Halo said between gulps of air as the tears steadily streamed down her pale cheeks. "I don't want you to go."

I didn't have the guts to tell her she was probably right but the truth was, I needed to forget her. She's young, still has another year to go in high school, and I needed to be free to do what I wanted. I could be a decent guy when I had to and do the right thing. The other guy in me couldn't let her go that easily.

"Now that's where you're wrong, Halo. I'll never forget you." I meant it, too. She was my first girlfriend so how could I forget her? Hell, she was basically my first everything. We started dating when I was a senior, and the band was playing gigs at parties, weddings, and any bar that would let us through the door. We even played at open mic nights just for the experience.

"Somehow, I feel like you really believe that, Carter, but deep down my gut tells me you'll leave me behind for someone on the road. Do you even plan to come home anytime soon?" I hated the look she gave me with those deep violet eyes of hers, but I didn't want to give her false hopes either.

"I can't say exactly when we'll be home. We've booked a bunch of places KeeMac's managed to line up, and we'll be adding more dates along the road. He's been working like a madman making arrangements. Hell, I don't even think we're getting paid half the time in anything other than drinks, but we've got to do this, Halo. We both knew it was coming, and now the time's right. We have to jump on the chance when it's offered. It's that 'right place at the right time' thing. You know I'm right, sweets." I pulled her in close and kissed the top of her brown head. Damn, she smelled so fucking good, and that's a memory I won't forget anytime soon. The girl bathed everything in vanilla like she was addicted to it or something. My dick was addicted to it, too.

"Well," she pulled away from me, standing up as straight as an arrow and brushed the tears from her cheeks. This was a side of Halo I loved. She would man up and be tough when she needed to be, and right now was definitely one of those times. "I guess this is goodbye then." The look on her face hurt to see, but she put up a great front. My girl was strong like that. She faced things head on even if she was dying on the inside. She rarely let people see her weak side. Damn, I'd only seen it a few times.

"Wait. We've got another day together. Come over while I pack all of my shit. Besides, we still have tonight." I tried to pull her back in, but she held up her hands, palms outward, keeping me at arm's length.

"No, I need it to be over now. I don't want to spend another minute more than I have to obsessing over you leaving. You're going no matter what I say and honestly, I don't want to stop you from pursuing your dream. You deserve this, the band, too. Besides, it's only dragging out the inevitable."

Tears streamed harder down her face again as she said the words that tore us both to pieces. "This is goodbye, Carter." She turned around and started for the door of her house.

"It doesn't have to be goodbye forever, Halo. You know that, right?" I called after her. Damn, why was this so fucking hard to do? It's the right thing, but at that minute it sure as hell didn't feel that way.

She stopped at the door and looked over her shoulder. "Yeah, Carter, I think it does. I'm not a sharing kinda girl."

The pain in her voice wrecked me, but I had to keep telling myself I believed it was for the best. Deep down, this hurt.

I wanted this tour, didn't I? I wanted the freedom. I need experiences that life on the road provided. At nineteen, I should be having the time of my life—playing music in a kickass band, living on the road with my best friends, and plundering through one-night stands like a sex god. My rep with the ladies needed to be built, one night at a time.

"Goodbye, Halo. I'll always love you, girl," I said to myself as she walked through her parents' front door and closed it without another look back. "And I'll never forget."

Carter

Eight Years Later

I walked into the studio to another new face at the reception desk. Seemed like 13 Recordings went through receptionists like water.

"Oh, Mr. Sheridan, what can I do for you?" Yeah, too much perkiness for this early in the fucking morning.

"Cash or Peri around today?" I hadn't checked in with either in a while, and we were preparing to head out on another damn tour. I loved the life, but shit, this was getting fucking old with me.

"Yes sir, Cash is in his office. Just a moment, and I'll see if he's available."

Like hell she would. I'd come and go as I pleased. "Don't bother," I mumbled as I walked passed her to the doorway leading to the offices. "He'll see me."

She jumped up and ran around the desk thinking she was going to stop me. I almost laughed hard. The pixie with her five-inch heels thought she stood a chance.

"Stop, little girl, and go back to your phone and *People* magazine. I'm telling you, he'll see me." The crazy thing practically launched herself at me and almost took us both down before I could catch her and straighten us up. "What the fuck are you doing?"

"I was trying to stop you to tell you that you can't barge in there. Someone important is in there, and he asked not to be disturbed. But no, you, 'Mr. Rock Star, and I can do what I want', went barrelling in like you own the place or something."

I stood there holding all ninety-five fucking pounds of feathers, who obviously had a death wish or something, and thought is this chick for real? "So, Miss Farmer..." I read from her temporary badge, "... you want to tell me who's in his office that's so damn important you're willing to attack me?" I put her down on her own two feet and glared down at her.

"Uh... well... I'm not supposed to say." She refused to look anywhere but the toes of her fancy little size four "fuck me" heels. I stuck my index finger under her chin and slowly raised it until her gray eyes met mine.

I growled, "Who's in there?"

"A woman." She swallowed the fear. "Someone he knows."

The look she gave told me there must be something more going on than she wanted to reveal. "A woman?" I lost some of the growl this time.

"Yes, and he told me he wasn't to be disturbed unless it was an extreme emergency." I let go of her chin, but she still held my eyes, only now the look grew challenging.

"So, if you don't mind, please wait until I can inform him you're here."

"Well, Miss Farmer, I do mind." I whipped around her and stomped to Cash's door knocking on it as I reached to open the handle. Hmmm. Locked. Before I could push on it, the brave little thing wedged her minuscule hot body between Cash's door and my six-foot-two hard body.

"I mind, too. I do what the boss says. So, allow me to get him for you." She turned and knocked again on the door and spoke through it. "Cash, there's someone here to see you who refuses to wait." The aggravation in her voice struck me as comical coming from her.

Only a second had passed before the door cracked open. "What is it Carter? I'm tied up right now with a client."

"Oh, really? Anyone I know?" I saw nothing and no one behind him.

"No, actually you don't. So what do you need that's so important you try to bust in my office?"

"I wanted to talk to you about some things I want to be supplied on the tour." I tried glancing around the little space he spoke through with no luck.

"Tell Peri. She's the one running Assured Distraction's tour."

"Peri's too busy with her family right now." I peered over his shoulder.

"No, she was in this morning. Did you even bother to go to her office?"

"No. I wanted to talk to you." My anger grew by the second. He purposely hid this someone and now I had to know why.

"Go talk to her, Carter. She'll handle it." He tried to shut the door, dismissing me.

With a fast move of my boot in the space, I stopped him. "When can I talk to you? Do I need a fucking appointment these days?" My need to speak to him wasn't all that necessary, but now he had me intrigued at who the hot little number was he kept me from seeing.

"I'm going to be busy for most of the afternoon. I'll call you later and talk about your list of demands. I'm sure that's why you're here." He cramped my foot more in the slot.

It only took a hard look in his eyes to see the moderately frantic stare, so I decided to back off. "Okay. You do that. Call me today, dickwad. We need to talk."

"I'll be sure to." He slammed the door, and I heard the lock snap in place.

Miss Farmer's sweet little ass led us back to her desk. "I guess you're still not going to tell me who's in there." She leaned over to the top of the counter, crooking her index finger in and out calling me to share a secret. I bent over so our noses almost touched. Damn, her Tinkerbell look made me want to laugh.

"Hell no," she whisper-yelled in my ear. What a tease. She sat and flipped open her magazine.

"Right, little girl. I'll remember this. We're family here, and I'll be sure to put in a good word with the rest of them for you." I received a glare over the magazine before I pulled out my phone and dialed Ryan's number as I walked toward the door.

"Dude, you and Peri home?" I made sure to say it loud enough so Miss Farmer would hear it.

"Me and Tuck are chilling by the pool. Come on out."

Tucker was swimming like a fish now. I couldn't believe the little guy had turned five years old. Where'd the baby go that we all took turns walking around holding, feeding, rocking while on tour after his birth? Seems like yesterday. He'd quickly grown into a tall kid for his age.

"Hey, Tuck. Cannonball!" Ryan yelled as he displaced half the water in the pool as he landed.

"Daddy. You make big wave. All the water gone. Momma's gonna be mad."

"Nah, she'll be happy we're having fun. She'll come swim too when she gets home."

I stood watching father and son from behind a pillar on their patio. Ryan's living the good life. Sometimes I wish I had this, but then I think no way. Tied down to one girl all the time? Not for me. I needed variety. The sole responsibility was on my shoulders for keeping the bad-boy image up with our fans. The rest of these pussies have succumbed to the picket-fence syndrome. Not me. No way. Not anytime soon, anyway.

"Hey Carter, why ya hiding back there?" Ryan called.

"Just watching Tuck playing like we used to do when we were kiddos."

Ryan pulled himself up out of the water just as Tuck did his own version of a cannonball off the board.

"Yeah, it's happened so fast. Just yesterday we were bringing him home from the hospital and now look at him. Thinks he's a damn teenager. Hell, he'll be texting the women next thing you know." We both laughed knowing this was true.

"By the time he's that age, kids won't be texting, they'll have something better. We had pagers back in the day, remember?"

"Yeah, we did. Kept that thing constantly beeping in junior high with those hot little babes."

"Some of us did anyway. Gunner, not so much. Remember how jealous he would get? We'd have to call his number just to make him feel better." We laughed loud and hard. Gunner was such a geek in junior high, and now he had his sweet little cherry pie, as he liked to call her.

"Poor Gunner. Such a smart, dumbass back then. So glad we weren't like that." I knew deep down the joke was really on us because we were such pricks back then. Ryan liked the long-term girl where I was still the same now, love 'em and leave 'em.

"Beer?" Ryan held out a cold brew.

"Hell yeah. If we're sitting out here, I'll need one." I popped the cap and took a long pull.

"What's up, dude? You sounded pissed on the phone." Ryan did the same and said all of this without ever taking his eyes off of Tucker. He had this dad thing down.

"I was over by the studio today and stopped to talk to Cash, but he was holed up in his fucking office with someone. That feisty new receptionist, Miss Farmer, tried to stop me. You met her? She goes about a full buck of nothing but sass." I raised my hand to indicate her diminutive height.

"No, but Peri likes her. Says she's a 'take no shit' kinda girl. So, who do you think he was hiding in there?"

"No damn clue. He didn't say, and Tinkerbell wouldn't spill. Just when I thought she was gonna come through, she blew me off like a speck of dust."

The bastard had the nerve to laugh at me. "What?"

"Nothing. I know you're not used to being owned by a female."

"Shit, I'll show her little fairy ass what it means to be owned one of these days."

As the last word left my mouth, Peri came outside in a see-through flowy thing with her bikini under it. Ryan's wife's beauty and sweetheart personality made her the perfect woman for him and the band.

"Hey, Peri." I stood and kissed her pale cheek. The alabaster skin set off her fully-colored tattoos.

"Hello, yourself, Carter. Who were you talking about?"

Great, she'd heard what I said.

"I've been at the studio."

Before I could finish what I wanted to say, Peri cut me off. "So you've met Johnna?" The shit-eating grin I received said she knew exactly what my next sentence would be.

"Yeah, I hear she's been taking lessons on how to exert her authority from some of the best." I gave her a look. Peri could be a hardass if needed.

"Why, whatever do you mean, Carter, honey?" Her southern belle accent fooled no one considering Peri transplanted from Cali to Austin several years ago.

"You know exactly what I'm talking about so don't give me that 'honey' shit. Little Miss Farmer thinks she knows how to exercise her control on whoever comes in there, and I'm damn sure not succumbing to her high-handed bullshit."

"So what'd she do, forget to fall at your rock-god feet and offer up worship?" Peri stole Ryan's beer to take a sip, but he stole it back before she could.

"Hell no, I didn't offer her my best effort for that. I wanted to see Cash and the little she-bitch thought she was going to stop me."

Ryan jumped up and landed in the pool next to Tuck. "Dude, let's swim to the big rocks. I think Uncle C and Mommy are going to have a discussion."

"He's gonna be in trouble, isn't he Daddy? He's saying words that make Mommy get red in the face."

Ryan started laughing. "Yeah, he is, but Mommy's got it taken care of. Race ya." The two headed off toward the waterfalls.

"So she did her job and that made you mad? We hired the right girl for the job then."

"You want someone treating your best clientele like shit?" I asked her.

"No, we want her to follow directions, be discreet, and keep the office running smoothly. What was it you were trying to see Cash for that I couldn't do for you?" Peri finally sat down so I didn't have to look up at her.

"I wanted to talk about some specific items that need to be on the damn bus when we leave, and I just happened to be close to the fucking studio. I stopped by but your door was closed so I asked... polite as fuck I might add... if he was there. She refused to disturb him. The real kicker is he was hiding someone in his office. That's what started the whole shit show with her."

"If you were mean to her, I'm gonna kick your ass," Peri said with such a calm voice that it kinda scared me.

"Hell no, I wasn't mean to her. It was the other way around. She got vicious in a heartbeat. Got between me and his door before I could blink. Told me what I could do with my demands."

"Good for her," Peri smirked, which was all kinds of wrong because that's my move. "I was there this morning discussing her role in the office. I must've said all the right things."

"What little pixie gets between a grown-ass man and what he's after and expects to win the fucking battle?"

"Okay, I get it. She thwarted your attempt to see what was going on, and it pissed you off. Carter, just because she's small doesn't mean she can't be forceful."

"She's got some lady balls. I'll give her that," I smirked at Peri.

"You should also know she's got her sights set on someone else already, too. Don't be getting any ideas about exploring her 'lady balls', please."

"Not a problem. She's sure as shit not my type."

"Sounds like it. So, who was in Cash's office?

"Hell if I know. Cash refused to say."

"Hmmm. Now you've got me wondering. Oh, wait. He did say something this morning about a country singer he went to see play last week coming by today."

"Country? Are you fucking with me? Cash isn't into country."

"You know how that music bleeds over to rock and pop these days. You can hardly call most of it country anymore. Look at Hayden. He was country all the way when he came from East Texas and now he's opened for AD. Cash mentioned this new artist likes to do duets with males so maybe Cash is thinking about the two of them teaming up for a few songs."

"What's his name? Would we have heard of him?" Maybe he'd be good for Hayden's career. Broaden his appeal. Not that the kid needed it. His music's outstanding, and the ladies love him. He has a huge following after opening for us.

"No, it's a she. She's a local girl who's getting a name for herself here in the Austin area. Cash kept hearing great things about her so he went to watch her set. I think her name's Victory."

"Victory, weird name." I finished off my beer and stood up for another. I held it out offering one to Peri, but she declined.

"Doctor said no more beer for me." She looked me square in the eyes. "And no, I'm not pregnant..." long pause, "... yet."

"So another little Powell on the horizon?" I lifted an eyebrow.

"On the horizon, but not in the oven." She smiled and rubbed her hand over her naturally rounded tummy. Peri was a real woman with softness in all the right places. I knew what Ryan saw in her. Hell, everyone did. She was a sweetheart, a best friend, a kickass tour manager, and a great mom to little Tucker and his cousin, Crew Devillier, Hayden's son.

"Hey, I'm sure Ryan's enjoying all of the practicing."

"Practice makes perfect, and I know this because perfection is sitting there on that rock by the falls." She motioned out to Ryan and Tucker.

I followed her line of sight to the father and son having a serious discussion with their feet flipping water. Damn, that was a photo waiting to happen. "Want me to go for a swim with Tucker to allow for some spontaneous practice? You can never get too much in, you know." I wiggled my eyebrows up and down.

"As good as that sounds, I think I'll take a raincheck? Wrong time of the month for that."

"Dammit woman, that's TMI spewing from your mouth." I didn't need to hear that. Living on the tour bus with Chandler was bad enough since she never held back on that whole hormone explosion. I knew why God didn't give me sisters.

"On those words, I guess I'm going to hit the road."

"Don't let my honesty run you off. I'm sure you've got a swimsuit here still. Jump in with the boys."

Ryan yelled at me. "Don't go, dude. Come swim with us. We need another team member to play volleyball if Peri's getting in too."

Peri took off her cover-up and walked into the pool. "Your suit's in your drawer in the laundry room. Come on."

"Guess I'll stay awhile then. We get first serve, though," I yelled as I opened the back door.

Victory

"You really think we can make my music work?" I said flipping through the contract lying on Cash's desk.

"I know we can, Victory. Your sound is outstanding and will appeal to the audiences Hayden attracts. He has quite the following already. His last solo tour did better than we expected. You'll open for him, and then the two of you will sing a couple together. It'll be great exposure for you. If everything goes well, we'll start adding more duets. When y'all return from this tour, we'll get you both in the studio to create an EP that will drop before joining the big tour with Assured Distraction."

"You know, I've never actually toured before." I looked at him gauging his reaction.

"Gotta start somewhere. This fifteen-show tour will fly by, and you'll be back in the studio in no time. Hayden knows touring already. He'll help you. It's the kind of man he is." He looked at me like he was expecting an immediate answer. I didn't know if I was prepared enough for all of this.

"What the hell. Let's do it." I picked up the pen and signed my name before I could change my mind. This was what I'd been working for, wasn't it? I played every bar in a fifty-mile radius of Austin ten times over. I'd be living on a tour bus for a short time with all of Hayden's backup band. I could do this. Dammit, I deserved to do this.

I stood up and offered my hand to Cash, and we shook on the deal.

"There's only one more thing I need to tell you, though."

"Yeah?" He raised his head and dropped my hand. "What's that?"

"I'd prefer to keep this under wraps for a while. Like, get out on tour without everyone who is signed with 13 Recordings knowing about the tour."

"Is there a problem I need to know about?"

"No, there's not a problem, but I want to see how things go before I make a splash here in Austin. What if it doesn't work out? I've lived in this area my whole life. I'd hate to make a fool of myself with all of your big-named bands."

"Well, yeah, I guess we can try. AD is finishing up their next album, and then they'll be leaving on the U.S. tour. I want you and Hayden to join up with them. There's no reason why you should meet up with them before you leave in a couple of days. Can you be ready to go by then? I realize this is very short notice, but I knew when I heard you during your two sets I caught, you were exactly what I've been looking for."

"Great." I hardly got that word out when someone knocked and tried to come in the room. Good thing I locked that door-handle lock when I came through it.

He spoke to Carter through the door, and I jumped behind it before he opened it. I didn't want Carter to have any knowledge of me being there. I wasn't here to see him, and I prayed it'd be some more time before we faced each other again.

So much had happened since he left years ago with AD to start their career. I secretly cheered his success with AD, but he never needed to know that. Getting signed by 13 Recordings was the beginning of an outstanding journey for them and when the band skyrocketed after joining Steele on tour, they were set for a lifetime of fame.

Eight Years Ago

I looked at my guitar leaning sadly in the corner by my closet door. I tried hiding it behind the door, but that was too much. My guitar was such a big part of our time as a couple. We played together before he joined the band. Every time one of us learned something new, we couldn't wait to teach the other. I took lessons, and he taught himself how to play. When his friends decided to form a band, he learned to play the bass, and that's when he truly fell in love with music. He could play an acoustic as well as anyone I knew but with the bass, he was on another plane in his head while he played. It was like he was born to add that sound to a band.

It also marked the time when we stopped spending as much time together. Those guys were older than me and naturally could go play places I couldn't go. My parents didn't like the idea of their little girl hanging out with a bunch of older guys. They would never allow me to go to a bar if that's where they played that week, so I rarely was able to see them perform live.

"My parents won't let me go to those bars in Austin, Carter. You know that."

"I know, Halo, but we have to play there. When you turn eighteen, you can come, too. What a rush it will be to have you there watching us. Just knowing you're in the audience will be awesome." He pulled me into him and wrapped his arms around me.

We'd hugged before, but he held me there for longer this time. I can't say I minded it either. Carter was super hot, but he never seemed to act like that's what he wanted with me, and I was good with it. We had a great relationship playing guitars, hanging out, laughing, and just having fun together without adding emotions to it.

All of that changed when he leaned back, and he raised my chin up to look at him. He slowly lowered his head, and I knew what was coming. The first kiss, magic overwhelmed my senses. His soft and smooth lips gently slid across mine. The feeling mesmerized my seventeen-year-old senses. I'd been kissed before but nothing like this. This felt like a man and woman kiss, like a let's do more kiss.

When he broke the kiss and moved far enough back to look at me, I thought my bones were Jell-O. The molten look of lust clouded his half-hooded eyes. Then he kissed me hard. I wrapped my hands around his neck and kissed him hard right back. Damn, I swear to God this was the experience of a teenaged girl's lifetime.

He slid his tongue across the seam of my mouth to allow him entrance, and I let him. If we weren't kissing, I would have begged him for one more. It was that good of a feeling going on in my brain as our tongues rubbed across each other's in frantic movements.

As fast as it started, it was over. Carter slowly backed away from me.

"We better not do that in your bedroom, Halo." His smile alone could've convinced me to drop my panties on the spot, but his words kept that from happening.

"Oh, okay. Did I do something wrong?"

"Hell no. You did too much right."

That comment kinda confused me, but I wouldn't argue with him. "Right. Too much right." I didn't know how to respond. I couldn't think anyway, and now he was confusing me. "Now, exactly what does that mean, Carter? Too much right."

He smirked at me. "Let's just say, that kinda kiss can only lead to no good in your bedroom, and your parents trust us to be playing music. That was some sweet music all right, but not the kind we should be playing." He gave me a quick laugh.

"So, you thought it was a good kiss then?" He was confusing me with every sentence that spewed from his beautiful lips.

"Yeah, Halo. The best. Now pick up your guitar, and let's go over some of the songs we are going to be doing at the show."

"Okay." I floated on air the rest of the evening. His words 'the best' were playing havoc in my head.

That night of two kisses in my room became the first of many followed by dates and lots of making out and the rounding of bases. Before school was out and he graduated, he slid in at home plate, and I stumbled head over heels in love.

Eight Years Later

"I'll be ready to go. Just tell me when and where." The calm exterior I exhibited on the outside in no way indicated what happened on the inside of my head. To put it plainly, freaking the hell out came closer to a description. I'm going on tour with someone who toured with a megaband. My brain screamed "Squeee!" but my mouth spoke like a normal twenty-something. I hoped Cash didn't feel the sweat on my palms. I considered wiping them on my jeans before I took his hand but thought that would look even more awkward.

Cash stepped from his office. "Johnna, please call Camille and see if she's available to work tomorrow? We need a quick makeover done and some wardrobe for Victory. If she's not available, let me know ASAP."

He turned to me. "Camille will see that you're prepared to do this before you leave. She's great at what she does." Was he kidding? She could do whatever the hell she wanted to make me look ready. At this point, she could probably shave my head and paint me purple, and I would be okay with it.

"I guess I'll head out then and get prepared so I can be with her all day tomorrow." I tried to sound nonchalant about it all but damn, a girl could only keep her excitement in for so long.

"Great idea, and I'll have the contracts ready for you before we leave. They'll be the standard contracts but for the tour time only. Once we see how this is going to work out, we'll look at something on a more permanent basis for you." He'd been staring at papers on his desk and finally looked up at me.

"I can't thank you enough for what you're doing, Cash. I look forward to meeting with Hayden as well."

"Yeah, we need to get Hayden in here. I'll get him on the phone shortly. Would you be opposed to meeting with him this evening if he's available? I've been keeping him up to date on our meetings, and he's completely on board with the idea."

"Sure, that's great. I'm willing to do whatever it takes to be ready. Give me a call." I shook his hand again and made my way to the front door.

I prayed all the way to my car. *Please don't let me run into him. Please let him be somewhere else today.* I didn't want to run into any of the other AD band members either, but I doubted they would recognize me anyway. Carter would, and that might be disastrous at this point. I wasn't exactly hiding from him, but I didn't want to meet up this way either.

I never set out to capture the attention from someone at the same label where they were signed. I didn't invite Cash to my set at the bar. So why did I freak out about this?

The simple answer, Carter Sheridan. How would we react to seeing each other again? I loved him then, but that was a long time ago. I was sure we both had changed drastically since we said goodbye.

I'd had a lot of time to grow up. Now I knew what I wanted in life. I had a life plan in place, my eyes on the prize. I decided to give this music thing a couple of years of my life. I had a college degree behind me to fall back on if it didn't pan out. I worked and saved while I went to school so I could live to play music now. If I made money along the way, that was icing on the cake for me. If it was meant for me to be a musician, then something good would have to happen in the time I allotted.

With Carter, though, he lived in the spotlight and had practically been since the day we parted. It wasn't long before Cash discovered them, just like me. He led AD to the big time, especially after they hired the girl, Chandler Chatam, in the band. Now she's one of the hottest females in music. Of course, it helped that she and Assured Distraction's lead singer, Keeton MacDonald, were together. Their stage presence sparked gossip that made legends.

Whew, made it. I sat in my car and exhaled a loud breath. I needed to get my head on straight about everything and dealing with a reunion with my ex was not part of my plan. I drove away with so many different ideas rolling around in my brain—meeting Hayden, playing for bigger audiences, singing duets with a star, running into Carter. Ugh. It all sounded great until I got to him.

Carter

I found myself sitting across the conference table from the rest of the asshats in the band a few days after visiting with Ryan and Peri. Attending meetings was not my idea of the way to spend the day, but Peri and Cash called this meeting so I decided to go. They didn't call joint meetings too often.

"Okay, now that you're all here, I want to go over the release of the new album," Peri began. "We are planning a release party for next week in L.A. since that's the start of the tour. It's the perfect place to hold a huge extravaganza. The concerts at the Staples Center and the parties at The Ritz-Carlton. We've already lined up some great industry people to attend and word is it's the party to be seen at, so tickets are already hard to come by. When it's done, we'll be heading out to Seattle and move on from there. I know better than to give you guys too much info at once, but the schedule's on your phones and in your email in case you need it."

"I'm glad to see you playing Seattle again. It's been a while since you've been in that part of the states," Cash added. "I haven't looked over Peri's schedule yet, but I'm sure she's done an outstanding job of booking." He smiled at her when he said it, and we all hoorahed over Peri's abilities to do her end of the business. The band couldn't ask for a better tour manager.

"Are we playing any festivals?" Gunner asked. "I fucking hate playing those in the summer. It's too damn hot if we hit the south."

"We are hitting a few, but they're all in the north. I knew you guys would throw a little bitch tantrum if I did that to you," she smirked at us because she knew us all too well. "The four of you will be traveling in the band's bus, and Ryan and I will be behind in our RV with the boys and a nanny."

"What about Hayden?" I asked assuming he would be opening for us again especially if Crew was going, too.

Cash jumped in. "Hayden is going on a short tour on his own with a new opening act that will actually be doing some duets with him. They're working on their music now and are leaving today for fifteen shows. Then the two of them will be joining AD, provided it all goes well."

"Who's opening for him?" Chandler asked.

"A new female singer I found here in Austin. I caught two of her shows and she's good, damn good. Her vocal style works well with Hayden's. They both lean toward a country sound but these days, country sounds a lot like rock so it's hard to say. I did hear the locals at one place call it country rock. Leave it to Austin to find a way to market to every demography of music."

This comment made us all laugh. Assured Distraction never wanted to be associated with country music but when Hayden came along, and his songwriting stood out more than any we'd heard and his vocals the same, we had to rethink music. We would always be rock and roll, though.

Cash continued, "This new female artist..." he glanced down at the papers in front of him. "Victory is her name. She's got the looks to backup her musical abilities, so I feel confident she's going to help take Hayden to the next level."

"Victory, I like it," Chandler said. "I also like the idea of not being the only female on the bus." She looked around the table at the rest of us. "Not that I don't love you guys, but having a female to offset your humor, smell... well, everything actually, will be a huge plus."

"Awe, Chandler, you wound us. Everyone except your fucking boy toy there," I said as I nodded toward KeeMac. "I'm sure I speak for everyone when I say we go out of our way on the damn bus to make sure you are treated like a princess."

"I'm so sorry, Carter, and it's just like I know you go out of your way choosing the perfect groupies at every damn venue to bring home so we can hear them/her screaming your name *All. Night. Long."* Her emphasis on those words accompanied three hard hip thrusts. The little shit had my movements down. Everyone else must have thought so too since the group laughed.

"Why thank you, cupcake." I stood and took a quick bow. "I never knew you could do me so well." I turned to KeeMac. "Does she do me well in bed fucking, too?"

"No, prick. She does not *do you* anywhere, especially in the fucking bed." KeeMac pulled her over and kissed the top of her head. "Do you, babe?"

"Great," Peri rolled her eyes. "Looks like the fun's ramping up already."

Everyone started laughing. Our band family rolled this way all of the time. If we couldn't laugh and make fun of each other, how would we ever make it?

"So when do we get to meet Victory?" Chandler asked.

"Probably not until she and Hayden show up to join the tour. Touring is new to her, so I decided her meeting you bunch of fame-whores before they left probably wasn't the best plan. I'll be with them when they meet up with you guys. Maybe you can all remember that and ease her into your constant fucking antics, please."

I jumped up. "Sure thing, boss man. I'll try to keep down the *All. Night. Long.* screamers." I pumped my hips like Chandler, then stopped and looked at Cash. "Wait just a damn minute, so she and Hayden will be on the bus with us, too? Don't you think that's going to get a little crowded?"

"That's only six of us. Besides, you think she's going to cut down on the shit you do with your groupies?" Chandler asked me.

"Hell yeah. I like room to spread out. If you know what I mean?" I winked at her.

"Don't wink at Chandler, you douchebag. I don't even want her thinking about you and your skanky hookups."

KeeMac never took his eyes off Chandler when he spoke. Those two were inseparable, and we knew it from the day she joined AD.

"Dude, she's the one who brought my sex life into the fucking convo. I try to keep my fun and games to myself, but hey, if she wants to get up in my junk, I'm willing to share or let you two join. The more the merrier, right Gunner?" He texted on his phone the entire time we were in the room which wasn't like the old Gunner.

He looked up from his phone. "What the fuck, Carter, don't bring me into your shit. Those days are over, and you damn well know it. I've found my one. Maybe you should do the same, dude."

"Fuck that. I'm ready to rock and roll anytime, anywhere. The rest of y'all got your dumb asses tied down and can't partake of all the willing women. I'll have Hayden with me pretty soon so we can make it our business to hold up the rock-star image."

"You do that, Carter, but try to stay out of the tabloids on this tour with any negative publicity. We don't need naked pictures of you and a bunch of groupies surfacing like they did on the last tour. You make my job so much harder when you do stupid shit," Peri added and looked down at her tablet. "So if we've set Carter straight, and Cash's done with you, I'm finished as well."

"I'm done. Carter, did you want to talk to me now? You seemed so insistent the other day when you tried to bust into my office," Cash asked me.

"Yeah, about that. Why were you so protective over who was in your office? Who was it?"

"If you must know, it was Victory. Oh wait, the term 'none of your business' comes to mind. She's shy when it comes to you guys. She asked me if it would be possible to get in and out without having to run into any of you pricks that practice here. She was nervous enough when I spoke to her after the set she played, so I thought it was best to keep her meeting low-key." He kept looking at his phone as he spoke.

"So she has her mind made up about us all already, and we haven't even met her? Damn, we aren't that big of douchbags."

This caused Cash to look up. "Are you shitting me? Have you met this group when you see a beautiful girl? It's like fresh meat in the lion's cage."

"She's beautiful, huh? Can't wait to meet her, and I promise to start out on my best behavior just for you and Peri."

"Just keep your hands off her and let her get used to being around you guys before you show your true selves is all I ask."

"Sure thing, boss man. Hey, wait a fucking minute, that's wrong. I'm the boss. You work for me."

"And while that's absolutely true, someone has to be the adult, and you've never been known for that particular quality."

"Yeah? Try telling that to the ladies. I'm an adult from head to toe."

Cash shook his head and smirked. "Keep telling yourself that, and I'll keep doing my job making sure you appear that way."

We parted with us both laughing. I could be a damn adult if I had to, but where was the fun in that? If the beautiful ladies liked me this way, then I'm fucking happy to oblige. It was a win-win for both of us.

I lounged by the pool waiting for the call from the town car to pick me up. I crawled home this morning with Zach, our bodyguard that went out with me last night. I only had a few hours of sleep and nursed a damn hangover. Not a good way to start this day, but I could sleep on the plane to fucking L.A., so I wasn't overly concerned. The concert tonight technically started the tour to promote our fourth album, *Pleasure*.

As usual, Chandler, KeeMac, and Ryan wrote most of the music for this album. Everyone contributed to the lyrics and one song was completely Hayden's. He wrote it for our band to sing about Crew and Tucker. Those two kids added a new side to our lives in their five short years. Even I could hardly remember what it was like before them.

Hayden and Ryan both made great dads. I sure as hell don't know how Hayden managed being a single dad. The fact that he and Crew lived with Ryan, Peri, and Tucker made his life a hell of a lot easier. I knew I couldn't fucking do it. I hadn't finished raising me much less raising a baby, and Hayden was only eighteen the day Crew arrived in this world. Crew and Tucker never lacked for adult guidance with the band around. Built-in uncles and Chandler were always there for them. Now with Gunner and Lola together, a new aunt was added to the mix. Lola being a pediatric nurse made for a great bonus, too.

I grabbed my phone off the side table when it chimed a text.

Hayden: *Dude, you should have been with me last night. This new chick Cash found is awesome*
Me: *Oh yeah? You should have been with me when I was picking up the twins last night*
Hayden: *Trying to one up me*
Me: *More like me up two*
Hayden: *LOL, maybe next time*
Me: *So the girl. She any good*
Hayden: *Hell yeah she is. Plays guitar like a pro and her voice is killer*
Me: *a babe*
Hayden: *hell yeah to that too. Gorgeous*
Me: *plays, sings, and arm candy. Did you hit it already*
Hayden: *NO and you can't either. We work together. She's older*
Me: *too old? A MILF?*
Hayden: *fuck no. She's like a year younger than you. Like I said, OLDer*
Me: *Fuck you, dumb ass. I'm not old*
Hayden: *yeah keep thinking that. we'll see who all the chicks run to when I get there with y'all*
Me: *LOL ok. Keep the new chick in line and I'll keep the real women happy*
Hayden: *whatever. Later*

Carter

Another text came from the car out front, so I walked to the door to let them get my bags while I showered and dressed. I was going to miss my house, especially my bathroom and bed. They bought the bus pimped out in the best of everything, but it still had a minuscule shower and bunks. Everything that could be upgraded had been, so we were at least comfortable. It sure as hell wasn't my California King bed, my shower for several people, and my tub that held as many as I wanted in it.

The first of the band's entourage walked up the steps to the plane when we arrived. The rest of AD arrived about the same time as I did.

Ryan, Peri, and the two boys stepped out of their limo with their bodyguard beside mine.

"Uncle Carter, Uncle Carter!" The words came in unison from Tuck and Crew as they both ran to me. Damn, I loved these little guys. Having them call to me made me feel all warm and fuzzy on the inside, but I'd damn sure never say that shit out loud. I'd be the ass-end of jokes for the rest of my life.

"We get to fly on the plane," Crew yelled. "Daddy's gonna meet us when we get to... to... I forget."

I scooped them up, one in each arm, and hugged them close. They were all boy, but I still loved holding them. They smelled like little kids' shampoo and soap when I kissed their heads. A few years ago holding a kid would have scared the shit out of me but now, I loved being with them. I actually looked forward to lying on the floor and building Legos or playing with their superhero characters. Who would've ever thought I could pull off being the fun uncle?

"Is it California?" I asked.

"No, Uncle C, another place."

"Help me out here, Tucker. Where are we meeting Hayden?" His dark brown eyes, like his momma's, looked serious.

"I dunno. I think Momma told us, but I was shooting webs out of Spiderman's hands all the way here." Pkewww. He shot it on the top of my head.

"Little dude! How am I supposed to see if you cover me in spider webs? I might fall down."

"No you won't, Uncle C, it's only pr'ten."

"I think that's pretend, dude."

"That's what I said, pr'ten."

"Okay, I guess that's close enough." I laughed.

Crew yelled over to Peri. "Ri Ri, where's my daddy?"

Peri laughed when she heard him call her the name he christened her with as a baby. "He's meeting us in Denver."

"Yeah, that's it. Denver, Uncle C." Crew's blue eyes looked so serious. "He's got a girl with him now. Did you know that?"

"A girl. Ewww. We don't like girls, do we guys? What do we say about girls?"

Together we yelled, "Girls mean trouble."

"Carter!" Peri raised her voice. "I told you to stop telling them that. Boys, girls are not trouble. I'm a girl. Channey's a girl. Y'all like her."

"Oh yeah, Uncle C, we like Mommy and Channey." Crew was so serious about it.

"Well, guys, I agree. Only some girls mean trouble." I put them both on my shoulders and carried them over to the plane before putting them down on the bottom step. I bent down and pulled them in for a secret. "We have to say that about Mommy 'cause we don't want to hurt her feelings, so we'll only say that about other girls when she's not around. It's our secret. Okay?" They both nodded their little heads. "Now head on up the steps but be careful and don't fall. I'll stand here and watch you."

"What bullshit were you telling my kids?" Peri asked behind me.

"Just guy stuff, Mom."

"It better not have been vulgar. I'll kill you in your sleep if you teach them bad words."

"Peri, would I do something like that?"

"In a heartbeat. I know you too well, Carter." She smiled as she said it, but she could put the fear of God in all of us when those momma bear claws came out.

As the plane reached its cruising altitude and leveled out, everyone started moving about and talking. We hadn't spent much time together after our part of the album was done and handed off to the producers to work their magic.

Sitting down next to me, Gunner ordered a beer from the flight attendant. "What about you, Carter? Don't you want something to drink?"

"No, thanks." I shook my head at the tall guy serving us today. Gunner gave me a funny look.

"What? I'm still hungover from last night's fun and games."

"That the reason you're still wearing your damn sunglasses on this dark plane?"

"You fucking know it. My head is hurting like a son of a bitch. I'm going to sleep some so I can play with the boys later."

"Yeah. I thought I would get on the floor with them after I finished this."

"How you been, Gunner? Haven't seen too much of you since Lola came into your life."

"Good. Real good, actually." He has a smile on his face before he sipped from the bottle.

"Enjoying life together?"

"You know it. She's the best, and she puts up with my shit."

I laughed. "Oh yeah? You better lock that down. Might not find another one willing to do that."

"Don't I fucking know it." He glanced around to see where the boys were.

"Yeah, you better be afraid if Peri hears you." We both laughed. "I never thought there would be a day when we were all so damn pussy whipped or trained to watch our mouths."

"The kids don't need to hear that shit, though. I agree with her on that." He took another long pull of the cold beer.

"I know. We never heard that kind of language out of our parents at their age or if we did, we didn't understand it."

"Right, and that's the way it should be," Gunner added.

"So when are you and Lola going to pop one out?"

"Ha! No time soon. We have a lot of practicing to do first." He laughed as he said it. "Lola's enjoying her job, and I want her to quit when we have a kid. I'll be damned if a stranger will be raising my kid, and she won't have it either."

"Not to mention she would need to be on the fucking road with us."

"Hell yeah, she and the baby'll be with me. Pretty soon we'll look like a damn circus caravan if we all have separate buses to live on with a shit ton of kids in tow."

"Yeah, we may have to buy a bigger plane and start flying to every venue," I offered as a possibility.

"No, I don't want that either. That would mean living in some damn hotel every night. Lola would probably rather have a rolling house like Peri does."

"That big bitch they live in cost more than a lot of fucking houses." Gunner nodded his head agreeing with me. His next comment took me completely by surprise.

"Makes me wonder how long we'll do this after all of us are married or have kids or both."

"What the fuck are you talking about, Gunner?"

"Carter, we can't live our lives like this forever. Being on the fucking road all the time is no way for a family to live. Once the kids start school, we'll have to either hire tutors or stop touring. It'll be a cold day in hell before I leave Lola behind with my kids."

I couldn't say anything. I honestly didn't know how to respond to his statement. I never considered what our fucking lives would be like after all of these guys married and popped out babies. The thought of me being married? Oh, hell no. I didn't know if I'd ever get married. I liked my freedom. I damn sure loved having a different woman in my bed. I liked having a couple at a time if the participants were down with it. Hell, there was a time that Gunner and I shared two or three women in the same room.

Now that Hayden was my wingman, that didn't happen too often. He wasn't down with sharing unless he was wasted and whiskey dick wasn't always a good thing with the ladies. It's a good thing he's young.

"Carter?" Gunner called my name. "You asleep behind those dark shades?"

"No, man. Just thinking about how our lives have changed. We had some great times in that old van in the beginning, even before Chandler took Jacoby's place."

We spent the next hour of the flight reliving some fun times on the road with all of the women we shared and the drunken nights before we stumbled back to the bus.

When the pilot announced to prepare for landing, Gunner and I both were on the floor with all of the superheroes spread around. The four of us conquered every antihero in the universe and a few out of it. The entire cabin of the plane offered places to set up our forces to fight the bad guys, hiding behind furniture and rolling under tables as we saved the world. Gunner and I were both still kids and having two five-year-olds to entertain with their wild imaginations allowed for a great way to spend a few hours.

"Uncle C?" Crew buckled in beside me.

"Yeah, dude? What's up?"

"Do you think my daddy wants a girlfriend?"

I noticed him watching Chandler and KeeMac cuddling on the couch while we used their legs and feet to hide behind.

Oh, wow. *How do I answer this?*

"Well, Crew, that's hard to say, but I think the answer will be yes. I mean when he's ready."

"How will I know he's ready?" He put his little hand on mine that laid on the armrest. I took it and held it tight while the plane was coming in for a landing.

"Little dude, I don't think that's something you have to worry about. You know your daddy loves you more than anything in the world, right? I don't think he'll get a girlfriend without talking to you first." I felt sure that was the truth. I wouldn't want to lie to him.

"Will he marry her so I'll have a real mommy like Tucker does?"

Shit. This was getting deep. I didn't know if I was the right guy to be answering these questions.

"Now that's something I can't answer for you, Crew. He'll only marry her if she loves you like he does. That's a fact." My brain rolled over looking for the right answers.

"What if the new mommy doesn't want a boy like my mommy didn't?"

Oh my God. *Why was he asking me these things?* My heart broke for him. Did he think about this a lot? That fucking bitch of a mother of his, Krissy. I would like to strangle her dumb ass right this very minute. *Who does this to a child?*

I unbuckled him and pulled him into my lap. This earned me a death stare from Peri and Ryan, but I shook my head no. I hugged the little guy as tightly as I could. The lump in my throat melted a little as I kissed the top of his head.

"You know what, Crew? There are so many people sitting right here on this plane who love you and will always make sure you're wanted. Heck, even a crazy guy like me would be happy to have you as my little boy any day of the week. But you see, Crew, I know your daddy pretty well, and I honestly don't believe he would ever choose a girl that didn't love you as much he and we all do. You're too special to everyone to not have the best mommy ever."

Was that enough? Hell, I floundered in unchartered waters here.

"You mean, you would let me come live with you if you got a wife, and we could be a real family?"

"Dude, you're always welcome in my house, but I think I'd have to fight your dad to get you away from him. He loves you too much to let you go. What's that he always tells you about loving you?"

He perks up and smiles at me, and just like that the lump was back. "He loves me more than there are stars in the sky at night in Texas. That's why we count them all the time. We get beside each other on the lay-down pool chair with all of the lights off. We count as high as I can go, like a hundred million trillion."

"Whoa, that's a lot of stars, dude. It's a good thing we live in Texas so you can see so many."

"Yes, sir, and sometimes we see a shooting star, and he tells me to wish on it. You want to know what I wish for every single time?"

Dammit, I knew what was coming. "Sure, Crew, what do you wish for?"

"I always wish to be able to sing like my daddy 'cause he's the best singer ever."

Okay, not what I expected him to say but thank God. I dodged a bullet on that one. "Yes, sir, young man. You are right about that. Your dad is the best singer ever but don't tell UncKee—his own rendition for Uncle KeeMac—that. It might hurt his little feelings."

I had never been so fucking happy for a five-year-old attention span in my life. That was some heavy shit we were talking about. I needed to tell the others about it soon. He's obviously thought about this to ask those kinds of questions. I wondered if he'd mentioned it to his dad yet. I guess I've gotta watch what I say around the two little guys more. I never realized how much they took in at this age. Obviously, he'd already internalized a lot of what he heard or saw.

I kept him in my lap until the plane rolled to a stop and waited for the attendant to open the door. I kissed him on the top of his little head again and stood him up. He grabbed my hand as we started toward the door. Guess my little buddy and I were partners now since he didn't have to share me with anyone.

Victory

Hayden met me in one of the rehearsal rooms. I opened my guitar case with my back to the door when I heard it open. A little tingle pulsed through me thinking it might be one of AD, but they weren't supposed to be in until this evening so I knew it had to be him. I turned and saw this gorgeous man walk through the door shutting it behind him. Just one look told me it probably didn't take him long to develop a huge following of groupies all vying for a chance to get a piece of him. They probably fought over who could get the closest to him onstage. He was definitely hot in a young guy sort of way. His age didn't matter to me if he could play and sing. I'm not old, but he still had the little boy face that would attract a lot of the younger crowd unless he let the scruff grow on his face like he tended to do.

The onstage experience and touring with AD made him a perfect partner for me. My stage experience in smaller venues, bars to be exact, gave me some credit. I needed to bring my best work to this meeting so he would be impressed with my talents. I caught Cash's attention and didn't even know he watched me the first time. Now I planned to do the same thing to Hayden so he knew I deserved this opportunity.

"Hello, I'm Victory," I said as I offered him my hand.

"Hey, I'm Hayden. Nice to meet you, ma'am."

"Oh God, no, just no. You can't call me ma'am. I'm not that old." I tried to brighten my strained smile, but he knew I wasn't angry.

"Yeah, I'm just programmed that way. My mom and grandparents teach old-school manners and ma'am is one of them. It's a habit drilled in from birth in the south." His perfect smile proved the honesty of his words.

"I'm from Texas, too, and understand completely. Damn kid, we're going to be partners, and I'm not having you remind me I'm getting older by the day." My plastered-on smile started hurting my cheeks with the fakeness of it. I finally dropped it for a more natural one since my nervousness dissipated with each sentence.

"You're not old at all so don't think that way, and I promise to try and drop it." He let go of my hand and opened his guitar case on the top of a cabinet. "You do much writing?"

"Yeah, I do some covers in my sets, but I prefer to play my own music." I tuned my guitar preparing to play.

"I feel the same way. I play all of AD's music as well, but I damn sure prefer mine. I've written a few songs for them, too."

"Really, which ones? I'm familiar with all of their music."

"*Life Worth Living*. You know that one?"

"No, is it new?"

"Yeah, it's about my son and one of AD's sons. Those two little monsters are like brothers."

"That's great. Which one from AD?" I tried not to read anything in the gossip magazines about AD. The trash those rags could spin out of something innocent appalled me. I honestly didn't want to see what or who Carter was doing. The few times I found myself staring at the thin newsprint in the grocery-store line, he filled whole pages with beautiful arm candy or some gorgeous supermodel type wrapped around his body in a suggestive pose. His man-whore status became etched in stone, and he looked proud of it.

"So you call them the little monsters?" I laughed thinking they were probably spoiled, rotten kids.

"No, we do have a lot of names for them, though… Bevis and Butthead, Spiderman and Batman, the James Gang, Thing Two and Thing Two, Shake and Bake. Depends on what they're doing at the time. Sometimes it's terrorizing the nanny and sometimes saving the world. You know typical little boy shit."

"And of course, they have real names?" I asked.

"Ryan and Peri's son, Tucker. My son's name is Crew. They were born a couple of weeks apart. We live with them, too. It's a long story, but we're all good now. Peri's made sure of that."

"Cash introduced me to Peri at his office. Seems like a great person to work with."

"She's the best and the reason we all live together. That girl wouldn't take no for an answer. You'll love her. She takes care of everyone."

"Sounds like you found a gem with her."

"Crew and I both did. Ryan's one lucky fucker. Those two were meant to be together. You'll see it the first time you meet them."

"Great. I look forward to it."

"So, Victory, let's see what we're going to do together here. You even heard any of my damn songs?" His laugh made him sound like he was joking.

"I've heard all of your songs. I went home and YouTubed the hell out of your music."

He laughed out loud at that. "I hope it sounded half-way good. I honestly don't know how some of that shit got on there. I don't even bother to look at it anymore. Scares the hell out of me."

Now it was my turn to laugh at him. "Hey, at least people like your music and gigs enough to record you."

"Before this is over, I have a gut feeling everyone will know about The Hayden Victory. Hey, I kinda like that." He said the name again. "You know, not like my name is Hayden Victory, but The Hayden Victory like it's a thing all by itself."

"I think you're getting ahead of yourself. You haven't even heard me play or sing. What if it's shit?"

"First off, I know for a fact you have to be outstanding to have impressed Cash. The guy's ability for finding talented singers proceeds him. And second, Peri wouldn't line up AD with anyone fucking lousy. I told you, she's very protective when it comes to her guys and Channey."

"Channey? Who's that?" I strummed across my strings while he tuned a little more.

"Oh, that would be Chandler Chatam, musical genius. The girl's a music prodigy, but you would be too if your dad was Ryder fucking Steele."

"Yeah, I heard about that somewhere."

"She's great, though. Channey's what the boys call her. She loves them like they were hers."

"I have a hell of a lot of people's names to learn if this all works out."

"Then let's give it a whirl and see what ya got."

He launched into his hottest tune on the market. Of course, I recognized it right away so I joined him. When the lyrics began, I backed him up softly to get a feel for his pitch and the rhythm. When he reached the guitar solo in the middle, I continued to play the accompanying part while he tore up the music. We came back together after it, and I think we both knew this would be a success. Our voices blended perfectly together.

It didn't take many songs before we began feeding off each other. He listened to some of my songs and after one time through, he joined me. Our harmonies were on point.

"Damn, that was outstanding, Vic." Hayden stood up and fist bumped me.

"Yeah, after the first song, my gut told me it would be kickass music."

"It's more than kickass. It's fucking fierce, babe. Fierce." He didn't have to use words at this point. His opinion was all over his face. "We gotta get Cash in here."

Cash walked through the door clapping his hands. "I knew it when I heard her at the bar. She's got the sound you need on some of your songs, Hayden, and vice-versa. Don't get me wrong, you both have a great sound on your own, but I think on certain songs you could come together and make them da bomb."

I started laughing immediately, and I couldn't stop. "Da bomb?"

"Wrong term these days?"

"How should I know? It just sounded funny coming from you."

"You know what I'm saying, right Hayden?" Now he wanted Hayden to backup his attempt at street slang.

"Yeah, I know." Hayden smirked and turned to me. "Sometimes you gotta overlook the old man. He still thinks he's a teenager."

"Dammit, I keep telling you I'm not an old man. Stop with the fucking old jokes."

"At least he hasn't forgotten how to use that word." Hayden and I both started laughing, and finally, Cash joined in.

"Okay, all jokes aside. I listened to most of what you played through the headphones. With some more rehearsal time, I think you'll be ready to hit the tour stops we have lined up and join AD in L.A."

Hayden turned and looked at him. "How much more time do we get?"

"Tomorrow." He grinned at us both.

"Fuck, I knew you were going to say that." Hayden was pissed.

"What's got you so angry? You knew this was coming up quickly," Cash asked him.

"I wanted to be there when we put Crew on the plane with the band. Shit, I hate sending him off like that."

"He goes with Peri and Ryan all the time. Besides, he'll be with Tucker."

"I know, but dammit, he's my kid, and I like to tell him bye before he leaves with other people. You know I'm not fucking wild about flying, and he's getting on a plane without me." Hayden's concern grew more intense with each sentence.

"Shit, that's really the problem, isn't it? You don't want him flying without you." Cash didn't outwardly laugh at Hayden, but I could tell he wanted to. That wasn't fair to Hayden. He was scared for his son.

"Right. I like to be with him on a plane. I couldn't live if something happened, and I wasn't there holding him."

He saw Hayden's real fear and offered sincere advice. "He'll be fine. I promise. You know Peri wouldn't let anything happen to him or let him be scared. She loves him like her own."

"I know you're right, but shit, it doesn't make it any easier on me. We'll both be fine. I'll FaceTime him before he leaves." Hayden picked up his guitar and turned to me raising his eyebrows. "You ready to do this?"

"Sure. Practice 'til we fucking feel it. Right?"

"Hell yeah. We need to be *da bomb* on the stage." We both laughed and that broke the tension. Cash left without laughing which only made us laugh harder.

On the fifth day, we were in San Diego, and I knew Hayden was ready to get this mini tour put to bed. He called Crew every day to talk, sometimes more than once. He introduced him to me over FaceTime, and I thought him adorable right up until he asked his dad if I was his girlfriend.

"No, son. She's my partner onstage. We sing together."

"Channey and Unkee sing together, and she's his girl." The adorable child obviously never missed a thing going on around him.

"Yeah, that's true, but Victory's my friend so don't worry."

"Okay, Pops."

"Pops? Where'd that come from?" Hayden shrugged his shoulders at me.

"Pops, he's the lollipop dad on Cartoon Network." Crew's tone made Hayden sound like he was behind the times and needed to catch up.

"You and Tuck watching a lot of TV?"

"No Daddy. You know RiRi won't let us. She sets the timer and when it goes BZZZ, we have to stop. It's okay 'cause we get to play with our superheroes. We built a fort under the table. You should see it, Daddy..."

I walked away so the two of them could discuss fort building. Little children kind of scared me. How did people know what to do with them? At my age, I should want to be thinking about that but no. Hell no. Maybe when I reached my thirties. Right now, I had things to do.

I strummed on my guitar working on a new song when Hayden ended the call.

"I wondered where you went," he said walking over.

"I wanted to work on this idea that keeps spinning in my brain trying to get out to my fingers." I played the opening riff for him.

"Sounds like a great start." He picked up his guitar and began looking over what I'd written and added to it. Before we knew it, the music for an entire song with some words appeared on the page on the music sheet. Hayden and I seemed to feed off each other's talents while we wrote. Our thought streams flowed together when it came to songwriting. The process banked off our minds and hit mid-stream causing a whirlpool of music for us to pull from. If one of us started to drown, the other was there with the perfect note to float the music to the bridge.

"Damn, Hayden. I love it! I fucking love it." I stuck up an open palm, and we high-fived each other.

"I don't know where you've been all my music life, but I'm so damn glad you found me." His genuine smile stretched across his face.

"We need to kiss Cash!" I said enthusiastically.

"That would be a 'hell no.' You can do the kissing," he said with a smirk.

I laughed and punched him on the arm. "Come on little daddy pops, I think we deserve a drink before the show."

"Now that would be a 'hell yes!'" We picked up our guitars and headed out.

Carter

The roadies had the Center loaded in, and we needed to do a sound check. We hardly ever did it anymore, but we hadn't played there before so KeeMac wanted us to look it over and make sure it's what we previously discussed with the technicians. This show kicked off the new album, and the band liked the first show to be perfect so it set the wheels in motion for an outstanding tour.

"What do you think, KeeMac?" Peri asked from mid-auditorium.

"What do you think, Peri? You're the one standing where our adoring fans will be screaming and yelling." He hit a note on his guitar with a little whammy added to it for effect. We all knew the changes wouldn't be made from her comments, but she liked being part of it somehow so we humored her.

"Very funny, guitar boy," Peri yelled at him. The guitar's loud sound sucked the other noise from the auditorium.

"Okay, let's head back to the hotel. I'm starving," I told the rest as I handed my bass off to my tech.

"Yeah, you slept through breakfast in the penthouse with the rest of us," Peri told me.

"Oh I ate breakfast, it just didn't have any nutritional value," I smirked in her direction.

"You're nasty and watch your mouth around the boys with talk like that. Keep your slutty groupies away from them, too. Ryan and Hayden told you this on the last tour."

"If Ryan would share, I wouldn't have to bring home extras." I knew this would get a rise out of her.

She reached around and popped me on the back of the head. "Dumbass. That'll never happen."

"Owww. That hurt. Abuse. Abuse," I yelled, feigning mock injury.

"You probably deserved a hell of a lot more than that." Ryan walked up laughing.

"Little shit thinks we need to share so then he doesn't have to bring groupies around anymore."

"Fuck that. Do you know who you're talking to?" Ryan gave me a hard stare.

"Yeah, but never mind. I didn't know she had a damn mean streak in her still. Thought you'd whipped all that out of her."

"Dude, what the fuck are you talking about? I think all that sex made you psycho."

"I'm talking about your wife. She's feisty and strikes back." I rubbed the back of my head.

"And, what's that supposed to mean?"

"I thought you would have gotten her to submit to your pleasures after all this time." I smiled when I said it because the idea of Peri being a submissive was so fucking ludicrous, I couldn't hold it in.

Peri's right arm came straight out at me with her palm facing forward. My first instinct was to duck thinking she was going to slap me. Instead, she shoved the palm in my face to shut me up. "The bullshit noise spewing from your mouth, I can't even deal with right now." She whipped around and stomped off.

"Do you even stop and think before you vomit dumbass shit from your mouth? Now she's gonna be mad at me thinking I told you she was my submissive when you know damn good and well, she's not." He actually sounded pissed off.

"Yeah, I thought it was pretty funny. She knows that we all know what a ball buster she can be and would only ever be a top. Wait, wait, wait. Maybe she's the dominatrix in this scenario and you're the sub. Dude, don't tell me you let her put a harness on and lead you around like an animal with a ball in your mouth."

"Listen here, asshat, you stepped across the line." When he said that, I doubled over and couldn't help myself from hitting the floor laughing so hard.

When I finally straightened up, Ryan glared at me.

"Dude, calm down. I was just messing with y'all. You two are too easy."

"Yeah, and you're twenty-seven going on fourteen with the sexual habits of a pervert." He took off after Peri and left me still laughing.

I looked around at the others still left watching us and shrugged my shoulders. "These guys are too damn serious, and we're just getting started."

The new stage design for the tour KeeMac and Chandler helped create looked like the best we had ever used. It wasn't just the new album cover but an enhanced version of it. Our fans would recognize it, but when the tiles appeared to open with pictures of all of us from past tours, it created more of an interactive look. The fans who attended past concerts would recognize the pictures, and the new fans would get an insight into some former times.

We ran out to the cheers and screams ready to play to a packed house, and our adrenaline began pumping. KeeMac took his mic and spoke to the crowd like he always did.

"Heeellllooo Los Fucking Angeles!" he yelled into the mic. "We're Assured Distraction, and we're here to get this fucking party started." That's all it took to get the audience ready to rock the house down.

Ryan started into the opening riff of the number one hit song off our last album. The sound in the audience was so over the top if we pulled our in-ear monitors, we couldn't hear ourselves think. The fans yelled and screamed and sang along to the words KeeMac poured out. The entire concert rocked along for the next hour and a half, and then we added two encores. Exhaustion took over when we finally exited the stage, but with the adrenaline rush the band exudes when we're done, we all have our own way of coming down.

KeeMac and Chandler still demand an empty dressing room for some hot sex. Ryan wraps around Peri and pulls her away to a private location, which leaves Gunner and me. Only this time, Lola waited for him offstage. He picked her up, and she wrapped those long beautiful tanned legs around his middle. She ran her hand over his slick head kissing him like there was no tomorrow.

It left me with strangers mulling around waiting. I handpicked two beauties who were hugging the stage eyeing me the entire night. I felt like one of the girls had been backstage with me before, but I couldn't remember where. As I made my way off the stage and we all bumped fists acknowledging the great concert we just handed our audience, the two were waiting for me.

I grabbed the dark-haired one I recognized and kissed her breathless before I spoke a word to her. I wanted to judge what I had to work with here. She responded in kind which got me more worked up than I already was. That girl kissed like a suction cup with a split tongue. I broke the kiss and wrapped one arm around her neck while I pulled the redhead in for the same thing. She was a little more tentative in her approach, but the kiss heated me up in a whole different way.

"Well, ladies, let's go see what we can scare up backstage." They both nodded in agreement. The night would end on a good note. Literally, fucking good. After a couple of beers, the three of us left to find an empty room, but Peri stopped me in the hall.

"Where do you think you all are going? You have to be at the hotel in thirty minutes and dressed for the party." She ran her eyes over the two women, and I could tell she tried not to let her face reflect her thoughts. Passing judgment wasn't in Peri. She found something in everyone to love.

"Sweetheart, Peri. Would I be late to my own party?" I winked at her.

"Okay, big guy. I'm holding you to that." She smiled at me then turned and walked away.

"Ladies, shall we?" The women both smiled at me nodding their heads.

The first dressing room waited patiently for some usage, and I planned to exercise that option. I ordered both the girls to strip as we walked through the door. "Ladies, we are a little short on time as you heard the boss inform me. Let's get our own party started the best way I know, without clothes."

The redhead laughed as she whipped the black top off revealing a luscious set of perfect double D's spilling out of red lace.

"Yeah, that's what I'm talking about."

These girls were talented in different ways, and I worked them both to put good use to those abilities. While the dark-haired beauty started on unzipping my jeans, the redhead continued stripping down unleashing her rocking body for me to savor.

As the forked tongue wrapped itself around my hard cock, I sucked one of those beautiful huge tits in my mouth lavishing one pink, pert nipple with my tongue while I played the other like the tuner on a radio. This managed to get a low moan out of the redhead's throat that matched the moan out of mine as that tongue and suction applied pressure to my dick like I've never felt before. When she slid down and took my balls in her mouth, while massaging the taint behind them, I wanted to blow on the spot.

I held back, though. Don't ever let it be said that I left a woman unsatisfied in the Carter caisson of carnal kicks.

"Ladies, let's take this party to the couch." I pushed the redhead to the couch and after lying down on my back, I pulled her over my face to gain access to the love spot at the bottom of her landing strip. The knowledge didn't escape me that my tongue flirted with the natural redhead. While I pleasured her with my mouth, the dark-haired darling continued to show me all of her talents with a stellar blow job. Damn, she swallowed me down with each deep thrust I made. I couldn't help myself once I figured out her throat would flex around my shaft.

The redhead and I howled about the same time as I blew my load and she showered my face. I hadn't had a squirter in a while. Not many women actually came that way, so when I find one, I felt like I'd hit the jackpot.

"Damn, Carter, I haven't done that in ages. What did you do to me?"

"It's a secret only a few of us know about. If I shared it, I'd have to kill you." We both laughed. I opened my eyes to see dark brown ones peering over the milky white skin of the redhead who was resting her head on the couch back while straddling my chest.

The look said, "what about me?" and I knew I owed her for the outstanding blow job. I couldn't send her home unsatisfied.

"We were saving the best for last." I nudged the redhead. "Don't you think we owe your friend the same pleasure?"

She laughed and nodded her head. "Come here, babe. You know I wouldn't let you go home disappointed. She slid off me, and I got off the couch.

"I really want this cock inside me, dude. You think you can make that happen?"

"Sure, but I gotta have a little recovery time so I think we need to warm you up. Right red?" I barely finished that question when that long tongue found its way into the redhead's mouth while she twisted, turned, and pinched on her friends' ample tits making them stand at attention. "Damn, girls. You'll get the ol' flag pole standing straight with that kind of action."

Watching these two go at each other was fucking hot. They obviously weren't strangers to each other's desires because before I could lift a finger, they were loudly moaning. My dick stood at attention ready to go for round two faster than I had been able to do in a while. Guess it'd been too long.

I flipped the newest guest of honor over and pulled her to her knees and then rolled on a condom from my pocket. As I moved my sheathed sword up and down her slick path to heaven, the redhead laid down under her and continued to pay close attention to her friend's tits. I finally sunk into the tight, heated tunnel. "Fuck, that feels great on my cock. Let me feel you clench down on it, babe. I know you can do that for me." Damn, could she ever.

The redhead added her fingers for some clit action as I drove home on her friend, but these two didn't stop there.

When I pulled the dark brown hair back and leaned over for a hot kiss, I saw she was offering her friend some clit action, too.

"Sweet cheeks, you better give that honey pot a little pinch and get her there fast 'cause watching y'all go at each other is going to make me nut in a hurry." This earned me a ram that hit home because she pushed herself back on my dick while I pumped forward. I swear, my dick hit the other end. She only had to do that a couple of times before she started screaming about coming hard causing me to join her in the sexual nirvana. The redhead must have liked the sounds because her body seized up letting us all know she rounded out the party.

We all collapsed together on that couch but only for a brief moment as the one on the bottom had to be in pain from our weight. I rolled off to the floor leaving the two women sprawled together. Looking around, I spotted my jeans and pulled them to me. I knew I needed to get out of there for several reasons. One, Peri would have my head if I arrived too late at the party, and two, these girls were so damn hot, they could talk me into a longer *go-at-it back* in my hotel room. The latter could not happen tonight so I pulled my jeans and shirt on, kissed the two sleepy women, and left them lying on the couch.

I strolled into the party thirty minutes later ready to celebrate the night with all of my best friends. Champagne flowed, and we spent the evening enjoying the groups of people who showed up to wish us luck on our new album. Networking and ass-kissing ran rampant in that ballroom, too. Everyone in AD secretly hated these parties but knew what a necessary evil to our success they were. All we ever wanted to do was play music and have fun. Shaking hands and making nice didn't fall into either of those categories.

"Hey, Carter," KeeMac said walking up to the table where I was standing watching the dance floor."

"Yeah, what's up?"

"Where were you?"

"What do you mean, I've been right here since I arrived." I looked at him dumbfounded.

"Yeah, I see that, but you looked like you were a million miles away with that stare."

"Oh, that? Just thinking about how much I fucking hate these kinds of parties. I'd much rather be at one of our houses playing guitars, singing a little, and drinking some damn good beer."

"Hell yeah, that'd be a much better time, but you know we gotta do this shit, too."

"Doesn't mean we have to like it. As much as I wasn't looking forward to getting back on the bus, at least there we can be us and not standing around bullshitting people we really don't care about."

"Shhh." Peri snuck up behind me. "Someone might hear that."

"I know but honestly, I don't fucking care," I told her.

"No, none of us do. It'll be over soon. Y'all want to come out to the RV when we're done and have some real fun?" Her smile was contagious, and I nodded my head.

"How much longer until we can sneak away from this place? I've had enough of this bubbly shit for one night." I held out my stemmed flute to her.

"Me, too." The words came from behind KeeMac. Chandler looked around his side.

"Hey, cupcake. You're bored, too?" I asked her.

"Hell yeah. Is this someone's idea of a good time?" She looked straight at Peri.

"I just do what I'm told. Tonight's agenda included a party to kick off the new album. Don't hold it against me."

We laughed as she looked like she was genuinely hurt by our words. "Girl, we're only giving you shit. We'd never take it out on you. Besides, I bet you feel the same fucking way."

"I do. So, if we spread out and wait around making small talk to a few people close to a door, we can slip out one at a time without anyone noticing," Peri offered, and we all laughed and nodded. "It's a plan then. The RV, thirty minutes?"

"You're on," the group said and slowly walked away.

"I'll find Lola and Gunner and let them know," I quietly told Peri as I walked by her and she nodded.

They were in total agreement when I found them. We each found a spot on the outside of the bullshit ring and spent time making small talk with strangers and then slowly disappeared one by one. It felt great the second I pulled that tie off my neck and stuffed it in my coat pocket. I fucking hated ties. Whoever invented them must have been a masochist of the worst kind.

Victory

"You know if we leave now, we can be in L.A. where AD is in about two hours, right?" Hayden seemed pumped at the idea of meeting up with them. I didn't want to see them any sooner than necessary. The longer we put that off, the better I'd be.

"Yeah, but we have three more venues to play before we join them in Portland. I vote we wait." I could see his enthusiasm falter with my comment.

"What is it you have against meeting them? They're all great people. You're going to love them. I can't begin to tell you how much they've helped me in my career much less personally. I know they'll have so many awesome ideas on how to take us to another level."

"I'm tired's all. We've been traveling and performing straight since we left Austin. Guess I just don't want to go any more than we need to in one day." I tried to make that sound convincing, but even I knew what a lame excuse it was.

"Woman, you are too young to act this damn old."

"Ha, ha. That song's already written, Hayden." I forced a laugh when I said it.

"No, really. Let's go up there tonight, and we can sleep in tomorrow morning. They have one more day before they leave L.A. so maybe they can catch our show. I know Peri can get us a room in their hotel if I call her now."

"I don't want to inconvenience them and besides, we already have rooms closer to our venue." My excuses were starting to sound desperate now, even to me.

"We won't inconvenience anyone. They always book extra rooms for big parties in case someone unexpected shows. They always get used, too."

"See, someone else will need them instead of us." I got more nervous by the minute. I knew this would end badly for me.

"Look, if you don't want to party with the band, you can go straight to your room. I can crash anywhere when the party shuts down. I don't expect you to stay in the same room anyway." Hayden must have really wanted to meet up with them to be begging like this. He turned those big blue eyes on me and that's all it took. The kid was too damn cute for his own good.

"Okay, if that's all right with you. I'll go on to my room, and you can party all night with them. As long as you're ready to be onstage tomorrow night, I'm good with it." I knew I'd give in to him. One bat of those long lashes, and he knew he sucked me into his plan. He was worse than my little brother when we were children, and he wanted his own way.

"Great. I'll call the bus driver and tell him we'll be ready in twenty minutes. You can do that right?"

"Sure, Hayden. I'll be ready." I smiled at him, and he jumped up and hugged me.

"You're going to love the band. Just wait and see."

Just wait and see. I could wait another lifetime before I saw Carter Sheridan again. A whole fucking lifetime.

The bus rolled into L.A., and it might as well have been twelve noon instead of twelve midnight. The city noises of people, cars, and music filled me. I'd never been to L.A. before so I couldn't contain my excitement. Hayden toured through here with AD more than once so he knew what to expect. The enthusiasm he spoke with of the places we passed said it still amazed him, too. Unlike any big city I had visited, some of the sights were bigger than life in my eyes.

The bus turned into the front of a fancy hotel and a parking attendant met us at the door. People everywhere watched as we descended the steps assuming we were a big-named act arriving. When they didn't recognize us, they continued down the sidewalk disappointed which suited me fine. I didn't know if I would ever be prepared for all the fame that went along with being a superstar like

Hayden already seems to be. Everything he talked about evolved around making it big like Assured Distraction.

"I texted Peri, and they're here. She said they do have a couple of extra rooms, and all we've got to do is go to the front desk for our keys," Hayden told me as he rounded the front of the bus with both of our bags.

I tried to take mine but he held on tightly, always the gentleman.

"Let's go get our keys. I'll drop my bag in the room, and then I'll find the party and the women." He wiggled his eyebrows.

"You do that, man-child. I'm sure those ladies are the real reason the bus burned the road up from San Diego to L.A." I laughed at him. No doubt he loved the ladies, and they loved him. His looks were going to get him in trouble one day. I'm sure he's exactly like Carter and the rest of the AD band members.

We approached the counter, and the girl looked up at him dropping the papers in her hand. "May I help you?" Her smile lit up the room as she perused Hayden's body.

"Sure can, sweetheart. Peri O'Connor left keys for us."

"Let me check. What's your name?" She tore her eyes away from the kid. Damn, I knew he would cause a riot when he got as well known as AD.

"Hayden Devillier, ma'am." He turned on that charm every chance he got.

"Oh, okay, Mr. Devillier. Yes, we have two keys for a two-bedroom suite. You'll also have to use this key in the elevator for access to that particular floor." She gazed up at him. I'm sure she tried to decide if he was someone she should recognize.

"Thanks, ma'am." He really poured on the southern drawl.

"You're very welcome, Mr. Devillier. The elevators to the left will provide you access to your rooms." She gave him her best come-hither look, and I tried hard not to laugh.

We walked away from the desk. "You're terrible Hayden. That poor girl's resistance to your charms flew out the window on the first ma'am. Do you do that on purpose?"

As we stepped into the elevator, he turned around and looked at me with a goofy grin that made me finally let go with the laugh I had been holding in.

"Who? Me?"

"Yes, you, dumbass. You were doing that just to get the girl all worked up while she did her job."

He leaned over to whisper a secret in my ear. "Bet her panties were wet when we left." Then he started laughing, too.

"Yuk, TMI. I don't need to know what you think about action in a girl's panties, Hayden. Never." I popped him on the back of the head.

"Oww. What was that for?"

"For saying something inappropriate to me."

"I only stated a fact." He couldn't stop smiling.

"A fact I had no need knowing."

"Okay, okay. I'll be good…" he said and then softly added, "… for now."

"I heard that."

I'd forgotten about Assured Distraction possibly being on the same floor as we walked down the hall. Loud noises of laughter and talking came from one of the rooms we walked by.

"Hey, this is probably the band or some of them. Let's stop here and let them know we made it."

"No, I'm tired. Give me my bag, and I'll go to my room." I prayed the door didn't open to their room.

"I'll take it to your room, then. Come on."

I waved the card past the reader on the door. The green light gave me access, and I walked right in turning to Hayden. "Okay, you can go. I'm going to take a shower and climb in bed. I'll see you in the morning." The look he gave me let me know he had something on his mind.

"What?"

"You're acting weird. What's going on?"

"Nothing. I'm tired and ready for bed. See you in the morning." I took the room on the left and shut the door with him standing there staring at me. I leaned against the door waiting to hear the outside door close behind him. He made no sound indicating he intended to leave. I knew my actions appeared rude shutting him out that way, but I didn't want Carter coming down the hall finding me. I wasn't ready to spring myself on him because I had no clue how he would react to seeing me. Hayden finally shut the door, and I heard his steps as he walked back down to the fun and games with his rock-star friends.

I worried for the two-hour drive up here about what would happen if we ran into Carter tonight. I also thought about how everything needed to work out in the morning so we could be gone before the group woke up. I wanted to allude Carter until I couldn't any longer.

I ran different scenarios through my mind about our reunion while I bathed. Would he be happy to see me? Shocked at my being there? Surprised to find me on tour with his young friend? Angry that I had kept my identity from him? Mad at Cash for not telling him? So many questions ran on a constant loop in my brain, it exhausted me. The sooner the secret came out, the better off I'd be. The consequences might come at a high price. Carter possessed the clout to get 13 Recordings to drop me.

By the time I climbed into the clean sheets, my mind resembled Swiss cheese, full of holes. I envisioned falling asleep the moment my head hit the pillow. My brain proved me wrong, though. I tossed and turned with thoughts of Carter and our last time together. We were young and dumb then.

"Holy shit, dude," followed by loud laughter woke me out of a light sleep I finally found.

"Pretty fucking sweet, huh?" Hayden's voice came through the sleep fog, loud and clear.

"I can't believe Peri put y'all up in style, you little fucker," said the unknown voice.

"Shhh. My partner's asleep. We gotta be quiet," Hayden drunkenly spoke.

"Oh yeah, forgot about that. So spill kid. None of us knew anything about you becoming part of a duo."

"Cash and I talked about it some. He seemed to think we'd mesh. I gotta say, she's awesome. She sings like an angel, and we work together so well. Damn, I don't know how I sang without her already, and we've only been singing together a few weeks. It's like we're fucking made to sing together."

Hearing how he really felt made me smile. He told me several times he was happy with our work together, but I didn't know for sure. He might have been trying to boost my ego to make me feel better onstage. Drunken confessions sometimes came closer to the truth.

"That's outstanding, dude. Glad to hear it's all working out, but you didn't give me any important deets. Is she hot? You tried to tap that already?"

"Dumbass, don't talk about her like that, and you stay away from her." Hayden defended my honor. The sweet kid in him made me smile again.

"Whoa, got a little crush going on boy?" The stranger harassed him.

"Hell no. Victory's not on my radar that way. Besides, she's older than me and unlike you, I ain't looking for a hookup every time I walk out on that stage."

"You little shit. I've taught you all I know about finding the women, and it sounds like you're missing one right under your nose. Unless, she doesn't swing that way." The stranger's comments made me angrier as he spoke. We hadn't even met, and now I hoped we wouldn't. He's a first-class douche. I hoped Hayden forgets anything he's supposedly learned from this prick.

"That's none of my business, but she's drop-dead gorgeous. Wait 'til you see these wicked eyes she's got."

"Wicked eyes, huh?"

"Yeah, but they might be contacts. I don't know. Haven't gotten around to asking her too much personal stuff yet."

"Well, what the hell do you know about her? So far all I'm hearing is she can sing, she's hot, and she's got wicked eyes."

"She can play the guitar like she learned from a pro." We needed to spend some time talking if the only things Hayden could say about me was how I looked and that I'm talented. Wait, I don't care what the stranger thought anyway. Forget that talk.

Someone pounded on the door, and I had half a mind to barrel out there and remind them some people in this room liked to sleep. Good thing I didn't because the next thing I heard was an obnoxious female screech. I wondered if that was supposed to resemble a laugh.

"Hell yeah, boys! The party's arrived."

Oh. My. God. Please tell me this wasn't about to happen on the other side of this door.

It got quiet for a minute, and I could only imagine what took place before I started hearing some moaning. Really? Were these guys going through with this?

"Calm down boys, there's enough for both of you. I'm always down to be the middle of the sandwich."

I pulled my pillow over my head and considered going into the bathroom and turning on the shower. Please don't let her be a screamer. My prayers went unanswered, though. The longer the sexcapades went on, the louder the screeching got.

"Yeah baby, just like that."

"Yes, yes my fucking god. *Yes*!" she moaned and screamed and moaned some more.

"That's right baby. It's Carter, but you can call me God if you want to."

Please, what a line of shit. I wanted to scream at them to shut the fuck up. That hyena and her howls and screams were too much. Finally, after what seemed like hours, the obnoxious sex noises died down. I heard some muffled talking and then doors opened and closed. God only knew who remained in our room, glad that I thought to lock my door before I crawled in bed. The small clock on the nightstand read 4:00 a.m. Tomorrow would be a hell of a long day.

Halo

I woke up to someone banging on our door. Damn, this place held a lot of crazy people who didn't know the meaning of quiet. I glanced at the clock again to see it was after 10:00 a.m. I heard unexpected voices. A child yelled "Daddy" followed by laughing and talking. Hayden's son must be here to visit. I forgot the band had his son traveling with them, but I knew Hayden hadn't seen him yet. It was one reason he wanted to catch up with AD.

What should I do? I had no clue which band members might be there, but it sounded like the time to find out approached rapidly.

"Hayden, knock on her door and see if she's awake," a woman said. "I want to introduce her to Chandler."

"Yeah, I'm dying to meet her. Cash and Peri told us she's a perfect match for your duo," said another that I assumed must be Chandler.

I could meet the girls from the band and no male voices other than Hayden's came through the door. I climbed out of bed and ran into the bathroom to make myself a little more presentable before meeting more beautiful people. Was everyone associated with these people gorgeous? I had yet to meet an average-looking normal person with them.

I peeked through the door to make sure who stood in the room and only found the two women with two small boys and Hayden.

Okay, I could do this.

"Good morning," I greeted them as though I'd had a good night's sleep.

If they only knew.

"Hey, sleepy head." Hayden offered me a smile. "Glad you joined us."

"Yeah, good morning to you, too, sunshine." I wanted to light into him about all of the noise I endured in our room but thought better of it with the kids there. Turning to Peri, I nodded my head. "Hello, Peri. Good to see you again."

She immediately jumped up and gave me a hug. "We're so happy you both decided to come on up and join us. She backed up and looked at the other woman. "Victory, this is Chandler Chatam."

We both stepped forward and shook hands saying our hellos.

"It's great to meet you, Victory. We've heard so many awesome things about the new music you and Hayden are doing now. I know he's excited about it."

"Me, too. I love working with Hayden and am grateful that Cash believed in me enough to offer the opportunity."

Wow, did that sound like a line of bullshit. I was thankful for it but saying that out loud sounded so fake.

A squeak came from behind the couch, and I leaned back to see two little boys about to peek over the top. "Hey guys. Are you hiding back there?" They both came running around the end and one latched onto Peri and the other onto Hayden.

"What's this? Are you both being shy?" Peri asked the boys, but neither gave a response.

Hayden reached down and plucked Crew off his leg. "This is Miss Victory, Crew. Say hello to her." He wrapped his arms around his dad's neck but said a soft hello. "Dude, you need to look at her and shake her hand."

Hayden put him down on the floor and the precious child looked up at me and stuck his little hand out. "Hello, Miss Vic… Vic…" He turned and faced his dad. "How do you say that again?"

"Miss Vic-tor-y," he sounded out each syllable slowly.

The sweet face looked at me again still holding out his hand. I kneeled down so I could look into his big brown eyes. "Hello, Crew. It's very nice to meet you." I took his little hand in mine and shook it.

"Hello, Miss Vic-tor-y. Nice to meet you, too."

His infectious smile pulled one from me. How adorable he was and obviously they had all taken the time to teach him manners. Before I could let go of his hand, another sweet face jumped over beside Crew almost knocking him down.

"I'm nice to meet you, too."

"You are? So, you must be…" I let him say his own name.

"Tucker. I must be Tucker." He put his hand out to shake mine. The whole room started laughing at this imp's precociousness.

"What a pleasure it is to meet you, Tucker." The obvious shy act was gone. "I heard that one of you was Spiderman and one was Superman."

This started a tale from the two of them about superheroes that ended up with the three of us sitting on the floor. They informed me of everything I didn't know on the subject.

After a few minutes, Peri stood. "Okay boys, I think we better get back to the room and see if breakfast has been delivered. We ordered every item on the menu so you are both welcome to join us." Everyone turned and looked at me.

"Oh, no. I couldn't right now. I need to shower and return some emails. Y'all go ahead, though. I'll grab some coffee and be ready to hit the road when Hayden is."

"I swear the woman hardly eats," Hayden told the others. "I don't know how she does it."

Even if I could eat an elephant, no way would I go into that suite. My brain worked overtime trying to figure out how to get to our bus without being seen.

"Suit yourself. We're going to eat and then make our way down to the parade of buses," Peri told me.

"Are you sure there's nothing we can entice you with? I hate leaving you here with nothing to eat," Chandler questioned.

"No, no. I'm great. Y'all enjoy your morning. Honestly, I had so little sleep, I might go down, get in my bunk, and go back to sleep. Some people had a party out here last night."

I cut my eyes over to Hayden before he walked out the door.

His man-child face turned into a sheepish grin. "Sorry about that. Hope we didn't keep you awake for too long. We tried to be quiet."

"Don't tell me you and Carter brought groupies from the party last night to this room?" Peri gave Hayden an evil eye. "No wonder he's still asleep."

"Okay, I won't tell you, but it was only one." The door closed behind them before I heard anything else she said to him. I wondered if she figured out they had a threesome or if that's the way they always had their women.

With lightning speed, I raced to my room, threw clothes in my bag and dressed in record time, ready to make my escape. The last thing I wanted to see this morning after all of the sex noises they treated to me last night slept in his own room. Thank God.

I listened at the door before peeking out. The quiet allowed me to open it and look around for the stairs. I could go down a couple of flights and wait for the elevator or find another one further away from their doors.

I hoisted my bag over my shoulder and stepped out into the hallway just as the elevator opened. I took off for the stairs but before I could get to the door, two men stepped out. Not just any two men. These two were the epitome of hot rockers. Shoulder length blond hair that was pulled back into a delicious looking man-bun caught my attention. I'm usually not attracted to that look. In this case, I made an exception. The other had no hair at all. Damn, I knew I stared, but what female in their right mind wouldn't stare at the beautiful tattoos or faces of gods? Did I step into another dimension that included all of Mount Olympus?

I turned the handle to open the stairwell door before one yelled, "Stop. Stop right there."

I kept trying the door but before I could get it open, they stood on each side of me.

"Going somewhere, sweetheart?" the blond asked placing his big hand on the wall beside me cutting me off from the doorway.

"Yeah, I'm checking out. Just need to give the key back to the front desk." The answer seemed harmless enough.

"Is that so? Care to tell us why you are leaving with a huge bag from one of our rooms?" It was all I could do not to fall into a trance looking into this guy's eyes. They were a bright shade of blue-green.

"Actually, it was my room last night."

"Oh yeah? Who brought you onto this floor?" blond hunk asked.

I dug in my back pocket and produced the key. "This key brought me on this floor." Did they think I would roll over and play dead to their accusations? I had every right to be here.

"That's great but who gave you the key, honey?" the bald guy inquired.

Okay, I had to get this over with before that other suite emptied out, and I ended up face to face with the one band member I did not want to meet today. "Peri O'Connor gave Hayden Devillier and me a key to stay in that suite. My name is Victory."

They began backtracking on their rude alpha-male attitudes as soon as I said my name. I should have started the interrogation with it and I would have been on the bus already.

"I'm so sorry. We haven't met you and thought, well we thought..." Blond god stammered.

"I know exactly what you thought, and no, I'm not a groupie sneaking out of a warm bed." I tried not to sound pissed, but I knew it came out that way.

"Right. Uh, we're sorry. I'm Gunner Wallace, drummer for Assured Distraction." A massive paw came out to shake my full hands. "Here, let me get that for you." He tried to take my bag off my shoulder.

"That's okay. What is it about you guys needing to carry my stuff?" I put the key in my back pocket and shook his hand.

"And I'm Keeton MacDonald, the lead singer and guitar player, but everyone calls me KeeMac." He grabbed my hand from Gunner's and shook it, too.

"That's great. Now that we know I didn't rob the place, I'll be on my way, guys. Wonderful meeting you both, and I'm sure we'll be seeing y'all soon." I tried to go through the door again, but Zeus and the Titan wouldn't allow me to pass.

"Let us take this down for you. Hey, why are you leaving, though? Didn't the girls invite you to brunch?" KeeMac asked.

"Yes, they did but I'm not hungry so I'm going to the bus now to get some sleep. Not much sleep going on in our room last night." I didn't want to repeat this story again.

"Yeah?" KeeMac raised an eyebrow.

"I'm not the one to blame. Talk to the others. They'll give you the story. So, I'm going. Y'all join the party in your suite." I grabbed my bag from the floor. "And yes, I can get it myself but thanks." I didn't give them time to stop me as I ducked under their arms and took off down the stairs letting the door shut on its retracting hinge.

After catching the elevator two floors down, I leaned against the back wall and closed my eyes. Damn, I thought I might never wash my hand again after having the pleasure of touching those two. They obviously didn't recognize me, but I sure recognized them. The guys that were in high school didn't resemble the men they had become. Stalking their pictures online and in magazines didn't do justice to how these two looked in person. When the elevator came to a halt on the ground floor, I picked up my bag and took off for the bus. Forget returning the key, I needed to get on that bus before I ran into anyone else.

I stepped on our bus and went straight to my bunk. I made it without being seen by anyone important. No one knew me, so it was safe to say I wouldn't attract attention like the group that would come down with AD. I began to question if I was cut out for this life.

Carter

I looked around as I walked into the living room of the suite where everyone ate brunch and made too much noise for my head. "Do y'all really have to make this much fu... loud noise to eat?" I realized the boys played on the floor before I made the mistake of dropping the f-bomb. The two momma bears' growls would hit me prior to their extended claws.

"Sounds like you didn't bother to keep your noises to yourself last night in the other suite. Apparently, you kept Victory awake half the night," Peri's mother voice informed me.

"Yeah, where is she? I hoped to meet her since the kid couldn't give me anything more than vital stats." An open bottle of pain reliever called to me from the kitchen counter. "I don't remember drinking that much last night, but my head sure as hell feels like it."

"I think we killed a bottle of tequila between the three of us before our guest left." Hayden's dumbass looking grin said all I needed to forget about the night before.

"Oh, yeah. That almost slipped from my mind."

"Must have been a memorable lay if you've forgotten her already." Gunner smirked at me over the top of his phone.

"Daddy, how did Uncle C disremember where he laid down last night? He just now got up." Crew looked to his dad for an answer.

Well, shit. I'm glad the kids rode in their own RV instead of being on the bus with us.

"He's got a headache this morning, Crew, and it's hard to remember when you first wake up with a headache. Isn't that right Carter and Gunner?" Hayden shot us both looks to remind us that little ears listen to everything we say.

"Back to my question. Where is Victory this morning?" I asked again.

"I met her Uncle C. You'll like her 'cause she's real pretty, and you like pretty girls." Crew looked at Tucker, and they both wrinkled up their noses.

"What's wrong with pretty girls?" I asked the dynamic duo.

"Me and Crew don't like girls. Remember 'girls mean trouble?' They cause problems and ain't nothing but trouble." Every male in the room laughed. Chandler and Peri didn't which made us laugh harder.

"That's right, little dudes." I stuck my fist out to meet theirs in a bump while I noticed the red faces on the girls.

KeeMac swallowed a piece of bacon whole before he said, "Crew's right. She is real pretty. Gunner and I met her in the hallway. There's something about her that seemed familiar, but I don't know what. But, we kinda made fools of ourselves with her."

Peri rounded on KeeMac. "Please tell me you didn't embarrass the poor girl. We don't even know her yet, and she's going to think we're awful."

Gunner spoke up. Guess he figured he might save KeeMac from Chandler's wrath. "We mistook her for someone else coming out of the suite next door."

"And?" Peri wouldn't let it go.

"And we thought she was one of the groupies walking out with a bag full of stuff from the room. In our defense, she was carrying a big duffel bag and acted like she was sneaking out." Gunner dug the hole deeper with every sentence. Some dumbasses never learned.

"You let her go when she told you who she was, right?" Chandler joined the inquisition.

"Yes, and cupcake, we offered to carry the bag down for her, but she wouldn't have it. She threw that thing over her shoulder and took off down the stairs in a run," Gunner finished.

"Down the stairs? Why would she do that?" Peri asked.

"Who knows, you women and your stuff. For all they knew, that bag could have been full of shoes." Ryan finally decided to step in and help the guys out of the mess with his wife.

"Hey, back to me, please. Am I the only one who hasn't met her?" I asked the gang.

"No," Ryan answered. "I haven't met her either. I was just trying to help these two asshats out."

"I think I'm going back to bed and let y'all duke it out, but can you be quiet please?" I headed for the bedroom as I spoke.

"No, you may not. We are leaving shortly. If you're going to sleep, go get in your bunk on the bus," Peri informed me.

"Shit, already?" Peri shot me the mom look again for my language. How could she expect us to not use words we said every day? I needed to work on that.

"Yes, already. Go get your things together and go sleep off your headache on the bus."

I hated tour manager, Peri, sometimes. She could bust our balls with the best of them.

Hayden and I carried our bags and Crew down to the buses.

"I want to go with you, Daddy."

"I know, little dude, but you can't this time. You have to stay with Tucker and the nanny until we join y'all in a couple of weeks."

"How many weeks are a couple?"

I hated seeing Crew separated from his dad but not nearly as much as Hayden. The look both of their faces said it all.

"It's only two weeks, and I promise we'll talk on your tablet every day. It'll be like I'm right there with you."

Crew's bottom lip looked like it was going to drag the ground. Man, I didn't think I could ever have kids and be in a band. As much as the two boys had a great life, keeping them away from their parents seemed too hard to deal with.

I stepped up to Crew and squatted down beside him. "Hey, dude. Let's go look at the new video games you have. Maybe I can ride in the RV with y'all for a while, and we can play."

"But, RiRi said you supposed to go to bed and sleep."

I had to smile at his language. "Well, RiRi doesn't know everything, but don't tell her I told you that. It'll be guy info only." I knew better than to usurp her authority. She'd have my head for it. Our secret made Crew smile.

Hayden spoke up. "Yeah, I'll go sit in the RV until it's time to go, and you and I can play a few games before the buses leave. Besides, Victory's asleep on my bus, and we don't want to wake her either.

Looked like I still wouldn't get to meet her. "I get the first game." I grabbed Crew up and ran to the RV. My head be damned.

Two weeks flew by just like Hayden told Crew they would. AD played six venues in that time, and we killed it. We mixed the new music with our old stuff to keep the crowds happy. The radio stations along the way helped by playing the new tunes and introducing them to audiences everywhere. The album opened in the top five its first week out with so much hype 13 Recordings put out there prior to the release.

Peri scheduled several radio interviews along the way. We loved it because our fans would show up outside. By fans, I meant groupies, and by groupies, I meant hot, willing women. There were always willing chicks around, but living on a bus could serve as a major cockblocker. Sometimes I wished for my own car and driver if they weren't into the idea of everyone on the bus being privileged to hearing loud sex.

My love life backstage seemed to be taking it on the chin, too. Being the only single one on tour before Hayden could join up, cut into the real after parties. Not that I couldn't handle having two or more beautiful women to myself, but fewer women wanted to hang around with only one of us to party with them. Some couldn't understand the basic concept of sharing.

Hayden and Victory were due in before our show tonight. They ended back in Austin, and the two singers flew out with Cash to join us in Tulsa, Oklahoma at the BOK Center. I believe Crew and I were equally excited to see Hayden. Peri relayed to us that Hayden and Victory killed their tour. They had outstanding numbers on ticket sales, and Cash wanted them writing music along the remainder of the tour so they could start working on their first album together the minute we arrived back in Austin. Peri kept a great watch on sales and their social media sites for hits, something I never do. Social media and the internet are the bane of my existence with all the lies and shit they report and the gossip they spread.

AD arrived at the Center about an hour before our set started like we usually do. We liked to chill before sweating for an hour and a half. KeeMac walked onstage and basically incited the fans into a frenzy at every show, and our adrenaline needed to be flowing with his first words into the mic. The Oklahoma fans showed the same enthusiasm to rock as every venue we played.

The dark stage held only enough light bleeding over from the audience for Gunner and me to find our way to our marks. My tech handed over my bass and stepped off. Those guys had cat eyes considering the way they could slip around the stage in the dark without making a sound.

Ryan and Chandler quickly followed us to their marks with KeeMac on their heels. He basically ran onstage which served to get him pumped up for his opening line, "Hello fucking Tulsa, Oklahoma. How y'all Okies doing tonight?" Couldn't take the southern speak out of us, no matter how much we traveled or how often people made fun of our drawls.

Assured Distraction's music kept the crowd on their feet for over an hour straight. Then, KeeMac and Ryan would do a song together or KeeMac and Chandler would sing. Tonight the lovers sang while the rest of us cooled down offstage guzzling bottles of water. The music stopped sooner than we thought and for some reason, the spots stayed on and the house lights came up, too. Great, some tech in lighting didn't get the memo on what happened next. Those of us backstage made our way back out waiting on those dickwads to get their heads out of their asses and take care of the problem.

When the three of us reached our marks, we looked up to see KeeMac holding Chandler's hand keeping her center stage.

"Okay, audience. Tonight we're going to deviate from the normal schedule for a few minutes. I hope you don't mind." Of course, the fans loved seeing something unexpected so they went wild.

"It's never been a secret that our beautiful keyboard player, Chandler Chatam, and I are in love."

Screams from the audience deafened the stage, and he waited to continue speaking through the mic.

"But tonight I have something new to add to our love story so I need you all to hold down the noise so everyone can hear what I want to say." It only took a second for total silence to overtake the huge crowd.

He took both of Chandler's hands, and the priceless look she gave him had us all smiling. "Chandler, our entire lives together have been in front of an audience. You auditioned in front of a small audience for the band, and we all immediately decided you were what AD needed to make us complete. Our rehearsals and recordings always happen in front of an audience. The shows we do take place in front of great audiences like this one. So tonight, in front of this crowd, I want to ask you a question that you have to answer in front of our fans."

He got down on one knee right there in the middle of the stage under hot spotlights, held her hands in his and looked up to Chandler. "As hard as we fought it, I think we knew we loved each other from the moment you came to audition. One look at you took my breath away, and then you played and sang and showed us all the talent and beauty you possess. You captured my heart with a single song Chandler, and now I want to let everyone know that I need you to keep my heart in a safe place for the rest of our lives. Chandler Chatam, will you do me the honor of marrying me?"

KeeMac pulled an aqua blue box from his pocket and popped it open. Tears spilled over her lower lashes and slipped down Chandler's cheeks as she nodded. "I need words here, Chandler. You're killing me."

He stuck the mic in her direction and through the tears and lump that must have been in her throat she gave a shakey, yes. Then she took the mic from him and yelled into it, "Yes, yes, *yes*!" With that, she jumped into his arms wrapping her legs and arms around his body.

With the house lights up and all the stage spots shining brightly, I noticed Hayden standing in the wings watching the proposal take place. I saw a female standing behind him, but I couldn't see her face from my location onstage. I moved enough to catch a quick glance of her before she turned and walked away at a fast pace. I caught a swish of long dark curls floating behind a female body and in a blink she'd disappeared. Something about her walk made my brain go on search mode thinking I knew that walk, but I couldn't connect it to the long hair. So many girls had come and gone over the time we'd been in the business, it could've been any one of the women I entertained.

The audience went crazy over the awesome scene playing out in front of them. I don't remember us ever having a louder audience making the last thirty minutes we played seem unreal. Finally, after the third encore when we usually do two, we ended the concert. The party backstage celebrating the engagement was off the hook. All the well-wishers who wanted a piece of the couple meant the room was packed with lots of extras who normally don't bother showing up.

I finally caught up with Hayden and after we shook hands, I looked around for Victory. "Dude, where the hell is she? I believe I'm the only person who hasn't fucking met her."

Hayden looked around. "No idea. She walked in here with me before the encores finished. Did y'all really have to do three? Maybe she snuck out to the restroom." So many people milled around that finding anyone other than Chan and KeeMac proved impossible. "I'll introduce her when she gets back. How have things been going on the road?"

"You know, same thing different fucking city." I slapped him on the back. "I've missed my wingman, but that only made more pussy for me."

"Yeah, it's been different only traveling with a woman, too. She's great and all but not the same as having y'all around."

"So you saying having a female along for the fucking ride kept you from the other chicks?"

"Nah, I've had my share."

"What about her? She bag a few strays for the road?"

"Not once. Told her she damn sure could, and we would rock that party. She turned me down saying she didn't need any complications fucking up her life right now. Said she preferred spending her time practicing and writing music. I learned she's a hell of a champ at playing video games. I had to work my ass off to actually beat her a few times."

"Have we met her before? I caught a glimpse of her when KeeMac did the proposal and thought I might have recognized her. She took off before I could get a good look, though."

"I've never met her so it must've been before I started traveling with AD. I'm outta beer. You want another?"

"Sure, it's better than that shit they're spewing around. I'll take a Corona over bubbles any fucking time."

People started making toasts to the happy couple, and that took over the party. The amount of adult beverages consumed in celebration exceeded our usual limit in the green room, so we were all falling down singing and dancing on the way back to the bus. Good thing security did their job to make sure we all made it before we pulled out of the parking lot.

Halo

Shocked and awed. That's the only way I could describe what I witnessed as I stood in the wings at Assured Distraction's concert. Me, a country girl through and through, offstage watching rock gods perform magic before an audience I could only dream of singing to.

I peeked around Hayden's tall frame, and there he stood. Carter Sheridan. I stared at the boy I once loved more than life itself so many years ago. Tears formed behind my eyes as the lump in my throat worked to close my airway so I couldn't breathe. The boy I fell in love with standing there in no way resembled him, though. Instead, a breathtaking man faced the audience.

His bass hung low across his hips tethered to the strap across his back. The muscular, tattooed arms barely moved to play the rhythmic chords of the music. Dark hair formed a ponytail down his back. He always wanted to grow his hair longer than they allowed in school. Now I knew why. My imagination formed an idea of the body hidden under the tight black t-shirt he wore. As a teen, he could only be described as lanky, but he obviously transformed into a man with a ripped body if the stolen pictures paparazzi made available on social media were any indication.

Not that I stalked Assured Distraction's men or anything. It's not considered stalking if it automatically appeared on my social media feeds, right? Most of Carter's pics that appeared showed him with beautiful women in all states of undress. He never seemed to keep his escapades secret from anyone.

Since the band's popularity started requiring bodyguards to keep the crazies away, candid shots became more difficult to find. Women Carter associated with didn't seem to mind talking to the press in the beginning either, but apparently, nondisclosure forms now came first because information about him and the band rarely popped up online anymore.

Memories of our time together rushed me. I sucked oxygen in as stolen kisses in a school alcove, laughs as we snuck behind the gym for slow tender kisses, and the night we made the decision to become one lying in the back of his pickup under the stars. Our love shined bright then but somewhere along the way, four friends and a bass guitar came between us. I let it happen because if I tried to stop it, hate and resentment would have eaten away at what we had.

Breathe, Halo. Just breathe. I whispered to myself. *He's just a man.*

"Did you say something?" Hayden looked down at me.

"Just talking to myself."

"Step in front of me so you can see better." He took my hand and tried to pull me forward.

I put it on the brakes. "No, no. I'm great right here."

He let go when he felt my resistance. "Fine, but this is looking important. I have a feeling you're going to miss a perfect moment in AD's history."

"Looks that way to me, too."

The words KeeMac spoke came from the heart, but mine beat out of my chest for a completely different reason. I glanced around Hayden again, and Carter looked directly at me. I jerked back in a panic.

"Hey, I'm going back to watch it on the monitor."

Hayden nodded, and I took off. I held back to keep from running out the door, not wanting to draw attention from the people backstage. Bypassing the rooms behind the stage area, I went straight to the bus. I didn't want our eventual reunion to take place in a room full of strangers. Over the years I'd played our reunion out in so many different ways in my mind, and an after party celebrating an engagement never appeared on my reel.

The little oxygen I'd been holding in while I found a safe exit finally depleted, so when the cool night air hit my face, I sucked in a deep breath. For a brief minute, I didn't think about the inevitable. It appeared our first face to face since we parted when I was seventeen would happen on the tour bus. At least there wouldn't be a crowd of people. The group would only be his best friends. The idea of being stuck on that bus didn't appeal to me, but I needed to pull up my big girl panties and face reality.

My bottom bunk waited patiently for me to climb in as I took off my shoes and changed into yoga pants and a tank. This had become my nighttime attire on the bus since it was comfortable and covered enough for me to roam around the bus without feeling self-conscious.

I laid on my back staring at the bottom of the top bunk. My mind replayed the vision of Carter standing onstage watching his friends become engaged. As I remembered the profile of his perfect face, memories of our time continued the loop in my head. Love and loss intertwined in it, and tears slid down my temples into my hair. My heart begged my head not to remember the good and the bad, but my head won out in the end. I closed my eyes and willed myself to forget and sleep, and that wasn't easy.

"Y'all gotta be quiet. My roommate's already here sleeping. Shhh."

My sleep-fogged brain heard the whispered-yelled drunken voice of Hayden. Obviously, he had guests. I hadn't considered he might come back with others, but I should have.

Loud muffled laughter. "Tiptoe back to the bedroom. We can shut the damn door," he told the laughing woman.

Then a different male voice whispered. "Fuck, is it big enough for all of us?"

"Hell yeah, it is. Besides, we don't need that much room," Hayden replied. The intoxicated group tried to cover their laughter with absolutely no success.

"Wait, baby. You can strip me down when the door's shut, not here in the hallway," a female spoke.

"Fuck yeah, but it'd be better if you stripped for me. I'd enjoy it even more if you went real slow and added some bump and grind to it," the second male voice added. This earned him seductive sounding moans from the woman. No telling what he did to her to get that response.

Great, two males and two females in the back of the damn bus. How long would I have to endure this? I pulled my noise-canceling headphones off the shelf beside me. I invested in them the first week we were on the bus knowing I would probably need them at some point. I scrolled through my phone until I found some sleep music. Ugh! This was going to be a long-ass night.

The vibration of the wheels rolling down the highway slowly pulled me out of a dead sleep. I pulled the headphones off and peeked out the curtain beside me. The hall was empty and quiet which suited me fine. I didn't have a clue who I would find riding on our bus today, but I knew who I preferred not to have on it.

Even with the headphones, the sounds from the bedroom the night before left no doubt the kinds of activities taking place. Facing that group this morning would be awkward, at least for me. If they shared, like it appeared, they probably didn't care what I saw or heard.

I snuck to the side bathroom, used it, and brushed my teeth. I took the time to make my hair look halfway decent and made sure no leftover makeup from last night lingered on my face and eyes.

Coffee stood out next on the agenda. I'd perfected making it while we rolled down the road by the second morning on the bus. I started the water heating and popped in a fresh K-Cup. While I waited for the blue light to turn on to close the lever, I leaned against the counter and checked Facebook. There might be some video of the engagement posted, and since I basically missed it running out the door, I wanted to watch one.

The aroma of coffee dripping into my mug caught my attention just as I heard some sounds from the back. Hayden moved forward in his boxers which was about the best I ever got from him in the mornings. Finding ourselves stuck together as roommates, we quickly learned intimate details about each other. He didn't seem to have a problem sitting around in his underwear so why should I?

I met his eyes over the top of my mug. "Want me to make you a cup?"

"Please. I'd love you for it." My first thought was he loved women for everything which made me smile as I turned to start.

"Hey, I'm sorry if we woke you up last night. I know the girls were kinda loud."

I wanted to tear him a new one for it, but he looked too pathetic to start out bitching at him this early. His face had a green tint, and his hair stuck out in all directions. "It's okay. I knew those headphones were a score when I bought them. They cut out pretty much all of the sounds."

I handed over the cup, and he blew across the hot beverage before taking a sip. "Good to know."

"Wait now. That's not an invitation for wearing them every time I sleep. I could still hear, you know." I gave him my best stink-eye.

"I'm not sure we're going to have final say now that we're with AD." He smiled as he said it. "Carter loves the ladies and they love him right back, sometimes all night long."

I rolled my eyes. "Great." I wanted to add a lot more but kept it to myself. So Carter's back there with two women. My nerves leaped up a notch on the anxiety scale. I inhaled my coffee and fixed another. Normally one cup would've satisfied my caffeine fix until later in the day, but it didn't even come close today.

I finally felt brave enough to ask a few questions I might not like the answers to, but oh well. "So, who else is on the bus with us today?"

"Just Carter and Cash. We sent the women back to the venue in a cab. Neither of us likes to find them in our bed when we wake up. That won't happen at all when Crew sleeps here."

"Good to know." I looked at him thinking I might get more explanation.

"You should know that Crew's my first priority no matter what's happening. I take advantage of my time when he's not around, but I'll never be an absentee father. I'm all he has."

"That's not true. He has all of the band family."

"I know, but he doesn't have another parent. Ryan and Tucker are his real cousins, but it's not the same as having a mom and dad. His happiness and a stable life's the most important thing in my life. If it comes down to it, I'll quit touring before he's hurt in any way."

I nodded in understanding. This big kid had his priorities pointed in the right direction to be a dad. So what if he'd had a night off, he knew right and wrong when it came to his son. I had to admire him for that. Many kids his age didn't have what it took, especially on their own.

"I'm glad to hear that, Hayden. You're a good dad."

A little grin passed over his face as he leaned his head back on the couch closing his eyes. "Yeah, remember that when I do something stupid, please."

"Hey, they don't come with an instruction manual. It's more of a learn-as-you-go type thing."

"That's for damn sure."

"So tonight's our big night to open for Assured Distraction. Are we ready for this?" I watched his face to see if any nervousness surfaced.

"Hell yeah, we're ready. We were born ready, girl. You jumped on the ready train the minute you hit the stage on your own."

I wished I shared his confidence. "Good, keep telling me that. I'm freaking out over here, and you're trying to stay awake."

"We'll rock that fuckin stage. The audiences' screams for AD will be epic." He'd yet to raise his head off the couch, so his ego did the talking.

"Glad you're so sure of our abilities."

"Abso-fucking-lutely." His sentences were getting shorter each time he spoke. I reached over and took the cup out of his hand when his eyes never reopened. For all of his morning bravado, he wasn't awake enough to stay that way.

I drank the rest of his coffee while I continued scrolling through my feed. I passed all of the fan pics when I finally came to a pretty good video of KeeMac on his knee. The two of them looked so in love. The part of the video that captured my attention happened to be the hot bass player in the background. Damn, I couldn't believe how he'd changed into this man. My girlie bits woke up watching his easy motions as he moved around onstage. He and the drummer seemed to have an ongoing commentary as the two in front spoke words of love.

I clicked the button on top and turned off the screen. I didn't need to be lusting over the hot body I'd zoomed in on in a still shot. Enough of that. It would never happen again. We had our chance, and it didn't play out. Time to move on.

I pulled my guitar out at the foot of my bunk. Hayden and I were working on music like Cash asked us to, and I could get some private time to continue what we started. I hoped both guys would be happy I took the initiative. Hayden brought more to the table in this duo so I felt like I needed to up my game to prove my worth.

With the score in front of me, I studied it a few minutes. I softly strummed a few chords when the bathroom door slammed, and the shower started blasting. So, either Cash or Carter had finally woken up. I prayed for the former and continued trying to work on the music. It proved useless. All I could think about was Carter in that shower. Warm water gliding down his body over those pecs, dripping off those pierced nipples. Would he have deep cuts in his abs like the pictures sometimes showed? That said, watermarking a path through them on its way down to…

"Shut the fuck up!" I said it out loud and woke Hayden.

"What?" He jumped from the couch.

"Oops, sorry. I was talking to myself."

He glared at me. "You always tell yourself to shut up, especially while you're working?" He nodded to my guitar.

"Yes, no. I don't know." I shrugged my shoulders about the same time we heard the water shut off which caused me to look in the direction of that door.

"Who's awake?" He looked at me.

I lowered my head and stared at the strings on my guitar. "How should I know? I'm busy, remember?"

I felt his stare continue, but I didn't want to make eye contact with him.

"Look, Victory. You had to meet the entire band sooner or later. They're just men like the rest of us. Yeah, they're rich and famous, but they put their pants on one leg at a time like us mere mortals do." He laughed as he started making himself more coffee.

The door popped open, and Cash walked out looking ready to meet the day. While we never dressed in more than necessary to be comfortable, Cash had on his business casual attire.

Hayden studied him a second. "Where you going, dude? Last time I checked we were stuck on this bus most of the day."

"I'm going the same place you're going, dumbass, because we ARE stuck on this bus all damn day." He noticed the dripping coffee. "You making that for me?"

"Hell no. I had a cup and some little shit coffee gremlin took it while I snoozed on the couch waiting for it to cool." His eyes shot over to me.

"Don't look at me. I've been working like the boss asked."

"Kissing ass is not a good quality, Vic," Hayden informed me with a smirk.

"Speak for yourself, dipshit. Her work ethic leads me to believe she's serious about the new music."

Hayden scratched his middle finger up the side of his face and then laughed. "You know I'm all about the new music but damn, I gotta wake up first."

I leaned over looking down at the paper again when I heard stomps coming up the hall. I wanted to turn and look but held back knowing my hair covered my face. *How long could I put this off?* When the door to the bathroom slammed shut, I looked around. The two men looked down the hall, too, then they both started laughing.

"Yeah, it's alive," Cash said, then turned to me. "Rules to live by. Don't speak until spoken to before noon. Don't make eye contact, if you value your life."

"And no sudden moves, unless you want something flying in your direction. Got it?" Hayden added to the list.

I nodded at the two rule makers. Since when had he become so hard to wake up? Oh yeah, since he became famous. We were given a few more minutes of reprieve when the shower turned on again.

"Good," Hayden said. "At least he'll be more awake when he gets out here to meet you."

"Oh yeah. I forgot you hadn't met everyone in AD yet. You're in for a treat with this one," Cash spoke as he continued staring at his phone. He got up and moved to the table to open his laptop. "Guess I'll get busy on some work so the two of you can get on with yours."

"Nope. Not starting until Carter's had his first cola of the day."

I put my guitar down. "I suppose this means stop what I'm doing, huh? He drinks cola for breakfast?" I didn't remember this about him. Of course, his mom would've had a fit if she'd seen him drink that first thing. As a health nut, she didn't even like him drinking coffee.

"Yeah, every single day," Hayden informed me.

"Does he have a stomach left?" I shook my head as I said it. "That shit's really hard on your stomach."

"I'm pretty sure you've probably stalked him enough online to know what his stomach looks like, Victory. His abs are all over Instagram. We give him shit about it all the time." Hayden looked at me when he spoke which was the wrong time. "Yep, if the color of your face and neck are any indication, I'd say you probably have a Pinterest board full of his abs and chest and probably his arms, too." He had the nerve to laugh at me. "What else you got of Carter on that board, Vic? Since you're glowing, I'll bet you caught those naked shots that were leaked last year. You harboring a little fangirl crush on the bass player?"

I knew his teasing was all in fun but damn, this was not going to play out well when the real news flashed for everyone in this entourage.

Cash jumped in at that point. "Please tell me you aren't going to fuel his damn ego. It's already so big we've considered buying another fucking tour bus for it."

"You have nothing to worry about in that department guys. Why would he give a shit what I think when he's got the pick of the ladies every night? They're willing and waiting for the nod to security."

"Yeah, but you know dipshit bass players. They're only in line in front of the drummers for getting women. Their wildassness is usually directed straight at KeeMac and Ryan when it comes to hot panties flying through the air. You might be on to something, though, with KeeMac and Ryan officially off the market. Maybe those two bastards should offer Carter up centerstage instead." Hayden started laughing and Cash joined him. "Like that's ever gonna happen."

"Like what's gonna happen?" his voice cut through the laughter. The gravelly tone I recognized immediately slid through the air and straight to my heart. The hairs on the back of my neck stood straight up and goosebumps went down my arms. How could he affect me this way after all these years? I'd been kidding myself if I thought he wouldn't.

I peeked through the strands to see Hayden watching me. What was he expecting me to do, jump up and throw myself at Carter? Start screaming like the girls hanging on the front of the stage? Faint at the sight of him? This wasn't a 1966 Beatles' concert. This was a man from my past. I could do this.

I sucked in a deep breath and let it out before turning and looking at Carter. He dug in the fridge for his morning beverage not paying any attention to the fact we'd never met.

"Carter, I don't believe you've met Victory." Cash took the lead on introductions.

He turned his dark gray eyes to me, and I met them straight on.

"Son-of-a-bitch!" he said in a tone I didn't quite understand.

"That's a helluva way to greet someone, Carter," Cash admonished him.

"That's a helluva thing to spring on a man first thing in the morning, Cash," he replied still staring at me.

"What's going on?" Cash asked him.

"What the fuck, Halo?" Carter threw out.

"Hello, Carter. Long time no see." *Very original, Halo.*

"Wait, you know each other?" Cash asked another obvious question.

"Yeah, we do. She's a blast from the past," he said it, picked up his bottle, and went back to the bedroom, slamming the door behind him.

"Well, it went better than I expected," I told the two remaining men.

Hayden walked to the front of the bus where I sat and kneeled beside my chair. "Who's Halo?"

"Me. My name is Halo Victoria Masters. Everyone offstage calls me Halo." My voice sounded monotone even to me. I couldn't muster the energy to have emotions since his acknowledgment took it all out of me. Why would I think he would be happy to see me? He made himself perfectly clear when we parted that he never wanted to see me again.

"Why are you just now telling us you knew him? We could have done some ground work before you met up with him again," Cash asked from his seat at the table. His tone loud and clear and filled with anger.

"When you first asked me to sing with Hayden, you never said anything about touring with Assured Distraction. If you'll recall, I hesitated to agree to sing with Hayden. I knew they had some connection, but I never dreamed I would end up traveling with the band until that day in your office. I made up my mind to be all in on this idea of working with Hayden before I came to you. Carter could suck it up. I told myself I'd give this music thing two years of my life, and I intend to. Two years is nothing in the music world so I figured if I made something happen in that short of time, then it was meant to be, and here I am."

"This could be a problem." Cash started to pace up and down the aisle. "Carter could put a halt to this before it ever gets started. You had to know that, Victory. Or is it Halo?"

"Doesn't matter if I'm not staying does it?" I snapped back at him.

"Now wait. No one said anything about you leaving yet." I could see the wheels turning in Cash's head. "We'll need to see what he says."

"I didn't realize 13 Recordings had Carter Sheridan as CEO," I continued to snap out comments that probably didn't help my case.

"No, he doesn't, but AD is one of our biggest investments so naturally, we tend to cater to them more than others."

I couldn't gather my thoughts fast enough for another comeback. I should've known it would be this way. They made the studio millions of dollars. I made them nothing. Hell, I was collateral at this point.

Who was I to think they would consider giving me this chance if he said no?

Clearly, he would be saying no.

Carter

The fucking shock I felt hurt all over me. I didn't need to wake up that way after the night I'd had. Hell, to be on the bus fucking strange women with Halo lying in the bunk twenty feet away made it even worse. *How could this happen?*

She did this. She plotted this from the beginning starting with changing her name. She never used Victoria; she hated the name. And Victory, that's just wrong. Who the hell chose a name like Victory for the stage? Yeah, my ex did, that's who.

It could've been avoided if she'd allowed me in Cash's office the first day. Nice how she hid from me all this time, too. Everyone's met her but me. Wasn't that convenient for her the morning in the hotel? Shit. The hotel. She stayed in the next room in the fucking hotel, too. Did she plan to cockblock me in all of these places or something? I showed her, though. We had a kickass good time that night.

Serves her right. She should've come clean to everyone from the beginning. She deserves all the heartache this is going to cause her. She's not staying on this bus or opening for AD. That shit's not going to happen. The label will bend on this one. Cash'll understand and make the cut before I have to take it to the label. This is my fucking label, and she sure as hell is not welcome here.

I spent too long feeling guilty over how we parted. It took me months to be able to look at another woman and not feel like a damn dog for cheating, even though I wasn't. Now, she's waltzed in here and established herself with a spot right under my nose. Nope, not gonna happen. She's gone at the first possible exit. Until then, I'd stay on the other bus. Damn, my fucking head pounded worse than my heart did. I covered my eyes with the night blinders and put the pillow over my head.

When I woke, the bus no longer rolled. After tossing and turning, I finally drifted off into a fitful sleep. Sleeping proved to be a bad idea because seeing her sitting there did nothing but conjure up dreams. I knew in my heart I did the right thing by ending it before I left, but it almost killed me. Temptation on the road for a kid my age back then would've destroyed us, and I didn't want to be *that* guy. My dream of one of our last nights together replayed in my mind.

Eight Years Ago

I took her out on the little bit of money I'd made from the gig the weekend before. I'd saved all of it so it could be a special night for her. After eating pizza at our favorite place, I took her to the pond on the back of our neighbor's property. The spot held magic for us both. We went there to be alone since most kids knew nothing of it.

"Come on, I want to show you something." I dragged her out of the front seat of my truck.

"It's still too cold to swim, and I'm dressed up."

"We aren't going swimming, crazy girl. You look too beautiful to mess up." I tucked her into my side, and we moved toward the tree line by the pond. The trees blocked the moonlight from the half moon shining down, but the glow from the flashlight I brought captured her sandaled feet and tanned legs from the bottom of her flowered sundress. Tanning in the hot Texas sun at all the fun places around Austin left her with a golden brown hue on her skin.

We reached the spot I'd set up for us earlier in the day. I reached down and flipped on the little camp light she'd given me earlier in the year. I hung it on the nail I'd put in the tree slightly above our heads. It lit the area of the blanket with a soft hue. Her stunning face had a warm glow capturing my attention.

I set this same scene before on the night she decided she wanted to gift me her virginity. It still stood out in my mind as the best night of my life. I hoped tonight would be equally great, but the guilt in the back of my mind of what I planned to do in a few days held me back.

"Feeling the need to get lucky, Carter?" She laughed as she ditched her sandals and sat down.

"I'm already lucky, Halo. I have you." I laid down on my back beside her.

"Awe, cheesy much?" She poked me in the chest.

"No, babe. It's the truth. You've been one of the best things to come into my life."

"One of the best?" She laid down on her side and turned to look at me propping up on one elbow. The vanilla fragrance floated softly toward me. I'd know Halo without opening my eyes from that scent.

I took her free hand and pulled it to my mouth kissing her palm. "Yeah, you and the band."

"The band? Uh huh? I see where I rate." I knew she liked fucking with me about the band. It was my life and had been since before her. We never fought over it because it was a given when we started dating that the band came first until we made it big.

"You always rate with me, little darling." I pulled her over and kissed her softly. "You know that."

"I know," she said as she crawled on top and laid her head on my chest. "I know."

"And you also know that you're making me horny lying on me like this, right?"

"You mean hornier 'cause when are you not? I'm feeling it loud and clear down there." Her light laugh and comment made me smile.

"Hey, what can I say, I'm a normal teenage guy." I wrapped my hands around her ass cheeks and ground her into my boner that my zipper left a permanent pattern on.

She sat up, straddling me and pulled the hem of her sundress over her head. A frilly bra with no straps kept my hands off her beautiful tits. "Girl, why'd you even bother with this damn thing?"

"Oh, I don't know. Maybe because it's pretty, and I like feeling pretty. I also know it drives you wild wondering what you're going to find."

"That's for damn sure. You always surprise me when I get your clothes off."

"Isn't that the point? Keep you guessing?" She winked at me. Winked! The little minx.

I pulled her down and kissed her hard. She opened her mouth, and my tongue dueled for control over hers. She sucked mine deep in her warm mouth when I ran my fingers around the top of the bra but didn't undo as she expected. I slowly ran my index fingers from the back hooks all the way around her until I got to the swell of each luscious mound. I teased her skin while I continued to kiss her causing her skin to react and spread goosebumps of anticipation. I dipped two fingers down inside the cups. I knew those sweet pink nipples would be standing at attention. I squeezed the stiff peaks between my index and middle finger just hard enough to hear her moan. I couldn't stand it any longer, so I reached around and popped the hooks apart with one hand and threw the lacy garment aside.

Her perky tits laid out for the taking, so I raised up and circled one nipple with a stiff tongue until it was wet and then blew a warm breath on it. She did the grinding this time.

"That's not all that's stiff, babe." This caused her to thrust her hips so she would move up and down the length of my suffering cock a few times before she rotated those hips around and around on me.

"I think someone's ready to come out and play, Carter." I slid her forward, and sucked the other peak in my mouth softly biting it, keeping just enough pressure with my teeth for her to feel a slight amount of pain.

Her pain turned to pleasure as she undid the button of my shorts and lowered the zipper. It felt so good to get that tight pressure off me. She pushed at the sides trying to free me of them so I lifted my hips and let her have her way, kicking them off my bare feet. The warm night air caused a sheen of sweat to form on our skin everywhere we touched.

"Still got a problem here, Halo." I tugged at the sides of her minuscule panties.

"Don't tear these off like you did the last ones. They're too—" the sides popped.

"Too late. Sorry, I'll pay for them." I slid the remainder of the silky material from her body.

"No, you're not sorry one bit! I think you take great pride in tearing my undies off me."

I couldn't help but smile. "Yeah, you're right. I do. But, I think you secretly like it, too." I laid back down taking her with me kissing her before she could continue her little tirade of pretending anger.

I rolled over placing her under me and looked down at her. "You're so beautiful, Halo. Your face." I kissed her. "Your body." I raised off her and looked down. I kissed her. "Your mind." I kissed her forehead. "Your heart." I kissed the area on her chest above her heart. "I love everything about you, babe."

She wrapped her legs around my waist digging her heels into my ass and pulled me tightly into her core. "Then make love to me, Carter."

I sucked her bottom lip into my mouth wrapping an arm around her leg and finding paradise. Her special honey waited patiently for me as I traced my finger along the crease. Dragging it up to find a swollen nub demanding my attention, my finger circled it before giving it a couple of light taps. Her thighs clenched tighter around my waist, and I knew she was already close. Damn, I loved this girl. Her response always ready to give me more than I deserved, especially tonight.

I forced my mind away from the slippery slope it headed for. I never wanted to discuss leaving. Knowing it would probably be our last time together, I needed this moment to be perfect before we had *the talk.* She deserved no less than the best. Her only mistake, falling for a guy like me. Our time together learning, exploring, and falling into a special love head first, meant our parting would be even more difficult than I ever imagined.

I pulled her pebbled nipple into my mouth as my steel cock slid up and down from where her crease began and ended. Running it over her back entrance, I teased her by rubbing some precum around it. This always got a loud no, but I only did it to excite her. She wasn't ready for that, and sadness hit my heart realizing I wouldn't be the one to have her there.

As my lips circled the other stiff peak, I slowly worked into the heated entrance that begged for the taking. Only the head breached her tight pussy as she sucked in a breath. Her taut body harbored tight muscles everywhere, and this spot was no exception. The feeling for me started out as my heaven but it took some work to get her to that point, too.

With her on the pill and us being exclusive for a year now, we let the condoms go after a couple of months. I wouldn't dream of jeopardizing her trust in me by cheating with another girl, even if having sex didn't exist.

"Damn, Halo. I swear each time it feels tighter. I fucking love it." I pushed in further, and she bit down on the skin of my collarbone. The sting made me want to drive in her, but I held back. Her thoughts were different from mine, and she grabbed my ass and pulled me into the hilt in one move.

"Babe, I don't want to hurt you. Why'd you do that?" I looked into intoxicating violet eyes for her reaction.

"I need you, Carter. I want to feel you. All of you. Now."

Who was I to question her motives? If she wanted it hard, even after asking me to make love to her, I was more than happy to go there.

"Hard, huh?"

She nodded with a seductive grin. That's all the encouragement I needed. I raised up and sat back on my calves pulling her body up to meet me as I began to move in and out of her in a forceful rapid movement. I wrapped my hands around her hips and watched as my cock set a rhythm with a pounding motion as I raised and lowered her to me. Her muscles began to spasm around me, so I moved one hand to her clit to add to the friction.

"Oh, God, Carter. Yes, just like that. Just like that. Don't stop. Don't stop." A rush of fresh liquid came from her as she gripped my cock in a vice hold. I didn't want this to end, but I couldn't help myself. It felt so good and so right. I exploded before she came down from her own release obviously extending hers if the noises and cries were an indication.

Several hard thrusts later I stopped the onslaught of thrusts, our bodies spent from the eruption of our pleasure. I laid over on her and enjoyed the comfort of her softness for a few minutes. Raising up on one elbow, I looked down at her and watched the tears slid down the sides from her closed eyes.

She knew our plans. I hadn't kept the preparations from her. We never spoke of what would happen, only that the band planned on hitting the road. Her tears broke me to pieces on the few times I caused them over our time together. Tonight I hated being the son-of-a-bitch causing it.

I rolled off her finally losing the close connection from being inside her. "Please don't cry, babe. Please?"

"Sorry, I know I'm being stupid about this. I've known all along what was coming." She grabbed her dress and pulled it over her head, then wiped the remainder of the tears away. I watched as the shield she built around her heart erected itself. She held her head up and looked at me. "Guess we better get back to town before my dad gets the sheriff out looking for us. His baby out with a rock and roll bad boy might lead to trouble." She picked up the remainder of her panties and laughed. "He's too late, huh?"

I couldn't take on her faked happiness. "Sure, if that's what you want to do."

"It's not what I want, Carter." She turned and her face said everything I never wanted to hear.

I pulled my shorts on and grabbed my shirt while she folded the blanket. No more words of significance passed between us that night. We had nothing more to say.

Carter

Present

I rolled out of the bed and opened the door. Someone played the guitar softly, and the music strains drifted down the aisle. Damn, I didn't want to do this, but I might as well face the facts and the sooner we got this out in the open, the better.

Halo picked at her guitar while leaning over a score in front of her. She heard my footsteps. I didn't try to hide.

I stopped at the fridge and pulled out another bottle of cola, unscrewed the lid, and drank down half. Finally, I turned to look at her. She was even more beautiful than I could possibly imagine on my own. Her brown hair cascaded down her back in soft curls. She used to gripe about it since that stick straight mess commanded the style then, and she fought the curls daily. Her teenaged body obviously gave way to that of a woman in all the best places from what I could tell.

"Quit staring at me and say something, Carter."

"Ahhh, now she chooses to speak." I couldn't help myself. Smartass took over too often.

"I speak when I need to." She shot me a glare through those violet eyes saying she would fight this battle. Well, that's just fucking great because so was I.

"Where is everyone?" The tone of my pointed question made me think she knew it, too.

"Cash and Hayden went over to the venue to look it over. They thought it might be better if we talked alone."

"Oh really? I don't have anything to say, Halo." I pointed my finger at her as I moved closer to her. "You, on the other hand, have a shit ton of explaining to do."

"I have nothing to explain to you. You're not my boss, Carter." She stayed seated holding the guitar on her lap.

"That's where you are partially wrong 'Halo.'" I air-quoted her name. "Why don't you start with Victory. What's up with that little gem?"

"Halo didn't feel right for the stage. Sounded too childish and Victoria too formal." She strummed across the strings. "I thought Victory sounded kinda badass."

"Badass? There's nothing badass about you, Halo. And yes, you'll always be Halo when we're talking." I sat down on the chair across from her. I wanted to be close to her. I needed her to feel as uncomfortable as I did.

"Whatever, Carter. Again, I don't have to justify anything I choose to do with my life to you."

"Why are you here, Halo?" I wanted to be an asshole to her badly, but if a harp sat across her lap instead of a guitar, she'd look like an angel sitting there.

"I'm here because Hayden and I are perfect together. Both Cash and Hayden think so. The mix of our voices works on so many levels. If you'd only listen to us, you wouldn't have to ask that question."

"Yeah, that's not going to happen. Sorry, but this is my gig, and you can find your own." Annnddd just like that, my dick-self was back.

"I don't want your 'gig'," she said using air quotes, too. She always had the smartass gene inside her, exactly like I did. "I've got one of my own already, thank you very much." She put the instrument down and stood. "I earned it all by myself since I was never good enough according to you and your little band to play or sing with y'all."

"My little band? Girl, did something big hit on that hard damn head of yours? We're rock gods now compared to when I left."

"Well, okay, Mr. Rock God. Let me bow down in your presence, oh great one." She bent over with her arms stretched out to offer praise and worship.

"Stop being a damn smartass. You fucking know what I meant." I took her hands and stood her upright.

"You stop being an over-exaggerated, conceited, condescending prick, and I will." She stretched her five-foot-five frame as tall at it would go.

"Wow, your vocabulary has improved. What did you do, go to fucking college or something?" I smirked right in her face.

"As a matter of fact, I did and graduated, too. If you'd ever taken the time to listen to me, you would've known I'm capable of many things, and I'm damn smart. Of course, you should've figured it out when I didn't bother chasing after you, begging you to take me with you after you dumped me."

We breached each other's personal space. "I did not fucking dump you, Halo. You knew the damn plan all along. Sitting around your last year in high school waiting and hoping I would return to you wasted your time. That was never going to happen."

She stood on her tiptoes to get closer to my face and yelled, "You conceited piece of shit. If you think I ever contemplated sitting around waiting for someone like you to come back for me, you're totally delusional. The thought never once crossed my mind. You left, and I quickly moved on. As a matter of fact, I moved on and on and on, if you're smart enough to catch my meaning. I dated who I wanted and did what I wanted with whomever I wanted without giving you a second thought."

I had no comeback to that little tirade. I just stared. Finally, she picked up her guitar and notes and moved back to her bunk, closing the curtain behind her. While it wasn't a real door, it offered privacy and separation. I think I might've needed it worse than her. What she said came across loud and clear. She didn't need me any longer and had lovers I could only wonder about. Thinking about that would get me in trouble. I knew it and so did she.

Back in the bedroom, I pulled out some jeans and a t-shirt, dressing quickly. I stomped my way to the front of the bus and pushed the button to open the door while I spoke into my phone. "Get me a car. I don't give a fuck how much. Get me a motherfucking car now."

I stepped off the bus and pushed the button closing it behind me. I would not be staying on this fucking bus. Women and liquor called my name and not the one on this bus. I'll have a whole fucking penthouse full. I dialed Peri's number. "Get me a penthouse for tonight and tomorrow night. I'm not staying here. Text me the location." I ended the call.

"So, Glendale, Arizona, let's see what you have to offer." I walked to the sidewalk and there was a brand new Corvette pulling to the curb.

"I need you to sign these papers, please," the porter said.

"Bang on that fucking door of that RV. Peri O'Connor will sign them." I slid down in the low-slung seat, adjusted it to my long legs, and left half the tires ground into the pavement.

I didn't have a clue where I planned to go. I'd never been to Glendale before. Hell, I hadn't driven in Arizona before. I pulled up a map on the car's navigation system and typed in bars. The first place that popped up was a strip club which suited me just fine, so I pushed destination and followed the voice to the spot.

Xplicit looked like it sounded. The cool darkness lured me in. I needed a drink, and I wanted to forget. Forget I'd ever seen Halo. Forget we were ever together. Forget I used to love her.

Big tits greeted me over the top of the bar. I looked up into a nice face to go with them. "What can I get you doll?"

Hmm, older than I expected. Fake tits were everywhere these days, though.

"Jack. Just bring me the bottle."

"Starting a little early, aren't ya?"

"Is that a problem? I can go elsewhere." I sounded like a douche even to myself. Fuck it, I didn't care.

"No, not a problem for me unless you plan to drink and then drive." Her hard look told me she wouldn't back down.

"Okay, just give me Jack, neat."

"Sounds better." She placed the short glass in front of me and poured it close to full.

"Figured we'd compromise and have a double." She winked at me, and I had to smile.

"You here to talk or just be pissed off?" She wiped down the bar on each side of me probably out of habit.

"I don't know yet. Let me give that some thought."

"Good enough." She left me alone to my drink.

I couldn't believe what had happened. How did Halo get mixed in my personal life? How did I feel about seeing her once much less every damn day? The possibility of this turning into a cluster fuck grew with every thought.

I drained the glass and banged it on the bar top to catch the lady's attention.

"I'm not a dog, boy. Don't be banging the glassware. My name's Cat. Call me when you're ready. I'm guessing that would be now?"

I nodded my head, and she swiped my glass. "What time do the women start dancing here?"

"In about thirty minutes, but if you're in a real hurry, they're already here. Probably could arrange a lap dance already." She sat the filled glass back in front of me.

"Sounds good. Can you take care of that for me?" I saw the look she shot my way. "Please." She kinda scared me. Please helped, though, because she picked up the phone behind her and spoke softly into it.

"Go sit over there against the wall. She'll be out shortly."

I nodded at her and picked up my whiskey. The bank of oversized chairs and small side tables ran the length of the wall making it easy access for the dancers. I heard a noise and saw a tall dark-haired girl strut her stuff out from the back of the room. The little top and bottom were a waste of money since it basically covered nothing on her nicely-shaped body. Her "fuck me" heels had to be six or seven inches tall. How could she dance in those things?

"Good morning. You look lonely out here all... by... yourself." She started right in on her grinding when I sat my drink down but not taking my hand off of it. I knew the rules. No touching on my part. Obviously, this didn't stop her, though. She was all over me. Her long legs squatted down in front of me as she slid her hands slowly up my thighs all while gyrating her hips on those fucking heels.

"What's your name?" I asked her.

"Passion, what's yours?" She smiled at me without missing a beat.

"Cash." I laughed when I said it. Cash would shit if he knew I used his name, but in her case, I'm sure she thought I meant "as in made of it."

"Ohhh, I like that name." Yeah, she thought it. I gifted her with a twenty beside her left tit.

This earned me a real smile from her. I liked this girl already. She snaked up between my legs making sure to rub the crotch of my jeans, and then turned her perfectly rounded ass cheeks and bent to push them toward me. This time I ran the twenty across the g-string creasing her. Each side of the bill touched skin, and it caused a slight reaction. When it got to the band at the top, I slid it under the blue spandex making sure I made some contact with her cheek while doing so. I needed to touch her.

I took a drink from my glass and before I could finish, she pulled on the ties on her back to let the bottom of the top go free. She stood and turned around and undid the tie at her neck. Two naturally beautiful tits spilled out from the material which surprised me since I expected them to be fake. I wanted to get my hands on them but knew better so I gripped my drink with one hand, the chair arm with the other.

"You want to touch them, don't you?" She flipped her long curls over her shoulder so my view of them was spot on.

I nodded trying not to appear overly eager. "How do you feel about that?"

She glanced at the bar and didn't see Cat. "It'll cost you."

"How much?"

"Hundred." A little steep but what the fuck.

I peeled off two fifties closer to the middle of the stack and tucked them in her bottoms, and she straddled my lap. The grinding never stopped. Her tits were so close now, and then she bent back over my knees and put her hands on the ground. Damn this girl had some moves. It stretched those luscious tits out in front of me. I shot a look in Cat's direction and then walked my fingers up her body until I reached the desired destination.

Wrapping my hands around them, I knew for a fact they were real. No implants in these sweet babies. Passion pulled herself back up to sitting with my hands still molded to the generous mounds. I teased the pink buds to hard peaks. This had to be exciting her, didn't it?

"Hands to yourself, big boy." I got my warning from Cat, loud and clear as she pointed to the sign. "No touching the dancers."

Passion shrugged her shoulders, and I removed my hands. It also removed my growing chub, too. She finished the dance as momma watched, while I added some more twenties along the way. A girl's got bills, I'm sure. Now she had quite a few of mine, too. I thanked her when she walked away, and she nodded over her shoulder at me.

"You through playing over there?" Cat interrupted my daydream of what I could do with the hot body returning through the door it appeared from.

"Yeah, I'm done," I said with disappointment.

"Don't look so sad, big boy. What happened, the old lady catch you doing something wrong?"

I shook my head as I moved back to the bar. "No, nothing like that."

"It sure must be something for you to be all hang-dog looking." I laughed at her expression. Hadn't heard that in a long time.

"My ex showed up unannounced and wants, no needs, to stay. I'm not having it."

"That is some bad news. Why does she need to stay?"

"She was employed to do a job where I work. They hired her, so now she needs to stay because it's a great opportunity, but it's my gig. She needs to find her own."

"I'm sensing you don't play well with others." Cat laughed at her own joke.

"Oh, I play really well but apparently so does she."

"But you have seniority, right?"

"Abso-fucking-lutely I do, which is why she needs to be gone."

"Are you in a position to make demands?"

"Hell yeah, I am." Her comment brought my anger back. "And that's exactly what I'm about to fucking do. Thank you, Cat." I threw a fifty down on the bar and headed to the door.

"Anytime, big boy. Anytime." As I looked back she put the fifty in her bra and wiped the bar off.

chapter FOURTEEN

Halo

My determination to not let him get to me crumbled the second I closed that curtain. He would never see me cry again. Tears remained unanswered the first time around, and I felt like this would be a repeat performance. I laid back on my pillow, then rolled over facing the wall. If he had the balls to open my curtain and continue talking, he could damn sure talk to my back.

That didn't happen. I heard him yelling for a car when he walked out the door.

So he was leaving? Good! No, great, in fact. Go the fuck somewhere else and leave me alone. I didn't need him or any man to make myself happy. I'd been down that route with him the first time and look where that had gotten me. Abso-fucking-lutely nowhere. So fuck him.

I heard the door to the bus close, and I whipped the curtain back to make sure he was gone before I screamed.

"Go fuck yourself, you fucking dumbass. I don't need your fucketty fucking rock-star life, and for damn fucking sure don't fucking need you."

With the tirade behind me, exhaustion took over. I pulled the curtain closed and cried until I drifted into a fitful sleep.

Movement on the bus woke me. My head pounded like a hangover. Crying did that to me. I looked at my mirror and hung my head. God, I looked like shit. I heard someone move down the hallway and stop outside my curtain.

"Halo? It's me, Peri." I knew who it was when she said my name, but I didn't want to open the curtain and face her.

"Halo, are you awake?" she spoke softly.

"Yes." That's all I could dredge up.

"Can you open the curtain?"

"No."

"I would like to talk to you, but this is kinda weird, honey."

"I know."

"Will you please reconsider opening it? It's just you and me. I'm all alone." Her soft voice calmed me.

I slid the curtain along the track enough to see her standing there looking down at me.

"Hey," she barely said aloud.

"Hey, yourself."

"You want something to drink? Coffee, tea, water?"

"No, I'm good. I'm not feeling well. My head's hurting badly. Must be the dryness or something." I could live with that lie, but she knew better.

"I bet if you got up and had some caffeine and ibuprofen, you'd feel better."

"Where's Hayden and Cash?" I didn't care about Carter, but the other two were important to me.

"They went to get something to eat after they came back from the venue. They didn't want to wake you." I figured they told her what happened from the look on her face.

"I guess they told you about Carter and me, huh?"

"Yeah, they gave me the brief version, but you know men. They rarely get the story right or complete most of the time. I hoped you might trust me enough to tell me the truth. I'm a great listener. And no judging here. Promise." Peri's personality shined through her words. The pin-up girl style she always wore with her beautiful tattoos and jet black hair cut with short bangs, made her look honest and true.

A barely-there smile touched my lips. "I guess I'll have a cup of coffee if you're having some too."

"Come on girl. Let's be besties and lounge in your elaborate kitchen." She laughed and made her walk the three steps to it. I swung my legs out and stood beside my bunk, head in hands. It really did hurt.

"So what did Cash tell you?" I asked as she joined me at the small dinette. She placed the pain reliever bottle in front of me with a bottle of water.

"He said you and Carter had some history, and he wasn't sure of the details, but Carter's super pissed behavior shined through when he left here."

"Yeah, I heard the tires spin all the way back here inside the bus when the ass left."

"Don't worry about him right now. He'll get over his mad. The man's like a big kid most of the time or an overgrown teenager."

"Tell me about it. He said hurtful things to me. He questioned my reasoning for being here, accused me of trying to latch on to his fame for my own gain, and made a lot more insinuations."

"That's rough. I'm surprised he stooped so low."

"Yeah, me too. I never expected him to be this angry. I suppose the biggest thing that bothers me is he feels like I instigated being here on this tour. That's so far from the truth. I never invited Cash to hear me sing, and I had no clue that he represented AD in the beginning. I certainly didn't volunteer to crash his party."

"You're right. Cash talks to people in venues all the time. He likes to hear from fans who's hot, who's worth giving a second look at. Your talent landed you on this bus."

"Thanks for the reassurance, Peri. I believe I needed to hear it from someone who knew the truth."

"I'm being honest with you, Victory. Wait, is that what you want us to call you? Hayden said that wasn't your name."

"No, my friends call me Halo, but I thought it sounded childish for a stage name."

"Halo's a unique name. I think I love it, so Halo it is. I'll tell the others unless you want to."

"I don't know how I'll face the others. I'm sure Carter will do whatever it takes to turn them against me." I hadn't thought about how the other band members would react to my being here. "It really doesn't matter. Carter assured me

I wouldn't be here long. He wants me gone from the tour, and he has enough pull to kick me to the curb."

"Yeah, I'm not sure about all that just yet. We need to hear what Cash says about it. Carter could go over his head and make demands. The label wants to keep AD happy." The pensive look she gave me over her coffee cup concerned me. "You know, let's not worry about that for now. Carter might've been throwing a little tantrum. When he gets back, his whole attitude could have changed about having you here."

"I kinda doubt that. I've never seen him so angry that he would hit below the belt like some of his comments did."

"Tell me, was your relationship volatile before? What were you to each other?"

"No way. We were magic together like a first love should be. You know where you can't spend a minute apart… a, can't breathe without sharing it kind of love?" Peri nodded her head as if she understood exactly what I meant.

"We occupied each other's mind twenty-four-seven. We never made a move without the other knowing it for an entire year. I know you'll find this hard to believe now, but Carter exemplified what a boyfriend should be. He lifted me up at every turn. I wouldn't be the guitar player I am now without his encouragement." I looked down at the floor remembering the nights we played guitars sitting on my bedroom floor.

"Are you sure we're talking about the same Carter Sheridan who is in Assured Distraction?" Peri asked me with all sincerity. "The Carter I know doesn't resemble what you're describing. Our Carter lives for three things... the band, partying, and women. And in that order, too."

"My Carter's kindness knew no bounds. His friends and family came first. I could tell you some stories about the wonderful things he did for anyone who needed it. He wasn't one of those jocks that felt like he was in a class all of his own. Even though he was definitely part of the cool kids, he never excluded anyone in any way, and he never allowed the people around him to treat people that way either."

"Hmm. I would like to meet this guy. Don't get me wrong. Carter isn't a bad guy when it comes to the band family but in the public eye, you're bound to know the reputation he carries with him."

"Yeah, I read the stories the tabloids put out about his escapades. In the beginning, I laughed about them but after a while, I began to believe what they published. Seemed like every city the band visited, a picture or story of him surfaced, but I'm telling you, that's not the Carter I knew."

"Did you ever think that maybe he tried to replace something he was missing?" Peri looked at me directly, trying to judge my reaction to this comment.

I tried to remain neutral. Those feelings were boxed up long ago, and they needed to remain that way. "No, I doubt that's the case. If you'd have seen his face when he realized it was me, you'd know that shipped sailed a long time back."

"I'm just offering a possibility to his reaction. I could be completely wrong."

"Yeah, I think you are."

"Okay. Come over to the RV with me. I'm sure my monsters are giving Nanny a run for her money. The bundle of energy they possess amazes me. I wish I could recharge that way with a little nap."

"Sounds good. Let me get dressed. I wanted to see your custom home anyway."

"I gotta say it's pretty awesome. Come on."

Stepping into that thing made me feel like I should remove my shoes and wash my hands, but then two screaming hyenas came busting out of a back room with little boats in their muddy hands and underwear. I turned and looked at Peri, surprised.

"Dudes, has your daddy been making mud pies in the bathtub again?"

"Mommy, we don't make pies. We driving tugboats on the missippi river." Tucker looked exasperated at his mother.

"I think that's Mississippi River, son."

"Dat's what I said, Mommy."

"Yeah, that's what he say, RiRi," Crew added his two cents.

"Why are you both wearing underwear in the tub... no river?"

"'Cause tug boats drivers don't go wifout clothes, Mommy."

I grinned at their developing language. Where one mixed some words, the other mixed completely different ones. Time would take care of this. Crew looked at me over his shoulder as he started back to the river.

"Miss Vic," Crew yelled. "Did you see my daddy this morning?"

I squatted down to meet his eyes. "Yes, I did. How about you?"

"Yes, ma'am. He's playing with Pops." Crew continued on to the bathroom yelling, "She's here, Daddy."

I looked at Peri. "Who's Pops?" I wondered if I'd missed meeting someone with the band.

"Oh, that's their new name for Ryan. He kinda likes it, too," she said with an easy smile.

Two big men came wandering out of the bathroom, and I wondered how all of those guys managed to fit into one RV bathroom.

"Glad to see y'all don't have on muddy underwear, too." Peri laughed at the two men with muddy hands.

"No, we couldn't drive the tug boats so we had to be the cranes that loaded stuff onto the barges," Hayden added.

"I want to know who's going to clean that mess up. I did it last time." I couldn't believe she let them do that more than once. Dirty water in the tub?

Ryan raised his hand. "We flipped for it. I lost."

I couldn't resist any longer. "Why do you let them do it anyway? Isn't that kinda nasty?"

"Heck yeah, it is. That's why we let them do it. They're kids. Kids need to get dirty," Hayden offered in defense. "They're too little to play in the river and can't on the road anyway."

"It'll be over my dead body that my child will ever be playing in the Mississippi River," Peri spoke up. Her force of words surprised me.

"No, I pray mine won't either, but we've got some sandy-bottomed ponds out behind my mom's house that they can play in and get dirty."

"I might go for that, but not a muddy river."

An argument formed between the two boys so the two older boys left to settle it. Peri turned and looked at me, and I couldn't help but start laughing.

"Don't encourage them by laughing at this scene. Your turn will come one day, and paybacks are a bitch you know." Peri gave me her famous stink eye look, but it didn't stop me from laughing.

It felt good to laugh. My emotions had taken over every minute in my head for so many hours that laughing turned into great medicine. At least for a few minutes. The door to the RV unlatched but didn't completely open. The voices weren't loud, but the words held a heated tone to them.

"I want her gone *now*, Cash." Obviously, Carter returned determined to continue his tirade over my being here.

"It won't be that easy, Carter. I've already told you this once. We signed a contract with her."

"I don't give a shit if I have to pay the contract out. I want her off the tour."

"And the label wants her on the tour. You're not bigger than the label," Cash replied.

"Then I'm off the tour. I'll get my shit and be gone shortly." Wow, Carter's anger flared even more than earlier. He couldn't leave the tour.

"You can't do that, dumbass. Stop and think what you're saying here, Carter."

"I've thought about it all morning. I can't do this with her under my feet every damn day. I won't fucking do it, so you solve this problem, or I'm out." He made the demand in slow and pointed words. I heard a car door slam and more squealing tires.

I looked at Peri and the other two who returned from the back. "Guess I'll go pack my stuff and get a flight out this evening."

"Wait, Halo." I pushed the door the rest of the way open and skirted around Cash who also yelled my name as I ran to our bus.

Carter

The sign read "Welcome to Sunny California," and I knew I had traveled west far enough. I whipped a u-turn in the parking lot of the visitor's center and headed back east down Interstate 10. This Corvette handled smoothly flying down the paved roads in the middle of nowhere. I needed to get one when we returned to Austin. There's plenty of open roads west of Austin, and the speed limits are higher than most places out there.

My phone rang, and Cash's name appeared on the screen so I accepted the call.

"Yeah?"

"Where are you? The band's got sound checks in a few, and you usually like to do your own."

I didn't have to do it, and he knew it.

"Let Gary take care of it today. I'll fucking be there in time to go on."

"That's cutting it close, Carter. Where are you?" Cash asked again and actually sounded worried.

"I'm flying down the interstate in BFE Arizona."

"Flying in a car, I take it."

"Hell yeah. This car's perfect for the open road. I'm buying one when we get home. Come to think of it, I might buy it and drive this badass between shows."

"I'm thinking that's not a great plan, but we'll talk about that later." I knew he had more to say.

"What else you got, Cash? I'm busy here." And by busy, I meant watching the miles tick off on the odometer.

"You come on in, and we'll talk about the situation with Halo."

"So she's let y'all in on the back story, I'm assuming."

"No, not too much to me. I think Peri talked more to her. You're my concern."

"That's bullshit, and we both know it. You're worried about your new jewel you've found and how to juggle us all."

"Dude, I'm not going to address that because you know it's a damn lie. Assured Distraction will always be mine. You guys are more than another band to me."

"Then why do I feel like the odd man out here, Cash?"

A very pregnant pause happened over the speaker.

"You are not the odd man out, Carter. Come back, and let's talk. Maybe if you talked to Halo everything could be worked out. She's willing to leave if you're adamant about it, but I hate to see her and Hayden not get a chance to make this work for them. They're solid when they sing together. If you'd just give them the opportunity, it could be the break they need."

Cash knew I wanted Hayden to make it big. His talent knew no bounds. He wrote music like no other, he sang any kind of music and made it sound like it was written just for him, and he could play almost every instrument on the stage. The gifts the kid possessed needed to be exploited but in a good way.

"Sounds like you're begging now, Cash." I laughed when I said it. I hated hearing him beg.

"Come back, Carter."

Well, shit. How could I say no when it meant so much for Hayden's success. But having Halo around all the time, I didn't know if I could do it. "I'm headed that way."

I arrived with plenty of time to get ready to go onstage. The others acted like I had deserted them or something.

"It's about damn time." Gunner gave me a fist bump. "We were thinking we might have to pull a White Stripes and play without a bass tonight."

"Fuck that. You know you need me out there to keep your dumbass from missing the beat."

"Yeah, yeah, you say that but hell, dude, you know it's the other way around." He popped open a beer and offered me one.

"Hell yeah. I've been in the damn desert all afternoon." I took a long pull on the cold brew.

"Was there a horse with no name out there?" I turned and looked at him. "Sorry, dude, couldn't resist. You know I grew up on classic rock."

"I do believe they are referring to another kind of horse, dickhead." We both laughed at the stupid conversation we were having. Leave it to Gunner to get me in a better mood.

"So what'd you find out there?"

"Not a damn thing except I made that Corvette stand up and go like a motherfucker."

"Nice. Lots of power?"

"Hell yeah, it does." The door opened and the rest of AD came through along with Peri.

"Glad to see you've decided to grace us with your presence. Where the hell you been?" she asked me.

"Out."

"Out? Out where? I've been worried to death about you taking off in that fast car. I could see you wrapping it around a tree somewhere as mad as you were when you left."

"Nope, no trees today. Just miles. Lots of them. But hey, I did wrap myself around a hot stripper earlier in the day."

KeeMac joined us. "A stripper? Dude, you went to a fucking strip club and left the rest of us to fend for ourselves?" This earned him "the look" from Chandler.

"Yeah, I didn't think the fiancés and wives would exactly go for that."

"Good thinking, Carter," Peri added. "At least some of your brain works correctly when it needs to."

"Don't start, Peri. I'm here aren't I?" I glared in her direction before finishing off the beer.

"Sorry, you're right. I'm glad you made it back in one piece and ready to go onstage." This time she offered me a slight smile.

"Come sit with me for a minute, trail boss."

"Trail boss?" She sat down and straightened the polka-dot skirt.

"Yeah, you're always hot on my trail when I stray from the fold."

"What's going on, Carter?" I loved Peri. She never stayed mad for long at any of us, even when we deserved it.

"I'm sorry I've been such a prick, but you should know that this is hard for me, too." I turned to face her on the couch.

"I know it is, but Carter, Cash believes in them. He wants to see Hayden succeed and right now, he feels like Halo and Hayden are the real deal. None of us want to see you hurting. Is this going to come down to that?" She placed her hand on top of mine.

I looked down at her petite hand with the tattoos covering the back and let out a long breath. "I don't know. What I do know is it's going to be difficult. I keep going back and forth on the idea. One minute, I'm like, 'hell no.' I set the rules, like today when I left the strip club. Then, when I think about what it could mean for Hayden, I change my mind and decide well, maybe I could make it with her around." I turned my palm over and squeezed her hand.

"We don't want to see this be a problem. We want it to work out for the best for everyone."

"I know y'all do. I need to talk to Hayden without her. Do you think you can arrange it tonight after our set?"

She looked at me with those golden-flecked brown eyes. “Yeah, I can do that for you. Can you not blow up before then even if you find yourself in the same room? Can you do that for me?”

I wanted to say hell no but knew better. I nodded my head and kept her hand in mine while I laid back on the couch and closed my eyes. I needed some connection right now, and Peri was always one to offer.

I felt like I flat lined at the show or maybe my mind couldn’t concentrate to make it my best. I played my bass the way I always did, but I just wasn’t feeling it. My mind flailed all over the place, and my attention to the audience completely failed to show up. Beautiful women knocked themselves out to capture my attention. Flowers, panties, and other random shit landed onstage as usual, but I couldn’t make myself care. When we took the first break for KeeMac and Chan to do their numbers, I sucked down two bottles of water. I knew Halo lurked around there somewhere offstage, but I tried not to think about her.

Hayden appeared at my side during the second bottle.

“She’s not here so stop looking for her.”

“I’m not,” I lied.

“Yes you are, so quit.” Leave it to the kid to call me on my shit. “She’s already back on the bus. Cash worked hard all evening to get her to stay. Her instincts told her to bolt, but he talked her out of it.”

"Yeah, did he beg her like he did me?" This conversation needed to happen elsewhere at another time.

"We'll talk after the show. Peri found me earlier and said you wanted to talk but not now. You're playing sucks enough already."

"Listen, you little dumbshit." I couldn't finish because he stood there laughing. I smirked at him.

"Go on, old man. Your turn to shine because you've been dull the whole damn show. You've still got time to redeem yourself, so do it."

"Fuck off, kid. I'll deal with your smart ass later, and who are you calling old? I know you're not referring to me." I walked back onstage with more enthusiasm than I'd had the entire first hour of the show and played my heart out.

When the final encore ended, the newly-engaged two did their usual sexing in an empty room. I wondered if that tradition would ever get old with those two. Peri met Ryan backstage, and he carried her wrapped around him to the party going on. Gunner's phone rang letting me know his evening plans just improved, especially since Lola would be joining the band next Saturday for a couple of weeks of vacation.

Hayden held out a longneck in one hand and a bottle of Jack in the other. "Which is it going to be tonight?"

I grabbed the longneck and took the cap off. The ice cold beverage felt so damn good on my dry throat. "I want to talk before we get too drunk to say the right things or remember them."

"Good idea. I thought maybe you would want something a little stronger depending on your frame of mind."

"I'm good, dude. Good." My dry throat appreciated another long drink. "Although, it might take a few six packs before the night's done." He picked up a six pack in each hand and made a motion with his head indicating for us to cut out of this party. I followed without question.

The back door to the venue opened to the cool night air, and we sat in the stairwell leading down to the parking lot. We could watch the roadies loading up the equipment while we talked and their noise filled in the gaps of silence that surely would occur.

After I finished two of the beers, I looked at Hayden. He still had that little boy look to his face. The kid had been dealt a shit hand so many times in his life. I knew he'd never admit having a baby at eighteen was part of that hand because the love he carried for Crew ran deep. That fucked situation only added to his worries early in life, but dammit if the kid didn't handle it better than some adults did at thirty.

"Hayden, I need to tell you some shit and the first thing is I'm sorry for acting like a complete douchebag since I figured out the situation. This whole fucked-up mess has nothing to do with you."

"You're wrong, Carter. It has everything to do with me."

"Let me finish, please." He nodded his head. "I don't know what Halo's told you, but I loved that girl with everything I had. Leaving her behind about killed me. You don't know how many times on the road I opened my phone to call her and tell her I was coming home. I would have begged her to forgive me if she would only take me back.

"The night before we ended it, I looked at her beautiful smile in the pics on my phone and knew I could destroy us in a heartbeat. Hell, she knew it, too. She told me so that night. If I did something to break her heart while on the road, it would end me. I swear to God, the hate created in me from that would never go away.

"The girl's stronger than anyone will ever know. She stood up to me and told me to go. Told me the band and I deserved each other. I wanted to have another night with her, but she wouldn't have it. So I ended it, cut the ties in one fast clean snip. I walked away and so did she. We never looked back that night." I stopped talking and stared out in the direction of the buses in the parking lot waiting on us. One of them sheltered her from me. One of them would open its door tonight, and we would find ourselves thrown together for months.

"Dammit, Hayden. It's gonna be a bitch dealing with each other in such close confines, but I'll do it for you." I closed my eyes and took a deep breath. "And for her."

Hayden's eyes were on me when I finally opened mine. "Shit, dude. I don't know what to say. I feel like a dick for asking this of you, but I need it, man. We need it. This is our big break, and we gotta jump in with both feet and make it stick. This tour could mean the big time for us. Do you know how many doors something like this opens for us? For me and Crew?"

"Oh fuck, don't bring that boy in this. You know I love the little shit. That's hitting below the belt."

"Yeah, but if it plays out for us, then I can give him the life he deserves without Ryan and Peri providing it for him. I don't want to mooch off of them the rest of his life."

"You know they don't think that about you two."

"They might not, but I do. I need to give him his own home and maybe with his own mom."

I remembered the conversation that brought me to my knees with the kid. I didn't have to tell him anything about the talk we had. Hayden knew what he needed for the boy already.

"Okay, Hayden. I will give it my best shot. This isn't gonna be easy. We have some shit to work through. You know that, right? Her hard head might be impossible to convince. She doesn't always play nice, she can be a real iron ass about some things."

"How well I know that already. When she makes up her mind something's gonna be a certain way, there's no changing it."

"Shit, I can tell you some stories. Our year together had some major road bumps, but we always made it over, sometimes we'd both would be kicking and screaming, though."

We finished off the beer with me telling him stories of the stupid stuff we got into. It felt good to tell them. I remembered why I loved her hard the first time around. Now we needed to be friends. I prayed the two of us could pull it off. People I cared about counted on us.

Halo

I walked back to the bus with a security guard I didn't know. It didn't matter much since no one knew me anyway. Hayden's fans populated the audience from the last time he toured with AD. The exposure made me feel special when we took the stage and people applauded, screamed, and yelled, but I knew the truth about who they aimed their praises at.

Hayden knew it, too, but never once failed to include my name when speaking to them. He always introduced us as a team. At twenty-three, he worked an audience like a pro, which helped me because performing for those huge audiences upped my fright factor to the top of the chart.

As soon as our set finished, I took off for the bus. The less opportunity I had of running into Carter, the longer I might stay on the tour. I'd never choose to leave because I owed it to Hayden and Cash, but every day the thought drifted through my mind.

The empty bus made me miss home. It seemed like someone always hung around the house to greet me or asked how the show went. Climbing the stairs to a deserted bus gave me a hollow feeling that I would never get used to. Can I live like this for several more months? Was the energy I put into doing the best job I had in me worth the loneliness?

Sure, the others went out of their way to make me feel included, but the one person I needed the approval from couldn't care less. And why? Why did I need Carter's approval for anything? He's the villain in all of this, not me. He hated me being here which boggled my mind. We didn't part on bad terms, really. He needed to leave, and I let him go. I never begged him to stay or take me with him, at least not too much. So what pissed him off so much? I wasn't here to make demands on him. Hell, I had hardly even seen him. Plenty of space in this entourage could keep us permanently apart.

The bus door opened and Chandler and KeeMac stepped up the stairs.

"Hey, Halo. We wondered where you'd run off to," Chandler told me as she plopped down on the couch by me. "Damn, I'm tired. I guess I forgot how much the heat could drain me. Then pile on the meet and greet, and it wipes me out."

"We did a couple of meet and greets after our shows. Nothing big, but they were fun. Hayden's fun to watch as he schmoozes around the room. Of course, his objective and mine were not the same." Chandler gave me a hug letting me know she understood exactly what I meant.

KeeMac leaned into the fridge. "The boy learned from the best. Between Gunner and Carter, the exposure to fun and games started early." He looked back over his shoulder at me. I suppose he wanted to judge my reaction to the comment since Carter's escapades were included in that.

"It's okay, KeeMac. I know he's been enjoying all the perks of the road since the band took off from Austin. It doesn't bother me for y'all to talk about him. I don't want anyone feeling like they need to walk around monitoring everything they say. I'm a big girl like that." I gave him my best smirk.

He stood with a beer and laughed. "Good to know, Halo. I'm not sure we're capable of that anyway.

"No, you're not," Chandler added. "All of you say exactly what's on your mind because there's no filter where this group of guys is concerned." She rolled her head in my direction. "So be ready for it. They do and say whatever comes to mind, sometimes it's filthy, sometimes it's vulgar, and sometimes it's just plain gross. I had a rude awakening when I joined the band."

"Babe, you know you loved it. It was our way of showing how much we were willing to accept little miss innocent into the cool kids' club. Chan here was the epitome of a virgin on every level, Halo, but we made it our personal goal to corrupt her at all costs." He laughed as he said it, but I felt like he told the truth. "We treated her like one of the guys from the get go, and she loved us for it."

"Some more than others," Chandler added.

"That's right, babe, but not some, just me." He sat beside her and pulled her against him.

These two were seriously in love. The way they treated each other and the ease in their shared affection made it so obvious. *Must be nice*, I thought to myself.

"Oh, I forgot to congratulate the two of you on your engagement. Will it be a long one or are there wedding bells in the near future?"

"We haven't decided yet. We have so many people and dates to coordinate a wedding with. It's going to be hard with my dad always on the go, too." She turned to KeeMac. "I have grandparents, aunts, uncles, and cousins to also consider."

The sparkle in her eyes told me she planned to have them all in attendance. When the story of her locating her real family after the death of her parents came out, it made all of the tabloids so I wondered what the real story had to be.

"Babe, maybe we could rent an island and fly everyone there. We could charter a plane and get everyone there at once."

"Not going to happen. If that plane went down, I would lose all my family at once. Nope, I'll never agree to one plane, but we could have it on an island that people could fly in from separate places, and we rent out a whole resort or something. That's a good idea, Keeton. Let's do it. Now we only need a date. I'll talk to Peri. She'll know how to get that coordinated with everyone's schedule." Chandler jumped up from the couch and started pacing up and down the aisle in front of KeeMac and me.

"Oh, God. Activate your safety shield, Halo, I think bridezilla just kicked in." That earned him a look from his fiancée, and I laughed at the two of them. What a ride that crazy train would be. "Babe, sit down. You're exhausted and wedding plans can wait until morning at least.

"You're right." Chandler fell back down between us. "I'm tired." She glared at him. "If you wouldn't come offstage ready to tear my clothes off every time, I might not be worn out."

"Babe, really? Don't even try to put all the blame on me. You know you are just as hot for me as I am for you. It's our thing, Chan. We get worked up onstage, and we work it out offstage. Do you know how many times I've left the stage with a stiffy? It would be embarrassing if the audience only knew."

"What?" I needed to add to this conversation. "Do you honestly think you hide that from the audience, especially down front? Dude, those women in the audience leave the show with lady boners every single time."

Chandler shocked me when she reached over and grabbed his dick over his jeans. "Yeah, *babe,* you just have a hard time keeping it in your pants." The tone of her comment and the word 'babe' made me think she didn't like the idea of other women lusting after him. She should be used to that by now.

"Does it bother you that women are like that, Chandler?" I honestly wanted to know.

"Nah. It used to in the beginning. I thought he did all that thrusting and dry humping the mic stand to upset me, but then I saw how much the women loved it. I knew he did it to get them excited and coming back show after show. *And,* I'm the only one he's doing that naked with, so I'm good."

"Wait now. You learned the trick, too." KeeMac looked around Chandler to see me. "Don't think she doesn't do it to drive the men wild. After Peri and Camille got a hold of her and dolled her up for the stage, she drove the guys in the audience wild. I think our ticket sales with men shot up overnight from her stage presence. Hell, we had to start making a t-shirt with Chandler being front and center by demand. They stayed sold out for the first year."

"What an ego boost for you, Chandler." Not that the information surprised me, but it did make me wonder if Hayden and I would ever have that kind of success together.

KeeMac came off the couch and looked right at me. "Hey, did Cash talk to you and Hayden about this? He needs to schedule a photo shoot with the two of you so you can have merch for sale, too. It's one of the best ways to get your name and face out there. You could actually do some t-shirt gun shots into the audiences before the auditorium gets too crowded. When fans hear about that happening, some will come in sooner to get free shit."

It was his turn to pace up and down. I looked over at Chandler and raised my eyebrows in question.

"Don't worry about him. He gets like this when he starts thinking about marketing. I do believe some university should give him an honorary degree in it. He knows more about marketing than most kids do when they graduate."

"Yeah, yeah. We should be marketing your stuff along with ours. Of course, y'alls won't sell as fast as ours but when they see it's there to buy, a lot will be snatched up."

He started spouting all of this business stuff, and I tuned out. That wasn't my thing, but I would mention it to Hayden when I could.

"We need to get some EP's made too. They can be the unplugged music recorded. Has Cash talked to y'all about doing an EP to get it in the fan's hands?"

I shook my head but honestly, I didn't know if he did or not. "We need to ask Hayden all of these questions. You lost me at merch." I smiled up at him.

"Girl, we are going to get Hayden and Victory out there. Or should it be Hayden and Halo? I'm kinda liking that name. Or what about only Halo Hayden or Hayden's Halo? That could be the band name. You could still use Victory as your name that way."

My face must have given Chandler a clue as to how lost I was because she leaned over and whispered, "Don't worry. It'll be fine. He'll talk to Cash and Hayden. Let them worry about it. I leave the marketing stuff to him and Peri. They both are geniuses with it. I'd rather write music than worry about selling it."

"Me, too. Writing music is so much more fun and rewarding," I whispered back.

KeeMac pulled out his phone and pulled up an app, then started talking into it. Guess he grew bored trying to make Chandler and me listen.

She saw it, too, and laughed. "Good. Let him and his phone have a talk so you and I can talk about more important things."

"Like what?"

"Like you. Tell me about yourself. I don't know you at all, and I want to."

"Oh, I'm not all that interesting."

"Girl, I know you're from the Austin area. I know you have some stories." She didn't let me escape her questioning so easily.

"I grew up in Dripping Springs really. Went to school there. Started dating Carter when we were at the end of our sophomore and junior years. He left after graduation, and that's about it."

"No, that's about the end of your story with him. Tell me the rest of your story. When did you start playing and composing music?"

We spent the next hour talking about our lives. Getting to know Chandler made me feel closer to her. KeeMac ended up leaving to catch up with Cash and Peri. His excitement over all of his ideas helped him find a second wind. Chandler and I killed two bottles of wine and were toast when he came back to the bus.

He had an intoxicated Carter and Hayden with him when he returned, though. They boarded the bus with KeeMac's help as he pushed them both on, one at a time. One look at Carter, and I knew it was time for me to head to my bunk. I planned to be asleep before he got there, but it went by the wayside with KeeMac and Chandler's appearance.

The men laughed at something KeeMac said behind them, but when they turned and saw us sitting on the couch, all laughter stopped. Right, my cue to head to bed.

"Oh, Halo. Don't leave now. The party's finally arrived." Hayden managed to sound sober, but the smile on his face told a different story.

"I'm tired Hayden. Chandler and I had a little wine so I'm ready to sleep."

KeeMac picked up the two empty bottles and shook them. "A little wine? This equates to a massive hangover for my girl."

"And some drunk sex, Kee." With those words, she jumped into his arms and wrapped around him. "Come on, babe. I'll let you do some kinky things to me." She tried to whisper it, but every one of us heard, and that made Keeton laugh.

He looked around at the three of us. "Duty calls, people, and I'm never one to shirk my duties when they involve kinky sex with my little love muffin, provided she doesn't fall asleep on me."

We all laughed at his comment. She left wet kisses all over his face and neck so I doubted that would be the case. "We'll be taking the bedroom. There better be clean sheets."

"Yeah, yeah. The cleaners came in today. It's all good," Hayden told the two lovers.

"Perfect," he headed down the aisle. "I'll lock the door in case any of you dickwads get any bright ideas."

All we could do is stare at them as the door slammed, and the lock clicked. An awkward moment happened with the three of us standing there looking in the same direction. Thank God Hayden broke the silence.

"Another beer, Carter?"

"Sure, why not?" He flopped down in the chair across from the couch. I remembered that I volunteered to go to bed and started that direction when Carter grabbed my hand.

"Don't leave. Have a beer with us."

My skeptical look made him continue, "Just one. Come on."

I glanced at Hayden. Was this the same guy who left here yelling about me this morning?

"Yeah, Halo. Just one," Hayden pleaded. Even drunk I could tell he needed me to be here so I sat back down.

"Okay, but only one. I drank a lot of wine tonight. I don't know about adding beer on top of it. I'm not fond of saluting the porcelain god, you know."

"Oh, I remember it well," Carter said, and I almost jumped off the couch. Walking down memory lane tonight? Hell no.

Carter didn't add to it, and I wanted to do a happy dance.

Carter

I cannot let this girl crawl under my fucking skin. I'm pissed, but I needed to make an effort to not be a douchebag. Sitting there looking all beautiful with her cheeks glowing a shade of pink from the damn wine buzz she was feeling, gave my dick a slight zing. I always knew when she'd had enough from that look since wine did that to her every fucking time. Beer didn't have the same effect, and she wasn't much for alcohol back then. Who knew now? She'd probably learned to like those little bitchy, foo-foo drinks with flavored vodkas or some shit like that.

"I missed y'alls show tonight. Wish I'd been there to hear the two of you play." Music had to be a neutral topic we could all play fair with.

"Yeah, it was good. You'll catch it next time, though," Hayden assured me. It took all I had in me to not look at her again. Dammit, I flat out wanted to stare, but I couldn't do it without looking fucking creepy so I leaned forward with my arms bent, elbows on my knees, and dropped my head.

"Cash knew what he was talking about when he said our voices were meant to be together. I think you'll be surprised, Carter," she finally spoke directly to me.

Ice broken.

I could damn sure look at her now.

"Is that right? Well, I know shithead over there can belt out a song in front of an audience. Seems like he was born to do it. I'll be anxious to hear you perform, and what y'all can do together." Okay, this grew fucking lamer by the second.

"Where'd y'all go after AD finished?" she asked.

Change of subject. *Good.*

Hayden spoke up. "We killed a couple of six packs on the steps and gave the roadies hell about the equipment. Those fucktard clowns are always good for a few laughs, especially with beer involved. We can dole out orders and the best comments to piss'em off."

"I bet they loved you for it, too." The smile ghosting her lips reminded me of so many fun times.

Damn.

"Yeah. We're good, though. That bunch's traveled all over with us so many fucking times, they know every single move to make without anyone telling them. We trust'em to do that shit right," I added. Not that it was necessary but I needed to keep the small talk going if there might be a chance she'd stay for a while longer.

"That's good," she added. Yeah, lame. She stood and stretched. My eyes immediately honed in on the thin line of milky white skin peeking out from the bottom of her shirt. The memories of how soft that spot felt under my rough fingertips and how it tasted on the flat of my tongue flitted across my mind. The dick twitch happened again.

"Guys, I'm too tired to finish this beer. My eyes won't stay open any longer, and the bunk's calling my name." She yawned behind the comment.

I stood. "Yeah, me too. It's been a helluva day. Think I'll find myself one, too, since the two horn-dogs took my real bed."

"Hey, at least you got to sleep in one some of the time already," Hayden added but stopped there with his comments that involved women we picked up. I knew having her on the bus would cause some blue balls along the road. Either that or I'd be going to a lot of hotel rooms on my own. That had to be better than causing shit on the bus.

"Yeah," she said. "I'll see y'all in the morning. Good night."

The slide of her curtain closing behind her ended our evening. I looked at Hayden, and he shrugged and smiled. It went okay for a first talk. I could live with it. I peeled off my jeans and climbed into my bunk. Fuck, I'd forgotten how narrow they were.

I laid there thinking about how a girl that used to be my whole world now slept three feet away from me, alone. We're adults now. We'd handle this fucked-up situation like adults. Hayden and Halo's immediate success depended on it. Why did I feel left out? I drifted off to sleep wondering where her head was at in all of this.

Halo

The bus ride might be harder than I thought. I felt his eyes on me as we sat making small talk which turned out better than I was prepared for. The muscles in his arms bundled to perfection as he leaned forward and looked down. Most of his tattoos had been added after he left. They made his arms look like canvases for an artist. The dark ink added to his smoking-hot look he left the first time with. The man he grew to be caused my body to respond simply by looking him over.

I wondered if I affected him in any way like that. Was that why he seemed afraid to look at me for more than a glance? I caught him through my lashes sneaking peaks in my direction. Did he remember the us from before? Did he see me as a woman now instead of the teenager he left behind?

Stop it, Halo. I needed to get over the idea that a reconnection might happen. His plans never included me, and I only fooled myself into thinking anymore would become of us. He made it clear the first time, and I needed to keep that on the front burner at all times. This slippery slope could cause a cold splash of reality to hit me in the face in the end. I needed to do my best to make sure it didn't happen.

Now here we both lay feet apart. Before, he would've slipped in my bed and made love to me, holding me close when our bodies slowed from the peak we reached. Now, he's sleeping, dreaming of past lovers who fulfilled his needs after a concert, while I only dreamed of what we could have been. Tears I held back forced a lump in my throat. I turned and faced the wall to silently let them slide away as sleep overtook my troubled mind.

Carter

I knew the bus stopped sometime during the night because the constant hum of the tires on pavement no longer filled the silent void inside my head. I opened my eyes for the first real morning of the tour and realized a few things. One, the hangover usually clouding my head didn't exist today. Good perk. Two, I hadn't paid attention when Peri told us the schedule so who knew where we were. Neither good or bad perk because honestly, who cared? Three, a beautiful woman with a hot body who inhabited most of my dreams all night camped out across the aisle from me. What should have been the best perk of all, probably wasn't even close.

I rolled out of the bunk needing to piss like a racehorse. Even without the hangover, I still held on while moving down the wall to the bathroom. I jerked open the door and dense, steamy fog billowed out but quickly dissipated when it hit the air. Beyond the mist, a vision stood in the translucent, waterfall glass door of the shower.

An image struck my brain, and I knew the morning wood I sported was going nowhere anytime soon. Halo stood facing me with her head tilted back as she washed white clouds of foam from her hair. The lines of soap and water slowly made their way down the enticing curves of her body. It passed over her perfect pink centered mounds to make its way between the roundness of her stomach and soft angles of her hipbones. The soapy bubbles disappeared between her legs and returned around her knees to slide off her feet into the drain.

I needed to shut the door but couldn't bring myself to do it. I took advantage of the situation like any good voyeur of the female body would. Yeah, the pervert in me wanted to start at the top of her head and watch as another round of bubbles made its way down, down, down. The further it went, the harder I got.

And then she screamed. Not a little yip kind of scream. A full-on blood-curdling scream. A wake-the-dead kind of scream. In this case, the kind of scream to wake the entire bus. All I could bring myself to do was cover my junk which was hard to do when my brain's caught up in a beautiful wet- body fantasy. A hurricane force wind wouldn't bring down my flagpole.

The loud screech brought everyone into the hall to witness my full mast and a fully naked woman. When my brain decided to wake up, I slammed the door.

"I'm so sorry, Halo. I didn't know you were in there. Why didn't you lock the door?" I offered through the closed door.

"What the hell, Carter. How long did you plan on standing there staring at me?" The awkward conversation continued through the door.

"I wasn't staring at you."

"Like hell you weren't, perv."

"Well, I was trying not to but damn, Halo, what did you expect? You're all soapy and naked and my sleeping brain didn't know any better. You can't blame this all on me."

"Ugh, go away." She peeked out the door and saw the group of people standing there. This time she squeaked.

I turned and faced the crowd. "Shows over, folks. Go back to bed."

Chandler started laughing. "Nice wood, Carter."

"Chandler," KeeMac yelled.

"What? It's obvious he enjoyed his peep show."

"Thank you, Chan. You can help me take care of it if you want." I smiled and pointed to it when I said it. "Since the dick's out of the bag, I didn't see any reason to hide it any longer."

"Yeah, fucktard, that will never happen," KeeMac informed me, but I knew that already. I just liked getting him all worked up about someone trying to get with his little cupcake.

The bathroom door opened and a vanilla scent hit me before a fully-dressed Halo appeared. It captured my thoughts before I could stop it. Memories of the scent filled me—the curve of her neck, the soft underside of her breast, the bend of her knee, the bone on her inner ankle—and penetrated memories safely stored away. Everywhere I'd once touched her, kissed her, ran my tongue over her body came at a full rush in my mind.

I fell back against the door she slammed behind her as the vanilla floated by me, and she climbed into her bunk. The others watched me with curious looks on their faces. I bucked up and fled into the bathroom to escape the stares. What the fuck? I didn't flee from scenes with women. I wouldn't allow her to get in my head this way. I had to put a stop to it before any feelings returned for either of us.

When I walked out, she'd gone back to bed which made me happy. I didn't want to face her right then. Instead, the band waited to see me.

"What time do we have a sound check?" I asked as I pulled a cola from the fridge and took a long drink.

"We're supposed to be in the auditorium at one," Chandler informed me. "We're going to go get some breakfast. You want to come with? Hayden's going to go, too."

"Nah, I think I'll hang out here and have some Cocoa Puffs. I asked Peri for them specifically, and I saw a couple of boxes when I scoped out the goodies she stocked the bus with." I looked through the kitchen storage because I knew they were there somewhere.

"I wanted to ask Halo to come too, but she didn't come back out after she went back to bed. I hated to wake her up if she went back to sleep." Chandler snuck down the hall and listened outside of Halo's closed curtain putting her finger to her lips telling us to shush. She tiptoed back to the front where we all stood watching her.

"She must be asleep. There's no noise at all behind the curtain. Let's just go." The two guys jumped off the bus, but Chandler turned and looked at me before she headed down them.

"Leave her alone, Carter. She doesn't need any of your dumbshit to upset her."

I looked up as I poured the cereal into the bowl. "Me? What would I do?"

"I don't know, but I do know you and that can only mean trouble. So be good."

"Oh, my dear little Chan, I'm always good. Just ask the women."

"Yeah, that's what scares me."

"You wound me, Chan." I clutched my chest. "Deeply."

"Eat your Cocoa Puffs, dickwad, and leave her alone." She gave me the fakest smile I'd ever seen and stepped off the bottom step. I sat down at the table with my phone and my cereal and the gallon of milk and scrolled through Facebook while I ate.

The curtain's rollers scraped with an irritating noise as it moved down the tracks. The gang left about thirty minutes before so I knew the two of us had the bus to ourselves for a while. We needed to talk before they came back, and I figured if her mood had improved since this morning's incident, now would be a perfect time.

She stood and pulled her hair through a tie a couple of times forming a messy knot on top of her head. The tight yoga pants and tank top hugged her body perfectly. Damn, she'd filled out in all the best places over the years. My staring screeched to a halt when she made a sound in her throat meant to attract my attention.

"Hey. Good morning." I smiled at her hoping to lighten her mood.

"Hey." She looked around the empty bus. "Where's everyone?" Sadly, not even a brief smile graced her face. She looked more nervous than anything else.

"Yeah, they all left to go get breakfast. Chandler whispered through the curtain to see if you wanted to join them, but she didn't get an answer."

"I guess I fell back asleep. I didn't realize I needed that much more. Exhaustion kinda took over." She glanced around some more. "Is it okay if I make some coffee? Looks like I'm going to be needing it today." She yawned and stretched arching her back like a cat after a long nap in a warm window sill.

That was a sight worth waiting for. Her tits stuck out, and I couldn't help but be drawn to them. Visions of their fullness formed in my head, and I knew I needed to find something else to think about fast.

"There's lots of things to eat in the cabinets and fridge if you want breakfast, too."

"Looks like you haven't outgrown your kiddie cereal." She nodded toward the box of Cocoa Puffs.

I grinned and slurped a spoonful in my mouth. "Guess some things never change."

"Ain't that the truth." A hint of sarcasm accompanied the comment.

"What's that supposed to mean? I've changed a lot since you knew me. You have no idea what kind of adult I am."

"An adult, huh? I wondered if you referred to yourself that way." She grabbed a bowl from the cabinet above her head and a box of something resembling horse feed when she poured it. Adding strange-looking milk only made it look worse. I grimaced as she took her first bite.

"Do you eat that shit every day? Looks disgusting and what are you pouring on it?"

"Yes, it's very good and that's almond milk which happens to be good for you. It's tasty and high in protein. I happen to love it." She took another big bite and crunched down on it.

"I'm surprised it doesn't break your teeth." The smirk I gave met a scowl from her.

"It's much healthier than the pure sugar you're slurping down."

"I'll keep that in mind, but you don't have to worry about me eating any of it. It's all yours."

"Good to know. So what's everyone doing today? Did we all get a sound check time?" If I didn't know better, I would swear she was actually trying to make polite conversation with me.

"Yeah, Peri left us a schedule. I haven't seen Cash since I got up. He must have left early with shit to do. He knows people in almost every city so I guess he's making connections." I kept my eyes on my bowl. I stared at her enough when she walked in to look creepy. She needed to feel comfortable around me if we were going to get off the acquaintance level.

"Do you do your own sound checks?"

I looked up and met her eyes. The violet color held me captive longer than necessary before I answered her, and damn, here again, staring at her.

"Yeah, uh, we do. The techs get it all set up, but we still like to double check if we can. Sometimes, it's not possible but usually there's time." I stuck the spoon in my mouth. Damn, her eyes got me every time. The unusual tint drew me in just as it always did, but I didn't have to allow it. The purple irises fringed with the soft, long dark lashes brought me to my knees more than once in our younger lives.

"Why are you acting so weird, Carter?" She glared at me when I looked up.

"What do you mean? I'm eating breakfast holding a conversation with an old friend. I don't see anything weird about that."

"Yeah, but you keep giving me this strange look like you're afraid to say the wrong thing. It's like you're making sure everything you say is the right thing. It's just me. Talk."

"I want to, Halo. I do, but you're right. I'm scared to say the wrong thing. I don't want our time together to add to the problems from before."

"Problems? Were there problems? Oh yeah, you left town and never looked back. Never called to check whether I was alive or dead. Never bothered to acknowledge I'd graduated or turned eighteen or twenty-one. Did you walk away and forget me? Was it that easy for you to move on?"

Carter

The comeback I prepared to give sounded wrong, so I kept my mouth shut for a few minutes. When I did open it, I weighed the words for the damage they might cause.

"Halo." I stopped. "I wanted to call. I planned to call several times and stuff just kept getting in the way." I stood and walked to the front of the bus putting some space between us. "A month passed and then it was two, and I felt like maybe I shouldn't. Maybe it would only rub salt in the wound. The responsibility for continuing to hurt you or make you angry or sad, ate at me. When I realized six months has passed, I decided to let it go. I walked away to keep from hurting you and calling might give you false hopes that I had no intentions of following through on."

"So kind of you to constantly be looking out for my feelings like that, Carter. I can't thank you enough." Sarcasm dripped with each word.

"Don't be like that, Halo, please. I want us to be friends. I can do this. I hoped you could, too."

"Friend-zoning me? Will that ease your conscience if I agree so we can get on with our lives?"

Damn, the words didn't win her over. "I'm not trying to win you over, Halo, but we can be friends while we're stuck on this road to happiness we've stepped on."

"Happiness, huh?" She smirked at me, but I gave her a full-on smile this time.

"Can we at least make it through a conversation?"

She looked at me hard for a while. Seemed like an eternity. "Yeah, I'm willing to try if you're sincere about it."

Thank God. The tour would be a much easier road to go if we could be in the same room without snipping at each other.

"That's awesome. So tell me everything. Start at the beginning of your senior year. How did you hone your skills on the guitar? How come you never sang when I was around?"

"Okay, stop with the twenty damn questions, please. My senior year flew by. After you left..." she looked at me hard and exhaled a deep breath, "... after you left, I had time on my hands so I continued practicing on my own. You'd taught me the basics and I took lessons, but I needed to find my own style, not play yours. I found a few other people in my class who played, and we all met up at different places a couple of times a week. We learned songs from each other and some of them were pretty good at singing. They encouraged me to backup some of the others since my self-consciousness kept me from going it alone. I practiced at home and finally decided to try it out with that group, and wa-la, here I am, singer extraordinaire." She ended with a smile. God, she was beautiful. Damn my stupidity for leaving her.

"You should take pride in what you've done. Cash says you and Hayden were made for each other. Own that shit, Halo. I believe you can do it." I stuck my fist out for a bump and she looked at it for a second. I thought she was going to leave me hanging, but she finally connected her small fist with mine.

"I guess I know all about your time since it's all over the media." This might go badly so I took a minute before I answered. I leaned back against the bench where I'd sat back down.

"You shouldn't believe everything you read or hear in the media, Halo. You know that, right? Those fucking vultures follow us around incessantly and become a damn nuisance. They destroy lives sometimes with the make-believe venom they spew." I stood and dumped my bowl in the sink.

"But some of it's bound to be true. How can they publish total lies?"

"I don't know, but believe me, they do. I've seen lots of couples, married and unmarried, split from it only to find out it was pure bullshit. Look how many celebrities have sued their asses and won."

"Then tell me some truths so I know the real stories about you and the band." She truly looked like she wanted to understand.

"We've had an incredible run with our music. We're the luckiest sons of bitches out there. With Chandler reconnecting with her dad, our road to fame became lined with yellow bricks overnight. Ryder helped us at every turn. That man is a god among men in the rock world, but I guess you knew this already." She nodded her head. I knew this wasn't the info she wondered about. The rumors of my sexcapades with the others found their way into print from the time we started getting a following. Gunner and I had all the women we could handle and then some.

I decided to rip off the Band-Aid and go for the truth. "Once we started touring with Steele, new opportunities came our way at every venue."

She laughed so hard at my statement I carefully concocted to gloss over the truth. When she finally caught her breath, she looked me in the eye. "I'm assuming by that statement that 'opportunities' is a euphemism for women, right? That's such a farce you're spinning there, Carter."

I smirked at her. "Yeah, I figured you'd call bullshit. The women were crazy after we started touring with them. He would invite us to Steele's after parties at these clubs and in his suite. KeeMac and Chan were together already, and Ryan had the bitch in the beginning."

"The bitch?" Guess this story escaped her need to know portal.

"Krissy. We rarely ever call her by name since all that shit went down. We just use 'the bitch.' Anyway, Krissy tried to catch Ryan up in a pregnancy scheme, but it blew up in her face when the timing didn't work out. The sad part, though, was Hayden finding himself a dad at eighteen. I can't tell you how fast we watched that kid become a man."

"Wait, so Ryan's girlfriend and Hayden had a baby together?" Her face told me she and Hayden hadn't discussed it.

"Well hell, maybe Hayden should tell you this fucked-up story. I assumed since y'all travel together, he'd told you this already." I stepped into this shit with both feet.

"No, I didn't know how he ended up with a five-year-old. I mean, I knew how, but I didn't know the details. I'd never pry like that. We talked and practiced and wrote together, but he never said much about life outside the band."

"Dammit, I should have known better." I felt like I'd betrayed Hayden. If they'd been traveling this amount of time together and he hadn't told her, maybe he didn't want her to know.

"I promise not to say anything. For one thing, I don't want to jeopardize our relationship. We're a helluva team now, and I need for it to stay that way, so don't worry. If he ever decides to tell me on his own, I swear, I'll act surprised."

"Swear, huh? Is this like a pinkie promise thing?" I smiled at her and got one in return for a change. God, this girl still had the ability to bring me to my knees with a simple gesture.

"You know what I mean, asshat. I won't spill."

"I know. I just like giving you shit." We both began to relax into an easy conversation. I skirted around the wild parties as much as I could, but I knew she could probably fill in the stories. She knew me. Sex with her as teenagers had been incredible, and I wanted it a lot like any other horn dog in high school but once I left, the women were freaks. Gunner and I learned to be freaks right along with them. No matter how I painted the picture, it sounded wrong. Before I could get on to other topics, she nailed me with the exact topic I avoided in my history.

"So, tell me the truth, Carter. Are the wild stories we've all read about you and Gunner real? You know the ones I mean, the wild orgies, the red light districts in Europe, the freakish parties that happened on the bus?"

Damn, she aimed straight for the gut. "Well, I don't want to lie about it. Gunner and I did find ourselves in a few wild-ass situations we didn't know how to get out of. We hung out with the crazies that accompany Steele everywhere they go. Those groupie whores would do anything to us if they thought they had a chance to get to sleep with someone in that damn band. They used us like fucking stepping stones, and we were definitely down for helping them out, however we could. I mean since we were gentlemen and all." The sheepish grin I gave her looked more like the bad wolf instead.

"Sounds like every twenty something's ideal life to me."

"You don't know how many mornings Gunner and I woke up in a bed full of naked bodies. Women we damn sure didn't even remember meeting found their way into our fucking hotel rooms. Of course, we weren't going to complain since we'd found our way into the women." Shit, that sounded bad. I wasn't talking to some roadie wanting the deets. This was Halo. We needed to move on to another topic.

"That sounds scary to me."

"Some mornings it did scare the shit out of me. Waking up to strangers isn't the rush guys make it out to be. After a few years, we started being a little more discriminating. We found our own women or they found us. We laid off the damn booze on those nights, too. Had to make the fucking security tighter, too. Then Peri stepped in and made anyone who got inside our inner circle sign NDAs."

"Good to know. So you and Gunner got the pick of the litter?"

"That's one way to see it, yeah. Then Hayden came along. Now it's the two of us skimming off the cream." She took all this information in without making a judgment. I knew this shit portrayed us as the biggest man-whores on the planet.

"Hayden's choices haven't always been the best on this trip. Guess he needed his wingman to help him out. He never invited me to go out with him, but he did tell me I could bring friends back with me."

"Hell yeah, you could have. He'd damn sure never be one to tell you not to. What's good for one's good for all around here." Another statement I chose to make that was probably gonna bite me in the ass.

"So, you'd be okay with me bringing guys back to the bus to spend the evening or night?" She looked directly in my eyes and waited for a response.

Shit, this had 'mistake' stamped all over it.

My mouth said sure, but my mind said hell no to this idea but what could I say?

Who was I to stop her from having guests back on the bus?

Shit, this was bad, and it hadn't even happened yet.

"You know, Halo, I won't lie. It's probably going to fucking bother me, but we're not each other's keepers. You have to do what's right for you. All I ask is for you to be careful, dammit. There's so many fucked-up pervs and freaks out there.

"Then there's the scumbags who are looking to catch you up in some kind of chicken-shit scandal. They'll take pics when you're sleeping. They'll slip fucking drugs to you to set you up. Be careful's all I'm saying, especially finding yourself alone. You'd be better off bringing them back here or in a suite with the rest of us. At least someone in the band would be around." My face must have sent a lot more of my feelings than what my speech said.

"I'm a big girl now, Carter. I've experienced a lot of things and know the rules of being with strangers. You don't have to worry. I'm not much of a party girl anymore like when we were together. Actually, I turned into more of a music geek."

"And as good as that sounds, I gotta say it worries me even more. You can't take risks out here. It's fucking dangerous. There are bodyguards. Take advantage of it." I knew she heard the anger in my voice. How could she miss it? "Please."

"Considering you gave up the right to tell me how to live my life about eight years ago, I'm afraid you're overprotective act isn't going to go far with me." She stood up and threw her dishes in the sink with a loud crash.

This conversation turned into a shit show so fast, I didn't know how it happened. "I'm not trying to tell you how to live, Halo. I want you to be safe, is all."

"Safe? You want me to be safe? How safe was I when I was with you? You were my everything and you walked off and left me like I was worth nothing to you. You broke me,

Carter. Totally broke me to the point I didn't know how to exist when you left me alone. I wanted to do bad things to myself when you left me. How safe was I then, Carter?

"Let me tell you how safe. I spent my senior year with a shrink, Carter, a damn shrink to get my head back on straight. The music I learned, it started out as therapy, Carter. Fucking therapy. How do you think I found the group of kids who played guitar in school? The counselor, that's how. She helped me find them, and then I found my way. Alone. I found my way back to being me." She whirled around and went back to her bunk and dug around coming out with tennis shoes, sliding them on as she hopped down the aisle.

I stood behind her. "I didn't know, Halo. I didn't know." I didn't know what else to say. I watched her punch the door opener, and she disappeared down the steps.

I'm not much of a runner. Actually, I don't run at all, but I ran from that bus like a fire tried to burn my ass. I couldn't believe I told him all of that. I promised myself I wouldn't go there with him. I never wanted him to know about my problems after he left, but when he started in on wanting me to be safe, I lost it. Damn him for getting to me that way.

The loneliness I felt after he left devastated me to the point I didn't want to live. I realized now how immature the thoughts of harming myself were. How could I believe it would help me cope with the situation I'd found myself in? He was my everything, and then I had nothing. Now I knew that my happiness came from within me, and not from the person I was when we were together. It took a lot of therapy to realize it. What hell I put my poor parents through to finally learn this knowledge.

To survive, I had to learn to be happy with me. I didn't need anyone else to provide me with happiness. I still wanted to be with other people and enjoy friends. I'd had a few boyfriends over those years apart but nothing serious. Maybe I feared getting serious again, but I didn't think so.

As I pounded the pavement in tennis shoes not really made for running, I came to a complete stop and put my hands on my knees trying to breathe. Why the hell was I running? I wouldn't run from him. He couldn't hurt me again. I wouldn't allow it. I survived his betrayal once. I knew I could do anything now. I turned and made my way back toward the venue.

I walked through the gate where I left from and waved to the guard.

"Wear yourself out?" the young guard said to me as I passed through.

"Yeah, something like that. Doesn't take me too long." Thankfully he didn't see me huffing and puffing like I did when I turned around.

"Gotta keep in shape to keep yourself looking good for those men on the buses, huh? You know, we could have some fun together, too. I'm as good in bed as those pretty boys. My package works as well as theirs." He had the balls to say that to me now? Not a good idea.

"Hell no, and just so you know, I stay in shape for me." I kept walking toward the bus.

"Yeah, but we all know the truth. Those guys always bring in the hot pussy. Makes all us working men jealous since you high-class hos won't give us the time of day." He stood up from his perch.

I walked a little faster because I was two seconds from ripping him a new one.

"See what I mean, you little cunt. You won't even stop and talk to me now." He yelled to me. "All high and mighty like you are someone important."

Oh no, he did not go that far. I couldn't take anymore. I whirled around to let him have it but before I could, Carter came around from the backside of our bus. He tore into the man with a death wish. Grabbing the guard by the collar, Carter swung him around, let go and gave him a good right hook to the side of his head.

"Who the fuck do you think you are talking shit to any of the band members that way? She is part of our tour, dickwad, and even if she wasn't, nothing gives you the right to speak to a woman that way." Carter's fist punched the guard's stomach, and I almost cringed. Almost.

"Don't ever disrespect another woman like that again." He kneed the man's jewels and sent him to the pavement.

Turning to me, he started to pull me to him for a hug, and then I guess thought better of it. He grabbed my hand, and we walked away from the bent-over security guard. I stopped him when we were a safe distance from the guard.

I couldn't let my crazy emotions get in the way. I wanted him to hold me. I grabbed him and hugged him. His big arms enfolded me in a tight embrace like he was genuinely worried for my safety. It felt like home, and I wondered if it felt the same to him.

It took me a few minutes of enjoying the embrace before I finally let go of him and backed away a couple of steps. "Thank you. I would have gone for the balls first thing."

Carter laughed. "Yeah, no doubt in my mind you could have taken him down, but I heard most of the dumbass remarks when I came around the bus. The idea of any man standing by while a woman was being so disrespected with those douchebag remarks doesn't ever sit well with me or any member of this band."

"Well, it's all good now so not to worry." We both stood looking at each other.

He broke the silence. "Hey, about this morning, I'm sorry. For everything. I had no idea and the dumbass kid that I was, assumed everything would all be okay. For a while, I became number one in my book, and everyone else was a long way down my list of priorities. I know you probably don't care about my excuses, but what I'm saying is the truth." He took a step toward me and grabbed both of my hands holding them between us.

"I was an overgrown prick to you, to the people around me. Hell, even to the other band members back then. I want to think I've outgrown all of that, but honestly, it might be my imagination. The band may say differently still."

I didn't have to initiate the embrace this time. He tugged me forward and wrapped me in his arms bringing his head down until our foreheads touched. I had a fierce need for him to kiss me right then. It would've been a perfect time to do so, but I couldn't bring myself to do it yet. The look he gave me said he wanted the same, but before anything happened, he pulled back.

"Sorry, I didn't mean to get up in your space. I don't want you to ever think I'm trying to take advantage of you. We're all in this together now, and I'm not about to do something to make it all weird for both of us." He let go on one side but kept his arm around me and lead me back to the bus.

"Do you think we can do this Carter? Can we be friends on the bus for this length of time we're stuck on it?" I looked up at him.

"All I can tell you is we can try, but if I do something to make you uncomfortable, I need you to call my shit on it. Don't hesitate. Damn, Chan and Peri don't ever miss an opportunity to call me out on anything so I don't want you to either."

We walked on the bus, and I turned and put my hand out to shake his. "That's all we can ask of each other then, to try and make it work." We flopped down on the couch and the door to the bus opened again with the band coming back from breakfast. This time, though, the entire AD entourage climbed on, kids and all.

Peri led Tucker up the stairs. "Oh, hey guys. We missed you at breakfast. You should have gone. The waffles were to die for." She cocked an eyebrow at Carter obviously trying to judge if something went on between us.

"Well, if you must know, I've been craving my Cocoa Puffs, and it just so happens that our band has this wonderful lady manager who treats us like royalty by doing little things like stocking the pantry with a couple of boxes. I spotted them first thing when I went through looking for the goods.

"Now, Halo here..." he pointed to me, "... is a different story. She had horse feed or chicken feed or some kind of grain, and it pained me to watch her eat it. Then, she topped it off with a run. How crazy is that? Me, I'd rather take a beating than run. Give me the gym and weights any day."

"So you went and worked out while she ran?" Peri asked.

"Hell no. I ate the rest of the Cocoa Puffs and played some Warcraft. I'm gonna get in a workout sometime today, though. Can't let this body get away from me." He stood and raised his shirt showing off the abs that the ladies seemed to swoon over. "Don't want the ladies looking elsewhere when they throw their panties."

"Mommy, why do girls throw panties at Uncle C? Don't they want them anymore?" If the lightning bolts coming out of Peri's eyes could have struck Carter, a funeral would be in our near future.

Peri turned and looked at Ryan. "Would you like to take your son back to the RV because he doesn't need to hear what's about to come out of my mouth?"

Ryan slipped up behind her and kissed the side of her neck. "You go on back to the RV, sweetheart. I'll take care of the man-child here." He nodded over to Carter who had a look on his face I couldn't quite identify. It might've been terror as he decided who he was more afraid of.

"Be sure to express my opinion completely, babe." She took Tucker's hand and led him off the bus.

It only took a second for the bus to clear out when everyone saw the look on Ryan's face. As I crawled into my bunk to get out my guitar, I heard a heated argument going on between the two band members. The door finally opened and closed signaling it was done.

I opened my curtain, and Carter held the controls to his game.

"Is the coast clear?" I ventured out of the bunk.

"Yeah, don't worry about him. He's all bark." He looked at me holding my Gibson. "Damn, girl, you still got that old thing?"

"It's not old. I love my guitar. It bears the scars of years of learning." I sat down across from him in the chair and the door opened again.

Chandler climbed the stairs and saw me. "Oh, are you in the mood to play? I haven't played my guitar in a while. Mind if I join you?"

"I would love you to join me. I didn't know you played guitar, too."

"Oh yeah. Keeton and I write most of the songs on the bus with our guitars." She came back to the front with hers. "This is my baby. I love her almost as much as I love Keeton, but don't tell him that." She whipped around and looked at Carter. "And don't you tell him either."

"Hey, my lips are sealed. Just us girls having girl talk." He smirked at the two of us.

"So how long have you been playing?" Chandler played a few chords while she did some fine-tuning.

"About nine years now."

"That's great. Are you self-taught or did you take lessons?"

I glanced up at Carter. "Oh, I had an instructor. He was pretty good most of the time, but he could be unreliable, too." I knew Chandler didn't know the whole story between us. The band's original keyboard player, Jacoby, left the band before their big break. Their music took them to stardom, especially after Ryder came along.

"Is that so? He or she?" She dug for the information, one question at a time.

"He, but he doesn't play rhythm guitar anymore. He moved on to bigger and better music, at least in his mind."

"Really? What's better than playing rhythm?" Chandler turned to Carter and arched her eyebrow? "Unless you're a bass player, and then you're just along for the ride with the real musicians."

"Real musicians, are you shittin' me? You know I'm the musician that keeps the band together. The rest of you dumbasses are only around to look pretty and attract a crowd." Carter tried to act indignant, but I knew better. The band loved giving him and Gunner hell about their abilities.

"So let me see if I got this straight. A guy taught you to play a great guitar, but he chose to give it up? What an asshat."

"Oh, a number of colorful terms describe him and his poor choices." I narrowed my eyes at him.

"I bet they do," Chandler added. "I bet they do." She strummed across her strings.

For the next few hours, we played a variety of music. Some of AD's hits and then a few songs Hayden wrote for us. I taught Chandler a few of my original pieces that Hayden and I included in our line-up.

"That's a beautiful tune, Halo. Did you write that one alone?" Chandler asked.

I glanced in Carter's direction to see him staring at her. "The music, no. The words, yes."

"I love the intro riff to it and the melody flows over you when you sing it like it's there to haunt someone. But the words do the real haunting. They leave you wanting more as though the story isn't over."

I nodded at her. I didn't have a reply, but Carter spoke up. "Maybe the story hasn't ended. Maybe it needs another stanza added to it. What about it, Halo? Are you completely finished with it?"

"Part of me wanted it to end a long time ago, but fate has a funny way of taking over sometimes. I guess we'll see in time."

Chandler glanced back and forth between Carter and me. I knew she figured out early in this conversation that a completely different story must be happening in the background. She dropped her head back to her guitar and started putting it away.

"Guess we better think about going over to the venue for sound check. It's about that time. I'll go find Keeton." She slipped from the bus, but I don't know if it was to find her fiancé or to escape the tension that built in the last few minutes.

"What the hell was that about, Halo?" He stood and walked toward me. "I thought we were going to call a truce between us."

"I don't know what you're talking about, Carter." I took a deep breath. "I didn't mean it to sound like an attack on you."

"I call bullshit. You obviously can't let it go, can you? Will I pay for my mistake forever?"

"Is that what I was to you, a mistake?" I stood and squared off to him raising my voice.

"Fuck no. You know that's not what I meant." He matched my volume.

"What exactly did you mean then?" I refused to back down. He'd added to the sparing we did when Chandler listened. I stepped closer to him.

"Choosing to let you go, Halo, and you damn well know that's what I meant." His eyes glowed with fire.

"So you admit what you did to us was wrong?" My heart beat faster with each word.

"Fuuuccckkk." He hauled me into him and attacked my lips with a punishing kiss. I responded with equal ferocity. When he wrapped his hands in my hair and swiped his tongue across my lips trying to gain access, my judgment flew out the window. I opened and let him in. My acceptance allowed the kiss to deepen, and I slid my hands around his neck feeling engulfed in his need or maybe it was mine.

The sound of someone clearing their throat brought me back to earth, and I pushed back breaking the spell. He let me go and stepped back looking toward the door where Hayden stood staring at the two of us.

"Sorry to interrupt this little reunion, but Cash wants us over at sound check, too." He turned and stepped off the bus.

I looked up at Carter, who stared at the floor. He refused to look at me which pissed me off. This scene was all on him, again.

Carter

What the fuck. I knew better. I needed to get my head on straight. Hell, I needed to get back to my old self. Having her around tempted me too much. Talking to her reminded me of how I felt about her before the band. I couldn't go back there, but she made it so damn difficult. I never wanted to fucking hurt her again, and this situation seemed to be plowing headfirst in that direction. All indicators pointed to hurt. I couldn't do it, so it had to stop now.

When KeeMac opened our show, the crowd screamed at their usual volume since the performance by Hayden Victory had them primed and ready to rock.

"Hello, fucking Phoenix! How ya doin tonight?" The roar of the crowd led into our set, and the noise didn't stop. The babes threw lingerie our way along with flowers and stuffed animals with phone numbers attached them. The women waited to get the nod from us, only now the nod only came from me. Ripe for the picking, I looked the scantily-clad beauties over. Shit, my mind still lingered on that kiss from Halo, but I needed to break this once and for all.

One blonde and one purple-haired lovely caught my attention when they started making out right in front of the stage directly in my line of sight. I usually stayed back closer to Gunner since we were the sound that kept the rest of these dickwads in line, but when I spotted that girl/girl action, I had to move closer making sure of what I saw. Damn, these women knew their actions had all of my attention. I gave the nod to our security who promptly went over and pulled them aside. They always had to sign non-disclosure agreements before coming backstage. The guards now made sure of that before leading them off to the room for tonight's meet and greet.

When the third encore finished up the night, we made our way offstage. With something special to look forward to after the show, I quickly wanted to get this meet and greet over with. The radio station that sponsored tonight's party brought in all their winners for us to meet. The women I brought in were for later in my own private party. I needed the after party to start ASAP. After Halo's kiss, I only had one thing on my mind, and it had nothing to do with meeting and greeting.

The radio hosts escorted the last of their group from the room, and we all breathed a sigh of relief. We loved meeting our fans, but standing around making small talk after a show when we were all fired up made it difficult. So many of the female fans stood and stared at us and that used to be freaky. We grew accustomed to making conversation with them by doing most of the talking.

"So ladies..." I opened with walking up to the two, "... are you both ready to have our own little party?"

Both women stood and attached themselves to each side of me. "Hell yeah," they said in unison.

The blonde slid her tongue around the outside of my ear and whispered, "Where do you want to move this Carter, party of three?"

The other slid her hand under my t-shirt and traced her fingertips over my abs. "I'll replace my finger with my tongue in a few minutes."

"I like where this is going, babes. Let's see if we can find an empty room around here." We moved toward the doorway. It opened to Halo and Chandler walking in.

Chandler spoke immediately, "Typical Carter, already found the women. So sad you've lost your best wingman this tour."

"Well, sweet Chan, my friends and I don't need a wingman for what we have in mind. Isn't that right, ladies?" I looked at both of them and then at Chandler and Halo. Chandler smirked, but the look on Halo's face almost sent me to the floor. I fought the urge to send the groupies out of the party alone.

Seeing that look on Halo's face took me back to the days we were still together. She would occasionally go to the parties where we performed. She quickly learned that girls wanted bad boys and playing in the band automatically classified us that way. Breaking up with her before we left on tour was necessary because of that image and those women. While I hated ending our relationship, leaving her at home waiting to see if I fucked up while on the road was even worse.

Now she saw it in living color right before her eyes. Leaving an after party with two beautiful, willing groupies draped all over me, cut her to the core. The way her eyes rolled over the women and then the glare she gave me said it all. She knew the score. Hell, maybe she even expected it so she could feel free to move on, too.

"See y'all later," I said to the Chandler and Halo. I didn't want to get into any more of a confrontation than Chan had already pulled me into.

Our threesome found an empty dressing room for our naked romp. While we were working up to some great sex, I couldn't bring myself to get into the ménage with them like I usually did. My mind kept replaying Halo's expression when she looked at the two women.

"You know, ladies," I finally said while my hard cock was buried deep in one's throat. "I'm not really feeling this tonight. I think we're going to have to call it a night."

"But we've just begun, Carter," purple hair said as she pulled my semi out of her mouth. "What's up with this? Don't you love us?"

"Oh, it's not that I don't love you, sweets. I have some shit on my mind and can't get into it. But hey, don't let me stop you from enjoying each other, or I know some of the roadies that would be honored to take my place to satisfy beautiful women like you both are." I zipped up my pants and tugged my t-shirt back on. "I'll take a raincheck until next time."

The two pouted for a minute until I promised them free tickets and backstage passes to our next show. I quickly kissed them both and went back to the after party. Slipping through the door, I saw not too much was going on.

I walked up to KeeMac and Chandler. "What's up guys?"

Chandler looked at me as KeeMac spoke up from talking with a sound engineer he knew from some other shows. "Not too much. The radio people left about five minutes ago, but you weren't here to thank them."

"Hey, that's your job. You're the big front man, remember and the rest of us are damn happy it's you and not us." I slapped him on the back.

"Where's Hayden this evening? I never saw him come in here."

"He came in and left pretty fast with an overenthusiastic Barbie doll. I'm surprised he's not back already if he's even coming here. He's either holed up in a hotel room with her or back on the bus, I'm sure." KeeMac finished off his last gulp of beer from the bottle.

I looked around but refused to ask about Halo. The room usually emptied out pretty fast when the band members weren't there to entertain.

"She left right after you did," Chandler finally spoke up.

"Who?"

"Oh please. You are such an asshat," she laughed as she said it.

"What are you talking about?" I continued to play dumb, but I knew I was so busted.

"Halo, dumbass. Halo. Remember her?" Chandler continued.

"Yeah, I remember. I also remember the two of us discussing moving on with our lives and being okay with the way things are between us." I didn't owe this to Chandler, but I wanted her to know I wasn't a complete douche when I came to Halo.

"That's good to know, Carter. I'm glad y'all had that talk. I wouldn't want you to be mad when you jump on the bus and found the back room occupied." She didn't take her eyes off me.

I guzzled the beer I opened when I walked in. "Wait, what'd you say?"

"I said I wouldn't want you going all apeshit when you get on the bus and she's in the back of the bus bedroom with the man she left here with. You know, 'what's good for one is good for all.'"

Shit. "Uh, yeah. That's abso-fucking-lutely right. I told her that, too. She's welcome to entertain whoever she wants on the bus. Hell, I plan to. Those two I was with just weren't doing it for me tonight."

"Is that right? I would've thought they were perfect choices for you. Thought you were always down for a Carter sandwich." Chandler's eyes bore a hole through me.

"Sure as hell am. Those two just didn't have what it takes, though. Gonna have to start being more discriminating when it comes to picking the women out of the fucking crowd. My standards need to be raised now that I'm on my own." My determination to make Chandler back down grew with each comment.

"Oh, really. I thought you didn't have standards. As long as they were pretty, clean, and willing, so were you."

"Damn, Chandler. That's a low opinion you have of me. I'm not that fucking desperate. I get the cream of the crop, especially with no competition now from the other pricks in the band."

"More like the pick of the litter," KeeMac added.

"Very funny, dickwad. You've been there before Chandler came and stole you from the fucking chick market."

"That's right, and he'll never be shopping at the chick market again." She wrapped her arms around his neck and kissed him. "Let's go to our dressing room, babe."

"Hell yeah, we can." He picked her up and started unsnapping the snaps on his shirt while kissing from her neck downward.

God, those two couldn't ever get enough of each other. I looked around the room and there was only a handful of guys talking music in one corner. Fuck, what was I going to do now? I had no intentions of going back to that bus where Halo entertained her guest. I pulled out my phone and called Hayden. Maybe his Barbie needed to go home already.

"Dude? What's up?" he answered.

"Not much. Where you at?"

"Sitting on the bus playing Warcraft with Halo. You?"

"Halo's with you?"

"Yeah, she didn't like all the crap in the after party so we came back here looking for something else to do."

Well, shit. That little lying Chandler. What the hell was she trying to pull?

"I'm headed that way. I'll play the winner." Chandler better watch out. The next time I saw her we would have some words over her need to piss me off. I grabbed a bottle of whiskey and took off for the bus.

I heard yelling and then laughing as I stepped on the bus. Halo and Hayden both screamed at the screen. These two got into the killing-to-win thing. I walked around the divider into the living area, and they were piled up on the couch trying to kick each other's ass on the TV screen.

"Dude, she's better than you and me both on this game. She'll kick your ass."

"Is that right? I never knew you had a mean bone in your body, Halo." She never took her eyes off the screen to speak to me.

"Hell yeah. I had a lot of time on my hands, and my friends were mostly guys who liked to play this kind of shit." Her intensity grew with each shot she made.

Hayden looked at me. "I thought you had guests for tonight."

"No, it didn't work out. Not the right ones for me." I didn't take my eyes off the screen as I spoke, but I knew Halo looked at me. "So, do I get to play the winner?" I sat down next to Halo and started watching her moves on the screen. Damn, she was good.

"Yeah, I'm about to have to go. I'm spending the night with Crew tonight. I know he's already asleep, but I promised him we'd stay together tonight. He needs to wake up in the morning seeing I followed through." I only prayed that I'd be the dad that Hayden was to Crew someday. He had me beat all over the place.

"Well, shit, you did it again." Hayden almost threw the controller. "This girl'll whoop your ass on this game, dude. Don't let her con you into thinking she's all girly about killing." He laughed as he stood and made his way to the doors. "See y'all in the morning, somewhere. G'night."

"Goodnight sore loser," Halo called after him, laughing.

"A rematch is in our near future," he said as the door closed.

"So, big bad rock star, you ready to get your ass kicked by a girl?" She leaned over and shoved me some with her shoulder.

"Hell yeah. I'm ready to own you with this game, girl. You don't have what it takes to be a player like me."

"I bet that's right." She gave me a funny look when she said it. I knew what she referred to, and it had nothing to do with whipping me in this combat game.

When the bus driver stepped on the bus and started it a few hours later, we were in a draw on winning. Her skills matched mine in each game we played. Not too long after we started, Chan and KeeMac came back on the bus, and she acted all innocent about the bed comments so I let it go. They proceeded to take the bed instead, so we continued to play the game a while longer.

Halo finally yawned. "I'm too tired to play another game. My mind's wasted, and I haven't even been drinking."

"Yeah, I know what you mean but I'm a little too keyed up to sleep now after taking out so many bad guys. You want to watch a movie or something?"

"Sure. I'm going to change, though. You choose one." She disappeared to the bathroom and returned shortly in little boxer shorts and a tank top, sans a bra. Shit, the girl was going to test me at every step.

"You choose, and I'll change out of these tight-ass jeans." I put on some basketball shorts and returned to some scary movie with only the TV screen providing lights in the room. At least it wasn't a damn chick flick. I could do scary, especially in the dark with her.

We sat up on the couch, and she pulled a small blanket over her leaning against my arm. The sweetness of her vanilla scent assaulted me. I swear it could get me hard thinking about running my nose down her body smelling that everywhere I went.

The movie's scary scenes caused her to hide her eyes behind the blanket or behind my arm. The longer we watched, the more she moved toward me, and the closer I wanted her. I put my arm around her tucking her into my side when her body gave a little shiver. I didn't know if it was fear or a chill, but I didn't really care at that point. Hell, I felt like we were in high school all over again sitting on her mom's couch with all the lights off.

A lull in the action let us both calm down a little, and I took the chance to look down at her. Her beauty that took my breath away as a teenager, did the same thing to me now. The soft brown curls framing her gorgeous face attracted my attention to her every time, but those violet eyes captivated and held me locked away in their depths.

I couldn't resist kissing her. I leaned down and ran my lips softly across hers in a tentative kiss to make sure. I leaned back to lose myself in those eyes, and she put her hand behind my neck and pulled me back into her. This time she parted her lips and deepened the kiss herself.

It didn't take any time to agree to her aggressiveness. I moved my tongue along the underside of hers and wrapped mine up and around hers. She rewarded me with a low moan as I slid it slowly up one side and over the top of hers. I picked her up and sat her on my lap so I could get to her more easily. She wrapped her arms around my neck so that we were touching from hips to the chest.

Her hardened nipples hiding behind the thin material of the tank rubbed across my pecs proving our arousal for each other matched. The firm peaks begged for my attention. One hand found its way under the hem of her tank and inched upward until I had the soft mound in my palm. I squeezed slightly before I slightly pinched the pebble between my thumb and index finger.

She broke the kiss on a deep moan, and I moved to her neck stopping to pull the soft skin between my teeth and slowly bite and then soothe with my tongue. Her hips moved in a stroking motion over my rock-hard cock. With her legs spread over each side of my hips, it separated her slit and through the thin materials we both wore, the heat of her core moved up and down my length.

I wrapped my hands around her hips to stop the movement before I embarrassed myself. It felt so fucking good that I knew it wouldn't take too much to make me blow my load like a damn teenage boy.

"If you keep doing that, I'm gonna come, Halo. It feels so fucking great." She whined a little until I replaced my dick with my hand under her sleep shorts as I slid a finger inside her wet panties. "Ugh, Halo. You're so damn wet, babe. God. The feel of your need makes me harder."

With her spread open, I easily accessed her stiff, swollen clit and circled it a few times without touching it. My fingers moved down to her opening and gathered the sweet juices she had waiting for me. I carried the desire back up, causing her clit to feel slick as I again circled it. She rocked against my hand wanting me to offer more relief to her growing need.

I held back and continued slipping back and forth from her opening to circling the nub until she bit my chest where she had been sucking, licking, and tracing my tattoos with her tongue and lips. When I thought she couldn't take it anymore, I slipped two fingers inside the hot channel while my thumb played havoc with her clit. It only took a few pumps and some pressure sweeping across her inner sweet spot as my thumb circled and pushed down on her clit. She came undone.

The sound from her throat, as she bit down on my skin just above my collarbone, made me understand how hard she came, but the honey that flowed down my fingers into my palm eluded to how badly she needed what I gave her. I felt like the king of the world at that moment. The king who needed to fuck this girl like there was no tomorrow, that is.

Her breathing finally returned to a steady pace, and I thought she might have fallen asleep on me. Instead, she sat up on her knees, pushed my shorts down freeing me. She pulled her panties to the side and slid down on my swollen hard cock. The shock must have been written all over my face. I didn't know if we would take it this far, but she had other thoughts.

"Don't think, Carter. Don't speak." She fucked me like it could be a once-in-a-lifetime gift, and I sat back and let her. I took it like a dying man knowing this would be my last time, and it was the best sex I'd had in years. I think I came as hard as she did when I fingered it out of her before, or maybe it was when I pinched her clit softly while she pumped up and down on me and cried out my name on a whispered breath. When we were done, she climbed off me and walked to the bathroom. I sat there looking down the hallway waiting for her to return up the aisle. She finally did never once looking my way. She climbed into her bunk and slid the curtain behind her leaving me staring.

What the fuck just happened? I sat on the couch asking myself that over and over until I finally climbed into my bunk and fell asleep.

The bus tires whirred continuing down the road. The comfort my bunk offered me was far more than simply a place to sleep. The cocoon allowed my privacy while trying to decide how today would go. Would he be waiting outside the curtain with questions? Would he pretend nothing happened? Would he expect that to happen every night?

While I hid, I asked myself some of the same kinds of questions. What did I expect to happen now? Would we be together now? The question haunting me the most was would he pretend nothing had happened? Could I handle that? The pep talk I gave myself to suck it up and be an adult allowed me to crawl out of bed and face the day.

Chandler sat at the table eating frozen waffles drowning in syrup.

"Morning sunshine." She gave me a bright smile.

I looked down at the floating bread. "That kinda makes me sick, Chandler. How do you eat stuff like that and stay so thin?"

"Yeah, I know it's bad for me, but they taste so damn good. I could eat them every morning, but Keeton gives me shit about it so I only eat them on the road. He can't bitch about it because they're easy to fix. Cooking's not really my thing." She shoved a huge dripping hunk in her mouth.

I opened the Keurig and popped a new K-Cup inside to make myself a cup of coffee before I looked at her again. "So the guys are still asleep this late?"

"Yeah, they usually sleep in after a show. Something about this bus rocking them."

"I figured when we woke up we'd be in Salt Lake City."

"You're asking the wrong person. I'm just along for the ride." She took another bite.

"I hear ya." We high-fived each other.

"Halo, I'm not usually one to pry into other people's problems. I leave that for Peri." She grinned at me. "But you and Carter? Are the two of you on the same page as far as relationships are concerned?"

"Relationships? I'm not sure what you mean. Neither of us wants a relationship." I opened the sugar and cream packs to load my coffee.

"I've never known him to have a girlfriend. Hell, I don't know if he's ever been in a long-term relationship." Her eyes held mine until I finally looked away. Did I tell her? Why hadn't he told them? I felt like KeeMac should've remembered me by now. Why didn't he tell Chandler about us? Our previous time together must've not seemed important to the band. Carter kept it hidden from everyone for a reason so maybe I should, too.

"Okay, spill Halo. KeeMac's only given me the barest of information and like I said, I'm not really nosy but I want us to be friends. I feel as though there's a story unfolding under my nose while I'm in the dark."

I took a deep breath. I didn't know exactly where to start and with last night's incredible sex, the confusion in my head screwed me up even more. I finally exhaled the air that I didn't realize I held in.

"I'm not sure Carter wants the band to know too much. He kept the information to himself all this time. Maybe you're asking the wrong person."

"Uh, no. You're the right person. He's a dickhead most of the time when it comes to discussing feelings, just like the rest of these dumbasses. I think he'd have us believe he's never had any. There's a lot more to the two of you than any of us know."

Wow, if she only knew. We both put aside our story for such a long time now. Obviously, the chemistry between us held on, though. I knew that alone couldn't keep us together, but sex might be all either of us needed right now. Could I do just sex to fulfil a primal need? The idea of sharing him didn't appeal to me. I wondered how he felt about sharing me with others.

When we were together before, our needs and desires ran rampant. We might have more control over carnal pleasures now. The idea needed to be given some more thought, but right now Chandler sought out some answers.

"Carter and I were in love when we were in high school. Let me rephrase that. I loved Carter in that first love sorta way. My entire being felt he made the sun rise and set. He was a grade ahead of me, and we spent his last year exploring our love and desire in every way possible. He constantly occupied my mind. I thought I did the same for him, too." I stopped to breathe deeply. I didn't want to make either of us uncomfortable with the rest of our story.

"He proved me wrong. Shortly after he graduated, the guys decided they needed to get out on the road and start building a following. They saved every cent they earned from the gigs they played around home during their senior year so they could live a while, and I think all of the parents kicked in some, too. Of course, their parents wanted them to get it out of their systems and go to college.

"They took off in a loaded-down van and trailer. KeeMac managed to set up gigs in bars and small venues as opening acts to begin with, but their popularity grew pretty fast. I guess you know the rest."

"That's a great story of the band's history but that's not exactly the story I wanted to hear, Halo. Where did the Carter-Halo story get sidetracked to?"

"Oh, yeah. I guess I left that part out." My lips turned up into a brief smile.

"Pretty convenient for you, huh?" She laughed. "Sooo?"

"Damn girl for someone who doesn't like to pry, you're like a little bulldog."

"Yeah, that's me, Bulldog Chandler, throw me a bone because I know how to use it." We both laughed.

"Better a bone than a boner," I told her, and we laughed harder.

From the back of the bus, we both heard KeeMac yell. “I gotta boner for you, babe. Come back to bed, and you can show me what you know.”

We looked at each other and fell over laughing on the couch. The mood lightened with all the laughter, and I felt so much better.

“Guess my story will have to wait now. You’ve got a hot guy calling for your assistance.”

“Babe, you know I need you. Please don’t make me come up there and show my super power to Halo. I don’t think we’re that good of friends yet.” He sounded pathetic.

“All right. I’ll be right there and you better be thinking of how you’re going to make it worth my time. Halo and I were having girl time.” She got up and winked at me, then made her way down the hall pulling his oversized t-shirt over her head.

“Oh, babe. I know all sorts of things I can do to make you happy.” She shut the door to the bedroom behind her.

I shook my head and gave a little laugh. Those two obviously knew how to make this work. Why couldn’t I figure it out? I laid my head on the back of the couch and closed my eyes but a noise captured my attention. Gunner and Carter argued over the next turn in the bathroom. Once they got that settled they both stumbled to the front.

“I need a Coke. Looks like someone’s been hitting my stash pretty hard already.” Carter stared at the contents of the fridge.

“Get out of my way, dickwad. Coffee is calling my name. One of these days you’re going to grow up and drink an adult breakfast drink instead of pure sugar that’s eating your insides with every drink.”

"Speak for yourself. Coffee is no better for you, and you damn well know it, asshat." Carter slammed the fridge with his foot while he screwed the lid off the cold drink. He put it to his lips and drank about half the bottle. "Ahhh. That's fucking good, right there."

I watched the two as they leaned against the counter, Carter drinking and Gunner waiting on his to finish brewing.

"Hayden tells me the two of you have combined your efforts on writing, and the tunes you're producing are fantastic. I'd like to hear'em sometime." Gunner's lips turned up on the ends in an almost smile.

"Yes, the longer we play together, the more our sound improves. Cash's very excited about it, too. Our crowds get larger at each concert, so I guess our music is attracting attention." I kept my eyes on Gunner while I spoke.

"Hayden's a gifted musician and a helluva great kid. I hope this move takes you both to the next level in your careers."

"Yeah, me too. He's been awesome to work with. I can only see our music taking off from here." I smiled at Gunner, glad to see him willing to give me a chance to prove myself.

"Stick with Cash, little girl. He'll make damn sure you both leap to stardom. He's got an ear for talent." The coffee finished, and he turned to add several scoops of sugar to the mug.

"I wondered about that. Didn't AD start with Cash? Why did y'all leave him?"

"We didn't leave him... he left us. Once he knew we'd made it, he passed the day-to-day operations to Peri so he could pursue more new acts. It's really his specialty. Don't think he doesn't keep an eye on our numbers. He takes it all in."

"But it's wonderful that he's talented enough to do that. It's like he has his finger in the pie for every band." This caused both men to almost spit what they were drinking.

Carter coughed and said, "Yeah, sweets, he does like his finger in a lot of pies. He hasn't found the perfect fucking pie yet, but he keeps trying them out."

I threw the couch pillow at his head. "You're so damn vulgar, Carter."

"Hey, it wasn't only me. Gunner thought the same thing." Gunner doubled over laughing at me.

"Yeah, but he didn't make a gross comment about it." Gunner's laugh boomed through the bus. "Only 'cause I couldn't catch my breath long enough to do so," Gunner finally added.

When their obnoxious guffawing finally calmed down, Gunner sat down beside me on the couch, and Carter took his Cocoa Puffs to the table and poured a huge bowl. Carter pulled out his phone and started surfing on it while he shoveled the chocolate sugar into his mouth. This effectively cut off the conversation with him, which suited me fine.

"Where were you playing when Cash found you?" Gunner asked.

"I played some small bars in Austin. A friend of a friend heard me play and recommended me to his dad who owned a little bar and grill in south Austin. He let me audition to play a couple of nights a week for tips. I didn't make much, but I got to play and that's all I wanted to do. I started getting a small following. When summer rolled around, another bar with an outdoor venue called and offered me three nights a week and paid me. Couldn't turn it down."

"Lots of bands get a start exactly like that."

"Yeah, one evening Cash came in and left me his card. I didn't think too much about it. But when he returned the next week, I started asking around about him and found out he was someone important. I dug his card out and gave him a call. He arranged for me to meet up with Hayden, and here I am on the bus with Assured Distraction. Seems like it was destiny."

A sound came from Carter's area. I couldn't decide what he meant by it. I never mentioned him when I told my story. I had no reason to. Gunner met me several times at their first shows, so he knew some of our history. I suppose my disappearance from their gigs answered his questions as to my importance in Carter's life.

"I've always believed about seventy-five percent of getting in this business is luck. Lucky you're in the right place at the right time. Lucky some bar owner needed someone to play that night. Lucky you sound good enough to catch someone's attention." Gunner stared down into his coffee.

"So true. It might even be a higher percentage than that." I turned and put my feet up under me on the couch.

"You have a fiancée, right?" I asked him.

He smiled. "Yeah, yeah, I do. Her name is Lola. She's a pediatric nurse in Austin. Thank God she's meeting us at the next venue for her four days off. I miss the hell out of that woman."

"That's great you'll get to spend time with her even with a job like she has."

His eyes said it all. He must truly be in love with her. They make it work being on the road.

"Do you think she'll ever travel with the band? It must be hard being away from her all the time." I wanted to probe this line of thinking, especially with Carter somewhat listening.

"It sucks balls not having her with me. I fucking hate it, but she needs to be happy, too. Right now, her being happy involves working with children. When we get married, I want to knock her up right away so we can have a few of our own. She's promised she'll travel with me so we can all be together. She wants to be home to raise our kids, and home means with me." The biggest grin spread across his face.

"That's wonderful you feel that way about home and family."

Carter took that opportunity to expound on the subject. "Yeah, the dude's so pussy whipped already, too. Can't do a damn thing without talking to the little woman about it first."

"Shut up dipshit. You know you'd give your left nut to have a real woman feel that way about you." Gunner glared at him. "I love her with all of my being and if that means I'm pussy-whipped, then so be it. I'd gladly have it that way than the way you and I were living before her."

"Right, right. You'd gladly give up a different free pussy every night for the same old thing. Something about that just doesn't sound like the best way to live to me," Carter responded to him.

My eyes played a tennis match between the two. With Gunner pouring his heart out over the love of his life and Carter siding with the single man's mantra, I didn't know who to believe. They both seemed perfectly happy with the way they lived their lives. I knew then I needed to step away from thinking Carter and I would ever be together again. The night before was my mistake. I wouldn't make it again.

Carter

The bus finally stopped at the venue in Salt Lake City. We had a day to kill, and the town's atmosphere looked like something we could do some damage in. The scenery around the city made me want to get out and do some hiking. Gunner rented a car and a hotel room for the time Lola would be here. The family people made plans to take the kids to do some of the historical things in the area.

"Chan, you and KeeMac want to go hiking? I looked up some trails in the area and there are tons of them. How about it?" I didn't want to go alone.

KeeMac came out of the bathroom. "Hell yeah, we want to go. Chan and I scare up some of our best fun beside a fucking trail. Ain't that right, babe?" He pulled her in and kissed her soundly.

"Yes, that's right but I'm not so sure Carter needs to be around if you're thinking of a repeat performance of some of our outdoor activities."

"Sweet Chan. I would never stand in the way when nature calls, and I'd always be happy to join in the fun and games." I wrapped my arms around both of them and hugged before KeeMac could push me back.

"No fucking way in hell you or any other motherfucker will join us for fun and games, dude. You know that." He wasn't mad, but his voice held a note of seriousness to it.

"Just kidding, dude. I'd never try to show your woman what she's missing."

"She's not missing anything, asswipe." He laughed and pushed me down on the couch.

"If you two have finished your pissing contest over me, I'll pack some snacks and we can have a picnic somewhere. It's a perfect day for it."

Chandler spoke up, "Hey, Halo. We're going hiking and on a picnic. You should join us and get off the bus a while."

Halo walked toward the front of the bus. "Where's Hayden going today?"

"They're taking the boys to some kind of dinosaur exhibit. I'm sure you could go if you wanted to or you can hang with us for the day in the outdoors. It'll be fun. Come on." Chandler gave her the pleading eyes, and Halo finally smiled and nodded her head.

Shit. Just what I needed, a double date with Halo. After the amazing sex she initiated the other night, I'd tried to steer clear of her. As fantastic as it was, I didn't want her getting any ideas that we'd be together or anything. Hell, the night after that, I couldn't even enjoy being with all the babes who offered up pussy on a fucking platter. I needed to avoid that shit at all costs for the remainder of the tour. I'd make sure we weren't alone on the hike. I couldn't have her jumping me every chance she had. Hell, I'm always happy for free and clear sex, but I knew this would come with strings.

A car service took us to one of the closer hiking areas. The boulders and red rock formations looked like something in an old west movie. I could picture a fucking cowboy coming over the top of a hill with his gun drawn shooting at a bear or some other wild creature. KeeMac and I kept the banter going back and forth on our abilities to survive in the wilderness until we arrived.

Chandler packed a lunch in a couple of backpacks, and we took off with a map from the ranger station. The day was perfect for hiking, not too hot or cold. The climb proved strenuous but well worth it. We chose a perfectly flat spot and spread the blanket to stop for a break.

"Hey, Chan. Remember the last time we spread a blanket on the ground? Monumental occasion, right babe?" He pulled her in for a hard kiss and then whispered in her ear making her turn several shades of red.

"Must have been a good one for her to blush that much after all this time," I told them.

"Hell yeah, it was," he said.

"So spill. You can't open that up and not tell the story." He had me interested now in what they could have done on a blanket in the wilderness.

"Keeton. You and your big mouth." She shoved him a little.

"Fuck yeah, it's a big mouth and you love every single thing this big mouth can do." He kissed her again.

"Okay. You two are giving me a chub, and I haven't even heard the story yet." I glanced over at Halo as she stared at the two lovers. "Don't you want to know, too, Halo?"

"Uh, I guess. Some things aren't meant to be shared."

"She's right, Keeton. Some damn things aren't meant to be shared with the world." Chan gave KeeMac the evil eye.

"But babe. This isn't even that bad. Hell, he's been on that fucking bus with us long enough to know how we roll."

Chandler rolled her eyes and gave him a small nod.

"When we were in Colorado to play at Red Rocks, we took a little side trip over to Garden of the Gods. It's a great place to hike, but it's an even better place for a spontaneous good fucking."

"Oh God." Chandler hid her face in KeeMac's chest which made me start laughing.

"Let's just say a blanket behind a boulder is a good place to get your rocks off." KeeMac laughed so hard he wiped tears from his eyes. "And yeah, the pun was intended."

Halo laughed at his dumbass comment. Her laugh always made me smile. She looked so cute when she really got into it and made the sweetest sound.

KeeMac and Chandler took off on the trail side by side talking and laughing about stupid things they did in the years they had been together. Now that they were engaged, who knew how long they would wait before getting married. Halo followed behind them, and I had the pleasure of staring at her excellent ass all the way up the trail.

The trail got steeper as we climbed, and Halo slowed some. "What's the matter little girl? Too hard a workout for you?" I teased her.

"No, I'm just pacing myself. The trail might get steeper, and I don't want to run out of juice before we reach the top." She looked over her shoulder and smiled at me.

"Oh, okay. I'll let that go then." I caught up with her. The trail width could accommodate two people easily so I moved in beside her. We used to talk about everything. Surely a civil conversation would come naturally between us.

"Hey." I looked at her.

"Hey, yourself," she replied.

"I know this is all foreign to you, but how's the whole tour going for you? We really haven't done too much talking."

"It's going okay. Great, actually. Hayden's skills are so much better than mine, and he's teaching me more and more, but he doesn't seem to mind."

"No, Hayden's a great kid. Not too much bothers him even with his full plate. He does love little Crew. I guess I've never met someone so unselfish. Crew means everything to him."

"Yeah, he told me he would give up singing if it meant making Crew happy or there was a need. That says a lot about his character. Most guys his age, hell most girls, wouldn't put their kid's happiness before themselves." She looked at me as though she wondered if I could ever be that guy.

"I know you think I couldn't do it, right?" Our eyes locked on each other.

"I don't know if you would or not, Carter. When you set your sights on something that you truly want, you're all in. If it was for someone else, though, I don't know."

I could read her mind on this subject. Was I ever all in when it came to the two of us? Looking back at my teen years, I was definitely a self-centered bastard just like most guys my age. Had I outgrown that at all? I hoped so but thinking about some of the decisions I'd made in the last few years, maybe not. Hell, I might never outgrow it. Is that how I wanted to live my life?

I looked at Chandler and KeeMac as they walked hand in hand in front of me. The sparkling diamond that he gave her in front of our audience a few weeks back represented the depth of the love he had for her. Shit, all you had to do was hang out five minutes with those two and you knew it, ring or no ring.

I thought of Ryan and Peri. Those two loved each other and little Tucker with such a strong unconditional love. Hanging out with their little family along with Hayden and Crew could sway the staunchest of bachelors.

Maybe true love wasn't something for me. When Halo was mine, I thought she was the love of my life, but I had a lot of growing up to do. I didn't know if I'd reached that grown-up stage yet. Hell, I didn't even know if I wanted to reach that stage, and if I did would she ever consider taking me back? Being a colossal dick to her when I left, didn't help matters. Learning to be friends again might be all I get from her this go around.

She spoke and startled me out of my own head. "What are you thinking so hard about over there?"

"I don't know. Just thinking about life in general. Being out here in nature like this can do it to me. All this vastness surrounding us puts our small lives into perspective. Don't you think?"

"Wow, who are you? The Carter I know doesn't know those deep thoughts." She smiled.

I knew she was joking, but it still caught me off guard. Is that what she thinks of me? Is that what everyone thinks? Damn, I'm a joke in my friends' eyes. I never wanted to be that guy. They'd grown up and left me behind. The more I thought of this, the angrier I became. I sped up in my pace and passed the lovers, keeping my stride moving faster with each step.

"Carter, I was only joking. I didn't mean to make you mad," Halo yelled after me. She ran trying to catch up but couldn't keep up with my long legs moving faster and faster. Finally giving up, she stopped, but I didn't. I settled into a fast pace and made the summit long before they all did.

My legs ached from the quick steep climb but nothing like my fucking mind did. I needed to get my shit together. This wake-up call came with a giant bitch slap to the face. What the fuck was I thinking? A beautiful woman loved me once. Hell, I excelled in being a loveable kind of guy. I needed to set my sights on finding that true love again, but how would I go about making her love me again? I fucked us up so bad the first time, it might be a no go for her. I closed my eyes and tried to remember the things I did before. Damn, that happened a long time ago.

"It's about time you lazy asses finally got here. A nap while waiting on you three freshened me back up for the climb down." I sat up from where I'd leaned back against a large boulder.

"Why'd you take off like that? We were supposed to be taking a leisure hike to enjoy the scenery," KeeMac asked me.

"I felt the need to have a few minutes alone with nature."

"If all you needed to do was piss, you could have told us, and the girls would have turned their backs." KeeMac smirked at him.

"Not that kind of nature, asshat. You know communing with nature, like meditation type stuff."

"Dude, you wouldn't know how to commune even with a pack of old hippies in the forests of Oregon."

"That's a damn lie." I sat up, climbed on the boulder, and crossed my legs over each other and put my hands palms up. I closed my eyes, touching my thumbs to my middle fingers. "Ommm, Ommm, Ommm." I peeked out one eye to see if I had their attention. All three of them were standing there on the verge of breaking out in laughter.

I closed my eyes and did the whole routine again. "Ommm, Ommm, Ommm." On the third one, I fell off the rock with a big push from Chandler. "What the hell, Chan? My metaphysical side just started getting the vibes," I said from lying sprawled on the ground.

"I had to do it. I couldn't allow you to look that stupid in front of Halo an ommm longer." She smirked at me. "You're welcome, Carter."

"Yeah, thanks. I hope you didn't break my playing hand." I bent my wrist around.

"Your hand gets more than enough workout so it's in good enough shape to take a fall," KeeMac added to the conversation.

"Good one, babe." Chandler fist bumped him.

"That's a damn lie and you both know it, but all of this meditation might send my life in a new direction. I've decided to give up the rock-star wildlife to walk the straight and narrow. I believe it's time for me to outgrow all the groupie shit. Don't y'all?"

The three of them all looked up at me with their mouths hanging open.

"You're gonna what?" KeeMac asked.

"Yeah, let's hear this line of bullshit you're spewing," Chandler added, but Halo said nothing. She narrowed her eyes at me and stared.

"I'm dead serious about this. The perfect groupie sex machine decided to call it quits." I sat down on the blanket with the rest of them still staring at me. "It's about time I made some changes. I need to better myself with intelligent women who have ambitions other than how many rockers they can fuck to use as a claim to fame."

Damn, I should've given this more thought before I launched my plan to get Halo back. I could end up with a huge right arm with no more groupies to entertain me.

"So, what do you plan to do to earn these smart women giving you a second look? Read a book or something?" Chandler started with a low blow to my fragile new plan.

"I read books." KeeMac looked me in the eye. "Well, I do when I'm off the tour. I have lots of books in my house."

"Your collection of vintage *Hustler* and *Playboys* don't count dickwad. She's talking about real books or at least some downloaded on your iPad," KeeMac laughed when he said it.

"Yeah, you know you can use those for stuff other than porn and playing games. They have apps for it." Chandler kept shooting me with zingers basically killing my project.

"Y'all just wait and see. I'm telling the three of you the truth. As of today, I'm changing my life. I'm going to better myself in all areas including the women." I picked up a sandwich and took a big bite out of it. Maybe this would end their need to undermine my idea with smart-ass comments.

"I think you can do whatever you put your mind to, Carter," Halo finally spoke up, and I almost choked when it sounded like she might defend me to the other two. "You used to do all sorts of things that were good for your body and mind. I'm not sure reading books could be included but other stuff."

"Like what, Halo? I've known him the least amount of time, but I've never seen him do anything that wasn't self-fulfilling." Chandler looked at her obviously expecting an answer.

"Well, let me see. He used to know a lot about history. He tutored me all the time when I took AP History in high school. He just knew that shit. I hated the class but wanted the college credit so he tutored me."

I'd forgotten about that. I still loved to read historical non-fiction and fiction books. I realized it had been forever since I'd opened one, but that didn't mean I stopped loving history. Wars and battles held my interest for hours. The strategic planning and how it evolved over history amazed me.

"So you're telling me that this dumbass over here voluntarily picked up books and read them for the knowledge?" The look on KeeMac's face made me want to laugh hard.

"Yes, and he remembers all kinds of facts that most people skip right over or at least he did in high school. I realize that's a long time ago, but he did excel at it back then."

Halo's memories of our time together surprised me. I hadn't thought about that in so long. The recent books on my iPad I'd read, even some lately about the wars in Iraq and Afghanistan, contained great information about the types of battles our soldiers fought. I'd also read several biographies of soldiers.

"I read all of the stories about Chris Kyle. He exemplified what a lot of the soldiers coming home from that crazy war go through. Even if some of it's been glamorized by Hollywood, at least more Americans might understand that those guys need help to live back in society."

"Who are you?" KeeMac asked. "I didn't know you had it in you to think about something besides sex, booze, and music."

"Hell yeah, I do. I got all kinds of deep thoughts in this brain." I tapped my head. "I haven't let them out to surprise this group because... because... yeah, I don't know why. I just fucking haven't."

"That's good to know, Carter. All these years I've been thinking you were a typical bass player. You've been holding out on me with your stored brainiac ways." Chandler patted me on the back.

I had a lot of time to think about what Carter would try to pull by making this announcement. I didn't trust him to follow through on his word. He'd broken that trust with me a long time ago. We still hadn't talked about my need to climb on and fuck his brains out on the bus. I didn't want to talk about it. I wanted to have sex, no questions asked.

I'd had a few lovers over the past eight years but none that I cared for. Pure and simple sex, that's it. Our quick encounter lit me up like fireworks. He knew exactly what buttons to push to make me come alive. But when I finished, I was done. He should have felt used because that's what I did, used him for sex that I needed at that moment, just as it had been with the few guys I let in my pants after he left me.

We arrived back at the bus at dusk. All four of us filled the ride with idle talk about the band, venues, and music. It turned out to be a fun afternoon after we got off the subject of Carter wanting to make changes in his life. I knew the three of us had our doubts about his ability to follow through, but the truth would be in his actions down the road starting with the show tomorrow night. Even in Salt Lake City's Vivint Smart Home Arena, there must be lots of beautiful groupies waiting their turn at the band.

Another radio station meet and greet followed AD's performance. The winners of their on-air contest claimed the big prizes of getting backstage to meet everyone. Hayden and I found ourselves in the middle of the party. Getting to meet people who actually knew who we were made me feel absolutely special. To know that people out there knew our names and our music thrilled us. Hayden experienced this before but not me. I didn't exactly know how to handle it either.

I leaned into him while signing a t-shirt. "Hayden, this is freaking awesome. They actually know my name."

"Yeah, it's wild, isn't it? Wait 'til you see what happens when AD walks in here. We'll be back to nobodies by then." We both laughed.

"Hey, I'll take my fifteen minutes of fame."

He nodded, and we did a little fist bump between us.

When Gunner, Ryan, and Carter walked in, Hayden's prediction came true. The fans screamed and mauled them before they could all pass through the doorway and the security guards could get them behind the tables to start the signings. Witnessing the excitement had to be the wildest thing I'd ever seen in my life.

The guys sat down at the table with us. Carter took the chair next to me so I watched him interact with the fans. His friendliness captivated the hearts of screaming girls from eight to sixty-eight. He said kind things, asked important questions, and made them all feel special while he signed whatever they put in front of him. I'd never seen this side of him before. I felt like I might be seeing a new Carter.

"Hello, ladies," Carter addressed two young teen girls. "Did you enjoy the show?"

All either of them did was stare and nod.

Carter laughed a little. "So how old are you both?"

This time they stared at him like he had grown a third eye. Again, he smiled and glanced at the woman standing behind them.

"They are both fourteen and for some unknown reason they've lost the ability to talk which would be a Godsend any other time."

"I'm sure it is. So, fourteen, huh?" The girls nodded. "And do you have names?"

The cute girls nodded but never said a word. Oh my God, how did the guys stand this? At least when Hayden and I signed, the people acted like they had some still active brainwaves.

The woman leaned forward. "This is my granddaughter, Emmy, and her friend, Paige. Girls please at least say hello so he doesn't think you're both hearing impaired and mute." This caused the girls to start laughing almost hysterically. What a weird thing to watch.

Carter signed the t-shirts the girls won, addressing each with their names. He stood and walked around the table and hugged the woman. He thanked her for taking the time to bring the girls to the show.

She hugged him back and said to the girls, "See what happens when you actually use your words girls? You get a real hug from a hot guy."

Carter laughed hard at her comment. He kissed her on the cheek, and the two girls looked on the verge of passing out. The woman shook her head and shooed them along.

"Well, looks like you won all three of them over at the same time."

"Hey, it's not hard when you have all of this to work with." He motioned to his body.

"Palleeasse. That's pathetic, Carter."

"Oh, babe. The women love me all the time, but I'm going to be more choosy about loving the women. At least random women, that is." He winked at me, and I stared at him as he signed the next CD case for two beautiful twenty-somethings. His polite conversation almost had me believing he told the truth. Doubts lingered in my mind, though.

The number of fans slowly dwindled down leaving the band, Hayden, and me talking in a group. We all sat together in the same room for the first time since the tour began with only the two little ones missing. I watched them interact like a big family. It made me smile and wonder if they enjoyed being together this much all the time.

Singing as a solo act never allowed me to feel this kind of closeness to others who understood music. I felt alone most of the time which made me want to give the duo act a try when Cash asked me. They seemed to be at home when they found themselves in this situation. I wanted to be part of this family. I wanted to feel at home.

With the room cleared, we worked our way to the bus. Only a few groupies made it backstage since the party had been arranged by the radio station. The DJs got to pick and choose who they allowed through the doors. I didn't need groupies to make me feel accomplished, but I felt sure Hayden and Carter probably thought differently, but Peri sent them on their way.

"You guys have plans for the night?" Peri asked the question in general, but I knew she directed it to those of us who were still single.

Hayden spoke up. "No, I'm worn out and want to wake up with the little man early so we can play in the dirt with the dinosaur toys before we hit the road again. I'm headed to bed."

That left me and Carter looking at her. "What about you two? Going to call it a night or head out to a club or something?"

I shrugged my shoulders. I didn't have plans, but I knew I couldn't sleep now if I tried. "I'm flexible if y'all want to go out." I looked at Peri not wanting to make it seem like I needed to be included with Carter's plans.

He turned to me. "I don't have plans, but we can go do something if you want." He turned to Peri. "Any good clubs around here? Doing some damage on a dance floor right now sounds like a plan."

I started laughing. "Really, you want to go dancing?"

"Hell yeah, sweets. I'm a badass dancer." He swiveled his hips and made a few thrusts. "I thought you knew that about me already."

"Must've been after my time. You used to hate dancing."

"That's before I knew I had moves that drove the women fucking crazy. Come on, we'll have some fun. You know you damn sure want to see my moves like Jagger." He danced around in the parking lot. I laughed watching him look ridiculous. Hot, but ridiculous. His moves suggested sex, and he knew it.

"Okay, if there's some place Peri knows we can go." She searched her phone and pulled up a country music place not far from the venue.

"Country music, huh? I don't know if they're ready for me on that kind of dance floor." He spun around again.

"It'll be fun. I know you have those moves. I've seen those before." My mind drifted back to the last dance we attended in high school. They played mostly country music back then where we lived. He led me around the floor with smooth moves, perfect twists, and turns.

"Yeah, I guess I can still do that. Like falling off a horse, huh?"

"Or a mechanical bull. I've seen you do that as well." I smiled when I said it.

KeeMac jumped into the conversation. "You mean this guy can do those line dances with his fucking cowboy boots on? I think Chan and I need to come with so I can make some YouTube-worthy videos. Hell, we'll go live from there. It'd be fucking epic."

"Keeton, the last thing we need to do is attract attention," Chandler told the dumbass. If we encouraged our fans over Facebook to come join us, the fire marshal would close the place down.

Peri jumped in. "I'm calling security to go with you. I know it'll be fun, but fans can get out of control quickly. He can take the car, too." She moved away and started typing into her phone.

"Sounds good. Let's fucking do it." KeeMac pumped his fist in the air. I thought their after-show dressing-room sessions alleviated some of his adrenaline. Guess I was wrong.

We sped down the freeway to the club. I never missed a chance to wear my skin-tight bootcut jeans. I paired them with a short lacy top and my red cowboy boots. Peri made Chandler buy cowboy boots before they left Austin, and she wore them occasionally onstage. Tonight they would get used for their original purpose. For once, I looked forward to being out having fun with this group. With KeeMac and Chandler along, some of the pressure would be off me.

Cowboy Cadillac proved to be the place everyone touted on Yelp. The music blared, the dance floor moved, and the beer flowed. The security guard led the way through the door first and paid our way. As the bouncer checked the

ID's, the others grumbled, but I knew it would happen. Thankfully we all had ours on us.

The huge man looked the names and faces over and when he got to KeeMac, he stopped and then smirked. "Kinda out of your element, aren't ya?" He turned and looked at the other two AD members and then at me. "Bringing some of your own groupies with you tonight? You didn't need to bother. They may be fans of country music, but they'll know you guys."

Carter stepped up to look eye to eye at the six foot something guy. "That would be a big no, dude. She's a star, too. This is Victory of Hayden Victory. Remember the name. You'll be hearing it more and more in the next few months." He turned from the guy and grabbed my hand. "Forget this dickwad. Let's go in."

We entered the loud, hot room and Carter headed straight for the bar. "Coronas, guys?" We all nodded, and he repeated it to the bartender. Once we grabbed the cold beverages that slid across the bar to us, we found a high top to sit down.

Carter whispered in my ear since the music blared through the speakers, "Sorry about that. I didn't plan to get all caveman, but that pissed me off."

"That's okay and thanks for setting him straight. I'll never be the star like you guys, but I appreciate you telling him. Who knows, maybe he'll remember my name." I smiled and nodded my head. His "Hulk" action made him look all badass to the people standing behind the rope trying to gain access to the crowded club.

"Let's go dance." He stood from his barstool, and I jumped down when he took my hand.

"Yeah, I want to watch this. I've never been to a dance hall like this." Chandler seemed excited to be doing something different for a change.

"I'm getting my phone ready. I won't post, though, until later anyway." KeeMac smirked at us.

Carter pulled me close to him and wrapped his arm around my shoulder for the slower tune while I put my hand behind his back. I prayed he didn't pull me in so it looked like I hunched his leg the entire song. When we were in high school, we danced that way all of the time just for the thrill it created. We didn't need that thrill now.

He led me around the floor as though we'd been doing it all our lives. Being this close to him, his signature cologne floated in the air around me, assaulting by senses with pleasure. The woodsy scent reminded me of how long it'd been since a man held me this close. My body screamed too long.

The next song sped things up, and he twirled me around the floor to the George Strait music everyone knew. Our rhythm flowed on the floor as though we hadn't ever stopped dancing together. The twists and turns dazed my senses with the sensuality of it all. People who'd never danced didn't know what they missed out on.

We both laughed when the song came to a close and he twirled me a final time, signifying the end of the dance. He hugged me to him and kissed the top of my head.

Halo

"Damn, Halo. I forgot how much fun we had dancing together to good music. Thank you."

"You're welcome. I loved it. I haven't been dancing in a long time." The look he gave me warmed me in all the best places. Those feelings messed with my head. I couldn't think of him like that. He obviously wasn't interested since he'd never mentioned the sex I initiated. For me, it scratched a long overdue itch. For him, it must've been uneventful.

KeeMac patted us both on the back when we reached the table. "Well hell, y'all look like some fucking *Dancing with the Stars* contestants out there. The two of you surprised the hell out of Chan and me."

"Yeah, Carter. You've been holding out on us. All this time you could've been teaching us about this country dancing. It looks like so much fun." Chandler jumped off her stool and mimicked the way I twirled Halo.

"That's right. We need to get the two of y'all out there to teach you how to cut a rug," Carter told them both.

"What? Why would we want to do that?" Chandler's confused face made us all laugh.

"Girl, that means dance. We need to teach the two of you how to dance." I laughed at her lack of Texas lingo. For a girl who grew up a Texan, she missed out somewhere along the way.

"Oh okay. I get it now." The three of us started laughing. After a couple more beers each, we changed partners and taught the two of them the basics so they could get out on the floor to dance together. They both picked it up quickly, so Carter and I were reunited after only a couple of songs.

The next song slowed things down and Carter once again pulled me in close. "This is more like it," his warm breath whispered in my ear. "It's great getting to hold you this close." He sang the familiar song as he led me through the crowds of people in smooth movements. "I really do miss this, Halo. Holding you and feeling your body next to mine takes my mind to all kinds of good places."

He held me tightly around the back of the neck so that my upper body seemed molded to his chest. My mind overloaded my brain with sensual feelings. What was he thinking? He barely acknowledges me after we have phenomenal sex, and now he's excited to be holding me pressed up against him. I didn't get it.

"I'm sure a lot of those women you bring home can dance this way, too. You didn't have to wait on me to show back up in your life."

"Just placeholders, Halo. Not a damn thing more."

"What the hell does that mean, Carter?"

"Those groupies only want one thing from us, to say they've fucked a rock star. They'll never be replacements for real relationships with the real women in our lives. KeeMac got laid every chance he had until Chandler came along. None of those women meant a thing to him. Hell, most of the time he didn't even know their names. Same thing with Gunner and me.

"Now Ryan, his story didn't follow that path because he wouldn't let it. He never got into the groupie thing. He went looking for long term and found Krissy, but she wanted him to leave the band and work a nine to five. Ryan couldn't do that. None of us could do that either. We're not built that way. They parted ways but not before Hayden got caught in her web that gave him Crew.

"Even after Gunner found Lola, he didn't readily give up the wild nights of sex. We still had our fair share of crazy women willing to do whatever we dreamed up. Once they decided they trusted each other, that lifestyle ended, but Hayden stepped in and took his place as my wingman most of the time. He still spends as much time with Crew as possible. I have a feeling that he's going to be looking for women instead of place markers very soon if my conversation with Crew is any indicator."

We moved onto a faster song, and he twirled me and even flipped me over a couple of times before the song ended. Why had I waited so long to go dancing? Stomping our boots proved to be a great way to spend the evening.

"That's so much fun." Chandler's breathless comment made us all laugh. "I didn't know it would wear me out so fast. I thought I worked out enough."

"Yeah, just means we need to be doing some more strenuous activities that require heavier cardio on your part." He wiggled his eyebrows at her. "I suggest we go home and practice it right now."

"Did I say anything about sex?" She glared at him. "Besides, I'll be too exhausted after all this."

"All you gotta do is lay there. I'll do all the work."

"Famous last words, Keeton." She rolled her eyes and smirked at him for a change.

A line dance came on, and I drug Chandler back to the floor to dance to *Copperhead Road*. "You'll learn to do it in no time. It's all repetition," I promised and we laughed the whole time because having too much beer first made it even funnier. When *Watermelon Crawl* came on right behind it, she took us both to the ground.

"What the fuck, Chandler?" KeeMac grabbed her and picked her up. "Babe, you have no business dancing without me holding you up. I think we need to go home and practice that cardio. You've got the whole ride home to sober up." They walked toward the doorway where our security guard stood.

"You want to go home, too?" Carter asked me as he stood me back up straight. "I hate to end the fun evening, but I think you two have had enough beer for one night."

I wrapped my arms around his neck. "Are you going to carry me off like my knight-in-shining-armor the way KeeMac did?"

He scooped me up and headed for the door. "Sweets, I'll be whatever you want me to be."

I laid my head on his shoulder and closed my eyes. He put me back on my feet when we reached the car. The guard opened the door to KeeMac and Chandler already going at each other like the world was about to end inside of the limo. I didn't know whether to climb in or not. Looking back at Carter, he shrugged his shoulders and motioned for me to get in.

I couldn't stand watching the intimate moment, but they seemed bent on having sex. The idea that Chandler seemed okay with an audience surprised me. She couldn't be that drunk. I turned red when he unzipped her jeans and put his big hand down her pants with her moaning the whole time.

I turned my head and looked at Carter who seemed to be enjoying the live show. When he felt me looking at him, he looked me in the eyes.

"I can't watch this," I said in a whisper. KeeMac must have heard me which shocked me with all the moaning Chandler did. He pulled a blanket out of the seat beside him and wrapped the two inside of it about the same time Carter pulled me across his lap. I again buried my face in his shoulder. His scent hit me with my face so close. I wrapped my arms around his neck putting my nose and mouth against him.

"Damn, you smell good." I didn't exactly mean to say it out loud, but I couldn't take it back once he'd heard my compliment.

He pulled back and looked down at me. Our lips barely a breath away. I licked my bottom lip in anticipation of him kissing me and damn, did he ever. More like devouring my lips would be a better description. He sucked my lower lip into his mouth and ran his tongue across it. God, what a feeling. It tingled and caused me to tingle all over. My lip popped out when he let go but not for long as his tongue slipped into my mouth to dance with mine.

I wrapped my lips around his and sucked it further in. A gruff sounding noise came from deep within him followed by his hand working its way down my side. He found the bottom of my shirt and slid under where he lightly traced a line across my middle. His calloused bass-playing fingers seductively dug into the bare skin. All I could think about was how the roughness felt when he stroked inside me.

When the kiss broke, I moved to the side of his neck just below his ear with easy access from sitting across his lap. I traced a line from his ear to the curve of his neck, biting and sucking as I slowly moved downward. I went back with my tongue soothing the small spots by making circles around the bites I left. He shifted under me, and I knew those bites achieved my desired intention.

"Sweets, I don't know if it's a good idea for you to keep that up in this car."

I whispered in his ear, "Oh really, because it feels like you're enjoying it a lot." I latched my teeth on his earlobe and carefully pulled until I found the edge where I added my lips to kiss it.

"Well, yeah. I've got a gorgeous woman wrapped around me, slinking around on my dick. What's not to enjoy?" I bit a little harder when he walked his fingers up my body making his way to my breasts. "The thing is, you seemed a little shy about the idea of watching Chandler and KeeMac.

I'm cool with a being the voyeur on occasion, but I'm not cool with allowing them to see you naked."

"Oh, no. You're right. I'm not into exhibitionism all that much."

"So, this needs to stay PG until we get back to the bus, but it doesn't mean we can't enjoy each other for a few more miles." He smirked at me as he put his fingers under my bra and released both the girls for his pleasure.

"No important parts showing, please," I said as he tweaked my nipple.

"Deal, for now." He captured my lips in a hard kiss as he continued to plump my breast in his hand. When he squeezed the nipple slightly harder between his thumb and index finger, I moved more across the solid wood under me. The movement earned me a harder squeeze and twist that zinged all the way down to awaken my lady parts so they rushed to be ready for their own attention.

"Damn, Halo. Stop moving. It's been a while, and I don't want to come in my pants like a little fucker on his first date."

Wait, what? He said it's been a while. What about those groupies he left with at the last venue? Is he trying to make me think he's not had sex since we were together? Surely not. He would never take women home and not complete the deed.

I looked at him with a puzzled look on my face. "What are you saying, Carter? You've had groupies on the bus."

"Doesn't mean I had sex with them." He drew circles around the pebbled peak, then licked his fingers and did it again, leaving a ring of wetness.

As much as I wanted to continue the celibacy conversation, his actions kept my mind elsewhere. When I started writhing under his hands, he moved to the other nipple and started the teasing all over again. I wanted to comment on his statement but my traitorous body had other ideas in mind. If he kept it up, holding off an orgasm wouldn't be an option. He tongue-fucked my mouth while he tweaked and pulled the rosy bud.

"We're here," I heard KeeMac tell Chandler, and she started straightening and redressing while we got out.

"If you promise to wrap your legs around me, I'll carry you on the bus so we can finish what we started." Carter kissed me on the neck. "But either way, this is far from over." His voice grew rough and deep.

My unsteady legs wanted to give away when he made that noise, but I assured him I could make it on my own. I climbed the stairs ahead of him, and he palmed both of my ass cheeks.

"Mmm. Can't wait to bite you in all the best places."

Halo

With KeeMac and Chandler occupying the bedroom for some time now, we decided to take a turn. There was no way he would allow them to take it over. Those two could take a bunk like the rest of us.

Carter opened the door to it as they climbed up the steps.

"Dude, that's our room and you know it," KeeMac yelled up the bus aisle.

"Not tonight, it's not. Our plans start with clean fucking sheets." He opened the small linen closet and pulled out clean bedding.

"What are you doing?" I didn't want to wait to change sheets. He'd tortured me enough on the ride home.

"I'm not sleeping in their wet spot, so let's change these."

"That's nasty." I nodded in agreement.

"Hell yeah, it is. The only fucking wet spot I'm rolling around in comes from the ones we make, and I'm all about that."

I popped him on the back of the head. "I really love it when you're trying to be all romantic."

"I try sweets, I try." He finished remaking the bed, and I freshened up in the bathroom. My reflection in the mirror showed the glow on my cheeks. He spent time during sheet changing to stop for hot wet kisses to keep the fires burning. His kisses could light a fire on water, but they made my core smolder waiting to be fanned into a full-blown flame.

I opened the door and KeeMac, Chandler, Hayden, and Crew sat in front of the big screen watching something. Thank God the loud animated show also had music. Only lying a few steps away from them in the bedroom, I decided we needed to keep the noise down to a minimum.

Chandler caught my eye and winked. She knew what thoughts ran through my mind since Carter and I experienced the sounds almost every damn night from them.

KeeMac spoke up, though. I believed he wanted to see if he could piss me off or at least get a response. "Don't mind us, Halo. We'll all be sitting up here watching this kids' movie. You know the one with all the loud crashes and booms in it that always drowns out other noises." He ended his sentence by giving me a smart-ass smirk.

"Yeah, thanks a lot." I ended my sentence by rubbing my middle finger up and down the side of my face.

Hayden laughed. I didn't know if it was from my gesture or KeeMac's comment.

The door opened to a totally nude Carter lying on the bed looking like some Playgirl Playmate of the Year. I rolled my eyes and laughed out loud.

"Really, Carter?" I couldn't resist.

From down the hallway, we heard KeeMac's comments.

"Dude, is she laughing at LDS? That's just not right, Halo." The laughter turned to near howling.

I turned to him. "LDS?"

"Think, Halo."

Hayden joined in. "Hell, Carter, all this time I thought the ladies laughed with you. I didn't know they laughed at your miniature package. Want me to come in there and show her how a real man is supposed to look?" The three amigos rolled from laughing so hard up front.

Carter bounded off the bed at the last comment. He actually looked pissed off. When he swung the door open and stomped off down the aisle, I ran behind him grabbing his arm. He twisted out of my grip.

"They're only kidding Carter, just joking with you." I thought he might take a swing at them which would have been even worse since he was free swinging buck naked.

He arrived at the living area in all his naked glory and instead of tearing into the three, Chandler included, he struck an Adonis pose.

"You see this fresh hunk of man meat, you three?" He turned and flexed his muscles in his shoulders and back. "I got every fucking thing it takes to please a woman without your help. And that goes for you too, Chandler."

Hayden jumped up grabbing Crew and headed out the door of the bus. Carter turned full on to them and struck another pose causing his abdominals to pop while his forearms joined in on the act.

KeeMac's face started turning red. "Dude, she does not need to see that shit. Go back to bed."

"Oh, hell no. Y'all started this." He turned to me and grabbed his semi stiffy and started pumping it. "Make me hot for you, sweets. Show me some of those gorgeous tits."

I started laughing when he looked over his shoulder at a now quiet duo. I pulled my top up and squeezed my boobs together so the cleavage became a deep V. I thought they were going to pop out of my bra. He continued pumping slowly up and down his now stiff cock. I thought he was coming back to me, but when he stopped and turned around with a full-blown hard-on, I screeched.

"*Carter*!" I grabbed the sheet racing to cover the flagpole standing at full mast. "She does not need to see that."

"Sweets, she's seen it plenty of times before. Just not in full-blown fuck mode. There'll be no more little-dick syndrome discussed on this bus." He took his turn to laugh at KeeMac and Chandler, whose face hid behind her hands.

"Okay, big boy. Show's over. Come to bed before they get mad or you get soft. Either way, I lose." I shoved him down the aisle to the bedroom door and closed it behind us.

"Sweets, now that I'm all hard and ready, I think we need to get you as naked as me." He pushed me back against the door and kissed me until I melted against him. My hands found their way up his smooth muscled back and a groan slipped from my throat. Just thinking about his hard body pushing against me caused my breathing to deepen.

God, his tight smooth skin felt good under my palms as I moved them down and over his fine ass cheeks, squeezing the muscles hard. He reached around and started trying to unhook my bra, but I backed away and swatted his hands.

"Lay down." I pushed him back on the bed. "I'll entertain you this time." I leaned over to the docking station for my phone and ran through my playlist to find the perfect music for my little show. I pulled up my love songs list, pressed go, and turned back to him. This beautiful man that I once loved lay there looking so hot, so ready. I hoped I could pull this off without making him laugh at me. He sought a woman who could fulfil his fantasies. I believed I needed to be her.

"I'm kinda loving this idea." He pushed up on the mattress coming to rest on the pillows with his hands locked behind his head. "Go, baby, go!"

The slow sensual music of The Weeknd's, *As You Are*, played while I ran my hands slowly down my bare sides to the top of my tight jeans and back up smoothing the skin to the bottom of my bra where I again pushed my tits together as much as I could, giving him a look of longing for his touch. I let them go and went up to the straps with my arms crossed pulling on the opposite side. With one finger, I pulled them down going impossibly slow. They fell as far as they could, so I reached around and unhooked the bra letting it fall down and off my arms to the floor.

I looked up at him when it landed, and he moved back to pumping his cock, but this time the burning desire in his eyes told me it was for an entirely different reason than before.

Looking at the hard, stretched skin in his hand, "Mmm. Is that going to be for me?"

"Babe, it's always been for you." His answer took me by surprise which almost threw me off my game.

My hands squeezed my bare tits and moved down to my nipples that quickly pebbled between my thumbs and fingers. I pulled until they were distended, and it caused some pain making me gasp and moan from the feeling.

"Yeah, sweets. Make it feel good like it would be if my teeth pulled and bit them." His gruff and seductive tone caused wetness to slip from me with a slight contraction inside me. "Your gorgeous face lights up when you touch yourself like I would."

I picked both breasts up from the underside and moved them close to my own mouth. When my tongue eased across my stinging nipple, his groan filled the room.

"Shit, sweets, I didn't know you could do that. It's fucking hot. I could nut right now watching you lick those sweet tits."

I gave him a sly smile as I lapped my tongue across the other nipple while I ran my hand down to the button on the jeans, flipping them open. I turned my back to him and ran both hands over my jean-covered ass before moving to unzip them.

"That's right. Mmm, that perfect ass. I want to see some more smokin' hot skin I know you're hiding under there."

I looked over my shoulder and blew him a kiss. "Keep teasing me. You know what payback is," he said in a low voice.

I stuck my thumbs in the waistband and swayed my ass back and forth to get the tight jeans down.

"Fuck yeah, babe. Wiggle that sweet peach and get it out of those fucking jeans."

I went commando under them because of their skin-tight fit, so when I finally got them over my hips, he realized my mode of dress.

"Damn, Halo. If I'd have known all night you were bare down there, I probably would've had my hand inside of those jeans before now." He squeezed and tugged on his hardness causing a drop to escape the slit eyeing me.

"Just wait. You'll see all my hidden treasures before this is done," I couldn't resist telling him.

The jeans passed my knees and then ankles before I bent over at the waist staring at him between my legs to give him a perfect look.

"Oh. My fucking God, Halo. You're killing me. Look at that pretty pink pussy waiting for my tongue to slide up and down."

Damn the man. He could say things in a growl that caused my inner muscles to do a quick spasm. I stepped out of them and turned the top half of my body toward him while I ran my hand down between my ass cheeks to my opening and back up.

I bent back over and put my hand through my legs to the top of my ass and ran my fingers back down, but this time when I reached the sweet spot, I pushed my middle finger in as far as it would go.

He came off the bed and knelt behind me. "That's the hottest fucking thing I've ever seen, sweets, but I'm afraid I have to take over from here." He pulled my finger out and put it in his mouth lapping at my juices as he moved it across his tongue and lips. Another spasm deep inside struck me. He spun me around so my forearms went to the bed but my ass still up in the air.

"Dammit, Halo. You make me so hard I don't want to wait, but I need more of this first." His tongue started at my ass and went all the way down to my drenched opening. His hand found my ankle and he spread my legs further apart allowing him easier access to my clit. The pointed tip of his tongue flicked it a few times before he plunged his finger inside me.

"Car… Carter." My mind fumbled across his name.

"Yeah, sweets?" He did the same thing again and added another finger this time scissoring them inside me. This allowed him to brush one across the roughed area in the front. Contact with that bundle of nerves sent me into a quivering mess.

"*Caaarrrtteerrr,*" I screamed when he purposely did it again. My orgasm built and crashed into me just as *Creep* by Radiohead started playing. He continued to work the area until my legs could no longer hold me from the intensity of coming so hard.

My upper body fell on the bed as my arms refused to support me any longer. He pushed a pillow under my hips before he polished the head of his stiff, smooth cock with a splash of my own juice teasing the last of my orgasm out of me.

Carter's warm body leaned down over me and kissed up my spine to my neck and then around to my jawline, and his lips eventually found my ear. He whispered softly, "That was so fucking hot to see your body respond to me, sweets. How about a few more to go with that one? This sweet body of yours makes me want to come all over it." I heard the condom wrapper open and knew he was rolling it on before he continued to slide his hardness up and down my begging channel. I barely calmed my breathing when he stopped at my entrance and pushed the head in and then out circling it.

"Carter, I don't know if I can stand too much of that merciless teasing."

"I know, babe, but I want you to want me as badly as I want you." He pushed in a little further. "Your body could control me, Halo. It calls to me on so many levels, but now that I'm having you this way, I don't know if I can ever let it go."

This comment confused me, but I couldn't deal with the mind fuck right then because the way he moved between my legs pushed all the right buttons. "Carter, please. Now."

"Oh, you want some more of this?" He pushed about half way in me, and I moaned from the exquisite torturous pleasure. "Like that, huh?"

All I could do was nod my head, but he pulled out and circled my slick opening once again. "Hold on, sweets. This is going to be some furious fucking. We've only played around at it 'til now, but the time for playing is over." He plunged in until his balls hit my clit.

Over and over he hit me that way, and my clit stood up and took the constant tapping.

"Oh my God, Carter. I'm gonna come again. That feels sinful."

"Sweets, it is abso-fucking-lutely sinful. I wish you could witness what I am every single time I pull back. Those swollen lips of yours try their best to suck my cock back every, fucking, time. It feels phenomenal and makes me want to shoot my load with every move I make."

I slid my hand down between my legs and when he buried himself deep inside me, I moved my fingers over his balls with a gentle touch surprising him.

"Babe!" he called out. He buried in deeper, and I wrapped my hands around the tightening sac. "What the fuck!" He didn't pull all the way out so I could continue to massage him. "Let's get this damn party started, sweets." I felt his wet thumb circle the tight bud facing him.

"Uh, no. Carter."

"I'm not going in. Just adding to the pleasure like you're doing." He circled it again before adding a little pressure directly on the virgin territory.

"You're making me nervous with your thumb there."

"I promise not to dive in without permission. So relax and get back to enjoying it."

He continued to circle and lightly press, and I finally let out the breath I held. It felt good once I wasn't worried about him diving in. He alternated the thrusting pace and rotating his hips. With his breathing coming faster and harder, I knew he was getting close.

"Babe, as much as I hate it, I need you to work on your clit for me because I can't hold out much longer." The hip he held firmly took some abuse from his strong grip, but it added to my pleasure now that I helped myself along.

My muscles started that quivering motion from before. I couldn't hold out any longer. Just as the convulsing muscles began working, he pushed in his thumb a little more, and I pushed back against him. It caused me to come fast and hard with the two of us rocking into each other with force. My inner muscles gripped his cock, almost refusing to let go, and he exploded inside me.

"*Fuuuccckkk. Fuck. Fuck,*" he groaned out as he rocked into me over and over until he slowed to a stop.

He crashed on top of me. The warmth of his body felt like a blanket offering security. After such an emotional action, my psyche needed the close connection. We lay there simply trying to inhale and exhale, trying to grip the pure sense of passion we shared. I don't know how long we lasted in the position, but I couldn't have moved if I tried. Every muscle inside and out felt the pain from the usage and damn, it was the best feeling ever.

Carter finally pulled out of me and rolled over on his back, his eyes closed. My eyes roamed over his beautiful features and his taut body and then returned to his face. His wide-open eyes looked at mine.

"You're simply beautiful, Halo. Everything about you. I had to have been a damn fool to even think about leaving you before. Why did you let me?"

I shrugged my shoulders. "I didn't think I had a choice in the matter, Carter. You seemed determined to go off and do your music thing without being tied to me in any way."

"I know, and I'm so sorry. I hurt you when my intentions were to not. But I did, in the worst kind of way." He ran his fingers across my cheek. "I'm kinda hating myself right now for it."

"It's behind us now, Carter. We can't change the past." He rolled over and pulled me into his arms.

"I know we can't, but together we can make a new future with better memories." I gave him a small smile.

Thoughts of his comments floated around in my mind. Was I even willing to try this again with him? We might still be great in bed but what about out of it?

Carter

This unchartered territory for me might bite me in the ass, but right now I needed this woman in my life. I didn't know for sure I could do it—it'd been so long since I considered having only one. My heart said this was right, but would both heads be on board with it? Hurting her twice might destroy us both.

I woke to look into violet eyes. Damn, what a way to wake up.

On my stomach, I moved my hand from across her middle to rearrange some wayward sleep and sex hair out her eyes—those eyes that captured me every time I looked at them.

I scratched out words in a husky voice, "Been awake long?"

"No." The whisper barely left her lips. "But I like watching you sleep. Your eyes act like they never calm down. Always moving."

"That's not all that's moving. As a matter of fact, the very thing is growing more like a steel pipe under me." I smiled at her. I rolled on my back and pulled her on top of me.

"Think we can do something to help this situation?" I asked with a smile on my face.

"Hmmm. I don't know. Can we?" With that, she started sliding herself up and down the side of my swollen cock. It didn't take long for her to create a slick line down it.

I reached down and swirled my finger around her clit causing her to arch her back. The curls in her hair hung seductively over her breasts ending almost at her stomach. God, the sexy look she portrayed rocking on my cock, breasts stuck out from the arch, glistening pussy under that small landing strip of trimmed hair. Fuck, I needed her badly.

I took a condom package out of the bedside table and handed it to her. She tore the package with her teeth and rolled it on my hard length.

"Damn, Carter. That's a lot you have growing there." She smiled at me with a snarky look before she rose up and positioned it below her entrance.

"I think it's my turn to offer you the same torture you made me endure." Halo used my dick in every way but what it was intended before she finally lowered herself ever so slowly down until it was fully seated inside her.

"Fuck, that feels so damn good." My morning sexed-up voice sounded like a growl.

She rocked forward and back and then swiveled around and around, never allowing more than a couple of inches to come out of her. I reached for her hot tits and captured them, squeezing and twisting on the nipples. She reacted with more frenzy than her initial slow pace.

"Rock, babe. That movement feels so fucking good having your sweet pussy swallow me up and possess my cock that way. When you clinch down on it, I want to take over but this is your sweet torture, and I'll take it."

She put her hands on top of mine causing me to plump her breasts harder. I moved back to the pink pebbles to tweak them, but she continued to hold her breasts in a tight grip.

"Dammit, Halo. I can't wait any longer." I sat up and she wrapped her legs around my back. I took a sweet tit in my mouth and toyed with the nipple while my hands found her hips. I needed to pump her on me a lot harder than she was capable of.

A few easy pumps up and down moved on to banging into her with all I had at this angle. It allowed me to go deeper each time but not as good at it could be so I flipped us over and pulled one of her legs over my shoulder. I slammed into her with a fury I didn't know I had in me. I knew she felt it too when she cried out. I tried to hit that inside sweet spot each time, and my pelvic bone rubbed that clit on each thrust.

"Right there, Carter. There, don't stop."

I continued the assaulting pace until she clenched and spasmed on me followed by a gush of her sweet juices. "Yes, babe. Yes. Yes. *Yes*!" I shouted to the rooftops.

"Really? Can the two of you get any louder back there? Shut the fuck up," KeeMac yelled and banged on the wall.

Chandler joined in mimicking me. "Yes. Yes. *Yes*, babe! Can't you be more creative, Carter? I'm embarrassed for your lack of words."

I looked down at Halo, and we started laughing. "Nothing like sharing an intimate moment with your closest friends, right?"

She nodded at me. The intense love making made it all worth it. I didn't care who heard us at this point.

"Guess they kinda killed the post-sexual bliss, huh?" I stood and pulled off the condom tossing it in the trash can before I opened the door and walked to the bath. I warmed the water and wet a washcloth before taking it back to Halo.

"Sweets?" She barely opened her eyes seeing me standing there. "Let me clean you up some." She slightly moved her leg, and I lay the warm cloth on her swollen pink sweet spot that I abused in the best possible way for breakfast.

"Mmm. Feels good," she whispered without opening her eyes. I threw the rag on the floor, laid back down, and covered us before falling back into a peaceful sleep.

The loud hum of the tires continued over the asphalt down. I had no idea where we were headed, but I knew we had a day off between shows. Spending it naked and in bed the entire time equaled the best plan ever. When her stomach growled loud enough to wake us, I turned and took in her beauty, one arm covering her eyes, the other across her stomach.

"Hey, beautiful. I think someone's hungry, and I'm starving. All of those extra-curricular activities work up an appetite."

She smiled without moving her arm. "I hope you're talking about actual nourishment because I'm completely out of energy and need real food."

I sat up and pulled some shorts out of a drawer beside us. "You keep clothes back here?" she asked as she sat up in the tossed bed covers.

"No clue who these belong to, but looks like they'll fit. It's this or go up to the bunks and give Chan another show."

"I think she's seen enough for a few days." Halo laughed at her own joke.

"Are you saying it's not worth seeing daily?" I turned and shook my hips causing my free balling junk to move back and forth.

"Uh, no and don't do that. It'll get ideas, and I'm too tired and sore."

"Sorry, didn't mean to wear you out."

"I just need food and recuperation time."

"Hell yeah. I like the way you think." I stuck my fist out for a bump, and she returned it.

Moving forward to the front of the bus, I pulled a Coke out of the fridge and pushed the button to warm the coffee water in the machine. Coffee, first thing, pleases her and right now I'm all about keeping her happy.

KeeMac stuck his head out of the curtain. "Dickhead. Make a whole pot, please. The rest of us want some, too."

"Asshat, I don't know how to do that. I didn't even know that thing would make more than one cup. Isn't that what it's used for?"

"Are you wearing my shorts?"

I nodded at him. "Yeah, I kinda like them. Feels good against my baby soft skin."

"You're commando under there? I do *not* need your junk leaving nasty spunk in my clothes. You're gonna wash them before I get them back."

"Yeah, yeah. Mr. GQ's afraid of a little jizz here and there. Like you've never done that to my clothes before. I could tell Chan some stories about strange places we've found your load."

"Not necessary," Chandler said as she made her way over to KeeMac and down the aisle dressed in a tight little tank and some boy shorts.

"Dude, I'd be more concerned about how my chiclet ran around half nude." I wiggled my eyebrows at Chandler.

"Shut the fuck up, Carter. I'll dress however I want to, and I'm not his chiclet. I'm a grown-ass woman."

"Ewww. Testy this morning. I like it. Fucking too difficult in the bunk so you had to forgo the sex for one night?" I loved teasing her.

KeeMac responded, though. "Anywhere, anytime. We're good. Now stop talking about her and our sex life. I'm not even awake yet thanks to all the banging we had to endure with you two three feet away. Can't you have sex without talking or yelling?"

"Hell no. If it's good, you gotta shout it to the rooftops." I turned to look at a thoroughly sexed Halo. "Aint that right, sweets?" She fell back on the bed and covered her head with the sheet.

"No use being embarrassed, sweets. It's a natural occurrence commonly enjoyed among adults." I stood over her with a cup of coffee. "Here ya go. Just like you like it. I stirred it with my finger so it would be extra sweet." She reached out without moving the pillow and took the mug, finally sitting up to take a sip.

"Shit, I hope he washed his hands first," KeeMac added, "Never know where they've been."

"Dickwad, I know exactly where they've been, and it's the sweetest taste in the universe." I wiggled my eyebrows at her, and it gained me a wicked smile from Halo.

When we all finally joined the human race for the day, we decided to do some jamming and see about using the time to write music. Halo and Hayden watched and then moved to the back of the bus to work on their own tunes. My heart felt like someone squeezed it when I heard her laugh out loud, a new sensation for me. I liked knowing she worked twenty feet away from me, but for some reason, I would have preferred it was with me.

"Stop looking back there. She's fine." Chan stopped strumming to look at me.

"I know. I wasn't thinking about her. The tune sounded familiar to me is all." Dammit, busted.

"Oh come on, dumbass. Admit it. You don't like her back there without you. What do you think Hayden's gonna do, jump her in the back of the bus with you sitting this close?" KeeMac goaded me.

"Hell no. I trust them both and besides she's not mine to issue a claim over. She's her own person and can make her own decisions."

"Really, because the look on your face every fifteen seconds when you look back there says differently." Chan knew she had me on this.

I didn't know about feeling all possessive over a woman. This kind of stuff bothered me. I liked a lot of women but care about them enough to wonder what they are doing in another room with another man? Whoa. Stop. I didn't do that. I turned so I couldn't see the back room at all.

We continued to work on lyrics. I didn't write very much, but they did allow me to contribute. I could play an acoustic guitar, too. I might not be Ryan when it came to rocking the music, but I knew how to play.

The sounds from Hayden's guitar sounded more country in nature from where we sat. I played country music with Halo when she was learning. Chords were chords no matter what style of music you played. I knew that there were some country music people who could easily cross over to rock, like Brad Paisley and Keith Urban. They both played guitar like they owned rock music.

"Dumbass, are you contributing to this or has your head gone off to Halo-land again?" KeeMac kicked me with his foot. I looked up at him. He and Chandler were both staring at me. I finally got up and put my guitar away. When I came back to the front, I turned on video games and played. I snuck a look at them when they didn't make any more attempts at the music.

"What? Y'all didn't like my input so I'll do something I'm good at." I moved through the screens looking for shit to shoot.

"We wanted you to contribute, Carter. You've been a little preoccupied today, though," Chandler softly said. "You can't concentrate when your mind's elsewhere. Why didn't you go back there and see about picking up their music and helping them out?"

"They don't need my help. You know as well as I do Hayden's songwriting outweighs any of mine." The two couldn't deny it. Hayden had the gift. Cash told him all the time he could make a living writing songs and never play another concert. Hell, about half the stuff AD played now he wrote or collaborated on.

"Doesn't mean they wouldn't let you sit in, though. Just go back there," Chan continued.

"Nah. I'll stay here." I attached my earbuds to my phone and played the game listening to some of my favorites, Alt-j, Twenty-one Pilots, and Foo Fighters. I had lots of music on my phone.

Carter

We arrived in Denver in the afternoon to a perfect day in the Mile High City. I loved this place. I planned to have a house of some kind in this state when time and money allowed. I had a shitload of money, but the investor worked it to gain more and more so when I decided to buy one, there would be plenty to have whatever I wanted.

The ladies decided to spend time shopping with the kids, so we rented out a gym for the afternoon. We found it hard to workout on the road, but Peri managed to find places all along with trainers more than willing to help keep the bodies we needed onstage.

The trainer today worked our asses off. We walked out knowing there would be pain tomorrow. We returned to the bus, cleaned up, and were ready to hit the town ourselves.

Hayden walked up beside me. "You want to go out tonight? I need my wingman. I'm taking the kids today for them so I can go out tonight while the kids sleep."

I didn't take the time to think before I agreed to go. We hadn't hit a city in a while, and I knew he wanted to prowl around to find some hot women to hook up with.

Meeting up with the women, Hayden took Crew and Tucker to the outdoor bouncing place for children giving Ryan and Peri a kid-free day. Those two left as soon as Hayden's taxi pulled away. They never looked back or commented.

I looked at KeeMac. "Guess they had other plans."

"Probably, since they hardly ever get anytime without Tucker. How are they going to make a new one if they can't get away from the first one?" He laughed as he said it.

Chan looked at both of us with a sparkle in her eyes. "They must have found some time because I think she might be pregnant. She bought a test while we were shopping. Maybe that's what they're doing."

KeeMac and I bumped fists. "Hell yeah, then they can spend the rest of the fucking day celebrating."

Kids. What the fuck did they do with these little guys? Hell if I knew. They depended on you constantly. Food, clothes, housing, play, teaching them shit, the list just went on and on. No woman in her right mind would think having a kid with me was a great plan since I'm still a kid, too.

Halo wouldn't want them, would she? What if she did? Would she want to have a couple with me? What if she wanted three or four? Wait, she might not even want me one way or the other.

"What are you thinking so hard about over here?" Halo stood beside me asking.

"Uh, yeah. Trying to decide what I wanted to do this afternoon."

"We thought lunch first sounded good. What about you?" She looked at me with a strange look. "Unless you have other plans already. Then I'll just go."

It hit me that every time she asked or invited me to do something, she always added an out for me. She gave me the opportunity to dodge time with her if I wanted. Didn't she want to be with me? This woman made my head spin.

"No, no. I don't have plans. Hell yeah, let's do this. I'm hungry." I hooked her hand around my arm, and we moved back over to Chan and KeeMac as their taxi stopped to get them.

We spent the afternoon eating good food and wandering around in downtown. Sometimes it's nice to be normal people, which was why we never went without caps and sunglasses. Otherwise, when someone would recognize us, and it was all over. We'd have to taxi to another location. Today, we managed to dodge fans and enjoy being free.

The sun started going down so we headed back to the bus. Who knew what we would find there with Peri and Ryan off taking pregnancy tests and shit.

The taxi pulled up, and we headed back to the RV to see what was going on. The lock thrown could have meant a couple of things. They left or were going at it like rabbits or celebrating. When the RV started moving, we decided it was one of the last two options.

The door opened and Ryan stood there with a huge smile on his face.

"What's going on, Ryan?"

"Come in. Come in," he invited. Peri stood there with an equally big smile. As soon as Chandler saw it, she started jumping up and down.

"*You're pregnant*," Chan screamed. The two met midway in the aisle and wrapped in a hug while they jumped. Hugs, fist bumps, high-fives, and well wishes ensued.

"That's great, Peri," Halo told her. "I know you're excited from what I saw this morning when we shopped."

"Yeah, we didn't want Tucker to be much older before we gave him a sister or brother." Her smile said it all, though.

"So when's it due?" Chandler asked.

"Who knows? Who cares? We're having a baby," Ryan said. He sounded like a new dad all over again. This pregnancy should go much smoother than the last one without all the drama.

Peri held up the stick with the plus sign. "I think I'm about six weeks along, but I'll fly back and see my doctor as soon as I can arrange it."

The girls all surrounded her with questions and girly talk about babies, something I had no interest in.

The door opened and Hayden ushered two wild children into the RV.

"Hey, Mom," Tucker said. His face clearly tired from all the play.

"Hey, RiRi." Crew leaned in from the other side of her. That was a sight. Two boys loving on her. I still needed to tell Hayden about mine and Crew's conversation about a momma.

Hayden leaned over so Ryan, KeeMac, and I could hear him. "Y'all want to go grab a beer and celebrate, man-style? Too bad Gunner's not going to fly in until tomorrow. He'd want to celebrate with us."

We both nodded and slipped out the door.

"Let me send Peri a text and tell her where I'm going."

"Tell her to repeat that to Chan. She'll be pissed if I leave and not tell her something."

"Those pussies must have some teeth in 'em." I clapped KeeMac and Ryan on the back. "Now, Hayden and me. We're free and easy. Come and go as we please. Get the women when we want them. Right Hayden?"

"Hell yeah, we are." We high-fived each other as Ryan called the car service. If we were going to celebrate we needed security around and a car on demand.

We headed to Tavern Downtown in Denver's LoDo section. It was a great place to hang out, have drinks, and watch a game with the best rooftop bar in the city. The women were pretty easy on the eyes there, too. Hayden wasted no time in making the rounds of single women who made themselves available. The rest of us found a great tall table to celebrate.

KeeMac pulled out his platinum card and handed it to the hot little cocktail waitress who had forgotten how to use words when he spoke to her. "Bring us three pale ales on tap and keep them coming. Oh, and three shots of tequila. We're celebrating."

She returned straight away and drooled a little before disappearing. We laughed knowing we still had the ability to cause this in strange women.

"To Ryan and Peri," KeeMac toasted.

"Salute," I said. Ryan bumped our shot glasses together, and we downed the smooth 1800 Tequila. The waitress appeared instantly with more shots.

"Dude, we can't do too many of these. Peri will have my balls on a platter if I come home stinking drunk. I haven't done that shit in ages."

Late into the night, we all stood and decided to call enough on ourselves. Hayden didn't answer when we called his cell. Looking for him in the crowded building would take forever, so I sent them home and we'd catch a cab. I moved around to the other floor and propped up at the bar to watch. He finally moved in front of me, and I grabbed his arm.

"We gotta go. The others left already." My speech slurred with every word out of my mouth. It was my brain's way of saying I'd had enough alcohol for one night.

"Wait a sec. I got some women lined up." Hayden wasn't as intoxicated as me, which I took as a good thing.

"Okay, but let's go soon." He nodded and took off again. The women flirting and enjoying the evening made interesting people watching. Some were viewing sports on the televisions while others laughed and pawed at each other, hands sliding in suggestive ways over writhing bodies. It all looked innocent until I paid attention to the sensual nature of the moves.

"Here we go, ladies. I give you, Carter Jones. He's a dancer at a club in Dallas." I looked at him like he'd lost his fucking mind. I didn't dance at a club, and I sure didn't strip which is how he made it sound.

The blonde attached to my right arm and ran her fake boobs all over it. "Want to buy me a drink?" I looked at her and my mind said, *uh no*, but my drunken mouth said, "Hell yeah."

Several drinks later, I found myself in the back of a cab with a blonde straddling my lap rubbing herself off on me.

Wrong, wrong, wrong.

She wasn't the one I wanted on me but my other head said, "Fuck yeah, we're getting laid."

"One for the road, guys?" A bottle of vodka appeared from her Mary Poppins purse.

Who carried a bottle of vodka around?

Hayden took a long drink before handing it to me. I don't normally drink vodka, such a sissy alcohol in my mind, but I tipped it up and slugged back several deep gulps. The ride continued that way until we arrived at some hotel somewhere in Denver. The location was lost on me, and Hayden didn't seem to care.

The next morning, something hot burned my face. I couldn't open my eyes and my head felt like exploding on impact. I barely raised my eyelids to catch the warmth that came from the beaming sun sneaking through slightly opened blackout drapes. I stuck out my hands on both sides of me to stop the bed from spinning around. Shit. I knew better than to drink this much. I needed to get one foot on the floor if a hand didn't stop the motion.

My hand didn't hit bed, though. It landed on skin. Naked skin. "Shit, shit, shit." I turned my head to the side and saw Hayden. "What the fuck?" I said out loud as I reared up off the bed.

"Nooo," I cried out from the pain in my head. Hayden's eyes slowly cracked open.

"Fuck, Carter. Stop yelling. It's too early to be awake," he managed to croak out. His tongue tried to move out of his mouth to lick his lips. "My mouth feels like the Mojave." His eyes swept some of the room. "Where are we and why are you in my bed?"

"Hell if I know." I looked down. "Clearly a hotel room, but how'd we get here? Shit, where the hell're my clothes? Shit, dude, we're naked together in a bed."

"You know I don't swing that way. If you're into it and all, it's fine, but you should've said something sooner."

"Fuck no. You know that's bullshit." I crawled to the edge of the bed and saw clothes on the other side of the huge room. My jeans lay waiting but no shirt. That's it. Just jeans. No wallet, no cash, no cards, no nothing. I did finally spot my Chucks.

"What the fuck, Hayden? What did you get us into?"

"I don't remember. I remember two hot women and drinking vodka in the cab. That's about it."

"Me, too." Shit, my head pounded. I pulled on my jeans and stepped into my shoes before crashing back down on the bed. "We need to get back to the bus. Where the fuck's my phone? You got yours? Call mine."

"I don't have mine either. This is some kind of fucked up. We've been robbed and left for dead."

"You think, dickhead? Only we're not dead, but I have a feeling we're going to wish we were." We needed to get in touch with Peri. This could be some serious shit we're in. Who knew what those ladies had of ours. Hell, my phone had all kinds of kinky shit in it. Thank God Peri insisted our phones be password protected.

"What's the number? I'll call Peri to come get us." Hayden held a house phone handpiece in his hand.

"How the fuck should I know? The numbers're in my phone." This situation got worse as minutes ticked by.

"Dude, really. I gotta get home. Crew's gonna worry if I'm not there when he wakes up." Hayden pushed the panic button on the urgency to leave.

"Calm down. We'll get home. Call the front desk and have them send up a manager."

Hayden explained we had a serious situation in our suite, and a manager appeared within minutes knocking on the door. It sounded like he knocked on my brain without the benefit of a skull between brain matter and knuckles.

"What can I do for you, gentlemen?" The prissy manager peered around the room.

"Look…" I started, slowly which was as fast as my brain could function, "… we have a delicate situation here that needs the utmost discretion on your and the hotel's part."

"I can assure you discretion is our middle name, sir. So what can I do?"

"We were robbed by the two women who brought us here."

The man instantly stood straighter. "No, sir. That does not happen at this hotel. We are a five-star hotel with excellent security," his speech stilted and formal.

"I don't give a shit if you have five gold stars. We were brought here by two women. I'm pretty sure they drugged us, and I know for a fact they robbed us because our billfolds and cell phones are gone. Hell, my shirt's even gone." With my head throbbing, I still managed to raise my voice too loudly. "Don't y'all have like surveillance cameras and shit?"

"Yes, we do, and we will get to the bottom of this. Then there's the payment for this suite as well." He glanced around to see if there were any damages.

"Dude, I don't even know how I got here much less how we paid for this."

"Someone put it on a platinum card by the name of Carter Sheridan, but the paper was signed by a Carter Jones." He glared at me obviously questioning the fraudulence.

I leaned forward rubbing my throbbing head. My hair fell forward in my hands, and I pulled it back away from my face. "Look, dude. The card's good, and we'll pay for any damages, but we need to get back to our bus, and we need to find the women who did this."

"Your bus? You live on a bus?" The man looked at me like my status in life descended to the depths of hell.

"Yes, we live on a fucking bus when we're touring." I looked at Hayden. The less info this guy knew, the better.

"So, you're some kind of traveling musicians?" He made it sound like we were gypsies.

"No, not like that. We're with a band."

"Uh, hm. Okay." I don't know if he didn't believe me or didn't like the idea we were in a band.

"You can use that phone to call someone to come here and take care of this situation." He pointed to the house phone.

"Yeah, that ain't gonna work either. We don't know the numbers because they're in our phones, which I told you were stolen." My patience wore very thin at this point. My head pounded, my shit was gone, and this guy was being a real prick.

"Uh, hm," he said again which pissed me off.

"Send someone out to Red Rock Amphitheater and our tour director, Peri O'Connor, with Assured Distraction, will come take care of this mess." The man looked at me with big eyes and then finally nodded in agreement. He walked to the door to leave. "And please send up a big pot of coffee."

"Right away." He closed the door, and I looked over at Hayden. "What a huge clusterfuck, Hayden. You know that, right?"

"Yeah, Carter. I'm sorry. I guess we should've gone home with the others."

"Hell yeah. We're going to have some explaining to do to a lot of people." My mind landed on Halo. Just when we were getting things going in the right direction, shit happens. I never planned to get with another woman last night. I only wanted to support the kid.

I didn't know if we were going to stay together, but I had a feeling this incident had some major repercussions attached to it, between us. One more time to lose her trust on being the kind of guy she needed, and once again, I'd fucked it up.

Halo

I woke up in my bunk and lay there thinking about last night. KeeMac and Ryan came home but not Carter and Hayden. I waited around until I couldn't hold my head up thinking they would arrive right behind the others, but that didn't happen.

I had no claims on Carter. His freedom to come and go and be with other women hadn't been relinquished because we had some mind-blowing sex a few times. He never mentioned giving up that freedom. Why would I even think he might want to have a relationship with me anymore now than the first time?

Yeah, he'd made some comments that could've been taken that way, but he never once spelled it out for me. I should have known better. He spelled it out plainly the first time. Was I that stupid to not see those rules still applied? Our sex was a matter of convenience for him. Yeah, I jumped him the first time, but we never talked about it. I didn't have any expectations from it which was why I never brought it up. He obviously made no attachment after our few times together. At his first chance, he took off to find another woman's bed to play in.

I'd heard him and the guys talking about all of their threesome and multiple partners while on the road. Maybe he finds having one partner boring. Hell, maybe he finds me boring. If that's the case, he can find another bus playmate because I'm not bed hopping on this bus. I lived for eight years without having a relationship. I gave myself the two years to see where life would take me. Right now, I think it's taking me back to Austin, Texas. Maybe that's where I belong.

I heard the bus door open, and Peri climbed on the bus. She opened the curtain to Hayden's bunk and pulled out a t-shirt and then did the same to Carter's. When she turned around to leave, she saw me watching her.

"Hey, Halo. Good morning." She gave me a weary smile and turned toward the door.

"Did they not come home last night?" I had to know.

"Uh, no. Carter and Hayden didn't come home. I'm going to get them now." She kept moving to the door but now I wanted to know more.

"Why are you going to get them?" I stood up from my bunk.

"Well… they're in a bit of a situation that needs some PR work done to smooth it over. Ryan and I are headed out to take care of it."

"Are they in jail?" I couldn't believe she was cleaning up the mess behind those two.

"No, not jail, thank God. Hey, I have to go, but they'll tell you when they get back. You have a sound check in a little while and then a show to perform. Cash's flying in to meet us this evening." She looked like she wanted to say more and then stepped down the stairs and off the bus to a waiting car.

I dressed quickly and tried to get down some toast. I knew the day would drag on if I sat around waiting for the results. I decided to go over and help the nanny with the boys. I bet Crew asked for Hayden when he didn't show up as expected.

Stepping into the RV, the boys ran to the doorway to attack. When Crew saw it wasn't his dad, he turned around and went back to play with the Lego fort they were building.

"So guys, whatcha doin' over here?" I moved to the Lego table.

Tucker spoke up immediately. "We're building a fort so we can keep the dinosaurs out."

"Dinosaurs attacked your fort?" I laughed thinking they had quite a gap in history going on there.

"Yeah, my daddy took us to see the dinosaur place at the exbit. They're cool." His pronunciation of exhibit made me smile.

"I think you mean, exhibit, little dude." I scruffed his hair.

"Yeah, exbit. You know where they got fake dinosaurs that're super ginormous big like the real ones would be until they all died." Crew knew what he meant.

Tucker joined the conversation with his own take on the massive beasts. "Yeah, we saw flying ones, and T-Rex ones, and fish ones. We saw a whole bunch more that I disremember their names."

"Well, I bet there're a lot of places in the United States that have more exhibits for the two of you to see. I bet Austin even has one with ginormous animals."

Crew looked at me carefully. "You know, Miss Halo, most of these are not animals. They're rectiles."

"Is that right?" I wanted to laugh. *Rectiles.*

"That's right," Tucker added. "Rectiles. We looked 'em up on the internet with my mom, and she read to us about 'em. Some are animals and some are rectiles."

"The two of you are so smart. I think maybe I better start studying these things so I can be as smart as y'all."

"We could show you, but we can't look at internet without Mom or Dad," Tuck added. "It's off limits."

"Yeah, off limits," Crew repeated. Obviously, they had been taught the term for meaning no.

"Do you know where my daddy is?" Crew continued.

"No, baby. I don't."

He gave me a strange look and leaned over to tell me a secret. "I'm not a baby anymore, Miss Halo. I'm a little man. My daddy told me no more baby for me when he took away my pull-ups. I had to be a little man when I started wearing underwear like his. Only mine has Spiderman and Superman on them."

"Oh, so Daddy doesn't like superhero undies?" I restrained myself to keep from having a good laugh at this information.

"No, he said daddies can't wear superheroes or people would think he was a superhero, and he's just a daddy, and the only person he can save is me."

"That's a big mouthful of words there, buddy. Can I call you buddy instead?"

He smiled at me. "Yeah, I can be a buddy, just not a baby. Tucker's not a baby either 'cause his mommy took his pull-ups away, too."

Tucker nodded his head and then spoke. "That's okay, though, 'cause now we get to take a whiz on the grass when we are home."

"Tucker, not supposed to say that to girls. You know what your dad said," Crew admonished his little friend.

"Oops. I forgot. Not supposed to tell girls we pee in the grass." He got close and whispered, "Don't tell."

I nodded my head. The door to the RV opened, and Hayden came in and picked up Crew hugging him close.

"Daddy, where you been? You said you'd build a fort to protect men from dinosaurs today."

"I know, little man. I know. I messed up, didn't I? We can do it now though because it looks like you haven't finished yet."

"That's okay, Daddy. We started but needed you to make it perfect."

The father/son bond between them touched my heart. His ability to take on a child at eighteen and be the daddy he needed to be made me understand how seriously he took this job. Well, usually. He still wanted to be a man, too. I also saw how tight they all were within this family. While Crew didn't have a mom, he had a house full of people who loved him so he never felt left out.

I wanted to quiz Hayden about last night. When he finally looked me in the eyes, I knew things must have been bad. The red road maps around his irises told a story of exhaustion and being hungover. Now he needed to man up and be a daddy before going to work onstage. Life on the road could prove to be too much for him with Crew in the end.

"I think I'll head back over to our bus and see what time we're supposed to be at sound check."

Hayden spoke up. "Uh, Peri said Cash will be there today, too. He's flying in right now."

"She mentioned that before she left here. Will he be here for the show?"

"I assume so. We may be flying back with him, too."

"Really? She didn't mention that." He caught the surprise in my voice.

"Maybe not. Gotta wait to see what Cash says."

I got the feeling we were talking about last night's fiasco instead of our performance. We were only going to be on the road with AD for part of their tour. This could be our last time to open for them. We're doing great on the road and our music downloads have exploded since we left. Maybe Cash wanted us back in the studio.

"Okay, well… I'll see you in a few." I wanted to get back to the bus and see what Carter had to say.

I climbed up the steps, but no one greeted me.

Hmm. Odd. *Where were they?*

I went back to my bunk and started looking at the clothes I planned to wear tonight onstage. I wanted to look good since it might be our last night.

A car stopped out front, and I moved up to look out the huge windshield. Carter, Peri, and Cash got out of the vehicle and none of them looked too happy. Maybe I'd wait to ask any questions if I ever got a chance.

Before Carter climbed on, he looked directly at me. I recognized the bloodshot look. He'd been drinking heavily last night. He opened his mouth and drew in a breath like he was going to speak and then shook his head and got on. I watched him walk past me and down the aisle still hoping for something from him, but instead he climbed into his bunk and shut the curtain.

He never said a word to me, but I'd seen the look before. *Guilt.* What could he have done to look guilty? Did he have sex with another woman? Why should he feel guilty? He didn't owe me anything.

I moved off the bus with my guitar. Cash and Peri were talking but stopped when they saw me. I nodded at Cash, put my head down, and walked toward the stage area. I passed it and went out into the beauty of the amphitheater. I'd never seen anything like it before. Chandler told me they'd played here when she first joined in the band. The natural beauty and the enormity of the rock formations took my breath away.

I climbed about halfway up the seating area to the middle before I took a seat. A strange feeling clawed at the back of my mind, but I couldn't put my finger on why. I'd done nothing wrong so why did I feel like things balanced on a cliff, ready to fall?

Cash appeared at the bottom close to the stage. "Oh, Halo. I wanted to talk to you."

He moved up the seating rows and sat next to me and looked out at the view. "This place is something else, huh?"

"Yeah. I've never seen anything like it. I feel small sitting here."

"This is one place that some bands think if they play it, they've made it. Kinda like playing the Garden if you're a New Yorker."

I laughed. Madison Square Garden, as if I'd ever get to play that place. "So is there something going on I need to know about?"

"Yes, there is. After this show, you, Hayden, and I are going home. Crew and the nanny are coming, too."

"Is there a problem?" My face reflected my feelings.

"No, nothing's wrong. You knew this test run wouldn't last, and we've decided to get you two in the studio to record an EP for release while the fire's hot. The label feels like that time's now, so y'all are going to record. Y'all been working on songs?"

"Yeah, we have. We've at least four that we both feel you're going to love."

"Just what I'd hoped to hear."

"Why didn't you ask Hayden?" I asked him.

"We sent him back to get him out of the situation. Negative press isn't what the two of you need right now."

"Yeah, okay." I didn't know how to respond but felt sure he and Peri knew the best thing for us.

"Carter can take the heat this time. His reputation proceeds him and people understand him getting into stupid shit. You and Hayden, not so much. We'd like to keep y'all away from anything that casts a shadow over you before the first CD drops."

"Sounds good. Are we playing tonight?" I probably wouldn't even see Carter again before we left. I supposed it'd be better this way.

"Yeah, we'll leave as soon as you're done. I'm anxious to hear your music in this venue."

"Me, too."

I knew before they came the police wouldn't be able to do anything. I couldn't remember much and barely saw the women before we started drinking in the cab. Our security men should have gone with us, and this wouldn't have happened. Bad planning on our part to send them home when we left.

Peri handed me a bottle of ibuprofen and a water. If the damn floor would stop spinning, I might be able to actually think, dammit.

"So, Mr. Sheridan, do you remember their names?" the cop spoke loudly.

"No."

"Do you remember what they were wearing?" He looked over the top of the notepad.

"Uh, dresses. I think." Shit. This was bad.

"Did you get their phone numbers?"

"No, and even if I did, I wouldn't know it since they took our phones."

"True." His radio keyed up from another person.

"Yeah, go ahead," he spoke into the mic attached at his shoulder.

"The hotel found your phones in the garbage cans out front. Guess they figured out they couldn't get into them and ditched them. Probably won't get any prints from them, though, but we'll dust to see."

"Good. Thanks." He turned to me. "Your lucky day, Mr. Sheridan. Seems the phones reappeared."

"Great." My enthusiasm lacked inspiration.

"If we find any prints that are usable, we might get somewhere, but if they're smudged from being in the bottom of the heap, we're pretty much done on leads."

"What about all the cameras in the place?" Peri asked.

"That's going to take some time to run through the tapes, but the hotel's security is looking into it now. The worker on duty gave us the time of check-in so that helped."

"Wonderful. Thank you, officer. We'll be looking forward to hearing from you about any progress. When can we expect the phones to be returned?" Peri's official voice made the cop take notice.

"Probably never unless we catch them quickly. They will be evidence and until this is solved, they'll stay locked up."

Peri turned to me. "When's the last time you backed up your phone?"

"No clue." I shrugged my shoulders.

"Okay. So we'll get a new one today, and they can transfer your data."

Ryan sat down next to me on the couch and spoke quietly, "You can kiss your data goodbye. I hope Hayden backed his up more recently than you did so he won't lose all of Crew's pictures."

"Yeah, me too." I didn't care about that phone. I'd replace it, but Crew's pictures couldn't be which made me feel like shit all over again, but this problem was all on Hayden. He found the women. I was along for the ride.

"Okay, Ms. O'Connor. We'll let y'all get back to work. The department will be in contact if anything else is needed."

"Thank you, officer." She shut the door behind him.

"What the fuck, Carter?" she rounded on me.

"Hey, I was just following Hayden's lead. He found 'em. He said let's do it, and I went with him. At least I didn't let him go alone with those two." What I wanted to say was I'd have rather been with Halo but held back.

"You should have known better than to drink something like that. You're a grown man acting like a damn kid."

"Hey, the last time I looked, he's a grown-ass man, too. Why am I getting all of the blame?"

"Because you know the rules. He's still learning them." Peri's face turned red, but she stopped talking. Then it turned a sickly shade of green, and she sprinted to the bathroom with Ryan on her heels. We all knew this routine. She landed in the ER the last time.

I heard Ryan consoling her as she lost all her lunch to the porcelain god. Not a sound my head or stomach wanted to hear right then unless I felt like joining her.

They walked out and Peri's look said all I needed to know. I walked to the door and held it open for her.

Halo looked at me through the glass of the RV. I couldn't talk to her right then, even when she stood at the doorway looking down at me. My head hurt, my stomach rolled over and over, and my conscience wanted to explode. I climbed the bus steps and never looked back.

I couldn't do it. The very thing I tried to avoid years ago had come back to bite me in the ass. I never wanted to hurt her. She's too perfect for me in this business. I needed to let her go on with her life without me in it. Even though I fell asleep, my head and stomach didn't let me settle down.

Someone shook me.

"What?"

"Get up asshole. It's time to go to the venue."

I rolled toward the voice I recognized instantly. "When did you get back?"

"A little while ago. I put Lola on the plane and came here." He leaned against the opposite bunk.

"I guess y'all had a perfect conjugal visit, huh?"

"You might say that." His smirk said it all. Gunner's entire way of looking at life evolved after he and Lola made a commitment to each other. At first, I hated her for it, but his happiness made him a new man so I got over my jealousy. He deserved to be happy.

Maybe I didn't deserve it.

Hayden and Halo were ready to go onstage when we walked to the wings. The audience's noise poured through the area where we stood, so we knew the time was close when security opened the doors to go through. I'd have to face her sooner or later, so it might as well be now.

The two stood just off stage waiting for introductions. They talked and laughed with some roadies. One reached out and brushed the hair over her shoulder. I knew that look on his face. Dammit, I found myself ready to tear into the dude, but what right did I have to go all caveman on him? Yeah, dumbass, none.

Halo turned when he looked over her shoulder toward Gunner and me. I did a head tip but didn't move any closer. I didn't need to interfere with her life any more than I had. If she wanted to get with this guy, she didn't need my permission. Our dressing rooms were around a corner, so I took off. I felt her eyes follow me until I was out of sight. Man, I was so fucked.

The music coming from the stage filtered in, and it sounded fantastic. A perfect but unique tone to Halo and Hayden settled over everyone who heard them. Cash knew what he was doing. He always did when it came to talent and once again, he found it with those two. They would make their mark in the world just like Assured Distraction did.

Our band's established name held its own in the rock world. The success we wanted materialized and made us famous. It wasn't overnight and neither would theirs be, but it'd happen. I needed to let her have her time in the spotlight without me dragging her down.

"Those wheels in your head probably need more oil in them if you're going to continue thinking that hard," Gunner landed beside me on the leather couch.

"Yeah probably. All the alcohol rusted them." I laughed. "I was thinking about how we've made it, and now it's Hayden and Halo's turn."

"Yeah, they'll be touring on their own when their album's done."

"I guess they'll be back in the studio when this tour's over?"

"No, Cash's taking them back with him tonight on the jet. They're done with this tour. The label wants them to cut a CD now."

"What?" I faced him to see if he was fucking with me.

"Yeah. Hayden told me before they went on they're leaving tonight. He wasn't too happy because of Crew and the nanny. He didn't like dragging Crew out of bed to get on the plane, especially flying commercial since we'll need the jet. Cash needs to get back quickly for some reason."

"Shit." I looked away. I'd never get a chance to talk to her before she left.

"Is that a problem for him to wake Crew up?" Gunner didn't follow my crazy train in my mind.

"No, but it's a problem not being able to talk to Halo before she leaves."

"Dude, you knew this was coming, and you knew better than to get involved with her again."

"Dammit, I know, but it happened anyway. I didn't initiate it either. She jumped me first but then backed away. Now, I've fucked up, as usual, and she's leaving to go home."

"Yeah. You probably won't get a third chance."

"Maybe I don't deserve a third chance." I got up and headed to the wings to watch her sing. It could be my last time ever.

"Thank you, Denver. Good fucking night." KeeMac ended our final encore. "We'll see y'all soon." We walked off the stage waving, throwing picks and drumsticks to the audience as we handed off our guitars to the techs who cared for their packing.

The after party going on tonight had people already in the room. For a small party, people were everywhere. They always got bigger fast when the fans wearing passes poured in following a check by security.

"Looks like another long night to me," Gunner said as he walked ahead of me through the door.

"Is this getting old to you?" I raised an eyebrow. He used to love a party like this.

"Hell yeah, it is. I'd rather spend my time with Lola any day." He caught my eyes darting around the room while he spoke. "Dude, I told you she'd be gone."

"I know, but I hoped you'd be wrong."

"Me? Wrong? Asshat, have I ever steered you wrong with info?" He laughed loudly making smile.

"Yeah, about a million times that I can count. Probably a million more I can't." We both grabbed a beer and tipped the necks in a toast to another great show.

KeeMac and Chan finally strolled in as we signed autographs and took pictures with the fans. Peri lined up some quick PR after the incident with the crazies in the hotel. When KeeMac sat down and pulled Chandler in his lap, he looked down the row at the rest of us.

"Y'all chat 'em up for us?" he asked.

"Hell yeah, we did since we never know how long the two of you are gonna go at it in a dark corner." Ryan wiggled his eyebrows.

"Right, babe?" He kissed her until she was breathless causing the crowd to clap and make suggestive comments. "We tried to be quick tonight. I promised her better since the back room will be empty." The smirk never fading. "Hey, will you please change the sheets before we get there?"

"Da fuck? We changed them after y'all. I think it's your turn." I couldn't resist giving it right back to him.

"Yeah, yeah. The good news is we'll get the room the rest of the tour. The bad news is you get the bunks and no girl!" He and Chandler both laughed at that. I didn't find it funny at all.

"That sucks balls, you know?"

"Oh, there'll be some ball sucking going on. Don't worry." The whole group laughed and signed CDs, shirts, and tits flashed at us. What a strange life we'd come to think of as normal.

The next show would land us in Philly. Thank God the buses dropped us at the airport, and we'd fly to meet up with them after a short break. That meant we were able to go home for a few days in between. I needed some down time, and maybe I'd get a chance to see where I stood with Halo.

When we touched down in Austin, we all woke ready to see our own homes for a change. I wondered where Halo lived now. We never talked about it when she showed up on tour. Guess I should've taken the time to talk to her about the normal things in her life. Maybe this fucked-up situation we had going wouldn't be so bad.

My mind told me to stay away from her. She didn't need my shit since her own life was about to take a huge turn for the better. Halo deserved it. According to Cash, she'd come a long way in the short time she'd been singing with Hayden. She must've been good before or he would've never given her a second look.

The car dropped me at my house. The lock made a hard click as I turned it. When I shut the door behind me, the sound echoed in the emptiness. Shit. My fucking life mimicked that sound. I looked around. Guitars, furniture, toys, hell, even the house. Just things. Things I accumulated over the years. None of this brought lasting happiness. It only represented brief moments of instant pleasure. Now, it stared at me with cold indifference.

All I had were things with no real meaning. Things to take up time, kinda like the women I'd been with since the band left on tour the first time. They were only something to mark moments until the next stop. I honestly had nothing lasting that counted. Is this what I had to look forward to when I grew old?

I had to get out of here. I couldn't do this now. I found the keys to my pride and joy in the garage, my 1965 Roush Shelby Cobra. One more toy that only provided momentary fun. I pulled the cover off of her and ran my hand over the sleek, shiny blue fender down to the round headlights.

She quietly waited for me to show her some love. Her patience for attention would only last so long, though. She would die a slow death looking for me. Maybe I should let her go so someone else could give her a real life. A guy who could love her the way she needed. A man who would use her body and soul until she could go no further without refueling. One who would know exactly how far to push her each time he touched the right buttons or found the sweet spot in her pedal. I knew I could never do that. My need for her grew too strong. She had to be part of me now.

The engine roared to life with a purr only this motor could make. I loved driving her, a wet dream on the open road. I needed space between me and my fucked-up mind. I turned west and headed out of Austin, leaving the city and traffic far behind. I took the back roads speeding toward the full ball of fire close to the horizon. Once I finally hit a highway, I opened her up and let her have her head to stretch those horses to full capacity.

The tires' whirred over the black pavement sang a song causing me to think of the melody I'd heard Halo singing. Was she in the studio this evening working on the new music? Maybe she was out with Hayden talking about what they planned to accomplish in the next month? She might be home relaxing from being gone for so long.

It seemed like no matter where I went, my mind drifted back to Halo. I wished she thought about me like that, but why would she? Her opinion of me and what I'd been doing for the last eight years hadn't changed. If anything, it seemed like I did everything to reconfirm the worst about me. I needed to do something about that.

I had serious doubts about whether she'd want me at this point, but I could make changes. I knew the right things to do. I just hadn't been practicing for eight years to be the kind of man a woman could count on. I needed to rethink my priorities. I wanted to be that man, the type of guy who people respected. The others had made this change, and they were no different than me.

My parents raised me to be a better man. Halo inspired me to want to do that now. I was a kid when we were together before. I could show her those days of hard partying, drinking to intoxication, wildly spending money, and chasing every skirt that caught my eye were over. Mostly being a man- whore had to go, as in buried and put away for good. A big shift in my life needed to occur so she would see the man I wanted to be for her.

I stopped the Shelby on the upside of a hill, and my eyes followed the lines of my headlights. My gaze traced the lines upward. I could clearly see with the bright lights. I had an uphill battle in front of me if I planned to do what was necessary to show her that man. I checked behind me and saw nothing but darkness.

"Yeah, you dumbshit, that's where you've been," I spoke the words aloud. Looking into the round side mirror for a few minutes, I finally flipped a U on the empty highway and sped back toward the glow of lights hovering over Austin. Bright lights looked a whole lot better than dark, empty space.

Carter

I walked in my house feeling different this time around. I had a purpose other than the band. The woman I knew was the one had waited long enough. A plan formed as I took stock of my home. The designer I used planned every space for my entertainment. I hated the black and chrome. The sleek but uninviting lines of couches only served one purpose—to seduce the women I occasionally brought here.

I never hung out in this room. I stayed in my man cave that I refused to let her touch. Tomorrow, this would change. It could all go. Start over. New, fresh, just like me. I scrolled through my contacts until I found her and sent off a text for her to show up early in the morning. She made loads off of me the first time, so I knew she would comply with my wishes.

I dialed my phone.

"Gunner?" I didn't wait for him to say hello.

"What's wrong?" His voice held some panic.

"I need your help. Can you come over, or I'll come there?"

"Dude, we just got home. I'm kinda in the middle of something spectacular at the moment."

"Shit, sorry. I forgot."

"What's going on?"

"Never mind. Can you come over in the morning? I need to talk."

"Talk? Like in exchanging feelings or some shit like that? My man-card is firmly seated between my legs."

"No, not feelings..." I hesitated. "Yeah, maybe some feelings. Hell, I don't know. Maybe you need to bring Lola with you."

"You need mine and Lola's help? Are you okay? Do I need to call 911?"

"No, dickwad, you don't need to call 911. I'm asking for some help from my friends who understand me."

"Awe, I feel special."

"Shut up, dickwad. I'd come for you."

"I don't want you to come for me. Not now. Not ever." We both laughed at that idea.

"Okay, okay. Go back to Lola, and I'll see you both in the morning."

"Yeah, we'll be there but don't expect us at the butt crack of dawn. We've got better things to do then."

"Right, but not noon either, please."

"Later." He ended the call.

I looked around some more and made mental notes about all I wanted changed. By the time I finished, my house would take on an entirely new appearance, one more like the kind of adult I planned to become. I walked into my bedroom, and it disgusted me thinking about the times women were in here and the things we'd done.

I decided to sleep across the hall in the guest bedroom. If someone had had sex in here, it wasn't me so I felt better about sleeping in it. I stripped and landed face first in the clean sheets. I knew I could sleep now.

The doorbell woke me up.

What the fuck? Who came over this early?

I slid my jeans back on and went downstairs.

"I'm coming. Quit ringing the damn bell."

I glanced at the large metal clock on the wall. "Hmm. Eleven already? I guess I needed some sleep."

I opened the door and Gunner and Lola stood there. The pissed look he gave me had me laughing.

"You little shit. You tell us to get here early, and you're not even out of bed." He barged past me, tugging Lola by the hand. "Where's the coffee? And where's breakfast? It's the least you can do making us give up our morning in bed."

"Uh, I'll make some. Have a seat." I gestured at the island in the kitchen and started on the coffee. "I'll order some breakfast and have it delivered."

"I didn't know some places would deliver breakfast," Lola said climbing on the tall barstool.

"I pay them extra so they don't mind. I do it all the time. They're used to it."

Gunner raised an eyebrow and glanced sideways at Lola.

"What? I like breakfast with or without company, and I sure as hell am not making it."

"You'd actually have to have groceries to cook and maybe some cooking lessons."

"If we lived here all the time, I'd get a housekeeper to do that but what's the point right now?"

Yeah, something else an adult would do, have groceries or a housekeeper. One more thing for the list.

"My decorator was supposed to be here early this morning. Guess she didn't get my message."

Lola pulled a card from her shorts pocket. "You mean Dream Designs of Austin?" she read from the card. "Looks like you might have slept through it."

"Shit. I must've been more exhausted than I thought."

She laid the card on the counter.

I poured them both a cup and put the cream and sugar between us before I pulled a cola from the fridge. I picked the decorator's card up and texted her begging her to return ASAP. Thankfully, she responded she would.

"Why are we here, Carter? And didn't you get this place redone when you moved in?"

I opened my bottle and drank down more than half.

"Diabetes much?" she said. Yeah, her nurse panties wadded up over my bad sugar habits.

"No, it's the way I like it." I drank another long drink. "Ahh. Perfect."

"Back to my question, short attention span," Gunner reminded me.

"Yeah, so, like I said it all goes together. I've come to some conclusions about my fucking life and myself that I don't like." They both stared at me. "Some changes are going to be made in my life starting now."

"Really? And you need us to do a self-improvement sitcom?"

"Dude, I'm being serious. Last night when I got home, this house felt like a dungeon, dark and cold. I'm not talking BDSM style either. No sir, no fun and games here. I hated it and myself for making it that way. I plan to change it all… the house, me, my life."

"And where do you plan to start on Carter's Big Adventure or is this going to be Carter's Playhouse?"

"It's not an adventure. It's a shift of thinking. A paradigm shift."

"A what? Have you been playing on your thesaurus app or something?"

"No, it's an about-face change."

"I know what it is, dickwad. I've never heard you talk like you have more than a third-grade education outside of music."

"Now that shit cuts deep, my friend."

"Don't 'my friend' me. I've known you a helluva long time, and you've been pretty fucking happy forever. Why the change now?"

"That's just it. Everyone thinks I'm only good for two things, music and fucking."

Lola snorted and spit coffee across the island. "Oops, sorry." She jumped for a napkin wiping herself and counter.

"Well, some people would say just fucking, but we'll leave that alone since I don't want Lola drowning in coffee." Gunner laughed at his own joke since Lola was still trying to recover from my statement.

"Yeah, yeah, said the drummer to the bass player. I get your fucking musician joke." I gave him a quick smile. "I'm serious, and I need y'all to be serious, too."

They both did their best to wipe the smiles off their faces. Lola sat up straight in her chair and gave me her best salute. "Okay, Carter. I'm ready. Lay it on me."

"Don't tell him shit like that. You know how he'll take it." Gunner's reaction to Lola's statement went exactly how I expected it to.

"See, right there. That's the shit I'm talking about. I can be more than the guy who doesn't have limits, who only thinks about where my next lay's gonna come from. I can be the man a woman needs. I can do adulting just like the rest of you."

They both looked at me like I'd grown a unicorn horn.

"What? Y'all don't fucking believe me do you?" Apparently, my disappointment in their ability to support me came across through my tone or statement or something. They quickly changed their expressions.

"Wait now," Gunner started. "It's not that we don't think you have it in you, dude. It's just that we've never seen you even want to do the adult thing before."

"Yeah, sure we do, Carter. I mean, I know I'm the new one around here so I haven't had much of a chance to see you handle too much that goes on, but I feel like you can do it if you set your mind to it." Lola's vote of confidence meant a lot to me. She didn't know me all that well and yet, her comment seemed genuine.

"Hell, Carter. You're no different than the rest of us SOBs, and we've proven we can grow up." Gunner pulled Lola over to him. "Maybe it just takes the right person to bring it out in us."

"That's what I mean, Gun. I want to make this change for me, but I want to make it for Halo, too. She deserves someone who can man up and walk beside her, not some jerk-off who only sees her as my next bed partner."

Lola narrowed her eyes at me. "Is that how you see her?"

"No. Well, yes, maybe before. Hell, I don't know. That's how I see me."

"No wonder she put on the brakes. You don't deserve someone like Halo if that's how you've always seen her."

"Don't I know it." I shook my head and hung it. "I'm fucked, and I haven't even started on me yet."

How did I let my life evolve into such a mess?

Lola stood and put a hand on my shoulder. "I don't think all is lost, Carter, but you're going to have to prove to her or any woman you set your sights on, that you can be the man a woman needs in her life. She's not going to let you treat her like a doormat that you wipe your feet on and then shut the door. From the little I've gotten to know her, Halo is stronger than that."

I thought back to our first break up. "She walked away from me even when it looked like it killed her. She gathered her pride, stood tall, and left me standing there. She'd do it again, too. Only this time, I won't let her go without a fight, no matter what it takes."

Lola laid her hand on my arm. "Yes, she'll walk if you don't fix it."

"So, if you two are through using tampons to measure your feelings, do you have a plan?" Gunner smirked at us both.

I looked at the two of them for a minute and then nodded. "To start, the bachelor palace has to go. What woman would want a place that looked this way?" I motioned around my streamlined kitchen with black and stainless everywhere. "It's fucking cold and impersonal. I want it to look like a kitchen where a woman wants to be, even if she's not going to do the damn cooking."

I moved over to the living area. "This all needs to go. Looks like a room you'd bring a high-priced call girl to. I want it gone. I want it inviting to guests. I want it to look like a home." The stripper pole in the corner needed to be the first thing, although we all had such fun with it.

I turned to Lola. "That's why I asked you both here. I need you to help me. When that design lady gets here, help me pick and choose the right things."

"This is a good start on material things, Carter, but you have to consider what you're going to do to change you," Lola said not as a suggestion but a need.

"Right, I've been thinking about what I'm going to do. You know giving up the life I've been living is going to be hard as hell."

She stood back and glared at me. "Oh really? Harder than watching a great person walk away, again?"

I let out a deep breath. "No." I knew I needed someone to call me out on my shit, but Lola liked to hit below the belt. "You're right."

"Then you better start thinking right now about what you're willing to do to be the kind of man she's willing to accept. A man to make her complete. Until you do, this right here..." she waved her finger around indicating my house changes, "... won't mean a damn thing to her."

My mind stood still. I didn't know where to go with this. The doorbell rang hauling me back to reality. Lola opened it and asked the decorator to come in.

"So, what are we going to do this time, Carter?" I looked between Lola and Gunner.

"Change is good, right?"

They both smiled at me.

My mind hurt. It didn't think in English anymore—I thought in musical notes and lyrics. I wondered if Hayden felt the same way. I needed to buy an air mattress and start sleeping at the studio. It would save me time and wear and tear on my body. We didn't eat or sleep in normal hours. We worked until we finished. Cash made us do everything over and over until he and the producers approved.

Hayden worked with Cash before, and even he thought Cash went a little overboard on the work hours. When we walked out of rehearsals on Friday afternoon, worn out and exhausted, he stepped out of his office.

"Can I have a minute?" He turned and walked back in, and we followed. "I've been listening to what the producers finished mixing. I have to say, I think you two have done a first-class job. The music projects a new sound we all feel will send you to the top of the charts in no time."

Hayden and I looked at each other and smiled. Finally, news that perked us up.

"That's great, Cash. We needed some good news. You've worked us like slaves for days now. We're worn smooth out," Hayden spoke, and I nodded to add emphasis to his words.

"Good, good. You'll appreciate your hard work when we hang that platinum album on the wall or you get an award down the line. I can't emphasize the importance of your freshman album."

"So what now?" I asked.

"You keep working until you're done. This EP needs at least five great songs and the full CD is going to need ten. How many do you feel are ready?" He leaned over the desk and folded his hands together.

I looked at Hayden. "We have five recorded already and three more ready to record."

"Great, great, but still some work to do." Damn, the man needed to shoot me now. I didn't think I could keep up this pace.

AD left to finish the tour. They weren't going overseas this time so it wouldn't be as long away as before.

It put space between Carter and me. I didn't have to think about him all the time which helped my emotional side. It also helped with my lyrics. A lot of emotions tied up in my heart about us flowed out onto the pages. With him not around, I could allow it because the luxury of acting on emotions wasn't there.

Hayden needed this recording to be over with so he could spend more time with his son. Crew missed his dad and with Peri gone, the sweet angel spent long hours with the nanny. The older woman's loving and fun personality made it easier for Hayden to be away, but he missed Crew terribly.

Sometimes our days and nights floated together. We would take breaks outside so we could see the sunlight and remember what it looked like. I didn't think writing music would be this overwhelming, but Cash pushed us to our limits. He wanted to get the CD out as quickly as we could following our tour. He kept saying, "the iron's hot, we have to strike."

I considered throat punching the guy sometimes and then Hayden would crack a joke and bring me back to reality. I finally decided if he could do it with Crew waiting for him, I should stop complaining. He clearly had more at stake than I did.

"Hey, we missed lunch. Want to walk down to the food trucks and get something? If we get out before he cracks his damn whip again, he'll never miss us," Hayden whispered to me.

"Let's do it." I turned on tiptoes and headed for the back door.

The bright sun caused my eyes to water when I stepped out.

"Halo, it's not that bad. No need to cry." He laughed at me.

"I'm not crying. Wait, maybe I am. I'm crying for my pillow. I'm so sad my brain is crying, too."

He smiled. "What would it take to cheer it up?"

"About twenty-four uninterrupted hours would work."

"Maybe I should have asked who would cheer it up." He looked at me as we continued down the sidewalk.

"Uh, no one at this point." I didn't want to think about Carter.

"What's going on with you and Carter? I thought y'all might be getting back together. You looked pretty content on the bus together."

"I thought that, too. Then he didn't come home when the two of you went out. He never tried to talk to me about it. We left, remember? He hasn't tried to contact me, and they were home for a few days after we got home."

Hayden stopped walking and gave me a strange look. I continued on saying over my shoulder, "Whatever. It doesn't matter anymore. He's clearly loving his life, but I refuse to live that way."

I stopped in line in front of a Vietnamese food truck, and he continued to Torchie's Tacos. We met up at a table a few minutes later.

"I need to tell you something, Halo. I never realized you were left out of that conversation after I came home that morning. I assumed someone would fill you in on what happened."

"I don't care, Hayden. You two are adults and can do whatever you want to do."

"That's how it looked to anyone who didn't know, but that's not exactly the truth."

"Sometimes the truth is all about perception."

"In this case, the truth is a lot worse than people were led to believe, especially for me and in a way, for us."

"Whatever the truth is, Carter didn't think I needed to know it. He never bothered."

"That's on Carter. He should've told you, but maybe he didn't for a reason."

"You're right, but he failed to give me one or have anyone else give me one. Anyway, I'm done with that situation. Moving on. Starting over. Having fun." While that all sounded good, it was a line of shit, and I knew it. I didn't know what I wanted to do at this point. I knew whatever I decided it wouldn't include Carter.

"When he gets back home, you two need to talk. He needs to explain and you need to give him a chance. Nothing good ever came from not talking, Halo. You know that."

"Yeah, but he doesn't or he would've at least tried to contact me by now."

Hayden looked at me over his taco and nodded.

We walked back in the studio and Cash stood talking to Johnna, the receptionist.

"Oh, glad you're back. Look, why don't you two take the weekend off? It'll be good to look at your music after some downtime. AD's last show is tomorrow night back in L.A., and I want to be there." He turned and looked at us. "Unless you want to go with me."

"No," we both said in unison.

"That's what I figured you'd say. Go home, rest, read mail, do whatever. I'll see you both on Monday."

He didn't have to ask us twice. We waved at each other and left the parking lot. I couldn't wait to put my head down on my pillow on my bed. My apartment may be tiny, but it was home and I desperately wanted to be there.

I rose up and looked at the clock. It was mid-morning. I'd slept since I got home and when my stomach growled, I knew I'd missed a few meals along the way. I stumbled out to the kitchen to put on coffee. My phone showed I'd missed a few calls and texts so while I waited for the dripping to finish, I opened the messages.

Peri: *Where r u? should have come with cash*
Gunner: *why didn't you come out here*
Chandler: *Girl, what were you thinking? You should have come to L.A.*
Carter: *Hey.*

That's it? "Hey"? What the fuck? Why did he even bother?

When the coffee finished, I looked at the calls. Besides the spams, Carter called three times but didn't leave messages. What was going on? He doesn't contact me after I leave and now all of a sudden he texts and calls?

"Dammit, Hayden. You little shit," I said it out loud. He had to have talked to Carter and told him what I said. Why would he do that? I made up my mind to call Hayden when I woke up enough to scream and yell. Hayden had no right to tell Carter what I said about him or us.

I filtered through my mail while I had my coffee. My phone pinged again. How did Lola get my number?

Lola: *you awake*
Me: *sorta*
Lola: *want to go to brunch? I'm off today and all alone*

Me: *sure, what time*
Lola*: soon, I'm starving*
Me: *me too. I'll see you in an hour*
Lola: *Kirby lane?*
Me: *sure*

I showered and dressed quickly. Traffic could be a nightmare. Lola waited on the bench out front for me.

"Hey girl." I hugged her.

"Hey, yourself. What've you been doing? I haven't heard from you since you've been home."

"That's because Cash has been killing us. I swear the man locked us away in the studio with only bread and water for weeks."

Lola laughed. "Gunner's told me how Cash gets when it's time to cut a new album."

"I wish Gunner offered that info to me. I probably would've stocked up on food and energy drinks."

"Maybe that's why Cash didn't tell you. Those things are bad for you, you know."

"Okay, nursey. I understand, but we were dying in there. Too many long days and nights in a row. We hardly went home the entire time."

"You should've called me to rescue you." We sat and looked over the menu ordering when the waitress returned with our coffees.

"I'm surprised you aren't in L.A. with the band." I wrapped my hands around the tall mug as I spoke.

"Gunner wanted me to, but I want to take off next week while he's home so I switched with some other nurses. I can hear them another time. I need some Gunner time first." She gave me a devious smile.

I laughed. "Oh, right. I get it."

"Actually, I hope I get it," she said with a smirk.

"You're bad. You know that, right?"

"If you only knew." This time she wiggled her eyebrows up and down.

"Are you trying to make me jealous, because it's working."

"No, you know Carter'll be happy to see you when he gets back home. Haven't you talked to him?"

"That would be a no." I stared into my coffee cup. This subject needed to be declared off limits.

"Really, because when he left here the last time, I thought he'd be in constant touch with you." She seemed sure of herself by the tone she used.

"I haven't spoken to him since before our last show with them. He came back to the bus the next morning after being out with Hayden and, I'm assuming, women. He glared at me and then climbed into his bunk. Oh, and then he left me one text, 'Hey.' That's all he said to me."

"His head's so far up his ass, he can't think for the lack of sunlight."

I started laughing at her statement. We thought exactly alike.

"You hit it dead on. Dead on."

The food arrived, and we both ate like it was our last meal. When I finished, I sat back and had another cup of their delicious coffee.

"So, how are things with you and Gunner?" I didn't want to go back to the previous conversation.

"They're great. He's ready to be home. He misses me."

"I bet so. Why don't you go with him more?

"I'm not ready to give up my job yet, but I'm getting there. He wants the band to hire me to be their full-time medical care provider on the road."

"That's a great idea. What're you holding out for?"

"I don't know. At first, I felt like he offered it as a suggestion just to get me on the bus with him, but it seems like those guys are always going to clinics for stupid stuff. I'm working on my Master's Degree now so I can be a nurse practitioner. I need to be able to write prescriptions when they're sick. I could see to everyone."

"That would be awesome. With the amount they employ, you'd be great to have along."

"I'm still thinking about it, but I'll probably give in by the next tour. What about you? Got any future plans? Have you been seeing anyone since you got home?" She looked me in the eyes like she wanted some definite information.

"Hell no. When would I have time? Remember, task master Cash?"

"Yeah, but you've had time to do other stuff, too."

"Uh, no. We haven't. The man kept us there day and night working. I'm surprised we got anything done after the first week or so from the exhaustion. He finally let us have this weekend off so he could go to L.A."

"So no dates with hot men? You're such a beautiful woman. I'm surprised they aren't beating down your door."

"I don't encourage fans to come see me, and we weren't playing in the area. Where would I meet men?"

"Don't you have friends around here? You've lived here a while, haven't you?"

"Yeah, but I've been concentrating on my music. I've had a few boyfriends in college but nothing serious since I took the two years off for this. My friends from school all left for jobs since getting one in Austin's hard to do. The competition's stiff."

"That's true. Well, what about Hayden? No interest there?"

I smiled. "Isn't he a cutie? More like a little brother to me, though. Besides, he spends all his time with Crew."

"Yeah, he and Crew are a team."

"The right woman will come along and snap those two up. She'll be a lucky woman to have them." She nodded in agreement.

"What about someone else working for AD? No one gets your juices flowing?"

The way she said it I laughed out loud at her comment. "My juices flowing, huh? Whatever do you mean by that?" I said it like an innocent teenager?

"You know exactly what I mean." She wiggled her eyebrows and leaned in to speak softly. "Like one of the hot guys you would want to push you up against the wall and kiss you like he meant it while rubbing his hardness up and down you making your panties all wet for him."

"*Stop*! You must really be missing Gunner." Just listening to her description made me move around in my seat.

"That's an understatement. I think I'm going to do that to him when he gets here." Her face turned red. "I can't wait to see him, but we're not talking about me. What about you?"

"I don't know." I sighed. "I really thought Carter and I might have another chance. I loved him something fierce before he left. In my mind, he loved me, too. Now I'm not so sure. He's been hot and cold around me. Then, whatever happened that last night before we came home he never told me about it, and he's only sent that one text. I'm not sure there're enough embers burning between us to give it another chance."

Lola gave me a funny look which made me wonder if she knew something I didn't know.

"Weeelll," she started.

"What?" She had my full attention.

"I'm not supposed to say anything, but I can see this project needs a little push." Her voice had a hint of mystery to it.

"Say about what?"

"He's decided to make some life changes."

"Okay. What kind?"

"Carter made some decisions while he was here to get his life in order."

"What kind of order? You're being too vague."

"I shouldn't be saying anything, but you need to know that you're involved in the changes."

"Me? Why? He doesn't even like me other than to have impromptu sex. You know, like I'm not much different than a groupie?"

"Girl, you are so wrong on that account." She had to be making this up.

"I gave him all the right signals when we were on the bus together. Hell, I even attacked him on the couch and initiated hot sex. He never even mentioned it after we were done. How can you say he's interested in me?"

"I know things." She smiled that devious smile again.

"Then spill. You're driving me crazy."

"I can't."

"What the hell, Lola? You can't start a conversation and leave me hanging like this. Besides, I might not want to be part of those 'things.' He's left me before, remember. I don't know if I trust his man- whore ways. The things I heard about him and Gunner." I stopped and looked at her. Maybe she didn't know about them.

"I know all about their menage days. We don't have any secrets because they almost cost us our relationship in the beginning. Gunner's big on honesty. I failed to disclose some things to him, and he decided to walk away because of it. Once we found our way back to each other, we had a long heart to heart and told each other everything. We vowed to always be open and honest from that point on, and we have."

"Wow, that's great you got all of that out of the way. I doubt Carter cares enough to do that with me. I'm not really sure I want to know all of that anyway."

"Let's just say, those two have been everywhere and done everything. Some things my mind can't unhear but wish it could." The laugh she gave me made me wonder what kinds of things she knew. "Do you think it's even possible you and Carter could have a relationship?"

"I don't know. When we split the first time, he wanted his freedom to explore the world. My heart didn't get it, but my mind did. He was young, about to go on an adventure of a lifetime. Things exploded for them on their first real tour after meeting Chandler's dad. Opportunities other bands only dream of were handed to them on a silver platter.

They deserved it because their music backed their claims, but it all happened so fast."

"That's true. They achieved greatness overnight compared to bands that spend years getting there." We agreed on that completely.

"I suppose now that they've achieved their dreams, he might want me back. I feel like I've been waiting for him my whole adult life when really, I didn't wait around. I've been busy doing what I wanted. Now, he's back, and I'm still here. It makes me look like such a loser."

"No, it doesn't. Maybe your mind knew all along he was the one. Maybe subconsciously, you've been waiting."

"Possibly. I guess I'll have to see how things go now. Our CD is about to be released. I don't know what'll happen then. I'll be gone touring so Carter's time will be his own."

"True. Separate tours will make life hard for y'all."

"Yeah. The temptation for him will be knocking at the bus door every night. I won't stand by for him to answer it if we get back together."

"No, you shouldn't."

The waitress came with our check. Clear skies greeted us outside.

"Don't be a stranger, Halo. I'm here if you need to talk or want to get together. I don't work every day. Oh, and don't mention the info I gave you about Carter. Let him have his day."

"I promise not to spoil whatever it is you didn't mention. You're a devil in disguise."

She smiled. "Call me."

"I will when Cash's through using me up." I hugged her goodbye.

I hadn't forgotten the things she told me. Now she had me guessing what all she didn't say to me. What would he want to plan? Guess we would see soon enough. They'd be home tomorrow.

Chapter Thirty Two

Carter

Waiting until I got home to see the changes in my house made me anxious. I prayed that between Lola and the decorator the transformation would please me. Lola might have been raised globe-hopping, but she knew what a house needed to be a home.

I knew when I drove up changes had been made. They painted the outside to a more pleasing shade with rock and beams added to change the style. I opened the front door and a pleasant fragrance of cookies baking wafted through the opening. Was I at an open house or something? Whatever it was, I loved the smell. I hoped they left me some chocolate chips in the warmer.

"Honey, I'm home." No answer. Dammit. I wanted someone here to greet me. I needed a significant other to make my life feel like I was living and not simply existing between tours.

I walked in, and was immediately overwhelmed with the perfection of it all. A warm feeling wrapped around me. I felt at home. It had a woman's touch everywhere I looked. The blacks and grays were gone, replaced by rich browns, deep reds and a touch of aqua here and there. It looked like Texas but in a place a woman would be happy.

It made me glad they hadn't used whites and frilly stuff. I didn't want it to go to the other extreme either. No one would ever describe whites and lace when talking about me. I texted Lola.

Me: *It's perfect, thanks*
Lola: *So glad. She will think so too*
Me: *Yall come over*
Lola: *This is Gunner. FUCK NO. Go away. Later*

I smiled at his comment. Yeah, he laid right where I needed to be, wrapped in a beautiful woman's arms that I loved.

Loved. Now there's another term no one would use when talking about me. I hadn't loved in such a long time, maybe I don't know how. I loved Halo. I told her in high school I loved her, and I meant it. She meant it, too. I'm the one who fucked it all up. I did the right thing letting her go, but now that time needed to come to a halt. I needed her love again. I would have her love again. She gave it easily to me the last time. I hoped she made me earn it this time around. Maybe my appreciation of her love would be the tie that bound us.

Her phone rang and rolled over to messages.

"Hey, Halo. Uh, this is... this is Carter. I thought if you were home, I might come by and visit. We need to talk. No, I need to talk. If you'll let me. Please." I hung up the phone. It dinged with a text.

Halo: *You can come over if you want*
Me: *I'll be there in twenty. Tell me where.*

I rehearsed all the things that needed to be said as I drove. She needed to know all about my life, or at least everything she wanted to know. Some of the shit I'd seen and done needed to be buried and forgotten. I bet Lola and Gunner discussed some of the same things in the beginning. I'd ask him first chance I had.

I pulled into the complex and found the building. As I walked to the door with her number, my mind replayed all the things I had to say. On the first knock, the door opened. Good, she was waiting on me.

"Hey."

"Yeah, that's what your text said."

"Oh, yeah. I forgot." I took her hand and pulled her to me for a hug. She moved easily into my arms. Damn, I missed this. Her shirt rode up under my hand on her lower back and treated me to warm skin, which made me want to continue sliding upward. I had no right to take such liberties with her body. Not yet anyway.

She pulled back. "Come in and sit down. Want a beer or something?"

"Sure, whatever you're having is fine."

"I'm having white wine, and I know you don't like it. Corona?"

"Yeah, great." We had small talk down.

"Guess you're glad to be home."

"You know it. Being on the road is fun, but being home is always better." I took a hefty drink from the bottle. "Speaking of that. I want us to talk, Halo. I mean really talk."

"What are we doing now, Carter?"

"I think we've been working our way around an elephant in the room since you showed up on the tour. I'm done with that. I want everything out. No more hiding."

"I'm not hiding anything, Carter. I'm sitting right here in the open. You see me. You know who I am."

"Yes, I do, and I want you to know I love what I see."

"Really, because the last time you looked at me, I don't think you saw me. I don't know what you were seeing, but it wasn't me."

"The last time I saw you, things were in a shit storm we tried to keep Hayden out of."

"What are you talking about?" How did Hayden have anything to do with this? He came home that night. Carter didn't.

"I'm glad I get to be the one to tell you so if you're mad, it's at me." He took a deep breath like he didn't want to say what was about to come out. "That night, Hayden found some girls at the after party, and he wanted me to go with the three of them. I couldn't let the kid go alone with these women. We hadn't ever seen them before."

"Uh, huh. Like he's not a big boy?" She smiled. Guess she thought that would help this story out some.

"Yes, no. Anyway. We got in the cab and Hayden and I were pretty wasted. I thought the women were, too. One of the chicks pulled out a fucking bottle of vodka in the cab, and we tipped that bitch back and drank straight from the bottle. I took several healthy gulps because I knew it was going to be a long night from the looks of those two." Damn, I hated telling her this shit. It already sounded bad. "That's pretty much all I remember. We ended up in a hotel room naked in bed together."

"All four of you? Must have been a big bed." She smirked at me.

"Hell no. Just me and Hayden."

"What? Wait, I didn't know you and he were like..." The look on her face told me where her mind went.

"No, no, no. You got it all wrong."

"Oh, really because it sounded like you and Hayden might have had a little M/M action going."

"Fuck no. We did *not!"* I raised my voice and then sat back and took a drink of my beer.

"Look, I woke up and looked around and Hayden was sleeping next to me. Not like touching me or anything. Just in the same bed."

"Okay. This is getting interesting, Carter." She smiled a snarky smile at me. Here I came in thinking she would be pissed off about the women, and she's basically laughing at me.

"Stop. It's not interesting. The whole situation went south quickly, and in the end, it could have been disastrous for Hayden's image. And on top of that, the skanks drugged us." Her expression sobered quickly. His reputation damaged their reputation. Now she's getting it.

"I woke him up, and we only found our pants. No phones, no shirts, no shoes, no wallets. They robbed us, took our lifelines, and left."

"Why didn't you call Peri to come get you?"

"We don't know phone numbers. I had to convince the manager to send someone to the bus to get Peri to come get us. When she arrived, we decided it made sense to get Hayden out of there. We'd been drugged, robbed, left naked. We didn't know what they had on us. We're still waiting to see if any photos surface, but it's been a while so we think they weren't smart enough to take pictures."

"So that explains why Hayden came back and you didn't."

"Exactly. My rep's already tainted with kinky shit from years of it, but Hayden's isn't, and he needs to keep it that way." I didn't take my eyes off her. I tried to judge her reaction to the story. "That's the whole story, Halo. I promise you it's the complete truth. I wanted to be the one to tell you, and I know you'll be quiet about it all because it affects you as well."

She nodded her head. "Right, I understand. Thanks for telling me."

"The thing is, Halo, this is the kind of life I've lived and you're about to live until you can't stand it any longer. I've loved every minute of it but like the others, I'm tired of being alone. I'm tired of the shit that goes along with this life."

"And yet, you choose to stay in it."

"Hell yeah, I love the music side of things. I love being in front of the audience, making music. It's the best life ever. The problem is all of this other shit's part of it. Are you ready to jump into this limelight? Are you ready to be on constant public display? If what Cash says is true, you and Hayden're headed for the big time."

"I love the music, too, Carter, but I'm not so sure about all this other stuff. It's so overwhelming already, and we're not even out there yet." She sat back next to me. I reached for her hand. I didn't want her to think I was making a move on her, but I needed to touch her or offer comfort or do something.

She laid her head on my shoulder and let out the breath she held. Damn, she smelled good, like vanilla, just like always. I kissed the top of her head and moved closer to her. Her warm body next to mine felt perfect pressed into me. She wasn't the young girl I took the virginity from so long ago. Her woman's body had all the right curves and soft places a man could get lost in. But now wasn't the time. I'd take it slow and make sure it was where she wanted to go.

"What are you thinking about, Halo? You're too quiet for you." I looked down at her.

"I'm thinking... what the hell have I gotten myself into?"

"Nothing yet, really. The thing is you and Hayden are on the edge. You can take the leap and fall into stardom where life quickly gets real. You'll be wined, dined, and put on display for the world. Everyone'll want a piece of you, literally and physically. There're so many fake people out there who'll want to use you for your name. Hell, the guys'll be in line to fuck you in every way possible, and that's literally and physically, too."

She laughed. "I'm not you, Carter. I'm not the rock god on stage making the women cream their panties with a smoldering look or a kiss blown their way."

"No, you're a beautiful woman who doesn't know the power she holds in her voice, her gorgeous face, her smokin' hot body when you twist and turn, and a perfect ass when you shake it. You'll have men kneeling in your presence for any crumb you throw at them." The look she gave me made me understand exactly how much she didn't believe what I said even though it was the absolute truth.

"Really, Carter. I think you're exaggerating a little bit."

"Like hell I am, Halo. I know what I'm talking about. I've lived it already, and you and Hayden'll live it, too."

Her laugh seemed forced. "I'm nothing like Chandler."

"Yes, you are. You're every bit as beautiful as her and you sing like an angel. Now your guitar skills are not quite hers, but…" She poked me in the side.

"I had a good teacher, remember?"

"I remember a lot of things, but I'm not sure you want to take a walk down that road tonight, do you?" My eyes narrowed as I looked at her. I'd love nothing more than to push her back on this couch and make sweet love her, but I didn't think we needed to go there tonight.

"You're right, Carter. Maybe we need to take another path this time around. A path adults would take instead of two horny teenagers."

"I don't know. Now that you say it, I kinda like that horny teenage route. It was hot when we were young."

"Yeah, but we aren't those kids any longer."

"You're right. We're full-grown consenting adults this time around. No sneaking around or no hiding from parents."

"Yes, and now we need to do the adult thing and be responsible."

"Shit, I hate responsible." I turned my lips up to a smile. "So I guess the adult thing to do is walk to the door, kiss you goodnight, and go home to an empty bed praying that I'll get lucky next time around."

"No. That's not what you're going to do."

Now she's talking. "Oh really?"

"We aren't through talking."

Dammit. I thought I'd said enough.

"What do you want to talk about?" I asked her.

"When you left me behind, did you ever think or wonder about me?"

Not what I wanted to talk about at all. "Yes, Halo. I thought about you a lot in the beginning. I told you I loved you, and I meant it."

"But you left without even looking back. You never tried to contact me."

"No, I didn't, and I did it on purpose. I knew what my life would become, and I couldn't do that to you. You were too perfect to ruin with the shit we did. Dragging you through the mud I slept in held all kinds of repercussions and none of them good for you. Hell, they weren't even good for me."

"Oh poor boy. You look like you've come out scarred for life."

If she only knew the things I'd seen and done. "You don't even want to know, sweets."

"You're probably right about that. Were there ever any long-term women?" She needed honesty, and I'd give it to her.

"No. None. We were never in the same spot long enough to find one."

"Gunner did."

"They didn't make a go of it until she moved to Austin. It's still hard on them now with them living apart so much because of the tours."

"I had lunch with her. She seems pretty happy but wants more."

"Yeah, and so does Gunner."

"I think she's going to join the band on tour next time."

"Great that'll make him happy when she tells him and when she follows through." So Gunner would have his woman. Ryan and Peri had their own little home on wheels—Tucker and a new one on the way. Chan and KeeMac impending wedding was on the horizon and will be on the bus together. Where does that leave me? Shit. Thinking this through made me sick.

Halo looked at me. "To me it sounds like everything for most of AD's getting tied up with a nice little bow. Except for you, that is."

"Yeah, you're right. We'll see. Anyway, are you through with the questions for me because I want this behind us?"

"I just have one more for you." She pulled away and looked directly at me. "Where do we stand, Carter? We've had some amazing sex, but that's all we've had. We knew the sex would be good, but there's more to life than sex."

"Wait, I'm still at 'we had some amazing sex.' You thought I was amazing?" I smirked.

"Shut up, dumbass. I'm trying to be serious."

"I know, sorry. You're right. We've gotta have more than just sex. We can have more. I want to have more, which is why I'm in the process of making changes."

"What kind of changes?"

"I want you to come to my house, so I can show you."

"Okay, I can do that."

"No, I mean right now."

We exchanged very few words as we rode to my house. I needed time to think about how I wanted to play this. She'd asked me point blank about us. I should've been prepared. We were being honest and that question was right at the top of the list. What did I want out of a relationship with her? I told her how I felt. I wanted us to be more than fuck buddies. Right now that's not even an option in my mind, and I doubted hers either.

I stopped the truck and ran around to open her door. I had something to prove and now I needed to step up and do it. I could be a "boyfriend." I had skills, didn't I? I helped her down out of the truck, and we walked to the door holding hands. This was nice. It's been a long time since I thought of a woman for something other than sex.

Containing my excitement made me act kind of childish, but I didn't care right then. I wanted her to see the improvements as perfect.

"I started here." I turned the key in the lock. It didn't sound as ominous as the last time I turned this key.

"Wow, it's beautiful, Carter. Not what I expected at all. It's so homey."

"I know, right? I wanted a house that felt like someplace people actually wanted to live instead of doctors' office cold. Although I could be convinced to play doctor sometime." The minute it left my mouth, I knew it was wrong. She turned and glared at me, and then she smiled.

"Playing doctor doesn't sound all that bad to me either but later." She wiggled her eyebrows.

"Right. Uh. We'll save that for another time then." I'd be more than happy to throw her down and do a thorough examination, but I doubted she meant at that minute. "So this is the living area." I pointed to the other side where the wall had been taken out so the kitchen flowed into it. "And that's my new kitchen."

"I love the colors you chose. They're masculine without being overly manly." Good. I hoped for this reaction even though I didn't choose any of this. The décor pleased me, and the fact she liked it made it even better.

"So what do you think? Is it a kitchen you could see yourself cooking in?"

Her head whipped around so fast I thought she might hurt her neck. "I don't know about that. What about you? Could you see yourself cooking here?"

"Absolutely, if I knew how, that is. I'm really more of a heat and eat or takeout kind of cook."

"Then we should look at lessons because so am I." I busted out laughing. I doubted we'd starve, but neither of us being able to cook amused me.

"Lessons it is then. We could have some fun learning to cook together. You know like a date-type thing that lasted over several weeks. Then we could come here and practice what we learned."

"True. Practicing always works."

"Right, and I like to practice, over and over until I get it right." I gave her my best-dimpled look, and she laughed.

"Get your mind out of the gutter, Carter." She poked me in the stomach.

"Yeah, okay. Kill the moment." I loved having an easy way between us. The constant need to say and do the right thing didn't exist when only the two of us were together. The two of us needed no feigned behavior. Being ourselves came naturally.

We toured the rest of the house so I could show off the improvements, some I hadn't even seen myself. Her reactions satisfied my decision to bring her here, and my desire for her approval grew room by room.

"Your home is beautiful. It's nothing like what I thought your taste would be."

"Yeah? Why's that? What were you thinking?" I asked even though I knew where she was headed.

"You surprise me, that's all. I figured it'd be more bachelor like, very sleek and modern with lots of black and steel. Honestly, I'm glad it's not. I hate that look. It's cold and impersonal. This style makes it seem like a home, not a place to throw wild parties or entertain women."

"What makes you think that's all I do? I wanted it to look like a home."

God, have I always been so predictable? This was exactly why I needed to make changes. I felt like such a douche. I know that's what she thought, too.

"Come on Carter. Paparazzi loves you. You make their lives easy."

"That's harsh, Halo. Harsh." I don't know why I'm even arguing with her about this because she's right. My shit's all over the internet. At some point over these past years, I took pride in giving them what they wanted. Seeing it through her eyes, I'm disgusted with myself. No wonder she feels about me the way she does.

"I'm sorry. I didn't mean to upset you, but you have to know this. You can't pick up a tabloid or go to a media site without seeing something that exemplifies your life."

I scratched the back of my head. "Yeah, I guess I can't argue that, can I?"

She shook her head no. We wandered back to the living area and sat down. I didn't know how to continue the evening. No matter what I did would seem wrong.

The silence grew awkward for both of us. I finally stood. "Hey, I'm not a good host at all. You want something to drink? I think I could use one." The wet bar stocked everything anyone could request.

"No, I'm good. You can take me home if you want." She sensed my uneasiness.

"What? No, I'm not ready for you to leave. I wanted to bring you here so I could share the real me with you. I'm not the same guy, Halo." I sat beside her. "I'm different from the kid you loved in high school."

"Oh yeah, I got that the first day." Her sarcastic tone let me know she remembered that Carter just fine.

"Yeah, but now, I don't want to be the guy you read about or saw online. I want to be a better man, Halo."

"Why Carter? Aren't you happy being that guy? Why change now?" She looked me straight in the eyes. Maybe she wanted to judge the truthfulness of my answer.

I blew out a breath. "You cut straight to the heart every time, Halo."

"I've always wanted honesty from you. We may be older, but there are some things about neither of us that will ever change and that's one of them for me."

"Right. I should've never doubted that."

"You didn't answer me. Why now Carter?"

Oh, man. I'm scared shitless. How's she going to react to the truth?

"Okay, but remember you asked for this so try to have an open mind."

We faced each other, and I took her hands as I said it. I needed some connection before I spilled the truth to her.

"I'm tired, Halo. Tired of being that guy. Tired of jumping from one bed to another, one woman to another. I want something more permanent in my life. Something lasting. I want us to give *us* another chance. We were in love before." Her eyes grew wider as each word passed my lips.

"I suppose some of me has kept what we had locked away since that day before I left. You straightened your backbone and stood up to me, but the look you left me with killed me. I hated myself at that moment, but the pride I felt for you right then, I never forgot. You were much stronger than me. I wanted to run after you and beg you to forget what I'd said. I watched you walk away thinking you'd be there the next morning to see me off.

"When you didn't show, I knew you did the right thing for you and for us. I guess I've been spending these years searching for what I didn't see standing right in front of me, a strong, beautiful woman who knew her own mind."

"That's bullshit, Carter."

Wow, not the reaction I thought I would get for pouring out my heart.

"You made the decision without even giving us a chance to try. It couldn't have hurt me any worse if you'd taken a knife and stabbed me in the heart and walked away. No, scratch that, you did stab me in the heart. I bled for months but somehow the wound healed, and I moved on."

We stared at each other, neither of us knowing where to go from here. It wasn't declarations of love but we did share honest and true emotions to each other. This could be a start.

"So, where do we go from here, Halo?"

"Nowhere, Carter. How can we? Our lives are not any different now than they were eight years ago. You're still in the band, and I've added another layer of complications by forming one, too. If anything, it's worse than before." She pulled her hands away and stood up. "I think you need to take me home."

"No."

"No?"

"No, I'm not taking you home. We aren't walking away this time. Together we can make this decision. Not you and not me, us."

"Seems like the decision is made, Carter. You'll go on with AD, and Hayden and I will do our own thing. Sometimes our paths will cross and sometimes they won't." She pulled her phone out.

"What are you doing?"

"Sending for an Uber. I'm going home."

"Please, no. Let's talk about this." She looked at me and the sadness in her eyes said it all. She wasn't willing to try. She didn't want to open herself up to the pain and heartache I could cause. What she didn't realize is that now she held the same option in her hands. Her actions could destroy me. Seeing her with another man would kill me. I want her.

"It's here already," she said as she turned to the door. I stood and watched her walk out. Once again, I wanted more time, and she didn't give it to me. Only this time, I knew I was the loser.

"Fuck, fuck, fuck," I said it loud and clear in the empty room. Without her here, I once again heard the echo. How could I fix this?

Halo

"Wait, Halo," Hayden called to me. "You're still coming in on the wrong notes. Where are you today? We need to get this nailed down."

"I know, sorry. I can't seem to get my head wrapped around the music today." Yeah, my brain exploded last night. I wanted Carter, badly. I couldn't do it, though. I would never allow him to hurt me again so at this point all we had was sex. We were good at that.

"So want to talk about what's going on?" Hayden's caring look made it even worse.

Tears welled in my eyes. "No, I just need to get my shit together."

"Looks like it's more than that to me." Why did he have to be nice? He needed to be a mean old bastard and treat me like dirt. Hating him would make it all easy. I could walk away and let him move on to success without me. He didn't need me to be successful. His country music career would escalate without me on board.

I finally looked at him. "I just have some stupid shit going on that's causing me to stress out. I'm fine. Let's try again."

His phone sounded like the something out of *Jungle Book*. "That's Crew's ringtone." He pulled it out and touched accept.

"Hey, little dude, what's up?" I looked down at the music to try to get my mind on what I needed to do to make this right.

"No, no. I'll be there. Call an ambulance now. No, now," he screamed into the phone. He dropped his guitar and took off with me chasing him.

"What's going on?"

"Gotta get to Crew. Either go or stay." We were in his truck, and I barely got my door shut before he floored the gas pedal. I buckled up and held on. I didn't dare try to ask questions. Hayden flew around corners, ran stop signs, and treated red lights like blinking lights. I did text Peri though thinking she might know what was happening, but she didn't reply right away.

The ambulance pulled into the driveway just ahead of us and the paramedics ran with bags over their shoulders in the opened door with the nanny standing there waiting. I prayed Crew was okay, but I didn't know. Maybe he just fell down or something. Kids got hurt all the time. So many different scenarios ran through my mind. Looking through the back windows, I saw they had a pool.

"Oh please let him be okay, God. Please," I whispered.

Crew laid lifeless on the couch which caused my anxiety to shoot up immediately. The blue around his lips made it even worse. I stood back and watched in horror as the paramedics quickly started on him. Hayden kneeled beside his lifeless little body and spoke calmly to him. He didn't get any response out of Crew. I knew Hayden had to be scared to death because I certainly was. I heard a noise and looked over to see the nanny crying softly watching the paramedics work.

I moved next to her and wrapped my arm around her shoulders. When she finally took her eyes off Crew, I gave her a brief smile but never got one in return.

"What happened, Nanny?"

"I don't really know. He played outside this morning, and I went in and out checking on him like I have done for months now. Hayden told me not to hover over him, so I usually sat inside where I could see him. I made his lunch, and I called out to him to come in to eat. When he didn't answer, I went out and he stood on the patio with the strangest look on his face. I noticed him coughing a little earlier, but didn't think too much about it. He came in and laid down on the couch still coughing so I went over to him. When I got a good look at his face, I knew immediately something was wrong. His little lips were turning blue. He was barely breathing when I called his dad and then 911."

She let out a sob. "I should have been out there with him the whole time. I don't like leaving them alone outside, but his dad said it would be fine."

"He's never had trouble before, right?"

"No, never. I have noticed in the last week him coughing some but nothing to worry about really. He's outside all the time with Tucker. With Tuck gone, though, he had to entertain himself today." She sniffled again.

As soon as the paramedics had him stable under a mask, they loaded him in the ambulance and left. Hayden climbed right in with them so I followed in his truck with the nanny. She cried all the way there telling me how sorry she was this happened.

"I'm sure it's nothing you did, Nanny. Let's hear what the doctor has to say." She nodded her head, but I knew she worried all the same.

They rolled Crew in, and he looked better from what little I could see. He was trying to talk to his dad.

"Be quiet, little dude. Let the people do their jobs," Hayden told him.

"I'm sleepy, Daddy," Crew spoke from behind the mask. "I don't get to sleep until I have my lunch, but I don't want to eat today."

"It's okay, son. If the doctor says you can sleep, you can skip lunch today." Hayden looked at the doctor who nodded. Hayden bent and kissed Crew on the forehead before the boy closed his eyes and slept. The group disappeared into a room, so I took Nanny to the lobby to wait.

An hour later, I'd had enough waiting. No one came out to tell us a thing so I started asking questions. The people behind the admissions desk wouldn't tell me anything since I wasn't related, so I shot Hayden a text. I looked up a minute later, and he stood at the door and let me in with him.

"What's going on Hayden? We've been worried to death out here."

"I'm sorry. I hated to leave him alone in there in case he woke up. The nurse is with him right now."

We stepped behind the curtain, and the sweetest face looked up at us smiling. I turned to Hayden. "You have to go get Nanny, too. She's made herself sick with worry."

"Shit, I forgot about her waiting out there, too." He left, and I walked beside Crew's bed.

"Hey there, little guy."

"Hi." His voice sounded hoarse. "I been sick."

"I see that, but you're getting better now, right?"

"Yeah, I feel funny, though." He turned his head away from me but looked back as the curtain opened with Hayden and Nanny coming in the small room.

"Oh, Crew, baby. You had me worried to death." Nanny's white hair shone from the lights above the boy's bed as she bent over to hug him.

"I'm okay, Nanny. I just couldn't take a breath."

Hayden and I stepped to the edge of the room to talk. "So what happened to him?" I asked.

"I don't know yet. I'm trying to let him calm down from all of it. The doctor said it looks like an asthma attack, but he's never had one before so I don't know how it happened. God, Halo, I can't tell you how scared I was. When I saw him lying on that couch so still and blue around the lips, it scared the shit out of me." Tears formed in his eyes. "I thought I was going to lose him."

I wrapped Hayden in my arms and held on. His love for that boy ran deep, and I knew his nerves were on the edge of breaking. He hugged me tight until he heard Crew give a small laugh. We turned and looked at him.

"Daddy, you need to hug me, not her. She's a girl."

"Dude, are you jealous of Miss Halo? She's my friend."

"But girls are gross. Me and Tucker don't like girls, except RiRi and Channey and Nanny. That's the only girls we like."

I smiled at Hayden as he spoke to his son. "Well, you have to learn to like Miss Halo, too. You know I need her. She's my singing partner, buddy."

"Okay, if you need her, I guess she's all right." He gifted me with a sweet smile.

Hayden sat down and pulled the chair up close to the side of the hospital bed. "Crew, dude, we need to talk a little bit about what happened to you." Crew's face scrunched up, and he turned his head away.

"I'm sorry, Daddy. I didn't mean to get sick."

"No, you have nothing to be sorry for, buddy. Getting sick is part of growing up, but sometimes we need to know what might've caused you to get sick so it doesn't happen again. The doctor said something could have started it, and that's what we have to figure out."

"Yeah, it was scary to me when I couldn't breathe. I couldn't breathe in a lot of air. It hurt me right here." He pointed to his chest. "And right here." He pointed down his throat.

"Right. We don't want you to hurt any place, and we sure want you to breathe." Hayden took Crew's hand. "So before you hurt, what were you doing? Were you playing in the dirt?"

"No. I didn't play in the dirt today." He wouldn't look at Hayden. I knew whatever he was doing must have been something he wasn't supposed to be doing.

“But you didn’t say what you were doing. Just tell me, Crew. You’re not in trouble,” Hayden assured the boy.

“Well, me and Tuck have a secret, and I’m not posed to tell.”

“Some secrets you can share if it means keeping you safe, though, and I know you wouldn’t want to let Tucker be unsafe and get hurt like you did.”

The little guy shook his head no. “I wouldn’t like Tucker to get hurt. It was scary, Daddy when I couldn’t get air.”

“So tell me what your secret is, and we’ll make sure no one gets hurt again,” Hayden spoke in soft tones to try to persuade the boy.

“Me and Tucker found something, and we want to keep it but you and RiRi might not like it.”

“It doesn’t matter if we like it. We only want to keep you both safe.” As hard as Hayden tried, his aggravated tone finally slipped in.

“Promise not to be mad at me and Tuck, Daddy?” His bottom lip quivered ever so slightly.

“Dude, I promise no matter what you say, I will not be mad at you for telling the truth. Not ever.” These kinds of comments built lasting honesty between the father and son, even if Hayden didn’t realize it yet.

Hayden squeezed the boy’s hand, and Crew finally spoke. “Me and Tucker found a kitten.” He spoke rapidly. “It’s really soft and its fur is yellow.” Using his hands, he formed a little small shape. “And Daddy, it’s a tiny kitty that makes a little meow like, ‘meeeooowww.’ We took some milk to it and it drank a bunch, and then it curled up in the towel we got from the towels in the laundry room so we left it behind the pool room, and it was warm and furry and soft."

Whew, so many words poured out of him at once, I had to smile. He looked so cute telling the story.

"Did you hold the kitten, Crew?" Hayden asked him.

"Yes, sir. We both held him the other day but today, Tucker's with his mom and dad so I got to hold it all by myself. I put it in my lap, and it crawled up under my neck, and I let it stay there. It was soft and warm and made a ddd noise when I scratched its head." He finally put his head down. "Can we keep it please, Daddy? If RiRi says it's okay, can we please? We've never had a cat. Can we please?"

"Crew, I know you'd love to have it, but I'm afraid that's what made you sick. The doctor asked me if we had a cat, and I told him no. He said that cats can sometimes set off what happened to you, so if we keep the kitty, it will make you sick again."

Tears rolled down his face. "Okay, Daddy. I don't want to not have air in my mouth, but what's going to happen to the kitty? It won't have any food if we don't help it. It'll get sick, too."

"No, we'll find it a new home where it won't make anyone sick. How about that? If I promise we'll find it a home, will you be all right with that?"

Crew nodded his head. "Yes, sir. Can I tell it bye, or will that make me sick again?"

"Yeah, I'm afraid it might cause you to not breathe again. Maybe you can wave at it through the car window. How about that?"

"Okay. If that's all I can do, I'll wave bye to it."

Halo

Hayden and I walked out leaving Nanny talking to Crew about the kitten.

"I'm glad you found out the cause of his problem so easily," I told Hayden.

"Yeah, now we have to find the cat and take it to a rescue place. I never thought about him finding a cat. It must've wandered away from someone's house around ours. I'll put the word out and see if it's one of the neighbors' but it has to go today. If it's a neighbor's cat, they'll have to keep it inside. We can't have Crew having an asthma attack from the kitten every time it gets away."

"No, I don't think you want to get that phone call again." When we rounded the corner, the waiting room was full. The band family all stood and sat in the small space.

"There you are. Those people at the desk wouldn't let us go back there. Said there were too many people already,"

Ryan told Hayden. “Peri was ready to take the nurse on, and we can’t have that. How is he?”

“He’s fine now, and we know what caused it, too.”

“What’s wrong?” Peri asked.

“He had an asthma attack caused by holding a kitten that the boys have been keeping behind the pool room.”

“What? Where did they find a kitten?” Peri couldn’t believe what I’d said.

“Who knows, but it’s living in a towel behind the pool room and apparently the boys have been feeding it milk.” Hayden gave them the rest of the news.

Ryan spoke up. “But Crew’s going to be okay?”

“Yeah, he’ll be fine and now that we know he’s allergic to cats, we know not to get one for the kids.”

“I’m kinda partial to dogs myself, anyway,” Ryan said with a smile.

“We’ll have to see about that. He might be allergic to those, too.” Hayden didn’t want to discuss pets of any kind right then from his tone.

“Right. No pets with any kind of fur. How does a fish sound?” Peri asked.

“Fish sounds good to me. They’re going to let him go in a little while so thanks for coming guys, but I think you can all go home now,” Hayden told the group.

“That’s great news, Hayden,” Carter spoke up. “Want me to give you a ride, Halo?”

I looked at him. Was he serious? We had this conversation already. We need to leave each other alone. “Uh, I think KeeMac and Chandler are taking me.” I hadn’t asked them, but I knew they would.

"Sorry, we were all riding the Harleys so we came straight here," Chandler told me. I looked at Gunner, and he shook his head.

"My bike only holds one person. Sorry, but I can call you a cab."

"No, that's fine. Carter can drop me off." I looked at him, and he got a huge smile on his face. We waited around a little longer until they released Crew. He, Nanny and Hayden crawled into his truck and sped away for home. The others climbed on their bikes and took off, too, leaving Carter and me standing there.

"You ready?" he asked.

"I suppose. You need to take me to the studio. That's where we were when Nanny called." It wasn't too far away from the hospital, thank God.

"Sure thing," he said. "My car's right over there." He pointed to this classic antique looking race car. I had no idea what it was, but I loved it so much that I ran over to it.

"Oh my God, Carter. What is this thing? I love it?"

"It's a 1965 Roush Shelby Cobra. She's a beauty, isn't she?"

"Oh. My. God. I fucking love it. Does it go fast?"

"Fast enough. Climb in." He opened the door for me. This car screamed fast and sexy to me. Yes, definitely sexy.

"What do you call her?" I asked him. Cars like this had to have a sexy name.

He smirked at me. "Lo."

"Lo? That's weird."

"Well, Hey didn't work for me so I went with Lo. So like, Hey Lo where do you want to ride today? Get it?" No smirk this time. He laughed out loud.

"You did not just say that?"

"Yes, as a matter of fact, I did, and that's exactly what I call her. Lo, so get over it."

I ran my hand over the sleek fender and across the dashboard admiring the curve in front of the driver while he rounded the front of it watching me. He stepped in and looked at me. "You need to buckle up, sweets. We're going for a ride, and it'll be fast and hard." Sex oozed from his mouth as he said it, but I didn't care. This car was made for speed and sex.

We drove out to the winding roads leading to Lake Travis. The car's performance as it hugged the pavement thrilled me. She took curves like she was designed for. Carter knew exactly what he was doing when he accelerated her into them. I loved the feel of the power under me as she hummed. The feel of her engine roared my libido to life. I throbbed at the sheer rumble she emitted.

God, this ride might lead to another.

Wait, I'm done with him. I'm supposed to be mad, but how can I be mad and ride this bad girl? Her open top liberated all the anger from me for now. I held my arms up as we took a curve and a dip in the road at the same time. My stomach did that funny thing only a dip can cause, and I loved every minute of the ride. I began to laugh as the lurching feeling subsided. How could I possibly stay angry? I think he had me at Cobra.

We finally came to a crawl when he entered Pale Face Park. We'd been here a million times as teenagers. He drove down to the lakeside and stopped. It was dusk, and the park had emptied out long before we arrived. He walked around the car and opened my side offering his hand to help me out of the low-slung vehicle. When he closed the door behind me, he trapped me between his and her hard bodies.

"Did you like that, Halo?" I could feel him growing behind the tightness of his jeans. The ride had obviously gotten to him as well.

"Yeah, Carter. Hmm, maybe as much as you."

"It doesn't happen every time, but yeah sometimes the thrill of the drive does get my engine going." He forced my legs apart with his foot and stepped between my legs in search of warmer parts of me. My senses were on edge already, and the closeness made it difficult to not push back against him. Hell, I wanted to push back against him. I wanted to strip him down and take advantage of him right here.

"You look a little flushed in the face, Halo." The way he rolled my name off his lips with such an erotic vibration to it, my breathing increased simply hearing him say it. "Did the ride do it for you?"

I nodded before I wrapped my hands behind his neck and pulled him down for a kiss. I wanted a real kiss that added to the fire down below, but he didn't allow it. Moving back from my lips, he kissed the corners of my mouth in a slow sweet fondle before moving across my jaw dropping light kisses and nibbles. He reached my ear and nosed his way across it before licking the outer edge from top to bottom where he took my lobe between his teeth. His bite was more like a clip as he slid his teeth down and off the edge in a slow caress.

When he returned to my lips this time, he launched an all-out assault on them. His tongue breached my lips and began a dance with my own to set me on fire for him. By the time he backed away, pulling my lower lip with him, I melted against him hanging on for dear life.

"What are we doing, Carter?" I pleaded.

"Shhh. We're two adults enjoying the moment, sweets. Don't think, Halo. Just feel." He put his hands under my ass and lifted me, pulling my legs around him. Picking me up, he made his way to the front of the sleek blue hood where he sat me down on the wide white stripe dividing her hood into perfect sections.

"Lay back, sweets, so I can make love to you while Lo provides you with her hard body for support." I laid back while Carter peeled my skinny jeans and satin panties down my legs. My shoes were long forgotten on Lo's floorboard. I stripped my tank top over my head and threw it over the small windshield.

My bare skin cooled quickly to the touch of Lo's cold hard steel. The smoothness of her body from years of waxing added a sexy feel to her as I slipped and slid around on her, loving the way it felt on my bare skin. Carter wrapped his hands around my ankles and moved them up on the hood, sliding me further up to her windshield so I could rest my head while I watched him feast on my body. Leaning over, he placed his hands on my knees and peeled them apart while inching down my inner thighs, opening me for all the world to see knowing he was the only lucky one.

His darkened eyes held mine while he kissed one thigh and then the other following his decent to the prize he sought. The final wet kiss, landing at the seam between my legs and the swollen bud that screamed a silent cry for attention, caused a loud moan of desire to bubble up from deep within me and escape without any thought to another human hearing.

"Like that, do you?" he questioned hovering over my needy pussy, and then his flattened tongue started its slow ascent from my opening to the top. By the time he reached above the bundle of nerves that wanted attention so badly, I bucked straight up on Lo's hood. His hand started where his tongue stopped and grazed my skin all the way to my throat pushing me back down.

"She'll like it better if you'll just lay back and enjoy the ride, Halo." His fingers found my left breast and squeezed the nipple, tugging, and turning. The pleasured pain it caused shot straight to my core where liquid gathered in anticipation of racing to the finish when he raced into the passage.

"Fuck what she'll enjoy. The sensations on this hood and your lips and fingers are almost too much."

He smiled at me this time. "I want you to love every minute."

Like he thought I wouldn't?

His mouth kissed a trail from my navel back to my slit where he spread me open and used his warm tongue to circle my clit and then draw a line down to my opening and back up to my clit again. He did this several times causing me to writhe around on the hood. It would have still been slippery, but now a fine sheen of sweat formed on my skin caused by the sensations his mouth and tongue treated me to.

When I didn't think I could take much more, he slipped a finger inside me so slowly I thought I'd die from the pure pleasure it offered.

"*Oh my God*, Carter," I screamed when it was fully seated in the perfect spot to curl upward and graze across the roughened patch at the same time he sucked down on my clit. As I came hard, he added another finger pumping in and out across the perfect internal spot causing the orgasm to go on and on. He finally stopped and pulled his fingers free from where my walls convulsed around them trying to swallow the digits further inside.

Slowly I caught my breath and looked up to see him staring at me. "That good, huh?"

"You know it was. You've obviously learned a lot of good techniques." I closed my eyes again and concentrated on sucking air in and breathing it out to calm my body and mind.

"Oh, sweets, we are just getting started on the tricks I'm going to treat you to, but right now I need to be buried deep inside you. It was all I could do to let you recover. This time when I enter this sweet spot..." he kissed me on the lips protecting my clit, "... you'll know it's me and never forget who this has always belonged to."

He pulled a condom from his billfold and threw it on my stomach. "Don't want it sliding off Lo's curves." He winked at me and made quick work of getting his jeans off where his dick popped from to stand at attention.

"Commando?" I grinned at him.

"Waste of time and one more layer between us. I don't want layers between us, sweets." He gave me a solemn look, and I knew he meant much more by that statement than what the words conveyed.

Leaning forward, he kissed me slow and easy but when I wrapped my legs around his back, his tongue went deeper into my mouth and mimicked exactly what his unsheathed cock waited impatiently to have a chance at. Taking his full length in hand, he reached my slit and moved from my clit to my back entry purposely skipping my wet entrance each time. I wanted to swallow him up as he passed over or slid around but he was having none of it yet.

He broke the kiss and looked down at me. "You are so beautiful, Halo. The sight you make lying out on my car, frantic with a growing anticipation in those violet eyes, makes me want to speed into you. I know I could get lost every fucking time you catch me looking in them."

"Yes, but right now, there's another location I would love for you to get lost in and never find your way out."

He smiled at me and rose up to grab the packet, opening it with his teeth so he could torture me some more with the smooth head of his swollen cock. He stood and rolled it on himself, made a slow ride through the valley once again, and finally drove it home without using the brakes. After the first few frantic times, he stood and grabbed my thighs to anchor himself so he could propel his body forward burying himself in my warmth.

He pulled my legs up higher almost bending me in half but the angle it provided hit the spot I needed to speed home once again.

"Carter," my voice started with a low rumble as I felt my desire building to another climax. "Carter," I said again, this time in a muffled sound as I bucked up toward him. "*Carter*," I screamed as I came hard again, but he roared to life and raced faster and faster until he emptied himself finally rolling to a stop.

"Damn, Halo." He pulled my legs down and laid over on my chest resting himself in my arms.

"Yeah, what you said." I closed my eyes knowing I could sleep wrapped around him all night long.

We had a quiet ride home. He held my hand even to shift the Cobra. The sweet gesture kept the connection until we reached the outskirts of the city. He stopped at a red light and looked over at me. "Sweets, where do you want to go tonight, my house or home?"

"Where do you want me to go, Carter?"

He pulled my hand to his lips and softly kissed the palm. "I want you with me, but I'll understand if you don't."

"I feel the same way. I'm at a loss as to what we can do or have, Carter. I want you. I think you know that."

"Yeah, and you know I want us to be together, but can we make this work? Do you want to make this work?"

"Part of me says yes, we can do this but the realistic side says, we'll spend more time apart than together. I don't want to have a part-time boyfriend."

"And I don't want to be one. Like I said, I want to be an us." He drove slowly until we were forced to make a choice on where I was going.

"Please come home with me, sweets. I need you." The smoldering look in his eyes said everything I felt so I nodded my consent.

Carter

Halo went to the studio hoping the two of them could pick up where they left off. We talked about whether Hayden could leave Crew with Nanny today, but the music waited on them so she decided to go in and continue.

I called her around noon thinking we could grab some lunch. "Did Hayden make it in?"

"No, he finally texted and said he didn't want to leave his son, and I told him I understood."

"Yeah, I'm sure it's hard on him."

"Why don't you bring me some lunch? I'll promise you a reward." Now, this flirty Halo was one I liked.

"Sure, but do I get to pick my reward?"

"No, but I'm sure you'll like it." She dropped her voice an octave. "I will do something very special for you."

Shit, how could I say no to that? "I'm on my way."

The next day when Hayden didn't show again, I knew Halo worried how this was going to play out for them. I decided to go in with her and see what more the two of us could do.

"Not here again?" Cash stuck his head in seeing us sitting with our guitars.

"No, I guess he's scared to leave him yet," Halo told him.

Cash came in and sat down with us. "I get it. I really do so this is going to sound callous, but we need to get this CD finished and ready to release. Do you think he would consider bringing Crew with him here?"

"I don't know, maybe. We'd have to ask him." Halo looked at me when she said it. I knew Cash's comments made her uncomfortable.

"What are you doing up here again, Carter. You're on a break from music remember?"

"I know, but I figured if Hayden couldn't get in again today, maybe I'd sit in and work on the songs with Halo until he could get his head back in the game."

"That's a good idea, but we need Hayden." Cash's tone verified the anger he refused to acknowledge.

"It's okay, Cash. Carter and I did some work a few days ago, and it turned out great. It was on some music Hayden and I were fighting with. Maybe the two of us can get it finished."

He rubbed the back of his neck and finally nodded, leaving the room without saying any more.

"I get that he's pissed, but what's Hayden supposed to do? Crew-man has to come first," Carter said after the door closed.

"I know, but I don't know how to help Hayden. We need to get this done since Cash has already started lining up the next tour."

"Yeah, I bet Hayden's even more worried about that. The way the two kids come and go on the tours and now with the two of y'all going in different directions than AD, it'll only make it harder on Hayden."

"I thought that, too."

Carter surprised me with a fresh new sound he added to the music. We always sounded good together before, but he chose to move on to the bass when he had the opportunity to play with AD. Being back together again, we were able to write and add to what Hayden and I had started.

At the end of the day, we both felt satisfied with the progress we'd made and hoped Hayden would be on board with the changes.

"Let's go get something to eat," Carter suggested about the same time my phone rang.

"It's Hayden." I answered it. I looked at Carter when I ended the call.

"He wants us to come by. I told him we'd pick up dinner for us all."

"Has Ryan's bunch come back from Colorado yet?" The three of them had taken a short vacation since they wouldn't be able to travel together when Peri started getting closer to her due date.

"No, not yet. So we only need it for Hayden, Crew, and Nanny."

We picked up barbeque for everyone. Crew loved it so we knew he would eat.

We visited and went over the new music. Hayden didn't seem interested in anything but tending to his son. I supposed if he were mine, I would feel the same way.

Nanny finally announced it was time to put Crew to bed so we stood to leave.

"No, guys," Hayden started. "Y'all stay so we can talk."

We sat back down and looked at each other. This didn't sound good, but we hoped maybe he had made some decisions.

When he returned, he sat down and looked at both of us. I had a bad feeling about where this was going.

"I'm glad y'all came out tonight."

"Yeah, we are, too. I've been wanting to see the Crew-man," I told him. "I'm glad to see him getting better each day."

"The doctor said he'll be fine, but no more cats. I think we made Crew understand why he can't have them. The whole thing scared him pretty badly so I doubt we'll have to remind him."

"I think it scared everyone," Halo told him.

"You just don't know the feeling that came over me when Nanny called and said he couldn't breathe. Scared the shit out of me." Halo and I both nodded. "That's why I wanted y'all to stay. I have something I need to tell you. Well, really just Halo."

The hairs on the back of my neck stood up. This was going to be bad. I knew it already.

"Halo, I've had a lot of time to think about my life with this situation. I thought my heart would explode on our way to the house after we got that call. After it all settled down, all I could think about was what if I'd been out on the road and Crew was here with Peri or Nanny. I might be thousands of miles away or worse, what if we get the chance to go overseas?"

I looked at Halo when she tried to talk. "But Hayden."

He held up his hand. "No, wait. Let me finish, please."

"Okay," she said.

"I can't do it, Halo. I can't leave him. He's only got me. What if I can't be there in an emergency? I can't do it, so I've decided to talk to Cash about getting out. I know I can be a studio musician and continue to write songs. I don't want to hold you back because God knows you're good, so you'd continue but as a solo act. We could finish the CD and market it as yours, not ours. I'm willing to give that up so I can stay here with Crew."

Shocked. That's the only way I could describe it. He wanted to give up a chance at a music career to stay here with Crew. Would I be willing to do this? Give up everything for my kid? I couldn't fathom the idea. I looked at Halo expecting to see shock and anger, but she completely surprised me. She seemed completely okay with this.

"You know, Hayden..." she said, "... if I was in your place, I'd do the same thing. Your child or your family should always come first. You have to do what you feel is best for that little guy. I'm honestly proud of your decision." She stood and hugged Hayden.

I stood and stared at the two of them. What the fuck? How could they feel this way? They were willing to give up everything for someone else. Did people really do this? They're fucking crazy.

"Are you sure about this, Hayden?" I didn't want to give my opinion to them since they honestly seemed all right.

"Yeah, I mean, I won't make the big money. I do pretty well with my songwriting, and I'd have to see about getting out of the contract with the label. I know Cash's going to be pissed about it, but oh well. My son comes first, now and always."

The look on Hayden's face made me realize he truly meant what he said. His son's health and happiness would always be first. The selflessness in that decision amazed me. I think he thought I was the crazy one staring at him the way I did, he and Halo both.

Halo looked at me. "I guess our work's done here, Carter. He's made his decision, and I'm not going to try to talk him out of it." The pride she felt in Hayden astounded me. Most people would be pissed about it, but not Halo. She understood the decision. She knew where his priorities lay.

"Well, okay. We'll be going then," I told them taking Halo's hand.

We climbed into the truck and headed out for my home. "Are you okay, Halo?"

"Sure. Some things will have to be changed up, but I'm good. You know I knew coming into this it might not work out. Maybe it wasn't meant to be."

"But your music is fucking good. What will you do?"

"I don't know until I talk to Cash."

"Aren't you mad though?"

"No, why would I be mad? We tried it. It didn't work. I'll talk to Cash and see how he feels about me going it alone. If that doesn't work, I'll do something else or use the degree I earned." She seemed perfectly content with the idea of never singing again.

The shock hadn't worn off me yet. Processing the idea skipped over my brain. It couldn't find a place to land so I could consider all of the ramifications of her not being part of a duo. We rode home the rest of the way in silence.

The next morning Halo and Hayden scheduled a meeting with Cash. I wanted to go with her and hear how this all played out.

"I can drive you in if you want," I offered.

"No, that's okay. I'm sure you have things to do."

"Sweets, there's nothing I would rather do than spend time with you." I nibbled on her neck. "Or maybe we could go back to bed now and spend our time playing with each other."

"I have to go now, though. You should have mentioned this earlier. Don't you have something you need to do today?"

"Oh yeah. Everyone's coming back in town today. I forgot."

"Convenient how that works when your mind is on sex."

"Hey, I forget everything important when I have you to entertain me, and besides my mind is always on sex like every other male I know." I kissed her hard this time.

She pushed me back before the kiss got carried away. "No, I have to leave now. Go see Gunner, that way you'll be busy, too."

"I'm busy already. I'd rather spend my time in bed." I rubbed my semi against her hip. "See, I'm busy or rather, we could get busy."

She rolled her eyes at me. "Yeah, yeah. I bet you say that to all the girls." This got my attention, but I knew she was only kidding.

"There are no other girls, and you know it."

She pulled me down for another kiss. "I know, babe. I know. Now I have to go." Halo picked up her keys and headed for the door. "Go play band with the boys." She blew me a kiss and left.

I watched her go. I still hadn't been able to wrap my head around the idea that she was okay with the whole thing. I thought about it more after we made love last night.

I liked her in my bed, maybe too much, like she said. Yeah, I thought about sex a lot but what guy didn't? Having her here made me glad I'd started on the changes I wanted to make in my life. I still had ideas I needed to follow through on them to show her my willingness to make sacrifices, but nothing like the ones she thought were okay in looking at Hayden's issues.

She'd been staying over most nights, and I liked it. When she comes home, I like being here to greet her, and I'm pretty sure she likes it, too. I could get used to having her here full-time, but I'm not sure she'd be down with that just yet. What we have isn't fragile like it was before, but it's not set in stone either. I'm taking it one day at a time trying not to push for too much at once. She's not pushing either which is good. She knows we'll both be leaving at some point. We have some concert dates scheduled in a month or so but not a tour. She has tour dates or at least, they had tour dates. Guess we'll see what happens today with Cash.

Halo

"You can't mean that Cash. We've worked so hard on the CD and you want to totally scrap the project?" I blinked back my tears. I don't know if I was angry or upset. I never considered that Cash would want to throw it all away.

"Yes, we can. We signed on with you and Hayden and now he's backing out so we'll back out."

"But what about me?" When I said I backed Hayden's decision, I meant it, but I thought there would be a way we could at least finish this CD and earn something for all of our hard work.

Cash ran his hand down his face. "We signed a contract with the two of you to do a CD and a tour to kick it off. I don't feel like I can go to the suits and tell them that we have a CD and we have one singer even though there's two on the CD. We paid you some up front. Fronted the musicians for the recordings even. Not having Hayden changes everything. You need Hayden to make your sound complete."

"So what you're saying is I'm good, but I'm not good enough to carry it by myself." I felt the tears welling up. I would not cry. I looked at Hayden, but I knew he wouldn't change his mind. I didn't want him to change it. He had a bigger obligation with his son.

Hayden stood and looked down at me. "I'm sorry, Halo. I truly am, but I can't do it. I have to put Crew first. I feel like a dick for doing this to you, but it can't be helped."

"I'm not blaming you, Hayden. I know you're doing what's right for your family." I tried to muster a smile for him, but I'm not sure it came out looking like one. I still have a long time that I had allotted for this idea. I could go back to playing in the local bars, but I wouldn't have any kind of recording deal.

"Look, I feel bad about this, but unless I can find another singer that works with you who sings country music, I don't know what else to do." Cash sat back down at his desk. "I'll keep looking."

"What about the music we've done already?" I needed to know.

"For now, it'll be put on the shelf. This happens all the time, Halo."

"Not to me it doesn't. I guess that's all we've got then." I looked at Hayden who shrugged his shoulders.

I stood and opened the door. "Are you going now, too?" I asked Hayden.

"No, I still need to talk to Cash." I knew what he needed to talk about already. I prayed that the studio allowed him to work here. He needed the money and benefits for him and Crew.

"Okay, I'll see y'all later then."

"I'm sorry, Halo. I truly am," Cash said, and I walked out.

The second I shut the car door, the tears flowed. How could this happen so quickly? One event and the domino effect took us all out. I started my car and drove around a while, since I knew Carter probably wasn't home, ending up at my apartment. I walked in the door and flopped down on the couch. Six months I'd been here and what did I have to show for it? A partially complete CD. What good would it do us or me? None.

I couldn't stand looking at the four walls of my small apartment so I grabbed some clean clothes and left for Carter's. His house sat empty when I got there, but the pool called to me. I chose a chair in the sun to drink a glass of wine. The sun felt wonderful from my chaise, and the next thing I knew I woke up in the late afternoon. That wine must have put me out. I raised up and wiped the drool off my face. *Nice, Halo.*

A noise came from in the house. Carter had returned, then he yelled, "Honey, I'm home." He did it every time he walked in the door.

I opened the large sliders peering in. "I'm here, Carter."

His smiling face turned to me. "Hey, there you are."

"Yeah, just waiting for you."

"Now that's music to my ears." He wrapped me up in a hug and kissed me soundly. "I fucking love coming home to an answer."

"You know you can get a Furbee for that," I said with a laugh.

"Furbee? They don't make those anymore."

"I could be one," I told him. I held my hands up as ears twisting them around rolling my eyes all around mimicking their odd behaviors.

"No, you could never be a Furbee. You're prettier than those devils. Now if we found one that had violet eyes, you'd look pretty close to the same." He laughed at his own joke.

"Real funny."

"So how did the meeting go? I expected to hear from you with some news."

"Not well, I'm afraid."

"Oh, how 'not well?'"

"Like I'm screwed 'not well.' Cash said without Hayden, the CD will be completely scrapped. He doesn't think I can carry it on my own. The project's going to be shelved for now."

"Forever, you mean?"

"Yeah, forever." My voice quivered a little. I couldn't help but remember all of the hours we'd put into the project. He hugged me again to his warm body. It felt wonderful to breathe in his comfort. My arms wrapped around his waist. I needed to stay right here for a while.

"We'll think of something. I promise."

"I've spent all afternoon thinking about it. I can't come up with a solution. Cash said that he would start looking for someone to replace Hayden, but it could take months. The CD needs to be finished and released. The label isn't going to let this go on forever." I turned away from him and poured myself another glass of wine.

"Are you drowning your sorrows in the wine bottle, sweets?"

"No, it's only my second glass. Why? I think I deserve to wallow in it for a while anyway."

"Yeah, but it's not going to solve this situation. I've been thinking, too. What if you and I did it?"

"Did what?" I said after taking a long drink.

"Finished the CD?"

"What? No. How will that solve my problem anyway? It's a sweet gesture on your part, but that's not going to work." I kissed his cheek but when I pulled away, he wrapped his arms around my waist and pulled me to him.

"But it could work for now. We could finish out the CD and then see how long before it releases. Cash could line up some local shows and maybe do some around Texas while we're waiting. You know, just try it out. See how it goes over."

"You can't go out on tour with me. You have a band, remember? A successful band."

"I'm aware of that, sweets, but this could be a side project. Lots of people in bands have side projects or solo projects going on." He kissed down the side of my neck.

"Don't use your kisses to persuade me." I tried to back away.

"Why, is it working?" He continued across my collarbone.

"No, yes, stop." I pulled away. "Are you serious about this?"

"Hell yeah. Let's do it."

I didn't know how to respond to his generous offer. It sounded too good to be true. To have someone from AD onstage with me would be awesome, but I didn't know if we could work it out.

"How do you think the rest of the band will feel about you doing this? They might be against it."

"Why would they? It's not like I do any real music writing for the band or that I'm quitting. You'll have to work around our schedule with planning stuff, though."

"And what about Cash? How's he going to feel about it?"

"He should be in total agreement with the idea, Halo. Hell, he's getting me." He held out his hands in a joking way.

"I'm serious, Carter. Will he go for it?"

"Listen. Cash works for AD remember? And another thing, this is a fucking great deal for him. He gets us, together, and he still gets a piece of the damn AD pie. How could he be against it?" Standing behind me, he moved my hair to the side and went back to kissing down my neck. "Now if you're through negotiating, I have some other things we can discuss."

I turned and faced him. "I'm trying to be serious here, Carter. This is my life we're talking about."

"Sweets, we damn sure have it worked out until we can run it by Cash." The kisses turned into little nips with his teeth causing me to melt when he ran his tongue over the spots to soothe his bites.

I found the hem of his t-shirt and ran my hands under it and up the valleys of his solid abdominals. His warm skin felt heavenly as I traced the path back down dragging my nails and causing him to suck in a breath. When I leaned forward and bit his small distended nipple through the shirt, he grabbed me and lifted me onto the island whipping my shirt over my head.

"My turn at that," he growled out as he popped the clasp on my bra and pulled until it dropped at his feet. "God I love your tits, Halo. They're so beautiful and perfect." He picked them both up, slightly squeezing them while his tongue circled around the pink of my nipple before sucking the hard peak into his mouth to work it over with his teeth. The other he continued to torture between his index finger and thumb. He pulled them both together and lavished both nipples alternately driving me insane with need.

I undid his jeans and pushed them down over his hips then used my feet to push them to the floor where he dropped his Chucks and stepped out. I wrapped both palms around his length and pumped up and down before using one hand to caress his balls which caused him to suck in a breath around my nipples.

"Fuck, that feels so good, sweets."

Taking my cue from him, I slid down off the granite and went all the way to my knees never taking my hands off him. He didn't try to fight it. Instead, a smile stretched across his face, and I knew he would be happy with my idea. I continued pumping him, swiping my thumb across the slit to collect the drops that leaked out so I could add some slickness to his hardened length. His head dropped back, and I knew he enjoyed my movements.

When I licked up the engorged vein running the underside of him, he let out a moan that shot straight through me landing between my legs causing my panties to be soaked through. I licked back down and took his sac in my mouth fondling the orbs with my tongue.

"Shit, Halo. This will be over before we start if you keep that up." He spread his legs a little more to allow me better access.

"Then I guess I better change tactics." I licked to the head and circled it with my tongue before taking as much in my mouth as I could and earning me a loud growl this time. I wrapped one hand around the section I couldn't take in, and between the two, I was able to manipulate and suck his cock like I knew he enjoyed.

He moaned again, and I looked up wide-eyed when I had him hitting the back of my throat. He watched as I did this over and over pumping him in and out of my warm mouth.

"The look on your face with me in your mouth makes me so fucking hot for you, sweets. I don't think I can stand it anymore. As fucking gorgeous as it is seeing my cock disappear between those lips, I need to watch my cock disappear into your tight pussy even more."

He pulled me to standing and made fast work of getting rid of my jeans, taking panties and jeans together before he sat me back on the island. "It's a perfect height," he said as he slid one finger between my lips and collected a coating of liquid to circle my clit.

I pushed up on my elbows to watch him manipulate me into a dire need for him which happened all too fast when he leaned over me and sucked my nipple back in his mouth. He had me bucking under him from the sensations he created with fingers and lips. The orgasm blasted through me when he bit down on my nipple and first tapped and then squeezed my clit with his fingers.

"*Carrrttter*," I screamed out. He continued the punishment dragging the clenching feeling out until I laid back on the granite, happy to feel the coolness under my hot skin.

He replaced the tapping finger with the head of his cock before he slowly took it down to my opening where he breached the tightness in one swift movement. As he seated himself balls deep inside me, I moaned from the pure pleasure I felt.

"Yeah, babe. Feels fucking fantastic, doesn't it?" I smiled up at him because words weren't possible. He picked up my legs and put them over his shoulders while he continued pulling out and pushing in with a slow, gradually increasing pace. The pace turned into hard surges hitting the spot that set me off into another breathtaking orgasm that I moaned my way through.

"You're perfect, Halo. Perfect in every way I need." He leaned down and kissed me before turning me over allowing my feet to hit the floor before he kicked them out and entered me again. He leaned over and kissed up my spine before taking the bulk of my hair in his fist and pulling my face from the stone surface. With his other hand gripping my hip, he drove in me until he shuddered and filled me with hot ropes of his cum.

He laid on my back and kissed me everywhere his lips could touch. "Damn, that was the best, babe. The very best."

I nodded my head because speaking would be impossible after that. He stood and swept me into his arms. “I’m going to clean you up now.” He walked to the big master bath and stood me long enough to let the water warm before standing me under the spray. He washed me from head to toe before doing himself and then wrapped us in thick fluffy towels. We made our way to the bed and slept for several hours before I rolled over and saw him staring at me.

Chapter Thirty Eight

Carter

"Have you been staring at me long?" she whispered to me.

"No, just a few minutes, but I heard your stomach growling and was trying to decide how long I'd let you sleep before I fed you."

"You feed me, huh? Like sugared grapes or something?" she smiled when she said it.

"Who eats that?"

"Food of the gods, Carter."

"Well, this god is thinking more like steak, so get up and let's go eat."

She must have liked the idea because she barreled off the bed and ran to the kitchen where we'd stripped for some excellent kitchen sex. She handed me my clothes, and we both dressed in record- breaking time.

I kept her hand locked in mine on my thigh all the way there. I had a lot of ideas playing havoc in my mind. I wanted her with me all the time. Our attachment grew daily, at least for me. I had a tough time reading Halo. She seemed perfectly happy with the way things between us were going. She was willing to give me a second chance, and I thanked God every day for it.

We loved each other before, and I knew I was already there again, but I didn't want to scare her off trying to label us. She might not feel the same way. Maybe the idea of falling in love with me frightened her. I'd done all I could to make her understand I wasn't that guy anymore. I'd grown up since we were together before. I prayed she saw it in me.

The Capital Grille in downtown had the best steaks in town, and the band frequented the place often so when we walked in, they knew me.

"Hello, Mr. Sheridan. Glad to see you back," the owner greeted us.

"Thank you. I'm hungry for one of your great steaks." I shook his hand. He led us to a quiet table for two in a secluded section of the restaurant. He pulled the chair out for Halo and seated her.

"I'll send your waiter over shortly." He left us and the waiter immediately appeared, took our order, and left us alone once he delivered our drinks.

Halo looked at me. "You were quiet driving over." She picked up her wine and took a sip.

"I think you wore me out."

"Pffft. I doubt that," she said with a smile. "What's going on? Are you having second thoughts with your offer?"

"No, no. I'm completely committed to the project. We're going to set the house on fire when we play." I took her hand across the table.

"Are you sure about this, Carter? I don't want to go talk to Cash if you're unsure in any way."

"Sweets, stop. I'm a hundred percent on board with this. We'll have some kinks to work out, but it's happening. We'll go see him tomorrow and figure out what we need to do. First thing, though, we need to get that CD done and released."

The food arrived, and we both ate until we couldn't take another bite. The steaks, cooked to perfection, melted against the side of our forks. We topped it off with a decadent chocolate mousse before we made our way back to the truck.

"What about Hayden?" Halo stopped before we crossed the parking lot.

"What about him?"

"We need to talk to him about this. He might not like the idea."

"Halo, really? He'll be thrilled. He's written most of the music and lyrics and when it's a hit, he'll collect a nice paycheck. What's not to like about that?"

"Yeah, that's right. I didn't think about it that way. He'll bring in a lot from the royalties. Okay, I'm excited now."

"You weren't before?"

"Well, yes, but I haven't had time to think it all through like the money and stuff."

I pulled her in and kissed her. "I guess that's what you have me for then. To think, that is."

"I can think of a lot of reasons I have you, and money isn't one of them. Now take me home and I'll show you some of them.

"You got it." I shut the door and sprinted to the other side. The smile on my face all the way home spoke volumes.

Everyone we approached with our idea liked it. Cash's over-the-top excitement had him glowing, since he knew adding my name to the mix would draw in crowds even if it would only be to see if I could do it. We finished the work on the CD and the release party information went out to all the right places. Cash lined up several gigs for us in Austin and the surrounding towns where country fans frequented. Texas never lacked for country music venues, and some were even calling trying to get us to play.

Our first show sold out in no time, and we knocked it out of the park. AD showed up, but the place had an upstairs for them so the attention focused on Halo and me. We all went out afterward and celebrated our success. Hayden came to the party, and he seemed genuinely happy to hear his music being played for the crowds who loved the tunes.

By the time we finished a month of Texas tours, there were calls coming in from all over the U.S. inquiring about bookings. We had to turn them down since AD had some shows scheduled.

"It's too bad we can't make some of these shows on the West Coast," Halo commented on the way home from the last venue for the tour. I took her hand in mine.

"I know, sweets, but we knew this was how it was going to go when we started. The good news is we were well received everywhere we went. So let's be positive."

"I know. It's just now we have our momentum going, and we'll lose it all with not doing anything for several months." I pulled her hand to my lips and kissed the soft skin.

"Maybe you can come on tour with us, so we don't have to be apart." I didn't want to leave her behind even if we weren't doing regular tour stops. What would she do?

"I can't go with y'all. I'm not in the band."

"You can too. There's always extras traveling with us. What's wrong with you being one of those?"

"No, I'm not going." She seemed adamant about her decision.

"Why wouldn't you want to go?"

"I'd be in the way. I'd have nothing to do."

"I can think of a lot of things for us to do." I wiggled my eyebrows at her.

"No, I'm not going." She wouldn't look at me anymore so I assumed she thought this conversation had come to an end. I didn't like the idea of leaving her alone for a couple of months. Sure, we would come and go some but overall, I'd be gone for two months.

"Really, Halo. What will you do?"

"Hmmm. I guess I can go out with friends, drink, party with wild women. You know, the usual things I do." I gave her the evil eye, and she laughed at me. "Carter, I'm a big girl. I can entertain myself. I had a life before you, remember?"

Yeah, that's what scared me. What kind of life did she have before we reconnected? More importantly, who did she have a life with?

"Would you want to get a job or something?" I asked. It seemed like a legit question. She'd hate sitting around.

"A job? I don't know. Stop worrying about it. It's not important." We pulled into the garage and she jumped out of the car as the door went down. It was cool in the autumn air, but the garage warmed from the truck motor. She walked to Lo and pulled her cover off. "I can think of something we can do right now." She took her finger and ran it down the sleek lines. "You know, here in the garage."

She pulled her tight-fitting sweater dress over her head and turned her back to me to bend at the waist to pull the zipper down on her boots, glancing at me as she went.

"No, leave those high heels on. I'll have you just like that."

We spent the next hour enjoying each other on Lo's hood before we made our way to the bedroom to recuperate.

Assured Distraction, with a pregnant Peri, boarded the plane at the private airstrip outside Austin. Halo dropped me off, and we spent a long time with slow kisses and sensual caresses while the others waited on the plane.

"I sure wish you'd change your mind and go with us."

"We've been over this a hundred times already, Carter. I'm not going. Now I want you to have fun, rock out on the stage, and leave the wild groupies alone."

I wrapped her up in my arms and kissed her hard one last time. "I'll see you in a few weeks, if not sooner."

"Sounds good. Now get on the plane."

I let her go and climbed the steps. This was bullshit. I didn't like leaving her behind. I fucking hated it.

"Dude, she'll be fine," Gunner said. "Lola and I do it all the time."

"I don't give a shit about what you do. I don't like leaving her behind."

"Right, we get that, but you can't help what your job is. We need you, dude." He leaned forward and pretended to cry into his hands. His wailing grew louder so that everyone started laughing.

"This is not fucking funny." I stood up and went to the bathroom. I was pissed at the whole group of them. I'd listened to my fair share of their whining when they parted from their girlfriends and wives. Now it's me, and they want to make fun of me? Fuck this.

I finally came out about thirty minutes later, glad the private plane's restroom had normal dimensions to it instead of like commercial planes. I sat back in my seat and rocked back closing my eyes. The plane took us to Miami so the flight lasted several hours. When I opened them again, Peri sat in the chair next to me. I laid my head on the headrest and looked at her.

"Hey, Carter."

"Hey, Peri." I offered her a brief smile. "What's going on?"

"I wanted to say I'm sorry for how that went down when you boarded. We should've realized it would be hard on you to leave her. We've just never seen you like this before."

"I've never felt like this. I love her, you know, and being apart is killing me. I fucking hate it every minute. Then to get on here with the people who are my best friends in the world and have them laugh at me, it was too much. I couldn't do it."

"We get it, Carter. We do. None of us realized you, of all people, had fallen so hard. So, I'm really sorry, and I know the rest of them are, too."

"Really?" I looked around the cabin of the plane. "It doesn't look like it."

"No, we do. I promise. You didn't see them when you stayed in the restroom."

"Yeah, I had a lot of time to think in there about this new direction I'm going in. I'm not sure I'm happy with it right now." I couldn't believe I admitted that to Peri. Hell, I couldn't believe I said it out loud at all.

"What do you mean, Carter?" Her face looked petrified when she asked this, afraid of how I would answer.

"I mean, I'm fucking miserable when I'm away from her. I hate it, and we just left."

"Yeah, it's going to be a long two weeks."

"That's what I'm saying. Too fucking long." I shut my eyes. I didn't want to talk about it anymore.

A miserable week went by. Halo and I talked on the phone, FaceTimed, and sent live videos. We even had some scandalous phone sex, but it wasn't enough. Both of us hated it, but Halo used all kinds of excuses to not join us. She went home to see her parents for a few days. She'd been out a few times with friends and those were the worst nights of my life. I worried every time she went. I could hardly play my bass. It's a damn good thing it's second nature to me, or I would have totally fucked the band.

By the end of the second week, I was fucking crazy. I needed her like I needed music and air. I couldn't do this again. I wouldn't leave without her. She had to come with me. By the time the plane needed to land, they almost had to hold me down to buckle my seat belt.

"Open the fucking door. She's out there." The attendant looked at me like I had lost my mind, and he was right, I had.

"Dude, you need to calm the fuck down." Gunner tried to hold me back.

As soon as the door opened, I ran off down the steps and right into her arms. "God, this is where I've been dying to be."

"I've missed you too, babe."

I wrapped her to my body as tight as I could, and then I kissed the hell out of her. "Let's go home." I picked up my bag, and we climbed in her car.

I turned in my seat and faced her. "This isn't working for me, Halo. I don't like being apart. I've given this a lot of thought, and I want you to go with me when we leave the next time."

"I can't do that. We've discussed this. What would I do?"

"I'm going to talk to the band about putting you to work. There has to be something you can do. I'm going to talk to Peri about it. She's going to be off on maternity leave, and you can learn her job and fill in for her when she's out."

"As good as that sounds, I don't want to manage a band." Halo seemed adamant about it.

"I don't really care what you do, sweets. I just want you with me. Why are you fighting me on this?" I asked. I couldn't understand it.

"I'm not fighting you, Carter. I'm not part of Assured Distraction. That's your band. You told me that when you left me the first time, and I've never forgotten it." Now the truth comes out. She's holding me to something I said years ago. I meant it then and had good reasons, but our lives were different now. I needed her. I loved her.

I needed to prove this to her. I wanted her to know I had changed since I left her at eighteen. We were kids. We needed time to grow up. That time had come now.

I ran my fingers through her hair and wrapped my palm around the back of her neck. "I love you, Halo."

"I love you too, Carter, but it's never going to work for us, is it? Music will always come between us." I could hear the strain in her voice.

"No, I won't let it." We pulled in the driveway and both got out of her car. "I need you badly, sweets. Let's go in, and I'll prove it to you."

We made it in the door and left a trail of clothes to the bedroom. I spent the night worshipping her beautiful body trying to show her how much I meant all the things I'd said on the way home.

Carter

Me: *I need to talk*
Gunner: *Sup?*
Me: *Can you meet me at The Bar in an hour*
Gunner: *Sure*

I needed to run my idea past Gunner before presenting it to the rest of the band. They weren't going to be happy with me, and I wanted Gunner to have my back on this decision before I talked to them.

After Halo and I had feasted on each other until completely sated, I lay awake thinking of how to solve my problem. I loved and needed her. I never thought I would feel like this about her or any woman for that matter, but I'd come to realize I didn't want to live my life without her. I thought of making grand gestures before and about making changes. The changes I made were only superficial.

House furnishings and wall paint were not the kinds of alterations necessary to have her. She needed more than that. She had to see I meant it when I said I was willing to do whatever it took for us to be together.

I walked in and sat so I could see the doorway. I practiced what I wanted to say to him. I knew he might put up a protest, but I thought he would come to see my side of it all. As the waitress brought my beer, Gunner walked in so I ordered another for him.

"This must be important for you to meet me in a bar in the middle of the day. Are we working undercover or something?" His happy mood made it worse for me. I hated telling him this.

"Yeah, it's important, and I'm telling you first because I want your support. You've gotta have my back on this."

"Dude, this does sound serious. What did you do, knock up a groupie or something?" He smiled when he said it because he knew better.

"No, nothing like that. We've all dodged bullets like that, haven't we?" The two of us had shared many fun times over these years with the band. We've been places we could only dream of when we started. We've shared women in some of the kinkiest of ways. The threesomes we've participated in would fill a book. They were all fun times that I don't regret, and I doubt Gunner did either.

Now he had Lola, and they were counting the days until they made it official just like Chandler and KeeMac. Hell, Ryan and Peri married not long after their son came along, and now they're having a second to add to their brood. Where did this leave me?

I looked him right in the eye. I wanted to judge his first reaction. "Gunner, I'm leaving the band."

"What the fuck did you say?" His face expressed it all. Shock.

"I'm leaving the band and if she'll have me, I'm joining Halo. We'll form our own and be together."

"Shit, I knew it. I watched you mope around those two weeks without her and knew you had it bad, but I never realized it would be like this. You've thought this through?"

"Hell, I didn't have anything else to think about all those nights in the hotels. I tried to convince her to join us in some capacity, but she wouldn't even consider it."

"Yeah, she'd not be doing what she was destined to do with her own music following us around all the time."

"No, she wouldn't." I took a long drink of my beer. I found it hard to swallow over the lump in my throat.

"Well, shit. I don't like it, but I understand. There's nothing I wouldn't do to make sure I had Lola with me, nothing. Yeah, we are apart right now, but it's only until we get things straightened out. Y'all though, there's no straightening things out for you two. You'll be passing each other in the night somewhere on the road, and that's never going to play out the way you want it."

"I love her, Gunner. I'm not going to be in a part-time relationship. It's all or nothing for me. That's the reason I broke it off with her the first time."

"Yeah, I know. Damn, it's some good/bad news."

"How do you think the band will respond to the news?" The idea of telling the whole band had me on edge. These people are my family. *Would they disown me for it?*

"They're not going to be happy, but I'm sure they'll understand in the end. No one wants to see you be alone, Carter. We've had a great run, but things change. Life gets in the way. It's going to be hard to replace you but hey, we're all replaceable."

"Yeah, I thought about that, too. You know there's a lot of bands out there that don't do their live music with a bass player. They bring them in with their recordings but not onstage. Maybe I could even do some of the recordings with y'all but not tour. We've got a few options if everyone's agreeable."

"For whatever it's worth, I got your back on this. Hell, I've always got your back, dude. You know that. We're family, now and always." We stood and shook hands with the added hug at the end. "Decide when and where, and I'm there."

"Thanks, man. I needed your approval to move forward. I'll let you know." He gave me a head tip and left. I wanted to talk some more about it all, but I knew he needed time to digest what I'd said. After all the time we'd spent together, I'd learned all of the band's ways of dealing with problems, and Gunner needed time to sort it out. The fact that he was down with my decision made me feel a lot better. Now I had to tell Halo. I knew her reaction would be a lot stronger and more vocal, for sure.

The band met at the studios the next day at my request. I knew it surprised everyone when I messaged and said we needed a meeting. I never called meetings. KeeMac or Peri kept that job on a permanent basis.

I walked in the practice room where everyone sat waiting for me. I purposely came in a late. What I had to say needed to be said only once.

"Well, well. Dumbass calls a meeting and as usual, he's the last one to arrive," KeeMac said with a joking tone to his voice. "What's so important we couldn't talk at someone's house?"

"I wanted it to be official, that's why." My serious tone caused them to all look up at me.

"What's up, man? Halo finally catch on and kick you out or something?" Ryan asked before looking at Peri with concern on his face.

"Okay, I came last because I only want to say this one time." I took a deep breath and looked at Gunner who nodded his head, knowing I needed the support.

"I've decided to leave the band." A pin hitting carpet made more sound than could be heard at that moment.

"What are you talking about?" KeeMac's face took on a new look.

"I'm going to take Hayden's place with Halo. We're going to form our own band and hit the road."

"No fucking way, dude." Ryan stood up. "You're not leaving the band. Who'll play bass for us and keep this dumbshit in line?" He nodded his head toward Gunner.

"I'm not joking. I won't be going with y'all when you leave next time."

"What's this really about, Carter?" Peri asked in a calm voice.

"What it's about is me." I took a deep breath and ran my hand down my face. I needed to come clean about a lot of things. "I love Halo. Hell, I've always loved her. I just took an eight-year break, but now I've found her again. I'm tired of being alone. I'm tired of a different woman every night. And now with all of y'all together..." I looked down the line at the group, "... I'm alone even on the road. I don't want to be that way any longer. So, I made the decision to join her since she can't join me."

Silence filled the room again. I knew my admission surprised them. Finally, Chandler stood and walked to me. "Congratulations, Carter. I'm glad you're ready to grow up and find your way. If Halo makes you happy and loves you like you love her, then you deserve it. When I told you to make a big gesture, though, I didn't mean this. Just so you know." She smiled and hugged me.

The rest of the band followed suit with the congrats and back slaps.

Peri finally asked, "What does Halo say about all of this?"

"Nothing yet. I haven't told her."

"What? She's going to have a shit fit with you. She'll never let you quit the band."

"She doesn't have any say so. I've already quit." That sounded all well and good telling them that, but I knew convincing her would be harder than them.

Chandler spoke up. "I can't believe you didn't discuss these changes with her first. What if she doesn't want you to join her?"

"Hey, why wouldn't she want me? With these good looks, perfect body, fine guitar player, and generally good person that I am, what's to turn down?" I joked, but I knew a fight would be on my hands. She might be small but she's stubborn.

"Yeah, you say that now. Can I sneak in and listen? It ought to be good," KeeMac said laughing. "I know Chan, and she'd kick my ass for making a huge decision like this without talking to her."

"Which of our women wouldn't?" Ryan added sneaking a sideways glance at Peri, who chose to ignore his comment.

"Be serious, Carter." Peri tried again. "How do you think she's going to take this news? I don't know her too well yet, but I know she's strong and determined when she sets out to do something."

"I know she is, and it's one of the things I love about her, but this is my decision to make. I plan for us to make it big. Maybe not big like AD big, but big. The country music scene crosses over so much into rock and pop. Her sound is great, and the two of us together did well when I filled in for Hayden. Who knows, maybe Hayden will find his way back to the stage and join us at some point. Hayden will continue to write songs for us." I meant everything I said to them.

The group did some more patting on the back, but I'd made it past the hard part. Leaving Assured Distraction happened to be the hardest thing I'd ever done, but I knew this group had my back no matter what.

"So, the last thing I wanted to tell you is that I'll help AD all I can to find a replacement if that's the route you go."

"Awe, shit," KeeMac said. "I hadn't even thought that far."

"The thing is, I've been doing some research and you know there's lots of bands that don't even use a bass player onstage. They usually pull one in for recording but go without on stage." I wanted them to know I hadn't made a snap decision about abandoning them. I'd done my homework, but most of this I knew.

"The Doors never used a bass and neither does The White Stripes. The Black Keys hardly ever use one onstage. The new group, The Yeah, Yeah, Yeahs, don't have one, so you see it's possible, and if y'all decide to replace me, I'll make myself available to help out."

"Seems like you've got this all worked out with the huge exception of Halo," Chan said.

"No bass might require you to do some backfill Chan, but I'm sure you'll figure it all out." I knew her musical skills. She could do almost anything when it came down to music.

"Okay, well, I guess I'm going to go tackle the tiger."

"Good luck, dude." Gunner clasped my shoulder. "I think you're going to need it."

The others followed behind him with the good wishes until Peri.

"Stop," she said loudly. "You're not getting off the hook this easy. Just because you don't play in the band doesn't get you out of being a member of the family. We still expect you at our houses, playing with our kids, bringing pizza since you don't cook. We'll all expect it, especially the boys."

Gunner spoke up, "Yeah, we'll call you the black sheep or the red-headed stepchild or something. You'll be that branch no one wants to claim. You know the one I'm talking about. It doesn't have any forks in the tree." Everyone started adding stupid family-tree jokes but we laughed, and I knew things were going to be okay with all of us.

"You told them what? Have you lost your damn mind? You can't leave the band for me." Yeah, she's pissed all right, but she didn't try to throw anything at me, yet.

"I'm not leaving for you. I'm leaving for us." I tried to take her hand but she pulled back.

"No, you're not. Call Peri and tell her to inform the band you've changed your mind."

"I'm not changing my mind. I'm leaving the band, and we'll start our own."

"Carter, we're never going to be big like AD. Never!"

"I don't give a shit about that. I have enough money. I could quit the band and invest the money and never work again."

"But it's starting over. It's playing small places. It's night after night on the road."

"Yeah, you're right, but this time it's with you, and that makes it perfect for me." She finally let me take both her hands. "Halo, I left you once to find me. Now, I'm home to find us and this time, I'm not going anywhere."

"I don't know Carter. This could all fall to pieces you know. What if we don't make it? What if our music doesn't make it? What if we bomb?"

"Sweets, what if the world ends tomorrow? We have no control of our destiny. You know that. AD will make it work, and we'll find our own way."

"Are you sure about this? If you're not one hundred percent, tell me now."

"I'm one hundred percent. There will be no more distractions for us."

Halo pulled the sapphire blue short dress up her thighs trying to wiggle into it. "Babe, why did you buy it so tight?"

"It has to be tight, Carter. If not, it'll fall off me and wouldn't that make a statement on the red carpet?" She finally got it where she wanted it and adjusted her tits so they were covered as best as they could be in the dress.

"Yeah, I would hate to see it hit the floor walking up those stairs to the stage." I sat at the foot of the bed watching her. She could go in a sack, and I'd be perfectly happy. Halo was stunning no matter what.

"Don't say that. It's been an honor to be nominated, you know."

"I know, and I'm thrilled, but winning isn't everything, is it?"

"No, winning isn't everything. Besides, look who we're up against. I'm so excited to be considered in the same category as the others." She adjusted her earring and turned to look at me.

"God, sweets, you look so beautiful. Can we stay home and let me undress you now and do magical things to this body under all that glitz?"

"Save it for later. We've gotta go."

As we stepped out of the limo onto the red carpet for the Country Music Awards, Halo squeezed my hand. We were up for Vocal Duo of the Year and New Artist of the Year. All of AD and the two of us had attended the MusicRow Awards where Hayden had won the Breakthrough Songwriter of the Year. We collaborated with him on everything we wrote and recorded almost everything he wrote. Now we would see how we fared against great acts that worked as hard as we had.

The next limo pulls up and Assured Distraction got out to walk the carpet with us. They weren't here for an award, but they couldn't let us do it alone. We needed to share the joy with them if we won.

After a gazillion pictures were taken, a reporter stuck a microphone in my face and asked, "How does it feel to be nominated on the other side of the music fence?"

I looked right into the camera and said, "Feels fucking great." I turned to the guys, and we high-fived my comment. I knew they would have to bleep the whole thing out, but I didn't care. You might take me away from being a rocker, but you'll never take the rocker out of me.

These are songs I love and listened to while I was writing this book. There's no rhyme or reason to the order or the song. I just enjoy the music, the lyrics, the tune or the performers. I love live music, too.

Notes about ACL Festival

This is a great music festival of rock and alternative music, and that occurs in Oct. of each year in Zilker Park in Austin, TX. It invites performers from all over the world to play for two weekends. This is a great time to visit ATX because the weather is usually outstanding. I had the pleasure of attending it for the first time with my daughter, and we had an awesome experience. Thanks, Lacy for putting up with me for a weekend of fun and games. Looking forward to this year!

Distracted No More

"Something to Believe" In by Young the Giant
"Talk Too Much" by Coin
"Somebody Else" by 1975
"You Run Away" by Bare Naked Ladies
"Sweet Disaster" by The Dreamers
"Put Your Money on Me" by The Struts
"Do I Wanna Know" by Arctic Monkeys
"Trouble" by Cage the Elephant
"Unbelievers" by Vampire Weekend
"Madness" by Muse
"Give Me a Try" by The Wombats
"Life Itself" by Glass Animals
"Fire Escape" by Andrew McMahon

This series has been the ride of a lifetime. I've met new friends who encouraged me to write more. I met readers who loved my guys and rejoiced in their accomplishments, laughed at their antics and argued in their defense for doing the ridiculous.

I have to start with **Deb Carroll.** She has been a champion, a friend, and a confidant. I'm so happy she found and rescued me. I'm excited we were able to meet in person in her beautiful part of the U.S. I'm thrilled she brought me into her world with enthusiasm an excitement. I'm thankful to have her every single day.

Thank you to my family for not complaining too much when I turned you down to go and do, so I could write, especially **Steve**. He takes over when I'm in my Thia mode, and I'm thankful for it. I love you all.

Thank you to **Mayas Jamarla Sanders** for dropping everything and reading. She's been invaluable for making suggestions for the book to be better. Beta readers don't get recognized enough. She's a first class reader and friend!

Thank you to **Chris Genovese** for understanding my rants and little meltdowns that happen often. I appreciate your friendship more than you'll ever know.

Thank you to **Trudy Baker Dowling** for constantly entering me in every author contest known to man! She has been awesome to keep me in the loop of winners.

Thank you to **Elaine Marie**. She's been with me from the beginning when no one knew my name. It didn't stop her from putting my name out so everyone would know it when they saw it.

Thank you to **Kyle Jones** and **Jordan Jones** for answering crazy questions about the music industry, showing me Nashville, and putting up with me in general. Who am I going to call when I move on to my sports series?

Thank you to **Jenny Flores** for including me on some fun rides and many more to come in the future.

Thank you to **Jonny James** for putting up with some poorly timed and worded texts (you know the ones).

Goodreads Links

Check out the books below and to add to your TBR list.

Assured Distraction Series

Assure Her (Assured Distraction Book One) – Keeton's Story

His Distraction Assurance Distraction Book Two) – Ryan's Story

His Assurance (Assured Distraction Book Three) – Gunner's Story

Distracted No More (Assured Distraction Book Four) – Carter's Story

Website

http://www.thiafinn.com

Email

author@thiafinn.com

Facebook

https://www.facebook.com/ThiaFinn/?fref=ts

Goodreads

https://www.goodreads.com/author/show/14206242.Thia_Finn

Growing up in small town Texas, **Thia Finn** discovered life outside of it by attending The University of Texas, only to return home and marry her high school sweetheart. They raised two successful and beautiful daughters while she taught middle school Language Arts and eventually became a middle school librarian. After thirty-four years, she retired to do her favorite things, like travel, spend time off-roading with family and friends, hanging out at the Frio River, reading, and writing.

She currently lives in the same small town where she grew up, with her husband and the boss, Titan, the Chihuahua. She can often be found stalking on social media, watching Outlanders, Vikings or Game of Thrones to name a few on Netflix.

Made in the USA
Coppell, TX
06 October 2023